A Touchstone Book

ZORBA
THE GREEK

by

Nikos Kazantzakis

◇ ◇ ◇ ◇ ◇ ◇ ◇ ◇ ◇ ◇ ◇

TRANSLATED BY CARL WILDMAN

◇ ◇ ◇ ◇ ◇ ◇ ◇ ◇ ◇ ◇ ◇

A Touchstone Book
Published By
Simon and Schuster

ISBN 0-671-85100-4

ISBN 0-671-21132-3 PBK.

MANUFACTURED IN THE UNITED STATES OF AMERICA

7   8   9   10   11   12   13   14   15

19   20   21   22   23   24   25   26   PBK.

ZORBA
THE GREEK

◇ 1 ◇

I FIRST MET HIM in Piraeus. I wanted to take the boat for Crete and had gone down to the port. It was almost daybreak and raining. A strong *sirocco* was blowing the spray from the waves as far as the little café, whose glass doors were shut. The café reeked of brewing sage and human beings whose breath steamed the windows because of the cold outside. Five or six seamen, who had spent the night there, muffled in their brown goatskin reefer-jackets, were drinking coffee or sage and gazing out of the misty windows at the sea. The fish, dazed by the blows of the raging waters, had taken refuge in the depths, where they were waiting till calm was restored above. The fishermen crowding in the cafés were also waiting for the end of the storm, when the fish, reassured, would rise to the surface after the bait. Soles, hog fish and skate were returning from their nocturnal expeditions. Day was now breaking.

The glass door opened and there entered a thick-set, mud-bespattered, weather-beaten dock laborer with bare head and bare feet.

"Hi! Kostandi!" called out an old sailor in a sky-blue cloak. "How are things with you?"

Kostandi spat. "What d'you think?" he replied testily. "Good morning—the bar! Good night—my lodgings! That's the sort of life I'm leading. No work at all!"

Some started laughing, others shook their heads and swore.

"This world's a life sentence," said a man with a moustache who

3

had picked up his philosophy from the *Karagiozis* * theater. "Yes, a life sentence. Be damned to it."

A pale bluish-green light penetrated the dirty windowpanes of the café and caught hands, noses and foreheads. It leapt on to the counter and lit the bottles. The electric light faded, and the proprietor, half-asleep after his night up, stretched out his hand and switched it off.

There was a moment's silence. All eyes were turned on the dirty-looking sky outside. The roar of the waves could be heard and, in the café, the gurgling of a few hookahs.

The old sailor sighed: "I wonder what has happened to Captain Lemoni? May God help him!" He looked angrily at the sea, and growled: "God damn you for a destroyer of homes!" He bit his grey moustache.

I was sitting in a corner. I was cold and I ordered a second glass of sage. I wanted to go to sleep, but I struggled against the desire to sleep, and against my fatigue and the desolation of the early hours of dawn. I looked through the steamy windows at the awakening port resounding with the ships' sirens and the cries of carters and boatmen. And, as I looked, an invisible net, woven from sea, air, and my departure, wound its tight meshes round my heart.

My eyes were glued to the black bows of a large vessel. The whole of the hull was still engulfed in darkness. It was raining and I could see the shafts of rain link sky and mud.

I looked at the black ship, the shadows and the rain, and my sadness took shape. Memories arose. The rain and my spleen took on, in the humid atmosphere, the features of my great friend. Was it last year? In another life? Yesterday? When was it I came down to this same port to say goodbye to him? I remembered how it rained that morning, too, and the cold, and the early light. At that time also, my heart was heavy.

How bitter it is to be slowly separated from great friends! Far better make a clean break and remain in solitude—the natural cli-

---

* *Karagheuz*, or *Karagöz*, meaning "Black Eyed." A puppet shadow-play given in cafés and common to Arabia, Turkey, Syria and North Africa. These plays were the only dramatic performances known to orthodox Mohammedans. The *Karagheuz* play, which is comic, can be compared to Punch and Judy. It derived its shadow technique from Java thanks to fourteenth century Arab traders. C. W.

mate for man. And yet, in that rainy dawn, I could not leave my friend. (I understood why later, but, alas, too late.) I had gone on board with him and was seated in his cabin amid scattered suit-cases. I gazed at him intently for a long time, when his attention was fixed elsewhere, as if I wished to make mental note of his features, one by one—his bluish-green, luminous eyes, his rounded, youthful face, his intelligent and disdainful expression, and, above all, his aristocratic hands with their long, slender fingers.

Once he caught me gazing lingeringly and eagerly at him. He turned round with that mocking air he assumed when he wanted to hide his feelings. He looked at me and he understood. And to avoid the sadness of separation, he asked with an ironical smile:

"How long?"

"What d'you mean, how long?"

"How long are you going on chewing paper and covering your-self with ink? Why don't you come with me? Away there in the Caucasus there are thousands of our people in danger. Let's go and save them." He began to laugh as if in mockery of his noble plan. "Maybe, we shan't save them. Don't you preach: 'The only way to save yourself is to endeavor to save others?' . . . Well, forward, master. You're good at preaching. Why don't you come with me!"

I did not answer. I thought of this sacred land of the East, the old mother of the gods, the loud clamoring of Prometheus nailed to the rock. Nailed to these same rocks, our own race was crying out. Again it was in peril. It was calling to its sons for help. And I was listening, passively, as if pain was a dream and life some ab-sorbing tragedy, in which nobody but a boor or a simpleton would rush onto the stage and take part in the action.

Without waiting for an answer, my friend rose. The boat sounded its siren for the third time. He gave me his hand and again hid his emotion in raillery.

"*Au revoir*, bookworm!"

His voice trembled. He knew it was shameful not to be able to control one's feelings. Tears, tender words, unruly gestures, com-mon familiarities, all seemed to him weaknesses unworthy of man. We, who were so fond of each other, never exchanged an affection-ate word. We played and scratched at each other like wild beasts. He, the intelligent, ironical, civilized man; I, the barbarian. He exercised self-control and suavely expressed all his feelings in a smile. I would suddenly utter a misplaced and barbarous laugh.

I also tried to camouflage my emotions with a hard word. But I felt ashamed. No, not exactly ashamed, but I didn't manage it. I grasped his hand. I held it and wouldn't let it go. He looked at me, astonished.

"Are you so moved?" he said, trying to smile.

"Yes," I replied, with calm.

"Why? Now, what did we say? Hadn't we agreed on this point years ago? What do your beloved Japs say? *Fudoshin! Ataraxia,* Olympian calm, the face a smiling, unmoving mask. As for what happens behind the mask, that is our business."

"Yes," I replied again, trying not to compromise myself by embarking on a long sentence. I was not sure of being able to control my voice.

The ship's gong sounded, driving the visitors from the cabins. It was raining gently. The air was filled with pathetic words of farewell, promises, prolonged kisses, and hurried, breathless injunctions. Mothers rushed to sons, wives to husbands, friends to friends. As if they were leaving them forever. As if this little separation recalled the other—the Great Separation. And suddenly, in the humid air, the sound of the gong echoed softly from stem to stern, like a funeral bell. I shuddered.

My friend leaned over.

"Listen," he said in a low voice. "Have you some foreboding?"

"Yes," I replied once more.

"Do you believe in such humbug?"

"No," I answered with assurance.

"Well, then?"

There was no "well." I did not believe in it, but I was afraid.

My friend lightly touched my knee with his left hand, as he was wont to do in moments of abandon. I would urge him to take a decision, he would oppose this, stopping his ears, and refuse; finally he would accept, and then he would touch my knee, as if to say: "All right, I'll do what you say, for friendship's sake. . . ."

He blinked two or three times, then stared at me again. He understood I was distressed and hesitated to use our usual weapons: laughter, smiles and chaff.

6

"Very well," he said. "Give me your hand. If ever one of us finds himself in danger of death . . ."

He stopped, as if ashamed. We who had, for so many years, made fun of metaphysical "flights" and lumped together vegetarians, spiritualists, theosophists and ectoplasm. . . .

"Well?" I asked, trying to guess.

"Let's think of it as a game," he said suddenly, to get out of the perilous sentence he had embarked upon. "If ever one of us finds himself in danger of death, let him think of the other so intensely that he warns him wherever he may be. . . . Right?" He tried to laugh, but his lips remained motionless, as if frozen.

"Right," I said.

Fearing that he had displayed his feelings too clearly, my friend hastened to add:

"Mind you, I haven't the slightest belief in telepathy and all that. . . ."

"Never mind," I murmured. "Let it be so. . . ."

"Very well, then, let's leave it at that. Agreed?"

"Agreed," I answered.

They were our last words. We clasped each other's hands in silence, our fingers joined fervently, and suddenly unclasped. I walked away rapidly without looking back, as if I were being followed. I felt a sudden impulse to give one last look at my friend, but I repressed it. "Don't look back!" I bade myself. "Forward!"

The human soul is heavy, clumsy, held in the mud of the flesh. Its perceptions are still coarse and brutish. It can divine nothing clearly, nothing with certainty. If it could have guessed, how different this separation would have been.

It was growing lighter and lighter. The two mornings mingled. The loved countenance of my friend, which I could see more clearly now, remained immobile and desolate in the rain and the atmosphere of the port. The door of the café opened, the sea roared, a thickset sailor entered with legs apart and drooping moustaches. Voices rang out in pleasure:

"Welcome, Captain Lemoni!"

I retreated into the corner, trying to concentrate my thoughts afresh. But my friend's face was already dissolving in the rain.

It was becoming still lighter. Captain Lemoni, austere and taciturn, took out his amber rosary and began to tell his beads. I struggled not to see, not to hear, and to hold on a little longer to the vision which was melting away. If only I could live again the moment of that anger which surged up in me when my friend called me a bookworm! I recalled then that all my disgust at the life I had been leading was personified in those words. How could I, who loved life so intensely, have let myself be entangled for so long in that balderdash of books and paper blackened with ink! In that day of separation, my friend had helped me to see clearly. I was relieved. As I now knew the name of my affliction, I could perhaps conquer it more easily. It was no longer elusive and incorporeal; it had assumed a name and a shape, and it would be easier for me to combat it.

His expression must have made silent progress in me. I sought a pretext for abandoning my papers and flinging myself into a life of action. I resented bearing this miserable creature upon my escutcheon. A month earlier, the desired opportunity had presented itself. I had rented on the coast of Crete, facing Libya, a disused lignite mine, and I was going now to live with simple men, workmen and peasants, far from the race of bookworms!

I prepared excitedly for my departure, as if this journey had a mysterious significance. I had decided to change my mode of life. "Till now," I told myself, "you have only seen the shadow and been well content with it; now, I am going to lead you to the substance."

At last I was ready. On the eve of departure, while rummaging in my papers, I came across an unfinished manuscript. I took it and looked at it, hesitating. For two years, in the innermost depths of my being, a great desire, a seed had been quickening. I could feel it all the time in my bowels, feeding on me and ripening. It was growing, moving and beginning to kick against the wall of my body to come forth. I no longer had the courage to destroy it. I could not. It was too late to commit such spiritual abortion.

Suddenly, as I hesitatingly held the manuscript, I became conscious of my friend's smile in the air, a smile composed of irony and tenderness. "I *shall* take it!" I said, stung to the quick. "I shall take it. You needn't smile!" I wrapped it up with care, as if swaddling a baby, and took it with me.

8

Captain Lemoni's deep, raucous voice could be heard. I pricked up my ears. He was talking about the water spirits who, during the storm, had climbed up the masts of his caique and licked them.

"They are soft and sticky," he said. "When you take lots of them, your hands catch fire. I stroked my moustache and so, in the dark, I gleamed like a devil. Well, the seas washed into my caique and soaked my cargo of coal. It was waterlogged. The caique began to heel over; but, at that moment, God took a hand in things; he sent a thunderbolt. The hatch covers were burst open and the sea filled with coal. The caique was lightened, righted itself, and we were saved. No more of that!"

Out of my pocket I drew a little edition of Dante—my travelling companion. I lit a pipe, leaned against the wall and made myself comfortable. I hesitated for a moment. Into which verses should I dip? Into the burning pitch of the Inferno, or the cleansing flames of Purgatory? Or should I make straight for the most elevated plane of human hope? I had the choice. Holding my pocket Dante in my hand, I rejoiced in my freedom. The verses I was going to choose so early in the morning would impart their rhythm to the whole of the day.

I bowed over this intense vision in order to decide, but I did not have the time. Suddenly, disturbed, I raised my head. Somehow, I felt as if two eyes were boring into the top of my skull; I quickly looked behind me in the direction of the glass door. A mad hope flashed through my brain: "I'm going to see my friend again." I was prepared for the miracle, but the miracle did not happen. A stranger of about sixty, very tall and lean, with staring eyes, had pressed his nose against the pane and was looking at me. He was holding a little flattened bundle under his arm.

The thing which impressed me most was his eager gaze, his eyes, ironical and full of fire. At any rate, that is how they appeared to me.

As soon as our eyes had met—he seemed to be making sure I was really the person he was looking for—the stranger opened the door with a determined thrust of his arm. He passed between the tables with a rapid, springy step, and stopped in front of me.

"Travelling?" he asked. "Where to? Trusting to providence?"

"I'm making for Crete. Why do you ask?"

"Taking me with you?"

9

I looked at him carefully. He had hollow cheeks, a strong jaw, prominent cheekbones, curly grey hair, bright piercing eyes.

"Why? What could I do with you?"

He shrugged his shoulders.

"Why! Why!" he exclaimed with disdain. "Can't a man do anything without a why? Just like that, because he wants to? Well, take me, shall we say, as cook. I can make soups you've never heard or thought of . . ."

I started to laugh. His bluff ways and trenchant words pleased me. Soups pleased me, too. It would not be a bad thing, I thought, to take this loose-knit fellow with me to that distant, lonely coast. Soups and stories . . . He looked as if he had knocked about the world quite a lot, a sort of Sinbad the Sailor. . . . I liked him.

"What are you thinking about?" he asked me familiarly, shaking his great head. "You keep a pair of scales, too, do you? You weigh everything to the nearest gram, don't you? Come on, friend, make up your mind. Take the plunge!"

This great lanky lubber was standing over me, and it tired me to have to look up to speak to him. I closed my Dante. "Sit down," I said to him. "Have a glass of sage?"

"Sage?" he exclaimed with contempt. "Here! waiter! a rum!"

He drank his rum in little sips, keeping it a long time in his mouth to get the taste, then letting it slip slowly down and warm his insides. "A sensualist," I thought. "A connoisseur . . ."

"What kind of work do you do?" I asked.

"All kinds. With feet, hands or head—all of them. It'd be the limit if we chose what we did!"

"Where were you working last?"

"In a mine. I'm a good miner. I know a thing or two about metals, I know how to find the veins and open up galleries. I go down pits; I'm not afraid. I was working well. I was foreman, and had nothing to complain about. But then the devil took a hand in things. Last Saturday night, simply because I felt like it, I went off all of a sudden, got hold of the boss, who had come that day to inspect the place, and just beat him up . . ."

"But what for? What had he done to you?"

"To me? Nothing at all, I tell you! It was the first time I saw him. The poor devil had even handed out cigarettes."

"Well?"

"Oh, you just sit there and ask questions! It just came over me, that's all. You know the tale of the miller's wife, don't you? Well, you don't expect to learn spelling from her backside, do you? The backside of the miller's wife, that's human reason."

I had read many definitions of human reason. This one seemed to me the most astounding of all, and I liked it. I looked at my new companion with keen interest. His face was furrowed, weather beaten, like worm-eaten wood. A few years later another face gave me the same impression of worn and tortured wood: that of Panait Istrati.*

"And what have you got in your bundle? Food? Clothes? Or tools?"

My companion shrugged his shoulders and laughed.

"You seem a very sensible sort," he said, "begging your pardon." He stroked his bundle with his long, hard fingers.

"No," he added, "it's a *santuri*. †

"A *santuri*? Do you play the *santuri*?"

"When I'm hard up, I go round the inns playing the *santuri*. I sing old Klephtic tunes from Macedonia. Then I take my hat round —this beret here!—and it fills up with money."

"What's your name?"

"Alexis Zorba. Sometimes they call me Baker's Shovel, because I'm so lanky and my head is flattened like a griddle-cake. Or else I'm called Passa Tempo because there was a time when I hawked roast pumpkin seeds. They call me Mildew, too, because wherever I go, they say, I get up to my tricks. Everything goes to the dogs. I have other nicknames as well, but we'll leave them for another time. . . ."

"And how did you learn to play the *santuri*?"

"I was twenty. I heard the *santuri* for the first time at one of my village fêtes, over there at the foot of Olympus. It took my breath away. I couldn't eat anything for three days. 'What's wrong with

* Rumanian author who suffered from tuberculosis. He wrote in French. His chief claim to fame was *La Maison Thüringer* (1933), the first volume of *The Life of Adrian Zograffi*—the man without convictions. C. W.

† A stringed instrument. A variety of cimbalom or dulcimer, usually played with a small hammer or plectrum. C. W.

you?' my father asked. May his soul rest in peace. 'I want to learn the *santuri!*' 'Aren't you ashamed of yourself? Are you a gipsy? D'you mean to say you'd turn into a strummer?' 'I want to learn the *santuri!*' I had a little money put aside for my marriage. It was a kid's idea, but I was still half-baked then, my blood was hot. I wanted to get married, the poor idiot! Anyway, I spent everything I had and more besides, and bought a *santuri.* The one you're looking at. I vanished with it to Salonica and got hold of a Turk, Retsep Effendi, who taught everybody the *santuri.* I threw myself at his feet. 'What do you want, little infidel?' he said. 'I want to learn the *santuri.*' 'All right, but why throw yourself at my feet?' 'Because I've no money to pay you!' 'And you're really crazy about the *santuri,* are you?' 'Yes.' 'Well, you can stay, my boy. I don't need paying!' I stayed a year and studied with him. May God sanctify his remains! He must be dead now. If God lets dogs enter his paradise, let him open his gate to Retsep Effendi. Since I learnt to play the *santuri,* I've been a different man. When I'm feeling down, or when I'm broke, I play the *santuri* and it cheers me up. When I'm playing, you can talk to me, I hear nothing, and even if I hear, I can't speak. It's no good my trying. I can't!"

"But why, Zorba?"

"Oh, don't you see? A passion, that's what it is!"

The door opened. The sound of the sea once more penetrated the café. Our hands and feet were frozen. I snuggled further into my corner and wrapped myself in my overcoat. I savored the bliss of the moment.

"Where shall I go?" I thought. "I'm all right here. May this minute last for years."

I looked at the strange man in front of me. His eyes were riveted on mine. They were little, round eyes with very dark pupils and red veinlets on the whites. I felt them penetrating, searching me insatiably.

"Well?" I said. "Go on."

Zorba shrugged his bony shoulders again.

"Let's drop it," he said. "Will you give me a cigarette?"

I gave him one. He took a lighter flint out of his pocket and a wick which he lit. He half-closed his eyes with contentment.

"Married?"

"Aren't I a man?" he said angrily. "Aren't I a man? I mean blind. Like everyone else before me, I fell headlong into the ditch. I married. I took the road downhill. I became head of a family, I built a house, I had children—trouble. But thank God for the *santuri!*"

"You played to forget your cares, did you?"

"Look, I can see you don't play any instruments. Whatever are you talking about? In the house there are all your worries. The wife. The children. What are we going to eat? How shall we manage for clothes? What will become of us? Hell! No, for the *santuri* you must be in good form, you must be pure. If my wife says one word too many, how could I possibly be in the mood to play the *santuri?* If your children are hungry and screaming at you, you just try to play! To play the *santuri* you have to give everything up to it, d'you understand?"

Yes, I understood. Zorba was the man I had sought so long in vain. A living heart, a large voracious mouth, a great brute soul, not yet severed from mother earth.

The meaning of the words, art, love, beauty, purity, passion, all this was made clear to me by the simplest of human words uttered by this workman.

I looked at his hands, which could handle the pick and the *santuri.* They were horny, cracked, deformed and sinewy. With great care and tenderness, as if undressing a woman, they opened the sack and drew out an old *santuri,* polished by the years. It had many strings, it was adorned with brass and ivory and a red silk tassel. Those big fingers caressed it, slowly, passionately, all over, as if caressing a woman. Then they wrapped it up again, as if clothing the body of the beloved lest it should catch cold.

"That's my *santuri!*" he murmured, as he laid it carefully on a chair.

The seamen were now clinking their glasses and bursting with laughter. The old salt gave Captain Lemoni some friendly slaps on the back.

"You had a hell of a scare, now didn't you, captain? God knows how many candles you've promised to St. Nicholas!"

13

The captain knit his bushy eyebrows.

"No, I can swear to you, when I saw the archangel of death before me, I didn't think of the Holy Virgin, nor of St. Nicholas! I just turned towards Salamis. I thought of my wife, and I cried out: 'Ah, Katherina, if only I were in bed with you this minute!'"

Once more the seamen burst out laughing, and Captain Lemoni joined in with them.

"What an animal man is," he said. "The Archangel is right over his head with a sword, but his mind is fixed there, just there and nowhere else! The devil take the old goat!"

He clapped his hands.

"A round for the company!" he cried.

Zorba was listening intently with his big ears. He turned round, looked at the seamen, then at me.

"Where's *there*?" he asked. "What's that fellow talking about?"

But he suddenly understood and started.

"Bravo, my friend!" he cried in admiration. "Those seamen know the secret. Most likely because day and night they're at grips with death."

He waved his big fist in the air.

"Right!" he said. "That's another matter. Let's come back to our business. Do I stay, or do I go? Decide."

"Zorba," I said, and I had to restrain myself forcibly from throwing myself into his arms, "it's agreed! You come with me. I have some lignite in Crete. You can superintend the workmen. In the evening we'll stretch out on the sand—in this world, I have neither wife, children nor dogs—we'll eat and drink together. Then you'll play the *santuri*."

"If I'm in the mood, d'you hear? If I'm in the mood. I'll work for you as much as you like. I'm your man there. But the *santuri*, that's different. It's a wild animal, it needs freedom. If I'm in the mood, I'll play. I'll even sing. And I'll dance the *Zéimbékiko*,* the *Hassápiko*,† the *Pentozáli*‡—but, I tell you plainly from the start, I must be in the mood. Let's have that quite clear. If you force me to,

* Dance of the Zeimbeks, a coastal tribe of Asia Minor.
† Butchers' dance.
‡ Cretan national warriors' dance. C. W.

14

it'll be finished. As regards those things, you must realize, I'm a man."

"A man? What d'you mean?"

"Well, free!"

I called for another rum.

"Make it two!" Zorba cried. "You're going to have one, so that we can drink to it. Sage and rum don't go very well together. You're going to drink a rum, too, so that our agreement holds good."

We clinked our little glasses. Now it was really daylight. The ship was blowing its siren. The lighterman who had taken my cases on board signalled to me.

"May God be with us," I said as I rose. "Let's go!"

"God and the devil!" Zorba added calmly.

He leaned over, put the *santuri* under his arm, opened the door, and went out first.

◊ 2 ◊

THE SEA, autumn mildness, islands bathed in light, fine rain spreading a diaphanous veil over the immortal nakedness of Greece. Happy is the man, I thought, who, before dying, has the good fortune to sail the Aegean Sea.

Many are the joys of this world—women, fruit, ideas. But to cleave that sea in the gentle autumnal season, murmuring the name of each islet, is to my mind the joy most apt to transport the heart of man into paradise. Nowhere else can one pass so easily and serenely from reality to dream. The frontiers dwindle, and from the masts of the most ancient ships spring branches and fruits. It is as if here in Greece necessity is the mother of miracles.

Towards noon the rain stopped. The sun parted the clouds and appeared gentle, tender, washed and fresh, and it caressed with its rays the beloved waters and lands. I stood at the prow and let myself be intoxicated with the miracle which was revealed as far as eye could see.

On the ship were Greeks, cunning devils with rapacious eyes, brains like the trumpery goods of bazaar dealers, wire pulling and quarrelling; an untuned piano; honest and venomous shrews. One's first impulse was to seize the ship by both ends, plunge it into the sea, shake it thoroughly to make all the livestock which polluted it drop off—men, rats, bugs—and then refloat it, freshly washed and empty.

But at times I was seized with compassion. A Buddhist compassion, as cold as the conclusion of a metaphysical syllogism. A compassion not only for men but for all life which struggles, cries, weeps, hopes and does not perceive that everything is a phantasmagoria of nothingness. Compassion for the Greeks, and for the lignite mine, and for my unfinished manuscript of Buddha, for all those vain compositions of light and shade which suddenly disturb and contaminate the pure air.

I looked at Zorba's drawn and waxen face. He was sitting on a coil of ropes in the bows. He was sniffing at a lemon and listening with his great ears to some passengers quarrelling about the king and others about Venizelos. He was shaking his head and spitting.

"Old junk!" he murmured disdainfully. "Aren't they ashamed of themselves!"

"What do you mean by old junk, Zorba?"

"Why, all these—kings, democracies, plebiscites, deputies, fiddle-faddle!"

Zorba had got so far beyond contemporary events that they had already ceased to be anything but out-of-date rubbish. Certainly, to him telegraphy, steamships and engines, current morality and religion must have appeared like rusty old rifles. His mind progressed much faster than the world.

The ropes were creaking on the masts, the coastlines were dancing, and the women on board had become yellower than a lemon. They had laid down their weapons—paint, bodices, hairpins, combs. Their lips had paled, their nails were turning blue. The old magpie scolds were losing their borrowed plumes—ribbons, false eyebrows and beauty spots, brassières—and to see them on the point of vomiting, you felt disgust and a great compassion.

Zorba was also turning yellow and green. His sparkling eyes were dulled. It was only towards the evening that his eyes brightened again. He pointed out two dolphins, leaping through the water alongside the ship.

"Dolphins!" he exclaimed joyously.

I noticed for the first time that almost half of the index finger on his left hand was missing. I started and felt sick.

"What happened to your finger, Zorba?" I cried.

"Nothing," he replied, offended that I had not shown more delight in the dolphins.

"Did you get it caught in a machine?" I insisted.

"What ever are you going on about machines for? I cut it off myself."

"Yourself? Why?"

"You can't understand, boss!" he said, shrugging his shoulders. "I told you I had been in every trade. Once I was a potter. I was mad about that craft. D'you realize what it means to take a lump of mud and make what you will out of it? Ffrr! You turn the wheel and the mud whirls round, as if it were possessed while you stand over it and say: I'm going to make a jug, I'm going to make a plate, I'm going to make a lamp and the devil knows what more! That's what you might call being a man: freedom!"

He had forgotten the sea, he was no longer biting the lemon, his eyes had become clear again.

"Well?" I asked. "What about your finger?"

"Oh, it got in my way in the wheel. It always got plumb in the middle of things and upset my plans. So one day I seized a hatchet . . ."

"Didn't it hurt you?"

"What d'you mean? I'm not a tree trunk. I'm a man. Of course it hurt me. But it got in my way at the wheel, so I cut it off."

The sun went down and the sea became calmer. The clouds dispersed. The evening star shone, I looked at the sea, I looked at the sky and began to reflect. . . . To love like that, to take the hatchet and chop and feel the pain. . . . But I hid my emotion.

"A bad system that, Zorba!" I said, smiling. "It reminds me of the ascetic who, according to the Golden Legend, once saw a woman who disturbed him physically, so he took an axe . . ."

"The devil he didn't!" Zorba interposed, guessing what I was going to say. "Cut that off! To hell with the fool! The poor benighted innocent, that's never an obstacle!"

"But," I insisted, "it can be a very great obstacle!"

"To what?"

"To your entry into the kingdom of heaven."

Zorba glanced sideways at me, with a mocking air, and said: "But, you fool, that is the key to paradise!"

He raised his head, looked at me closely, as if he wanted to see what was going on in my mind: future lives, the kingdom of heaven, women, priests. But he did not seem to be able to gather much. He shook his great grey head guardedly.

"The maimed don't get into paradise," he said, and then fell silent.

I went to lie down in my cabin and took a book. Buddha was still engaging my thoughts. I read *The Dialogue of Buddha and the Shepherd* which had filled my mind for some years with peace and security.

THE SHEPHERD: *My meal is ready, I have milked my ewes. The door of my hut is bolted, my fire is alight. And you, sky, can rain as much as you please!*

BUDDHA: *I no longer need food or milk. The winds are my shelter, my fire is out. And you, sky, can rain as much as you please!*

THE SHEPHERD: *I have oxen, I have cows. I have my father's meadows and a bull who covers my cows. And you, sky, can rain as much as you please!*

BUDDHA: *I have neither oxen, nor cows, I have no meadows. I have nothing, I fear nothing. And you, sky, can rain as much as you please!*

THE SHEPHERD: *I have a docile and faithful shepherdess. For years she has been my wife; I am happy when I play with her at night. And you, sky, you can rain as much as you please!*

BUDDHA: *I have a free and docile soul. For years I have trained it and I have taught it to play with me. And you, sky, can rain as much as you please!*

These two voices were still speaking when sleep overcame me. The wind had risen again and the waves were breaking over the thick glass of the porthole. I was floating like a wisp of smoke between sleeping and waking. A violent storm broke, the meadows disappeared under the waters, the bullocks, the cows and the bull were swallowed up. The wind carried away the roof of the hut, the fire was quenched, the woman uttered a cry and fell dead in the mud, and the shepherd began his lamentations. I could not hear what he said, but he was crying aloud and I was sinking deeper into a slumber, slipping like a fish down through the watery depths.

At daybreak I awoke, and there, to our right, lay the proud, wild and lordly island. The pale-pink mountains were smiling through the mists beneath the autumnal sun. Round our ship, the indigo-blue sea was still seething restlessly.

Zorba, wrapped in a brown rug, was gazing eagerly at Crete. His eyes turned rapidly from mountain to plain, followed the shore, exploring it as if all the coast and land were familiar to him, and that he were delighted to wander there again in his mind.

I went to him, touched him on the shoulder and said:

"Zorba, it's certainly not the first time you've come to Crete! You're gazing at it like an old friend."

Zorba yawned, as if bored. I felt he was not at all inclined to start a conversation.

I smiled. "Talking bores you, doesn't it, Zorba?"

"It's not exactly that, boss," he replied. "Only talking's difficult."

"Difficult? Why?"

He did not reply at once. His eyes roamed again slowly over the shore. He had slept on deck, and his curly grey hair was dripping with dew. The rising sun shone right into the deep furrows lining his cheeks, his chin and his neck.

Finally he moved his lips. They were thick and drooping, like those of a goat.

"In the morning I find it difficult to open my mouth. Very difficult. I'm sorry."

He lapsed again into silence, and once more his small round eyes were fixed on Crete.

A bell rang for breakfast. Greenish-yellow, screwed-up faces began to emerge from the cabins. Women, with their coils of hair coming loose, reeled as they dragged themselves from table to table. They smelled of vomit and eau-de-Cologne, and their eyes were cloudy, terrified and stupid.

Zorba, sitting in front of me, sniffed his coffee in a sensual way which was quite oriental. He spread butter and honey on his bread and ate it. His face gradually became brighter and calmer, the lines of his mouth softer. I secretly watched him as he slowly emerged from his wrapping of sleep, and saw how his eyes shone more and more brightly.

He lit a cigarette, inhaled with pleasure and blew the blue smoke

20

out of his hairy nostrils. He folded his right leg under him and made himself comfortable in eastern fashion. It was now possible for him to speak.

"Is this the first time I've been to Crete?" he began. (He half-closed his eyes and looked through the porthole at Mount Ida, which was disappearing in the distance behind us.) "No, it's not the first time. In 1896 I was already a fully grown man. My moustache and my hair were their real color, black as a raven. I had all my thirty-two teeth, and when I got drunk I swallowed the hors d'œuvres first and then the dish. Yes, I enjoyed myself no end. But suddenly the devil took a hand in things. A new revolution broke out in Crete.

"In those days I was a pedlar. I peddled haberdashery from village to village in Macedonia, and instead of money I used to take cheese, wool, butter, rabbits and corn. Then I sold all that and made a double profit. In every village I came to at dark I knew where to spend the night. In every village there's always a tenderhearted widow, God bless her! I'd give her a reel of thread, or a comb, or a scarf—a black one, of course, on account of the late-lamented—and I slept with her. It didn't cost me much!

"No, it didn't cost me much, boss, the good time I had! But, as I said before, the devil got mixed up in things and Crete took up arms again. 'Ah, to hell with her destiny!' I'd say. 'Can't that damned Crete ever leave us in peace?' I put aside my cottons and combs, took my gun and set off to join the rebels in Crete."

Zorba became silent. We were now following the curve of a quiet, sandy bay. The waves spread out here gently without breaking and only leaving a thin line of foam along the shore. The clouds had broken up, the sun was shining, and the rugged contours of Crete became serene.

Zorba turned round and gave me a mocking look.

"And now I suppose, boss, you think I'm going to start and tell you how many Turks' heads I've lopped off, and how many of their ears I've pickled in spirits—that's the custom in Crete. Well, I shan't! I don't like to, I'm ashamed. What sort of madness comes over us? . . . Today I'm a bit more level-headed, and I ask myself: What sort of madness comes over us to make us throw ourselves on another man, when he's done nothing to us, and bite him, cut his nose off, tear his ear out, run him through the guts—and all the time, calling on the Almighty to help us! Does it mean we want the Almighty to go and cut off noses and ears and rip people up?

"But at the time, you see, my blood was hot in my veins! How could I stop to examine the whys and wherefores? To think things out properly and fairly, a fellow's got to be calm and old and toothless: When you're an old gaffer with no teeth, it's easy to say: 'Damn it, boys, you mustn't bite!' But, when you've got all thirty-two teeth . . . A man's a savage beast when he's young; yes, boss, a savage, man-eating beast!"

He shook his head.

"Oh, he eats sheep, too, and hens and pigs, but if he doesn't eat men his belly's not satisfied."

He added as he crushed out his cigarette in the coffee saucer:

"No, his belly's not satisfied. Now, what does the old owl have to say to that, eh?"

He did not wait for an answer.

"What *can* you say, I wonder?" he continued, weighing me up. "As far as I can see, your lordship's never been hungry, never killed, never stolen, never committed adultery. What ever can you know of the world? You've got an innocent's brain and your skin's never even felt the sun," he muttered with obvious scorn.

I became ashamed of my delicate hands, my pale face and my life which had not been bespattered with mud and blood.

"All right!" said Zorba, sweeping his heavy hand across the table as if wiping a sponge across it. "All right! There's one thing, though, I'd like to ask you. You must've gone through hundreds of books, perhaps you know the answer . . ."

"Go ahead, Zorba, what is it?"

"There's a sort of miracle happening here, boss. A funny sort of miracle which puzzles me. All that business—those lousy tricks, thefts and that slaughter of ours—I mean of us rebels—all *that* brought Prince George to Crete. Liberty!"

He looked at me with his eyes wide open in amazement.

"It's a mystery," he murmured, "a great mystery! So, if we want liberty in this bad world, we've got to have all those murders, all those lousy tricks, have we? I tell you, if I began to go over all the bloody villainy and all the murders we did, you'd have your hair stand on end. And yet, the result of all that, what's it been? Liberty! Instead of wiping us out with a thunderbolt, God gives us liberty! I just don't understand!"

He looked at me, as if calling for help. I could see that this problem had tormented him a lot and that he could not get to the bottom of it.

"Do *you* understand?" he asked me with anguish.

Understand what? Tell him what? Either that what we call God does not exist, or else that what we call murders and villainy is necessary for the struggle and for the liberation of the world . . .

I tried hard to find for Zorba another, simpler way of explaining it.

"How does a plant sprout and grow into a flower on manure and muck? Say to yourself, Zorba, that the manure and muck is man and the flower liberty."

"But the seed?" cried Zorba, striking his fist on the table. "For a plant to sprout there must be a seed. Who's put such a seed in our entrails? And why doesn't this seed produce flowers from kindness and honesty? Why must it have blood and filth?"

I shook my head.

"I don't know," I said.

"Who does?"

"No one."

"But then," Zorba cried in despair and casting wild glances about him, "what d'you expect me to do with all your boats, and your machines and neckties?"

Two or three passengers whom the sea had upset, and who were now drinking coffee at a nearby table, revived. They sensed a quarrel and pricked up their ears.

This disgusted Zorba. He lowered his voice.

"Change the subject," he said. "When I think of that, I feel like breaking anything within reach—a chair, a lamp, or my head against the wall. But what good would that do me? I'd have to pay the breakages and go to a doctor and have my head bandaged. And if God exists, well, it's far worse: we're bloody well done for! He must be peering at me from up there in the sky and bursting his sides with laughter."

He suddenly made a movement with his hand as if getting rid of an importunate fly.

"Never mind!" he said regretfully. "All I wanted to tell you was this: When the royal ship arrived all decked up with flags, and they began to fire off rounds from the guns, and the prince set foot on Cretan soil . . . Have you ever seen a whole people gone mad because they've seen their liberty? No? Ah, boss, then blind you were born and blind you'll die. If I live a thousand years, even if all that remains of me is a morsel of living flesh, what I saw that day I'll never forget! And if each of us could choose his paradise in the sky, according to his taste—and that's how it should be, that's what I call paradise—I'd say to the Almighty: 'Lord, let my paradise be a Crete decked with myrtle and flags and let the minute when Prince George set foot on Cretan soil last for centuries!' That'll do me."

Zorba became silent once more. He raised his moustache, filled a glass to the brim with iced water and swallowed it in one gulp.

"What happened in Crete, Zorba? Tell me!"

"Do we have to start making big sentences?" said Zorba, annoyed. "Look here, I tell you, I do—this world is a mystery and man is just a great brute.

"A great brute and a god. A blackguard of a rebel who'd come from Macedonia with me—Yorga, they called him, a gallows' bird, a real swine, you know—well, he wept. 'Why're you crying, Yorga, you hound?' I said, and my eyes were streaming too. 'Why're you crying, you old swine?' But he just threw his arms round my neck and blubbered like a kid. And then that miserly bastard pulls out his purse, empties onto his lap the gold coins he'd looted from the Turks and throws them into the air by handfuls! D'you see, boss, that's what liberty is!"

I rose and went up on deck, to be buffeted by the keen sea breeze.

That's what liberty is, I thought. To have a passion, to amass pieces of gold and suddenly to conquer one's passion and throw the treasure to the four winds.

Free yourself from one passion to be dominated by another and nobler one. But is not that, too, a form of slavery? To sacrifice oneself to an idea, to a race, to God? Or does it mean that the higher the model the longer the tether of our slavery? Then we can enjoy ourselves and frolic in a more spacious arena and die without having come to the end of the tether. Is that, then, what we call liberty?

24

Towards the end of the afternoon we berthed by the sandy shore and saw finely sifted white sand, oleanders still in flower, fig and carob trees, and, further to the right, a low grey hill without a tree, resembling the face of a woman resting. And beneath her chin, along her neck, ran the dark brown veins of lignite.

An autumnal wind was blowing, frayed clouds were passing slowly over the earth and softening its contours with shadow. Other clouds were rising menacingly in the sky. The sun appeared and disappeared, and the earth's surface was brightened and darkened like a living and perturbed face.

I stopped for a moment on the sand and looked. A sacred solitude lay before me, deadly and yet fascinating, like the desert. The Buddhist song rose out of the very soil and found its way to the depths of my being. "When shall I at last retire into solitude, alone, without companions, without joy and without sorrow, with only the sacred certainty that all is a dream? When, in my rags—without desires—shall I retire contented into the mountains? When, seeing that my body is merely sickness and crime, age and death, shall I—free, fearless and blissful—retire into the forest? When? When, oh when?"

Zorba, with his *santuri* beneath his arm, his steps still unsteady, came towards me.

"There's the lignite!" I said, to hide my emotions. And I stretched my arm towards the hill with the woman-like face.

Zorba frowned without looking round.

"Later. This isn't the time, boss," he said. "Must wait for the earth to stop. She's still pitching, the devil take her, like the deck of a ship. Let's go to the village."

With these words he set off with long, determined strides, trying to save his face.

Two barefooted urchins, as brown as Arabs, ran up and took charge of the luggage. A huge customs officer was smoking a hookah in the customs shed. He scrutinized us from out of the corner of his blue eyes, took a nonchalant glance at the bags, and shifted momentarily on his seat as if he were going to get up. But it was too much of an effort. He slowly raised the hookah tube and said in a sleepy voice: "Welcome!"

One of the urchins came up to me. He winked with his olive-black eyes and said in a mocking tone:

"He's no Cretan. He's a lazy devil."

"Aren't Cretans lazy devils, too?"

"They are . . . yes, they are," the young Cretan replied, "but in a different way."

"Is the village far?"

"Only a gun-shot from here. Look, behind the gardens, in the ravine. A fine village, sir. Plenty of everything—carob trees, beans, grain, oil, wine. And down there in the sand, the earliest cucumbers, tomatoes, aubergines and watermelons in Crete. It's the winds from Africa makes them swell. At night, in the orchard, you can hear them crackling and getting bigger."

Zorba was going on in front. His head was still swimming. He spat.

"Chin up, Zorba!" I called to him. "We've scraped through all right. There's nothing more to fear!"

We walked quickly. The earth was mixed with sand and shells, and here and there grew a tamarisk, a wild fig tree, a tuft of reeds, some bitter mullein. The weather was sultry, the clouds were gathering lower and lower, the wind was dropping.

We were passing by a great fig tree with a twisted double trunk which was beginning to grow hollow with age. One of the urchins stopped and with a jerk of the chin pointed to the old tree.

"The Fig Tree of Our Young Lady!" he said.

I started. On this Cretan soil, every stone, every tree has its tragic history.

"Of Our Young Lady? Why that name?"

"In my grandfather's time, the daughter of one of our landowners fell in love with a shepherd boy. But her father wouldn't hear of it. The young lady wept, screamed and pleaded. The old man never changed his tune! One night the young couple disappeared. The countryside was searched, but for one, two, three days, a whole week, they weren't to be found. Then they began to stink, so the stench was followed and they were found rotting beneath this fig tree, locked in each other's arms. You see, they found them through the stench."

The child burst out laughing. The sounds of the village could be heard. Dogs began to bark, women to talk shrilly, cocks to announce the change in the weather. In the air floated the odor of grapes which came from the vats where raki was being distilled.

"There's the village!" shouted the two boys, and rushed off.

As soon as we had rounded the sandy hill the little village came into sight. It seemed to be clambering up the side of the ravine. Whitewashed, terraced houses huddled together. Their open windows made dark patches, and they resembled whitened skulls jammed between the rocks.

I caught up with Zorba.

"Mind you behave, now we're entering the village," I told him. "They mustn't get wind of us, Zorba. We'll act like serious businessmen. I'm the manager and you're the foreman. Cretans don't take things lightly. As soon as they've set eyes on you, they pick on anything queer, and give you a nickname. After that, you can't get rid of it. You run about like a dog with a saucepan tied to its tail."

Zorba seized his moustache in his fist and plunged into meditation. Finally he said:

"Listen, boss, if there's a widow in the place, you've no need to fear. If there isn't . . ."

Just then, as we entered the village, a beggar-woman clothed in rags rushed towards us with outstretched hand. She was swarthy, filthy, and had a stiff little black moustache.

"Hi, brother!" she called familiarly to Zorba. "Hi, brother, got a soul, have you?"

Zorba stopped.

"I have," he replied gravely.

"Then give me five drachmas!"

Zorba pulled out of his pocket a dilapidated leather purse.

"There," he said, and his lips, which still had a bitter expression, softened into a smile. He looked round and said:

"Looks as if souls are cheap in these parts, boss! Five drachmas a soul!"

The village dogs bounded towards us, the women leaned over the terraces to gaze at us, the children followed us, yelling. Some of them yelped, others made sounds like Klaxons, still others ran in front of us and looked at us with their big eyes full of amazement.

We arrived at the village square, where we found two huge white poplars surrounded by crudely carved trunks which served as seats. Opposite was the café, over which hung an enormous, faded sign: *The Modesty Café-and-Butcher's-Shop.*

"Why are you laughing?" Zorba asked.

But I did not have time to reply. From the door of the café and butcher's shop ran out five or six giants wearing dark-blue breeches with red waistbands. They shouted: "Welcome, friends! Come in and have a raki. It's still warm from the vat."

Zorba clicked his tongue and said: "What about it, boss?" He turned round and winked at me. "Shall we have one?"

We drank a glass and it burned our insides. The proprietor of the café-butchery, who was a brisk, tough, well-preserved old man, brought out chairs for us.

I asked where we might lodge.

"Go to Madame Hortense's," someone shouted.

"A Frenchwoman here?" I exclaimed in surprise.

"From the devil knows where; she's been all over the place. She's managed to avoid going on all the rocks you can think of, and now she's clung on to the last one here and has opened an inn."

"She sells sweets, too!" cried a child.

"She powders and paints herself up," someone else said. "She puts a ribbon round her neck. . . . And she's got a parrot."

"A widow?" Zorba asked. "Is she a widow?"

The café proprietor seized his thick grey beard.

"How many whiskers can you count here, friend? How many? Well, she's widow of as many husbands. Get the idea?"

"Got it," Zorba replied, licking his lips.

"She might make you a widower, too!"

"Mind your step, friend!" shouted an old man, and all burst out laughing.

We were treated to a new round and the café proprietor brought it to us on a tray, together with barley loaf, goat cheese and pears.

"Now leave these people alone. They mustn't dream of going to madame's! They're going to spend the night right here!"

"*I'm* going to have them, Kondomanolio!" said the old man. "I've got no children. My house is big and there's plenty of room."

"Sorry, uncle Anagnosti," the café proprietor shouted in the old man's ear. "I spoke first."

"You take one," said old Anagnosti; "I'll take t'other, the old 'un."

"Which old 'un?" said Zorba, stung to the quick.

"We'll stick together," I said, and made a sign to Zorba not to get annoyed. "We'll stick together and we'll go to Madame Hortense's. . . ."

"Welcome! Welcome to you!"

A dumpy, plump little woman, with bleached flax-colored hair, appeared beneath the poplars, waddling along on her bandy legs. A beauty spot, from which sprang sow-bristles, adorned her chin. She was wearing a red-velvet ribbon round her neck, and her withered cheeks were plastered with mauve powder. A gay little lock of hair danced on her brow and made her look somewhat like Sarah Bernhardt in her old age playing *L'Aiglon*.

"Delighted to meet you, Madame Hortense!" I replied, preparing to kiss her hand, carried away as I was by a sudden good humor.

Life appeared all at once like a fairy-tale or the opening scene of *The Tempest*. We had just set foot on the island, soaked to the skin after an imaginary shipwreck. We were exploring the marvellous coasts, and ceremoniously greeting the inhabitants of the place. This woman, Hortense, seemed to me to be the queen of the island, a sort of blonde and glistening walrus who had been cast up, half-rotting, on this sandy shore. Behind her appeared the numerous dirty, hairy faces radiating the general good humor of the people—or of Caliban—who gazed at the queen with pride and scorn.

Zorba, the prince in disguise, also stared at her, as if she were an old comrade, an old frigate who had fought on distant seas, who had known victory and defeat, her hatches battered in, her masts broken, her sails torn—and who now, scored with furrows which she had caulked with powder and cream, had retired to this coast and was waiting. Surely she was waiting for Zorba, the captain of the thousand scars. And I was delighted to see these two actors meet at last in a Cretan setting which had been very simply produced and painted in a few broad strokes of the brush.

"Two beds, Madame Hortense," I said, bowing before this old specialist in the art of acting love scenes. "Two beds, and no bugs."

"No bugs! I should think not!" she cried, throwing me a provocative glance.

"Oh, no!" shouted the mocking mouths of Caliban.

"There aren't! There aren't!" she retorted, stamping on the stones with her plump foot. She was wearing thick sky-blue stockings and a pair of battered court-shoes with dainty silk bows.

"Off with you, prima donna! The devil take you!" Caliban roared once more.

But, with great dignity, Dame Hortense was already going and opening up the way for us. She smelt of powder and cheap soap.

Zorba followed her, devouring her with his eyes.

"Take an eyeful of that, boss," he confided. "The way the trollop swings her hips, plaf! plaf! like an ewe with a tailful of fat!"

Two or three big drops of rain fell, the sky clouded over. Blue lightning flickered over the mountain. Young girls, wrapped in their little white goat-skin capes, were hurriedly bringing back from pasture the family goats and sheep. The women, squatting in front of their hearths, were kindling the evening fire.

Zorba bit his moustache impatiently, without taking his eyes off the rolling buttocks of the woman.

"Hm!" he suddenly muttered with a sigh. "To hell with life! The jade's never done playing us tricks!"

◇ 3 ◇

Dame Hortense's hotel consisted of a row of old bathing-huts joined together. The first was the shop where you could buy sweets, cigarettes, peanuts, lamp-wicks, alphabets, candles and benjamin. Four adjoining huts formed the dormitory. Behind, in the yard, were the kitchen, the washhouse, the henhouse and the rabbit hutches. Thick bamboos and prickly pears were planted in the fine sand all round. The whole place smelled of the sea, excrement and urine. But, from time to time, Dame Hortense passed by and the air changed its odor—as if someone had emptied a hairdresser's bowl under your nose.

As soon as the beds were ready we retired and slept without a break till the morning. I do not remember the dream I had, but I rose lightly and as fit as if I had come fresh from a dip in the sea.

It was Sunday, the workmen were to come on Monday from neighboring villages and begin work at the mine, so I had time this day to take a turn round the shores on which fate had cast me. Dawn was hardly peeping through when I started out. I went past the gardens, followed the edge of the sea, hurriedly made my acquaintance with the water, earth and air of the spot, picked wild plants, and the palms of my hands became redolent with savory, sage and mint.

I climbed a hill and looked around. An austere countryside of granite and very hard limestone. Dark carob and silvery olive trees,

31

figs and vines. In the sheltered hollows, orange groves, lemon and medlar trees; near the shore, kitchen gardens. To the south, an expanse of sea, still angry and roaring as it came rushing from Africa to bite into the coast of Crete. Nearby a low, sandy islet flushing rosy pink under the first rays of the sun.

To my mind, this Cretan countryside resembled good prose, carefully ordered, sober, free from superfluous ornament, powerful and restrained. It expressed all that was necessary with the greatest economy. It had no flippancy, nor artifice about it. It said what it had to say with a manly austerity. But between the severe lines one could discern an unexpected sensitiveness and tenderness; in the sheltered hollows the lemon and orange trees perfumed the air, and from the vastness of the sea emanated an inexhaustible poetry.

"Crete," I murmured. "Crete . . ." and my heart beat fast.

I came down from the little hill to the edge of the water. Chattering girls appeared with fichus as white as snow, long yellow boots, and skirts tucked up; they were going to mass in the convent over there, gleaming a dazzling white by the sea.

I stopped. As soon as they noticed me, the girls' laughter ceased. At the sight of a strange man their expression became one of wild distrust. Their whole bearing from head to foot was suddenly on the defensive, their fingers clutched nervously at their tightly buttoned blouses. Fear surged in their blood. For centuries the Corsairs had made sudden incursions on to the whole of the Cretan coast facing Africa, ravishing ewes, women and children. They bound them with their red belts, threw them into the bottoms of their ships and set sail to sell them in Algiers, Alexandria, Beirut. For centuries the waters round these shores, festooned with black tresses, have resounded with lamentations. I watched these frightened girls advance, clinging together as if to form an impassable barrier. It was an instinctive reaction, indispensable in earlier times and today repeated without reason. A bygone necessity dictated the rhythm of their movements.

As the girls passed in front of me, I quietly stepped aside, smiling. And immediately, as if they suddenly felt that the danger they feared had passed centuries ago, and that they had awakened in our age of security, their faces lit up, the serried line of battle spread out and, all together, they bade me good day in clear and light-hearted tones. At the same time the merry, sportive bells of the distant convent filled the air with sounds of rejoicing.

The sun had risen, the sky was clear. I crouched among the rocks, perched like a seagull on a ledge, and contemplated the sea. My body felt powerful, fresh and obedient. And my mind, following the waves, became itself a wave, unresisting, submissive to the rhythm of the sea.

Then my heart began to swell. Obscure, pleading and imperious voices rose within me. I knew who was calling to me. Whenever I was alone for a moment, this being cried out, in an anguish of horrible presentiments, transports and mad fears—waiting to be delivered by me.

I hurriedly opened Dante, my travelling companion, in order not to hear and to exorcise the fearful demon. I turned over the pages, reading a line here and there, or a tercet, and committing to memory the entire canto. Out of those fiery pages the damned rose howling. Halfway up the rocks, wounded souls sought to scale a precipitous mountainside. Higher still, the souls of the blessed moved among the emerald fields, like brilliant fireflies. I wandered from the highest to the lowest regions of the terrible house of destiny; I went freely about hell, purgatory and paradise, as if in my own dwelling. I suffered, I awaited or tasted beatitude, carried away as I was by those superb verses.

Suddenly I closed my Dante and looked out over the sea. A gull, its breast resting on the water, rose and fell with the waves, abandoning itself to them and enjoying the pleasures of abandonment. A youth, sunburnt and barefoot, appeared at the water's edge singing love songs. Maybe he understood the pain they expressed, for his voice had begun to grow hoarse, like that of a cockerel.

For hundreds of years, Dante's verses have been sung in the poet's country. And just as love songs prepare boys and girls for love, so the ardent Florentine verses prepared Italian youths for the day of deliverance. From generation to generation, all communed with the soul of the poet and so transformed their slavery into freedom.

I heard a laugh behind me and at once fell from the Dantesque heights. I looked round and saw Zorba behind me, his whole face creased with laughter.

"Well, boss, this is a fine way of going on!" he cried. "Here I've been looking for you for hours, but how could I know where to get hold of you?"

Seeing I remained silent, he continued:

"It's gone midday, the hen is cooked; the poor thing'll be dropping to bits, you know!"

"Yes, I know, but I'm not hungry."

"Not hungry!" Zorba exclaimed, slapping his thighs. "But you've not had a bite since morning. The body's got a soul, too, have pity on it. Give it something to eat, boss, give it something; it's our beast of burden, you know. If you don't feed it, it'll leave you stranded in the middle o' the road."

I had despised the pleasures of the flesh for years, and, if possible, I would have eaten secretly, as if committing a shameful act. But so that Zorba would not grumble I said:

"All right, I'm coming."

We started off in the direction of the village. The hours amongst the rocks had passed as time passes between lovers, like lightning.

"Were you thinking of the lignite?" Zorba asked with some hesitation.

"And what else d'you expect me to be thinking about?" I replied, laughing. "Tomorrow we'll start work. I had to make some calculations."

"What's the result of the calculations?" he asked, as he made his way carefully.

"After three months we must extract ten tons of lignite a day to cover expenses."

Zorba looked at me again, this time anxiously. A little later he said:

"And why the devil d'you have to go down to the sea to make calculations? Pardon me, boss, for asking this question, but I don't understand. When I have to wrestle with figures, I feel I'd like to stuff myself into a hole in the ground, so I can't see anything. If I raise my eyes and see the sea, or a tree, or a woman—even if she's an old 'un—damme if all the sums and figures don't go to blazes. They grow wings and I have to chase 'em. . . ."

"But that's your fault, Zorba," I said to tease him. "You don't concentrate."

34

"Maybe you're right, boss. It all depends on the way you look at it. There are cases even wise old Solomon . . . Look, one day I had gone to a little village. An old grandfather of ninety was busy planting an almond tree. 'What, grandad!' I exclaimed. 'Planting an almond tree?' And he, bent as he was, turned round and said: 'My son, I carry on as if I should never die.' I replied: 'And I carry on as if I was going to die any minute.' Which of us was right, boss?"

He looked at me triumphantly and said:

"That's where I've got you!"

I kept silent. Two equally steep and bold paths may lead to the same peak. To act as if death did not exist, or to act thinking every minute of death, is perhaps the same thing. But when Zorba asked me the question, I did not know.

"Well?" Zorba said mockingly. "Don't worry, boss, you can't argue that out. Let's talk of something else. Just now I'm thinking of the chicken and the pilaff sprinkled with cinnamon. My brain's steaming like the pilaff. Let's eat first, ballast up first, then we'll see. Everything in good time. In front of us now is the pilaff; let our minds become pilaff. Tomorrow the lignite will be in front of us; our minds must become lignite! No half-measures, you know."

We entered the village. The women were sitting in their doorways gossiping. The old men, leaning on their sticks, were silent. Under a pomegranate tree laden with fruit a little, shrivelled old woman was delousing her grandson.

In front of the café an old man with a grave, concentrated expression and an aquiline nose was standing erect. He had a distinguished air. He was Mavrandoni, the village elder who had rented the lignite mine to us. He had called the previous evening at Dame Hortense's to take us to his house. He said:

"It's a scandal for you to be staying at her hotel as if there were no men in the village."

He was grave, he weighed his words carefully as one of the leading villagers. We had refused. This had offended him, but he had not insisted.

"I have done my duty," he said as he departed. "You are free."

A little later he sent us two cheeses, a basket of pomegranates, a jar of raisins and figs, and a demijohn of raki. His servant said, as he unloaded his tiny ass:

"With the compliments of Captain Mavrandoni. It's nothing much, he asked me to tell you, but it's meant well."

We now greeted the head of the village volubly and cordially.

"Long life to you!" he said, placing his hand on his breast. Then he fell silent.

"He doesn't like to talk much," Zorba murmured. "He's an old stick."

"He's proud," I said. "I like him."

We were arriving. Zorba's nostrils were quivering joyously. As soon as Dame Hortense saw us from the threshold she uttered a cry and ran into the kitchen.

Zorba put the table in the yard under the leafless vine-arbor. He cut the thick slices of bread, brought the wine and set the table. He looked round at me wickedly and pointed to the table. He had set for three people!

"D'you see, boss?" he whispered.

"Yes, I see, you old rip!" I replied.

"It's the old birds who make the best stew," he said, licking his lips. "You take it from me."

He moved nimbly, his eyes sparkling. He hummed old love songs.

"That's the way to live, boss. Have a good time and the bird into the bargain. You see, I'm doing things now as if I was going to die next minute. And I'm making it snappy, so I don't kick the bucket before I've had the bird!"

"To table!" Dame Hortense ordered.

She lifted the pot and set it down in front of us. But she stood gaping. She had seen the three plates. Crimson with pleasure, she looked at Zorba and blinked her sharp, little periwinkle-blue eyes.

"She's got hot pants, all," Zorba whispered.

Then with extreme politeness, he turned to the lady and said:

"Beautiful nymph of the waves, we are shipwrecked and the sea has cast us in your realm. Do us the honor, my siren, of sharing our meal!"

The old cabaret singer opened her arms wide and closed them again as if she would have liked to embrace the two of us. She swayed gracefully, brushed against Zorba, then me, and ran, chuckling, to her room. Soon after she reappeared, twittering, flaunting her charms and dressed in her very best: an old shiny velvet dress, decorated with worn yellow braid. Her bodice remained hospitably open and on it she had pinned a full-blown artificial rose. In her hand she held the parrot's cage which she hung in the vine-arbor.

We made her sit between us, with Zorba to her right and me to her left.

We all three set to ravenously. For a long time we did not utter a word. We were feeding the beast and slaking its thirst with wine. The food was soon changed into blood, the world became more beautiful, the woman at our sides became younger every minute, the lines in her face were disappearing. The parrot, hanging in front of us in his green jacket and yellow waistcoat, leaned forward to watch us. He looked like some odd little fellow under a spell, or else the spirit of the old cabaret singer wearing a green-and-yellow dress. And above our heads the vine-arbor was suddenly covered with large bunches of black grapes.

Zorba's eyes were rolling, he flung open his arms as if he wanted to embrace the whole world.

"What's happening, boss?" he cried, in astonishment. "We drink one little glass of wine and the world goes haywire. Ah, boss, life's a rum thing. On your honor, are those grapes hanging there above our heads, or are they angels? I don't know. Or else they're nothing at all, and nothing exists, neither chicken, nor siren, nor Crete! Speak, boss, speak, so I don't go right off my head!"

Zorba was beginning to get lively. He had finished with the chicken and was beginning to look at Dame Hortense gluttonously. His eyes were ravishing her; they looked her up and down, slipped into her swelling bosom as if they touched her. Our lady's little eyes were shining too; she liked the wine and had emptied several glasses of it. The mischievous demon in the wine had carried her back to the good old days. She became once more tender, merry and expansive. She rose and bolted the outside door so that the villagers could not see her—"the barbarians," as she called them. She lit a cigarette, and from her little French retroussé nose began to issue wreaths of smoke.

At such times all the doors of a woman's being are opened. The sentinels relax and a kind word is as powerful as gold or love. So I lit my pipe and pronounced the kind word.

"Dame Hortense, you remind me of Sarah Bernhardt . . . when she was young. I didn't expect to find such elegance, such grace and courtesy, such beauty, in this wild place. What Shakespeare was it sent you here amongst the barbarians?"

"Shakespeare?" she queried, opening wide her pale little eyes. "What Shakespeare?"

Her mind flew back rapidly to the theaters she had been to. In the twinkling of an eye, she made a tour of the *café-concerts,* cabarets and taverns from Paris to Beirut, and from there along the coast of Anatolia. Suddenly she remembered. It was in Alexandria, a great theater with chandeliers, plush seats, men and women, bare backs, perfumes, flowers. All at once the curtain rose and a fearful black man appeared . . .

"What Shakespeare?" she asked again proudly, having remembered. "The one they also call Othello?"

"The same. What Shakespeare, my white lily, cast you on these savage rocks?"

She looked around her. The doors were closed, the parrot was asleep, the rabbits were mating, we were alone. She was touched and began to open her heart to us. It was like opening an old chest, full of spices, yellowed love-letters and ancient dresses.

She spoke Greek after a fashion, murdering the words and mixing up the syllables. However, we understood her perfectly. Sometimes we had great difficulty in suppressing our laughter, sometimes— we had drunk a good deal—we burst into tears.

"Well"—this is roughly what the old siren told us in her perfumed yard—"well, the person you're looking at now was never a tavern-singer, oh, no! I was a famous artist and wore silk underclothes with real lace. But love . . ."

She sighed deeply and lit another cigarette from Zorba's.

"I loved an admiral. Crete was once more in a state of revolution and the fleets of the great powers had anchored in the port of Suda. A few days later I also anchored there. Ah, what splendor! You should have seen the four admirals: the English, the French, the Italian and the Russian. All gold braid, patent-leather shoes and

plumed hats. Like cocks. Great cocks weighing from twelve to fifteen stone each. And what beards! They were curly, silky, dark,
fair, grey, red—and how nice they smelt! Each one had his own
particular perfume—that's how I could distinguish between them
in the dark. England smelled of eau-de-Cologne, France of violets,
Russia of musk, and Italy, ah, Italy doted on patchouli. My God,
what beards, what beards!

"Many times, when we were gathered on board the flagship,
we talked about the revolution. Their uniforms were unclasped and
my silk chemise was sticking to my skin, because they poured
champagne over it. It was summer, you know. We were speaking
about the revolution, having a serious conversation, and I caught
hold of their beards and begged them not to bombard the poor
dear Cretans. We could see them through the binoculars on a rock
near Canea. They looked tiny, quite tiny, like ants with blue
breeches and yellow boots. And they shouted and shouted, and they
had a flag."

There was a movement in the bamboos which surrounded the
yard. The old female warrior stopped, terrified. Between the leaves,
wicked little eyes were gleaming. The village children had sensed
we were junketing and were spying on us.

The cabaret singer tried to rise to her feet, but she could not.
She had eaten and drunk too much, she sat back in a sweat. Zorba
picked up a stone. The children scattered, screaming.

"Go on, my beauty! Go on, my treasure!" Zorba said, and pushed
his chair still closer to her.

"So I said to the Italian admiral—I was more familar with him
—I seized his beard and said to him: 'My Canavaro'—that was his
name—'please, my little Canavaro, no boom-boom! No boom-boom!'

"How many times the woman you see here has saved the Cretans
from death! How many times the guns were ready loaded and I
seized the admiral's beard and wouldn't let him 'boom-boom!' But
what thanks have I ever had for that? Look what I get in the way
of decorations. . . ."

Dame Hortense was angry at the ingratitude of men. She struck
the table with her soft and wrinkled fist. Zorba stretched out his
practiced hands over her parted knees and seized them, carried away
by a feigned emotion, and he cried:

"My Bouboulina! * For pity's sake, no boom-boom!"

"Hands off!" our good lady said, chuckling. "Who d'you take me for?" And she gave him a languorous glance.

"There's a God in heaven," said the crafty debauchee. "Don't upset yourself, my Bouboulina. We're here, sweetheart, don't be afraid."

The old siren raised her acid-blue eyes to heaven. She saw her green parrot asleep in his cage.

"My Canavaro, my little Canavaro!" she cooed amorously.

The parrot, recognizing her voice, opened his eyes, clutched hold of the bars of his cage and started to cry in the hoarse voice of a drowning man: "Canavaro! Canavaro!"

"Present!" cried Zorba, once more applying his hands to those old knees which had seen so much service, this time as if he wanted to take possession of them. The old cabaret singer wriggled in her chair and again opened her little puckered lips.

"I, too, have struggled valiantly, breast to breast. . . . But the bad days came. Crete was liberated, the fleets had orders to leave. And what is to become of me?' I said, seizing the four beards. 'Where are you going to leave me? I have got used to grandeur, to champagne and roast chicken; I have got used to handsome little sailors saluting me; I shall be four times a widow! What is going to become of me, my lords and admirals?'

"Oh, they just laughed—that's men for you! They loaded me with English and Italian pounds, roubles and napoleons. I stuffed them in my stockings, in my bodice and in my shoes. On the last evening I wept and sobbed so much the Admirals took pity on me. They filled the bath with champagne, plunged me in it—we were very familiar by then—and they drank the champagne from the bath in my honor. They got drunk and put out the light. . . .

"In the morning, I could smell all their perfumes on top of each other: the violet, the eau-de-Cologne, the musk and the patchouli. The four great powers—England, France, Russia and Italy—I held them here, here on my knees, and I went like this with them . . ."

* Bouboulina was a heroine of the war of independence (1821–28). She fought valiantly on the sea like Canaris and Miaoulis.

Dame Hortense held out her plump little arms and moved them up and down, as if she were bouncing a baby on her lap.

"There, like that! Like that!

"At daybreak they began to fire off their guns. I swear to this on my honor, they fired off their guns, and a white boat with twelve oarsmen came out to fetch me and set me on shore."

She took her little handkerchief out and began to weep, inconsolably.

"My Bouboulina," Zorba cried rapturously, "shut your eyes . . . shut your eyes, my treasure. I am Canavaro!"

"Hands off, I said!" our good lady simpered. "Just look at your handsome self! Where are the golden epaulettes, the three-cornered hat, the perfumed beard? Ah, well then! . . ."

She squeezed Zorba's hand gently and started to weep again.

It was becoming cooler. We fell silent a while. The sea, behind the bamboos, was sighing. It had at last become gentle and peaceful. The wind had fallen, the sun sank to rest. Two crows passed over our heads and their wings whistled as if a piece of silk was being torn—the silk chemise of the songstress.

The evening light fell like a spray of golden dust over the yard. Dame Hortense's fanciful lips caught alight and quivered in the evening breeze as if they wanted to take flight and carry the fire to her neighbors' heads. The golden light fell on her half-bared bosom, her parted knees which had grown fat with age, the lines in her neck, her worn-out court shoes.

Our old siren shuddered. Half-closing her little eyes, which were reddened by her tears and the wine, she looked first at me, then at Zorba, whose lips were parched, and who was fascinated by her bosom. She looked at each of us with a questioning air, trying to see which of us was Canavaro.

"My Bouboulina," Zorba cooed passionately, whilst pressing his knee against hers. "Don't worry, there's no God and no devil. Raise your little head, rest your cheek on your hand and give us a song. To hell with death!"

Zorba was on fire. With his left hand he twisted his moustache, and his right hand strayed over the intoxicated songstress. His words were breathless, his eyes languid. It was certainly not this mummified and outrageously painted old woman he was seeing before him, but the entire "female species," as it was his custom to call women. The individual disappeared, the features were obliterated, whether young or senile, beautiful or ugly—those were mere unimportant variations. Behind each woman rises the austere, sacred and mysterious face of Aphrodite.

That was the face Zorba was seeing and talking to, and desiring. Dame Hortense was only an ephemeral and transparent mask which Zorba tore away to kiss the eternal mouth.

"Lift your snow-white neck, my treasure," he repeated in his gasping, pleading voice. "Lift your snow-white neck and sing us the song!"

The old songstress rested her cheek on her plump hand, which was all cracked with washing clothes; her eyes became languorous. She uttered a wild and woeful cry, then began her favorite song, repeating it many times as she gazed at Zorba with swooning, half-closed eyes—she had already made her choice.

Au fil de mes jours
Pourquoi t'ai-je rencontré . . .

Zorba leapt up, went for his *santuri*, sat on the ground Turkish fashion, undraped his instrument, rested it on his lap and stretched his great hands.

"Oh! Oh!" he bellowed. "Take a knife and cut my throat, Bouboulina!"

When night began to fall, when the evening star revolved in the sky, and the coaxing voice of the *santuri* rose, abetting Zorba's aims, Dame Hortense, stuffed with chicken and rice, grilled almonds and wine, reeled heavily onto Zorba's shoulder and sighed. She rubbed herself gently against his bony sides, yawned and sighed afresh.

Zorba made a sign to me and lowered his voice:

"She's in the mood, boss," he whispered. "Be a pal, and leave us."

A T DAYBREAK I opened my eyes and saw Zorba sitting opposite
me at the end of his bed with his legs tucked up; he was
smoking and absorbed in deep meditation. His little round eyes
were fixed on the fanlight in front of him, which the first gleam
of day tinted milky white. His eyes were swollen and his unusu-
ally long, bare, scraggy neck was stretched out like the neck of a
bird of prey.

The previous evening I had retired early, leaving him alone with
the old siren.

"I'm going," I said. "Enjoy yourself, Zorba, and good luck to
you!"

"Good night, boss," Zorba replied. "Let us settle our little affair. Good night, boss. Sleep tight."

Apparently they did settle their little affair, for in my sleep I
seemed to hear muffled cooings, and for a time the neighboring
room shook and trembled. Then sleep overcame me again. A long
while after midnight, Zorba entered barefoot and stretched himself on his bed, very gently, so as not to wake me.

In the first light, there he was, gazing into the distance with his
lackluster eyes. You could see he was still sunk in a sort of torpor,
his temples were not yet freed from sleep. Calmly, fondly, he was
letting himself drift on a shady current as thick as honey. The
whole universe of earth, water, thoughts and men was slowly

drifting towards a distant sea, and Zorba was drifting away with it, unresistingly, unquestioningly, and happy.

The village began to be roused—there was a confused murmur of cocks, pigs, asses and men. I wanted to leap from my bed and cry: "Heigh! Zorba! We've work to do today!" But I too felt a great happiness in delivering myself up, silently, to the rosy transformation of sunrise. In those magic minutes the whole of life seems as light as dawn. The earth constantly changes shape in the wind, like a soft and billowy cloud.

I stretched out my arm; I, too, felt like having a smoke. I took my pipe. I looked at it with emotion. It was a big and precious one, "Made in England." It was a present from my friend—the one who had greyish-green eyes and slender fingers. That was abroad, years ago. He had finished his studies and was leaving that evening for Greece. "Give up cigarettes," he said. "You light one, you smoke half of it and throw the rest away. Your love only lasts a minute. It's disgraceful. You'd better take up a pipe. It's like a faithful spouse. When you go home, it'll be there, quietly waiting for you. You'll light it, you'll watch the smoke rising in the air— and you'll think of me!"

It was noon. We were leaving the Berlin museum, where he had been to have one last look at his favorite painting—Rembrandt's *Warrior*, with his bronze helmet, emaciated cheeks and his dolorous and strong-willed expression. "If ever in my life I perform an action worthy of a man," he murmured, as he gazed at the implacable and desperate warrior, "it will be to him I shall owe it."

We were in the museum courtyard, leaning against a pillar. In front of us was a bronze statue of a naked Amazon, riding a wild horse with indescribable grace. A little grey bird, a wagtail, perched for a moment on the Amazon's head, turned towards us, jerking up its tail, uttered two or three times a mocking cry, and flew away.

I shuddered, looked at my friend and asked:

"Did you hear that bird? It seemed to say something to us, then it flew away."

My friend smiled. " 'It's a bird, let it sing; it's a bird let it speak,' " he said, quoting a line from one of our popular ballads.

How was it that at this moment, at daybreak, on this Cretan

coast, such a memory should come into my head, together with that faithful verse, and fill my mind with bitterness?

I slowly worked some tobacco into my pipe and lit it. Everything in this world has a hidden meaning, I thought. Men, animals, trees, stars, they are all hieroglyphics; woe to anyone who begins to decipher them and guess what they mean. . . . When you see them, you do not understand them. You think they are really men, animals, trees, stars. It is only years later, too late, that you understand. . . .

The bronze-helmeted warrior, my friend leaning against the pillar, the wagtail and what it chirped to us, the verse from that melancholy ballad, all this, I thought today, may have a hidden meaning, but what can it be?

My eyes followed the smoke which curled and uncurled in the dappled light. And my mind mingled with the smoke and slowly vanished in blue wreaths. After a long interval, without having any recourse to logic, I could see with utter certainty the origin, the growth and the disappearance of the world. It was as if I had once more plunged into Buddha, but this time without the delusive words and insolent acrobatic tricks of the mind. This smoke is the essence of his teaching, these vanishing spirals are life coming impatiently to a happy end in blue nirvana. . . .

I sighed softly. As if this sigh had brought me back to the present minute, I looked round and saw the miserable wooden hut, and hanging on the wall a little mirror from which the first rays of the sun had just struck sparks. Opposite me, Zorba sat on his mattress, smoking, with his back to me.

The previous day, with its tragi-comic fortunes, suddenly flashed into my mind. The smell of stale violet perfume—violet eau-de-Cologne, musk and patchouli; a parrot, an almost human being transformed into a parrot and who beat his wings against the iron bars of his cage, calling the name of a former lover; and an old *mahone*,* only survivor of a whole fleet, who recounted ancient naval battles. . . .

* Here a coasting vessel with sails. This name is also used for barges and formerly galleys. It comes from the Arabic, *ma'on*. C. W.

Zorba heard my sigh, shook his head and looked around.

"We've behaved badly," he murmured. "We've behaved badly, boss. You laughed, so did I, and she saw us. And the way you left, without any fine words, as if she was an old bag of a hundred. What a damn shame! It's not polite, boss. That's not the way for a man to behave, let me tell you. She's a woman, after all, isn't she? A weak, fretful creature. A good job I stayed behind to console her."

"But what do you mean, Zorba?" I replied. "Do you seriously think all women have nothing else but that in mind?"

"Yes, boss, they've nothing else in mind. Listen to me, now. . . . I've seen all sorts, and I've done all kinds of things. . . . A woman has nothing else in view. She's a sickly creature, I tell you, and fretful. If you don't tell her you love and want her, she starts crying. Maybe she doesn't want you at all, maybe you disgust her, maybe she says no. That's another story. But all men who see her must desire her. That's what she wants, the poor creature, so you might try and please her!

"I had a grandmother, she must have been eighty. What a tale that old soul's life would make! Never mind, that's another story, too. . . . Well, she must have been eighty in the shade, and opposite our house lived a younger girl as fresh as a flower. . . . Krystallo she was called. Every Saturday evening, raw young bloods of the village would meet for a drink, and the wine made us lively. We stuck a sprig of basil behind our ears, one of my cousins took his guitar, and we went serenading. What love! What passion! We bellowed like bulls! We all wanted her, and every Saturday we went in a herd for her to make her choice.

"Well, would you believe it, boss? It's a mystery! Women have a wound which never heals. Every wound heals but that one—don't you take any notice of your books—that one never heals. What, just because a woman's eighty? The wound's still open.

"So every Saturday the old girl pulled her mattress up to the window, took out her little mirror and combed away at the little bits of thatch she had left, and carefully made a parting. She'd look round slyly, for fear someone saw her. If anyone came near, she'd snuggle back and look as if butter wouldn't melt in her mouth, pretending she was dozing. But how could she sleep? She was waiting for the serenade. At eighty! You see what a mystery woman is, boss! Just now it makes me want to cry. But at that time I was just harum-scarum, I didn't understand and it made me laugh. One day I got annoyed with her. She was hauling me over the coals because I was running after the girls, so I told her straight out where to get off: 'Why do you rub walnut leaves over your lips every Saturday, and part your hair? I s'pose you think we come to serenade *you*? It's Krystallo we're after. You're just a stinking old corpse!'

"Would you believe it, boss! That day was the first time I knew what a woman was. Two tears sprang into my grandma's eyes. She curled up like a dog, and her chin trembled. 'Krystallo!' I shouted, going nearer so as she'd hear better. 'Krystallo!' Young people are cruel beasts, they're inhuman, they don't understand. My grandma raised her skinny arms to heaven. 'Curse you from the bottom of my heart!' she cried. That very day she started to go into a decline. She wasted away and two months later, her days were numbered. Then when she was at her last gasp she saw me. She hissed like a turtle and tried to grab me with her withered fingers. 'It was you who finished me off. May you be damned, Alexis, and suffer all I have!' "

Zorba smiled.

"Ah, the old witch's curse has hit home!" he said, stroking his moustache. "I'm in my sixty-fifth year, I think, but even if I live to be a hundred I'll never lay off. I'll still have a little mirror in my pocket, and I'll still be running after the female of the species."

He smiled once more, threw his cigarette through the fanlight, stretched his arms and said:

"I've plenty of other faults, but that is the one that'll kill me."

He leapt from his bed.

"Enough of all that. Cut the cackle. Today we work!"

He dressed in a twinkling, put on his shoes and went out.

With my head bowed, I ruminated on Zorba's words, and suddenly a distant snow-bound town came to my mind. I was at an exhibition of Rodin's works, and I had stopped to look at an enormous bronze hand, "The Hand of God." This hand was half closed, and in the palm an ecstatic man and woman were embracing and struggling.

47

A girl came up and stopped beside me. She also looked and was moved at the disquieting, eternal embrace of man and woman. She was slim, well-dressed; she had a wealth of fair hair, a powerful chin and thin lips. There was something determined and virile about her. I normally hate inviting a conversation, and I do not know what urged me to turn to her and ask:

"What are you thinking about?"

"If only we could escape!" she murmured resentfully.

"And go where? The hand of God is everywhere. There is no salvation. Are you sorry?"

"No. Love may be the most intense joy on earth. It may be. But, now I see that bronze hand, I want to escape."

"You prefer freedom."

"Yes."

"But, supposing it's only when we obey that bronze hand we are free? Supposing the word 'God' didn't have that convenient meaning the masses give it?"

She looked anxiously at me. Her eyes were of a metallic grey, her lips dry and bitter.

"I don't understand," she said, and moved away.

She disappeared. Since then I had never thought any more of her. Nevertheless, she must have continued to live deep down in my heart, and today, on this empty coast, she reappeared, pale and plaintive, from the depths of my being.

Yes, I had behaved badly. Zorba was right. That bronze hand was a good pretext. The first contact had succeeded, the first gentle words had been exchanged, and we might gradually, imperceptibly, have embraced and been united, undisturbed, in the hand of God. But I had suddenly darted from earth to heaven, and the woman had been startled and had fled.

The old cock was crowing in Dame Hortense's yard. The white light of day was now peeping in through the little window. I leapt out of bed.

The workmen had begun to arrive with their pickaxes, their crowbars and their mattocks. I heard Zorba giving his orders. He had thrown himself into the work straight away. One felt he was a man who knew how to command men, who loved responsibility.

I put my head out of the fanlight and saw him standing, like a

48

great gawk in the middle of the thirty-odd lean, narrow-waisted, rough and weather-beaten men. His arm was stretched out authoritatively, his words were brief and to the point. Once he caught hold of a youngish fellow by the scruff of the neck because he was muttering and coming forward hesitatingly.

"Got something to say, have you?" Zorba cried. "Well, say it out aloud! I don't like mumblings. You've got to be in the mood to work. If you're not, get back to the tavern!"

At that moment Dame Hortense appeared with tousled hair and swollen cheeks. She was not made up, and she was dressed in a full, dirty gown and was shuffling along in a pair of long, down-at-heel slippers. She coughed the raucous cough of old singers, like a donkey's braying. She stopped and looked with pride at Zorba. Her eyes became misty. She coughed again, so that he would notice her, and passed close to him, swaying and wriggling her hips. Her broad sleeve almost brushed him. But he did not even turn round to look at her. He took a piece of barley cake and a handful of olives from a workman and shouted:

"Now, men, in God's name, make the sign of the cross!" And, striding away, he led the gang in a beeline towards the mountain.

I shall not describe here the work on the mine. It would need patience to do that, and I have none. Near the sea, we built a hut out of bamboo, osier and petrol-cans. Zorba used to awake at dawn, seize his pick, go to the mine before the men, open a gallery, abandon it, find a gleaming lignite seam and dance for joy. But after a few days he would lose the seam and he would fling himself down on the ground with his legs in the air and, with his feet and hands, make a mocking gesture at the sky.

He had taken to the work. He no longer even consulted me. From the very first days all the care and responsibility had passed from my hands to his. His job was to make decisions and put them into execution. Mine was to pay the piper. This arrangement, moreover, suited me fairly well. For I sensed that these months would be the happiest in my life. Also, everything considered, I felt I was buying my happiness cheaply.

My maternal grandfather, who had lived in a fair-sized Cretan village, used to take his lantern every evening and go round the streets to see if, by chance, any stranger had arrived. He would take him to his house and give him an abundance of food and drink, after which he would sit on his divan, light his long Turkish pipe, his chibouk, and turn to his guest—for whom the time had come to repay the hospitality—and say in a peremptory tone:

"Talk!"

"Talk about what, Father Moustoyorgi?"

"What you are, who you are, where you come from, what towns and villages you have seen—everything, tell me everything. Now, speak!"

And the guest would begin to talk at random, uttering truths and falsehoods, whilst my grandfather, sitting calmly on his divan, smoked his chibouk, listening intently and following the stranger in his travels. And if he liked the guest, he would say:

"You shall stay tomorrow too. You're not going. You've still things to tell."

My grandfather had never left his village. He had never been even to Candia or Canea. "Why go there?" he would say. "There are Candians and Caneans, peace be with them, who pass here— Candia and Canea come to me, so why need I go to them?"

On this Cretan coast today I am perpetuating my grandfather's mania. I have also found a guest by the light of my lantern. I do not let him depart. He costs me far more than a dinner, but he is worth it. Every evening I wait for him after work, I make him sit opposite me and we eat. The time comes when he must pay, and I say to him: "Talk!" I smoke my pipe and I listen. This guest has thoroughly explored the earth and the human soul. I never tire of listening to him.

"Talk, Zorba, talk!"

When he speaks, the whole of Macedonia is immediately spread before my gaze, laid out in the little space between Zorba and myself, with its mountains, its forests, its torrents, its *comitadjis*, its hard-working women and great, heavily-built men. And also Mount Athos with its twenty-one monasteries, its arsenals and its broad-bottomed idlers. Zorba would shake his head as he finished his tales of monks and say, roaring with laughter: "God preserve you, boss, from the stern of mules and the stem of monks!"

Every evening Zorba takes me through Greece, Bulgaria and

Constantinople. I shut my eyes and I see. He has been all over the racked and chaotic Balkans and observed everything with his little falcon-like eyes, which he constantly opens wide in amazement. Things we are accustomed to, and which we pass by indifferently, suddenly rise up in front of Zorba like fearful enigmas. Seeing a woman pass by, he stops in consternation.

"What is that mystery?" he asks. "What is a woman, and why does she turn our heads? Just tell me, I ask you, what's the meaning of that?"

He interrogates himself with the same amazement when he sees a man, a tree in blossom, a glass of cold water. Zorba sees everything every day as if for the first time.

We were sitting yesterday in front of the hut. When he had drunk a glass of wine, he turned to me in alarm:

"Now whatever is this red water, boss, just tell me! An old stock grows branches, and at first there's nothing but a sour bunch of beads hanging down. Time passes, the sun ripens them, they become as sweet as honey, and then they're called grapes. We trample on them; we extract the juice and put it into casks; it ferments on its own, we open it on the feast day of St. John the Drinker,* it's become wine! It's a miracle! You drink the red juice and, lo and behold, your soul grows big, too big for the old carcass, it challenges God to a fight. Now tell me, boss, how does it happen?"

I did not answer. I felt, as I listened to Zorba, that the world was recovering its pristine freshness. All the dulled daily things regained the brightness they had in the beginning, when we came out of the hands of God. Water, women, the stars, bread, returned to their mysterious, primitive origin and the divine whirlwind burst once more upon the air.

That is why, every evening, lying on the pebbles, I impatiently waited for Zorba. I would see him suddenly emerge out of the bowels of the earth and approach with his loose-knit body and long striding step. From afar I could see how the work had fared that day, by his bearing, by the way he held his head high or low, by the swing of his arms.

* The feast of Klydonas, held on the fifteenth of August. It can be compared to Hallowe'en. C. W.

At first I also went with him. I watched the men. I endeavored to lead a different type of life, to interest myself in practical work, to know and love the human material which had fallen into my hands, to feel the long-wished-for joy of no longer having to deal with words but with living men. And I made romantic plans—if the extraction of lignite was successful—to organize a sort of community in which everything should be shared, where we should eat the same food together and wear the same clothes, like brothers. I created in my mind a new religious order, the leaven of a new life. . . .

But I had not yet made up my mind to acquaint Zorba with my project. He was irritated by my comings and goings amongst the workmen, questioning, interfering and always taking the workman's part.

Zorba would purse his lips and say:

"Boss, aren't you going for a stroll outside? The sun and the sea, you know!"

At first I insisted, and would not go. I asked questions, gossiped, and got to know every man's history—how many children they had to feed, sisters to be married, helpless old relations; their cares, illnesses and worries.

"Don't delve like that into their histories, boss," Zorba would say, scowling. "You'll be taken in, with your soft heart, and you'll like them more than's good for them or for our work. Whatever they do, you'll find excuses for them. Then, heaven help us, they'll scamp their work, do it any old how. Heaven help them, too, you'd better realize that. When the boss is hard, the men respect him, they work. When the boss is soft, they leave it all to him, and have an easy time. Get me?"

Another evening, after work, he threw his pick down in the shed and shouted, out of all patience:

"Look here, boss, do stop meddling. As fast as I build, you destroy. Now what are all those things you were telling them today? Socialism and rubbish! Are you a preacher or a capitalist? You must make up your mind!"

But how could I choose? I was consumed by the ingenuous desire of uniting these two things, of finding a synthesis in which the irreducible opposites would fraternize, and of winning both the earthly life and the kingdom of the skies. This had been going on for years, ever since my early childhood. When I was still at school, I had organized with my closest friends a secret Friendly Society *—that was the name we gave it—and, locked in my bedroom, we swore that, all our life, we would devote ourselves to the fighting of injustice. Great tears ran down our faces when, with hand on heart, we took the oath.

Puerile ideals! But woe betide whoever laughs when he hears them! When I see what the members of the Friendly Society have become—quack doctors, small-time lawyers, grocers, double-dealing politicians, hack journalists—it rends my heart. The climate of this world seems to be harsh and raw. The most precious seeds do not germinate or are choked by undergrowth and nettles. I can see quite clearly today, as regards myself, that I am not stifled by reason, God be praised! I still feel ready to set out on Quixotic expeditions.

On Sundays we both performed our toilet with care, as if we were marriageable young people. We shaved, we put on clean white shirts, and went, towards the end of the afternoon, to see Dame Hortense. Every Sunday she killed a fowl for us; we once more sat down all three together; we ate and we drank; Zorba's long hands would reach out to the hospitable bosom of the kind woman and take possession of it. When at nightfall we returned to our part of the shore, life appeared simple and full of good intentions, old, but very agreeable and hospitable—like Dame Hortense.

On one of these Sundays, as we were returning from the copious feast, I decided to speak and tell Zorba of my plans. He listened, gaping and forcing himself to be patient. But from time to time he shook his great head with anger. My very first words had sobered him, the fumes left his brain. When I had finished, he nervously plucked two or three hairs from his moustache.

"I hope you don't mind my saying so, boss, but I don't think your brain is quite formed yet. How old are you?"

"Thirty-five."

"Then it never will be."

Thereupon he burst out laughing. I was stung to the quick.

"You don't believe in man, do you?" I retorted.

"Now, don't get angry, boss. No, I don't believe in anything. If I

* Named after the famous Friendly Society which prepared the Greek revolution of 1821.

believed in man, I'd believe in God, and I'd believe in the devil, too. And that's a whole business. Things get all muddled then, boss, and cause me a lot of complications."

He became silent, took off his beret, scratched his head frantically and tugged again at his moustache, as if he meant to tear it off. He wanted to say something, but he restrained himself. He looked at me out of the corner of his eye; looked at me again and decided to speak.

"Man is a brute," he said, striking the pebbles with his stick. "A great brute. Your lordship doesn't realize this. It seems everything's been too easy for you, but you ask me! A brute, I tell you! If you're cruel to him, he respects and fears you. If you're kind to him, he plucks your eyes out.

"Keep your distance, boss! Don't make men too bold, don't go telling them we're all equal, we've got the same rights, or they'll go straight and trample on *your* rights; they'll steal your bread and leave you to die of hunger. Keep your distance, boss, by all the good things I wish you!"

"But don't you believe in anything?" I exclaimed in exasperation.

"No, I don't believe in anything. How many times must I tell you that? I don't believe in anything or anyone; only in Zorba. Not because Zorba is better than the others; not at all, not a little bit! He's a brute like the rest! But I believe in Zorba because he's the only being I have in my power, the only one I know. All the rest are ghosts. I see with these eyes, I hear with these ears, I digest with these guts. All the rest are ghosts, I tell you. When I die, everything'll die. The whole Zorbatic world will go to the bottom!"

"What egoism!" I said sarcastically.

"I can't help it, boss! That's how it is. I eat beans, I talk beans; I am Zorba, I talk like Zorba."

I said nothing. Zorba's words stung me like whiplashes. I admired him for being so strong, for despising men to that extent, and at the same time wanting to live and work with them. I should either have become an ascetic or else have adorned men with false feathers so that I could put up with them.

Zorba looked round at me. By the light of the stars I could see he was grinning from ear to ear.

"Have I offended you, boss?" he said, stopping abruptly. We had arrived at the hut. Zorba looked at me tenderly and uneasily.

I did not reply. I felt my mind was in agreement with Zorba, but my heart resisted, wanted to leap out and escape from the brute, to go its own road.

"I'm not sleepy this evening, Zorba," I said. "You go to bed."

The stars were shining, the sea was sighing and licking the shells, a glow-worm lit under its belly its little erotic lantern. Night's hair was streaming with dew.

I lay face downward, plunged in silence, thinking of nothing. I was now one with night and the sea; my mind was like a glow-worm that had lit its little lantern and settled on the damp, dark earth, and was waiting.

The stars were travelling round, the hours were passing—and, when I arose, I had, without knowing how, engraved on my mind the double task I had to accomplish on this shore:

Escape from Buddha, rid myself by words of all my metaphysical cares and free my mind from vain anxiety;

Make direct and firm contact with men, starting from this very moment.

I said to myself: "Perhaps it is not yet too late."

◇ 5 ◇

"UNCLE ANAGNOSTI, the grandfather, greets you and asks if you would care to come to his house for a meal. The gelder will be coming to the village today to castrate the pigs. It's an occasion, and the 'parts' are a real delicacy. Kyria Maroulia, the gaffer's wife, will cook them specially for you. It's also their grandson Minas's birthday today, and you'll be able to wish him many happy returns."

It is a great pleasure to enter a Cretan peasant's home. Everything about you is patriarchal: the hearth, the oil lamp, the earthenware jars lining the wall, a few chairs, a table and, on the left as you enter, in a hole in the wall, a pitcher of fresh water. From the beams hang strings of quinces, pomegranates and aromatic plants: sage, mint, red peppers, rosemary and savory.

At the far end of the room a ladder or a few wooden steps lead up to the raised platform, where there is a trestle bed and, above it, the holy icons with their lamps. The house appears empty, but it contains everything needful, so few in reality are the true necessities of man.

It was a magnificent day, rendered very mild by the autumn sun. We sat in front of the house in the little peasant garden, under an olive tree laden with fruit. Between the silvery leaves the sea could be seen gleaming in the distance, perfectly calm and still. Vaporous clouds were continually passing in front of the sun and making the earth appear now sad, now gay, as if it were breathing.

At the end of the tiny garden, in an enclosure, the castrated pig was squealing with pain and deafening us. The smell of Kyria Maroulia's cooking on the embers in the hearth reached our nostrils.

Our conversation was confined to the everlasting topics: the corn crops, the vines, the rain. We were obliged to shout because the old gaffer was hard of hearing. He said he had "a proud ear." This old Cretan's life had been straightforward and peaceful, like that of a tree in a sheltered ravine. He had been born, had grown up and had married. He had had children and had had time to see his grand-children. Several had died, but others were living: the continuation of the family was assured.

This old Cretan could recall the old days, Turkish rule, the say-ings of his father, the miracles which happened in those days be-cause the women-folk feared God and had faith.

"Why, look at me here, old uncle Anagnosti who's speaking to you! My own birth was a miracle. Aye, upon my soul, a miracle! And when I tell you how it happened, you'll be amazed. 'The Lord have mercy on us,' you'll say, and go to the monastery of the Virgin Mary and burn a candle to her."

He crossed himself and, in a soft voice and gentle manner, began to tell his tale.

"In those days, then, a rich Turkish woman lived in our village —damn her soul! One fine day the wretch became big with child and the time came for her to give birth. They laid her on the trestle bed and she stayed there bellowing like a heifer for three days and nights. But the child wouldn't come. So a friend of hers—damn her soul, too!—gave her some advice. 'Tzafer Hanum, you should call Mother Mary for help!' That's how the Turks call the Virgin. Great be her power! 'What for?' that Tzafer bitch bellowed. 'Call *her*? I'd sooner die!' But her pains became more acute. Another day and night went by. She was still bellowing, and still she couldn't deliver the child. What could be done? She couldn't bear the pains any longer. So she started to shout for all she was worth: 'Mother Mary! Mother Mary!' But it was no use, the pains wouldn't stop and the child wouldn't come. And her friend said: 'Perhaps she can't under-stand Turkish!' So that bitch yelled: 'Virgin of the Roumis! Virgin of the Roumis!' * Roumis be damned! The pains increased. 'You're not calling her the proper way,' said the friend. 'You're not calling her the proper way, and that's why she won't come.' So that heathen bitch, seeing her peril, cries out fit to burst her lungs: 'Holy Virgin!' And straight away the child slipped out of her womb like an eel out of the mud.

"That happened one Sunday, and the next Sunday my mother had *her* pains. She went through it, too, the poor wretch. She was really going through it, my poor mother was, and she screamed: 'Holy Virgin! Holy Virgin!' But she wasn't delivered. My father was sitting on the ground in the middle of the yard. He couldn't eat or drink because of her sufferings. He wasn't at all pleased with the Holy Virgin. You see, the last time when that Tzafer bitch had called her, the Virgin had broken her neck to come and deliver *her*. But now . . . When the fourth day came, my father couldn't contain himself any longer. Without a moment's hesitation he takes his pitchfork and goes to the monastery of the Martyred Virgin. May she succor us! He gets there, goes in the church without even crossing himself, so great was his rage, he shuts and bolts the door behind him, and marches straight up to the icon. 'Look here, Holy Virgin,' he shouts, 'here's my wife, Krinio—you know her, don't you —you ought to, she brings you oil every Saturday, and she lights your lamps—here's my wife been having her pains for three days and nights and she's been calling you. Can't you hear her? You must be deaf if you can't! Of course if she were some Tzafer bitch, one of those Turkish sluts, you'd go and break your neck for her. But my wife, Krinio, she's only a Christian, so you've become deaf and can't hear her! You know, if you weren't the Holy Virgin, I'd teach you a lesson with the handle of this pitchfork here!'

"And, without more ado, without so much as bowing his head to her, he turned his back on her and was about to leave. But, great is the Lord, just then the icon made a loud grating noise as if it were splitting. Let me tell you if you don't know it already, icons make a noise like that when they're doing miracles. My father understood at once. He wheeled round again, knelt down and crossed himself. 'I've sinned against you, Holy Virgin,' he cried. 'I've said a lot of things I shouldn't, but let's forget it!'

* Muslim name for Christians or Infidels, from Roman. C. W.

"He had hardly got back to the village when he heard the good news.

"'Long life to him, Kostandi. Your wife has given birth to a son!' It was me, old Anagnosti here. But I was born with a weak ear. You see, my father had blasphemed, he'd called the Virgin deaf.

"'Oh, that's how it is, is it?' the Virgin must have said. 'Well, just you wait, I'll make your son deaf, that'll teach you to blaspheme!'"

And uncle Anagnosti crossed himself.

"But that's nothing," he said. "God be praised! She might have made me blind or an idiot, or hunchbacked, or even—God Almighty preserve us!—she might have made me a girl. This is just nothing at all, I bow to her holiness!"

He filled the glasses.

"Long may she help us!" he said, raising his glass.

"To your health, uncle Anagnosti. I hope you live to a hundred and see your great-great-grandchildren!"

The old man tossed off his wine in one go and wiped his moustache.

"No, my son," he said. "That's too much to ask. I've seen my grandchildren. That's enough. Mustn't ask too much. My hour has come. I am old, my friends, my loins are empty, I can't—much as I'd like to—I can't sow the seed for any more children. So what'd I be doing with life?"

He filled the glasses again, pulled out from his waistband some walnuts and dried figs wrapped in laurel leaves and shared them with us.

"I have given everything I had to my children," he said. "We've become poverty-stricken, yes, poverty-stricken, but I don't complain. God has all that is needful!"

"God may have all that's needful, uncle Anagnosti," Zorba shouted in the old man's ear. "God may have, but not us. The old skinflint gives us nothing!"

But the old villager frowned.

"Don't say that!" he chided severely. "Don't upbraid him! The poor fellow counts on us, too, you know!"

At this moment grandmother Anagnosti entered silently and submissively carrying the celebrated delicacy on an earthenware dish, and also a large jug full of wine. She set them on the table and remained standing with hands clasped and lowered eyes.

I felt some repugnance at having to taste this hors d'œuvre, but, on the other hand, I did not have the courage to refuse. Zorba was watching me out of the corner of his eye and enjoying my discomfiture.

"It's the most tasty dish you could wish for, boss," he affirmed. "Don't be squeamish."

Old Anagnosti gave a little laugh.

"That's the truth, indeed it is, you try them and see. They melt in the mouth! When Prince George—may the hour be blessed for him!—visited our monastery up there in the mountains, the monks prepared a royal feast in his honor, and they served meat to every one save to the prince, who was given a plateful of soup. The prince took his spoon and began to stir his soup. 'What are these? Beans?' he asked in surprise. 'White haricot beans, are they?' 'Try them, Your Highness,' said the old abbot. 'Try them and we'll talk about them afterwards.' The prince took a spoonful, two, three, he emptied his plate and licked his lips. 'What is this wonderful dish?' he said, 'What tasty beans! They're as nice as brains!' 'They're no beans, your Highness,' replied the abbot, laughing. 'They're no beans! We've had all the cocks of the neighborhood castrated!' "

Roaring with laughter, the old man stuck his fork into another morsel.

"A dish fit for princes!" he said. "Open your mouth."

I opened my mouth and he popped in the morsel.

He filled the glasses again and we drank to the health of his grandson. Old Anagnosti's eyes shone.

"What would you like your grandson to be, uncle Anagnosti?" I asked. "Tell us, so that we can wish."

"What could I wish, my son? Well, that he takes the right road; that he becomes a good man, head of a family; that he, too, gets married and has children and grandchildren. And may one of his children be like me, so that old folk exclaim: 'I say, doesn't he look like old Anagnosti—God sanctify his soul!—he was a good man!' "

"Maroulia!" he called, without looking at his wife. "Maroulia, more wine, fill up the jug again!"

Just then the wicket gate to the enclosure yielded to a powerful thrust from the pig and the pig rushed grunting into the garden.

"It hurts him, poor beast," Zorba said pityingly.

"Of course it hurts him!" the old Cretan said, laughing. "Supposing they did that to you, wouldn't it hurt you?"

Zorba fidgeted on his chair.

"May your tongue be cut out, you old deaf post!" Zorba muttered in horror.

The pig ran about in front of us and looked at us furiously.

"I do believe he knows we're eating them!" said uncle Anagnosti, who had been put in high spirits by the drop of wine he had drunk.

But we, like cannibals, went on quietly and contentedly eating the delicacy and drinking the red wine, as we gazed between the silvery branches of the olive tree towards the sea, which the sunset had turned pink.

At dusk we left the old man's house. Zorba, who was now also in high spirits, wanted to talk.

"What were we saying the day before yesterday, boss? You were saying you wanted to open the people's eyes. All right, you just go and open old uncle Anagnosti's eyes for him! You saw how his wife had to behave before him, waiting for his orders, like a dog begging. Just go now and teach them that women have equal rights with men, and that it's cruel to eat a piece of the pig while the pig's still raw and groaning in front of you, and that it's simple lunacy to give thanks to God because he's got everything while you're starving to death! What good'll that poor devil Anagnosti get out of all your explanatory humbug? You'd only cause him a lot of bother. And what'd old mother Anagnosti get out of it? The fat would be in the fire: family rows would start, the hen would want to be cock, the couple would just have a good set-to and make their feathers fly . . . ! Let people be, boss; don't open their eyes. And supposing you did, what'd they see? Their misery! Leave their eyes closed, boss, and let them go on dreaming!"

He was silent a moment and scratched his head. He was thinking.

"Unless," he said at last, "unless . . ."

"Unless what? Let's have it!"

"Unless when they open their eyes you can show them a better world than the darkness in which they're gallivanting at present. . . . Can you?"

I did not know. I was fully aware of what would be destroyed. I did not know what would be built out of the ruins. No one can know that with any degree of certainty, I thought. The old world is tangible, solid, we live in it and are struggling with it every moment—it exists. The world of the future is not yet born, it is elusive, fluid, made of the light from which dreams are woven; it is a cloud buffeted by violent winds—love, hate, imagination, luck, God. . . . The greatest prophet on earth can give men no more than a watchword, and the vaguer the watchword the greater the prophet.

Zorba looked at me with a mocking smile which vexed me.

"I *can* show them a better world!" I replied.

"Can you? Well, let's hear about it!"

"I can't explain it; you wouldn't understand."

"That means you haven't got one to show!" Zorba rejoined, shaking his head. "Don't take me for a simpleton, boss. If anyone's told you I'm a moon-calf, they're wrong. I may have no more education than old uncle Anagnosti, but I'm nowhere near so stupid! Well, if I can't understand, what d'you expect of that poor fellow and his blockheaded mate? And what about all the other Anagnostides in the world? Have you only got more darkness to show them? They've managed pretty well up to now; they have children, and even grandchildren. God makes them deaf or blind, and they say: 'God be praised!' They feel at home in their misery. So let them be and say nothing."

I was silent. We were passing the widow's garden. Zorba stopped a moment and sighed, but said nothing. A shower must have fallen. There was a fresh, earthy smell in the air. The first stars appeared. The new moon was shining, it was a tender shade of greenish yellow. The sky was overflowing with sweetness.

That man has not been to school, I thought, and his brains have not been perverted. He has had all manner of experiences; his mind is open and his heart has grown bigger, without his losing one ounce of his primitive boldness. All the problems which we find so complicated or insoluble he cuts through as if with a sword, like Alexander the Great cutting the Gordian knot. It is difficult for him to miss his aim, because his two feet are held firmly planted on the ground by the weight of his whole body. African savages worship the serpent because its whole body touches the ground and it must, therefore, know all the earth's secrets. It knows them with its belly, with its tail, with its head. It is always in contact or mingled with the Mother. The same is true of Zorba. We educated people are just empty-headed birds of the air.

The stars were multiplying in the heavens, and they were all hard, fierce, scornful and pitiless towards man.

We no longer spoke. We were both gazing with terror at the sky. Every second new stars lit up in the east and spread the conflagration.

We arrived at our hut. I had not the slightest desire to eat, and sat on a rock by the sea. Zorba lit the fire, ate, was about to come to sit beside me, but changed his mind and lay on his mattress and fell asleep.

The sea was dead calm. Beneath the volley of shooting stars the earth also lay motionless and silent. No dog barked, no nightbird shrieked. It was a stealthy, dangerous, total silence, composed of thousands of cries so distant or from such depths within us that we could not hear them. I could only discern the pulsing of my blood in my temples and in the veins of my neck.

The song of the tiger! I thought, and shuddered.

In India, when night falls, a sad, monotonous song is sung in a low voice, a slow, wild song, like the distant yawn of a beast of prey —the song of the tiger. Man's heart flutters and seeks an outlet as he waits in tense expectation.

As I thought of this fearful song, the void in my breast was gradually filled. My ears came to life, the silence became a shout. It was as if the soul itself were composed out of this song and were escaping from the body to listen.

I stooped, filled my palm with sea water, moistened my brow and temples. I felt refreshed. In the depths of my being, cries were echoing, threateningly, confused, impatient—the tiger was within me and he was roaring.

All at once I heard the voice clearly. It was the voice of Buddha.

I started walking rapidly along the water's edge, as if I wished to escape. For some time now, when alone at night and silence reigned, I had been hearing his voice—at first sorrowful and plaintive, like a dirge; then, becoming angry, scolding and imperative. It kicked within my breast like a child when the time has come for it to leave the womb.

It must have been midnight. Black clouds had gathered in the sky, large drops of rain fell onto my hands. But I paid no heed. I was plunged into a burning atmosphere; I could feel a flame flickering from both my temples.

The time has come, I thought, with a shudder. The Buddhist wheel is bearing me away; the time has come for me to free myself from this miraculous burden.

I returned swiftly to the hut and lit the lamp. When the light fell on Zorba, his eyelids twitched, he opened his eyes and watched me bending over the paper and writing. He growled something which I did not catch, turned brusquely towards the wall and fell fast asleep once more.

I wrote quickly, I was in a hurry. *Buddha* was completely ready within me and I could see it issuing from my brain like a blue ribbon covered with symbols. It was coming forth rapidly, and I tried desperately to keep up with it. I wrote; everything had become simple, very simple. I was not writing, I was copying. A whole world was appearing before me, composed of compassion, renunciation and air: Buddha's mansions, the women in the harem, the golden coach, the three fateful encounters—with the old man, with the sick man, with death; the flight, the ascetic life, the deliverance, the proclaiming of salvation. The earth was covered with yellow flowers; beggars and kings donned saffron robes; the stones, the trees and the flesh became lighter. Souls became vapor, the vapor became spirit, and the spirit became nothing. . . . My fingers were beginning to ache, but I would not, I could not stop. The vision was passing swiftly and vanishing; I had to keep up with it.

In the morning Zorba found me asleep, with my head on the manuscript.

◊ 6 ◊

THE SUN was already well up in the sky when I awoke. The
joints of my right hand were stiff from holding the pen so long.
I could not close my fingers. The Buddhist storm had broken over
me and left me tired and empty.

I stooped to pick up the pages scattered on the floor. I had neither
the strength nor the desire to look at them. As if all that sudden
rush of inspiration had been merely a dream which I no longer
wished to see imprisoned in words and debased by them.

It was raining softly, silently. Zorba, before leaving, had lit the
brazier, and I spent the whole morning coiled up in front of the
fire, with my hands over it, eating nothing, motionless, just listening to the first rain of the season, softly falling.

I was thinking of nothing. Rolled up in a ball, like a mole in
damp soil, my brain was resting. I could hear the slight movements,
murmurings and nibblings of the earth, and the rain falling and the
seeds swelling. I could feel the sky and the earth copulating as in
primitive times when they mated like a man and woman and had
children. I could hear the sea before me, all along the shore, roaring
like a wild beast and lapping with its tongue to slake its thirst.

I was happy, I knew that. While experiencing happiness, we
have difficulty in being conscious of it. Only when the happiness is
past and we look back on it do we suddenly realize—sometimes
with astonishment—how happy we had been. But on this Cretan
coast I was experiencing happiness and knew I was happy.

That immense thirsting, dark-blue sea extended right to the shores of Africa. A very hot south wind often blew, the *Livas*, which comes from the distant, burning sands. In the morning the sea gave off a scent like that of a watermelon; at noon it was covered with haze and still, its slight undulations being like immature breasts; in the evening it sighed and was the color of the rose, of the aubergine, of wine, a deep blue.

In the afternoon I amused myself by filling my hand with fine light-colored sand and letting it run, hot and soft, through my fingers. The hand—an hour-glass through which our life runs away and is lost. It was losing itself. I looked at the sea, heard Zorba, and felt my temples bursting with happiness.

I remembered how, one day, my niece, Alka, a little girl of four, while we were looking into a toy-shop—it was New Year's Eve—she turned to me and made this extraordinary remark: "Uncle Ogre, I'm so glad I am growing horns!" I was startled. What a miracle life is and how alike are all souls when they send their roots down deep and meet and are one! For I at once recalled a Buddha carved in ebony which I had seen in a distant museum. Buddha had freed himself and was bathed in supreme joy after seven years of agony. The veins on either side of his forehead had so swollen that they had burst out of the skin and become two vigorous, curling horns, like steel springs.

The fine rain stopped falling towards the end of the afternoon, the sky became clear. I was hungry and was delighted to be hungry, for now Zorba would come and light the fire and begin the daily ritual of cooking.

"Another of these things that never leave you alone," Zorba often said, as he set the pot on the fire. "It's not only woman, curse her—that's an endless affair—there's eating, too."

On this coast I felt for the first time what a pleasant thing it could be to have a meal. In the evening Zorba lit the fire between two stones and did the cooking. We started eating and drinking, the conversation became animated. I at last realized that eating was a spiritual function and that meat, bread and wine were the raw materials from which the mind is made.

After his day's hard work, before eating and drinking, Zorba was

66

dull, his remarks peevish, and I had to drag words out of him. His movements were listless and awkward. But as soon as he had stoked up the engine, as he put it, the whole grinding, weary machine of his body came to life once more, got up speed and started to work again. His eyes lit up, he was brim full of memories, wings grew on his feet and he danced.

"Tell me what you do with the food you eat, and I'll tell you who you are. Some turn their food into fat and manure, some into work and good humor, and others, I'm told, into God. So there must be three sorts of men. I'm not one of the worst, boss, nor yet one of the best. I'm somewhere between the two. What I eat I turn into work and good humor. That's not too bad, after all!"

He looked at me wickedly and started laughing.

"As for you, boss," he said, "I think you do your level best to turn what you eat into God. But you can't quite manage it, and that torments you. The same thing's happening to you as happened to the crow."

"What happened to the crow, Zorba?"

"Well, you see, he used to walk respectably, properly—well, like a crow. But one day he got it into his head to try and strut about like a pigeon. And from that time on the poor fellow couldn't for the life of him recall his own way of walking. He was all mixed up, don't you see? He just hobbled about."

I raised my head. I had heard Zorba's footsteps as he came up out of the gallery. Soon after I saw him approaching with a long scowling face, his arms dangling helplessly at his sides.

"Evening, boss," he said lifelessly.

"Hello, Zorba. How did the work go today?"

He did not reply.

"I'll light the fire," he said, "and prepare the meal."

He took an armful of wood from the corner, went outside, arranged the faggots artistically in a pile between the two stones and lit them. He set the earthenware pot on top, poured in some water, threw in onions, tomatoes and rice, and began cooking. Meanwhile, I put a cloth on a low round table, cut thick slices of wheat bread, and from the demijohn I filled with wine the calabash, decorated

with designs, which uncle Anagnosti had given us soon after our
arrival.

Zorba kneeled in front of the pot, stared into the fire and remained silent.

"Have you any children, Zorba?" I said all of a sudden.

He looked round.

"Why d'you ask me that? I have a girl."

"Married?"

Zorba started laughing.

"Why are you laughing, Zorba?"

"What a question to ask!" he said. "Of course she's married. She
isn't an imbecile. I was working in a copper mine near Pravishta
in Chalcidice. One day I received a letter from my brother Yanni.
Oh, yes! I'd forgotten to tell you I have a brother, a sensible, stay-at-
home money lender, a hypocritical church-goer, a real pillar of society. . . . He's a grocer in Salonica. 'Dear brother Alexis,' he
wrote me, 'Your daughter Phrosso has gone astray; she has dishonored our name. She has a lover; she has had a child by him. Our
reputation is ruined. I am going to the village to cut her throat.'"

"And what did you do, Zorba?"

Zorba shrugged his shoulders.

"'Ah, women!' I said, and I tore up the letter."

He stirred the rice, put in some salt, and grinned.

"But just wait, you'll see the funny side of this. Two or three
months later I had a second letter from my silly brother. 'Health
and happiness to you, my dear brother,' the fool wrote me. 'Our
honor is safe, you can now hold your head high again The man in
question has married Phrosso!'"

Zorba looked round at me. By the glow of his cigarette I could see
his eyes sparkling. He shrugged his shoulders again

"Ah, men!" he said with unutterable scorn.

A little later, he continued:

"What can you expect from women?" he said. "That they'll go
and get children by the first man who comes along. What can you
expect of men? That they fall into the trap. Mark my words, boss!"

He took the pot off the fire and we began our evening meal.

Zorba was sunk in deep thought again.

Something was worrying him. He looked at me, opened his

mouth and shut it again. By the light of the oil lamp I could see the worried and anxious look in his eyes.

I could not bear to see him like this.

"Zorba," I said, "there's something you want to tell me. Well, tell me. Come on, now, cough it up; you'll feel better afterwards."

Zorba remained silent. He picked up a small pebble and threw it with some force through the window.

"Leave the stones alone! Speak!"

Zorba stretched out his wrinkled neck.

"Have you got confidence in me, boss?" he asked, anxiously looking me in the eyes.

"Yes, Zorba," I replied. "Whatever you do, you can't go wrong. Even if you wanted to, you couldn't. You're like a lion, shall we say, or a wolf. That kind of beast never behaves as if it were a sheep or a donkey; it is never untrue to its nature. And you, you're Zorba to the tips of your fingers."

Zorba nodded his head.

"But I've no longer the foggiest idea where we're going!" he said.

"I have, don't you worry about that. Just go straight ahead!"

"Say that again, boss, to give me courage!" he cried.

"Go ahead!"

Zorba's eyes shone.

"Now I can tell you," he said. "I've been working out a big plan in my mind these last few days, a crazy idea. Is it on?"

"Need you ask me? That's what we came here for: to carry ideas into effect."

Zorba craned his neck, looked at me with joy and fear.

"Speak plainly, boss!" he cried. "Didn't we come here for the coal?"

"The coal was a pretext, just to stop the locals being too inquisitive, so that they took us for sober contractors and didn't greet us by slinging tomatoes at us. Do you understand, Zorba?"

Zorba was dumbfounded. He tried hard to understand; he could not believe in such happiness. All at once, he was convinced. He rushed towards me and took me by the shoulders.

"Do you dance?" he asked me intensely. "Do you dance?"

"No."

"No?"

He was flabbergasted, and let his arms dangle at his sides.

"Oh, well," he said after a moment. "Then *I'll* dance, boss. Sit further away, so that I don't barge into you."

He made a leap, rushed out of the hut, cast off his shoes, his coat, his vest, rolled his trousers up to his knees, and started dancing. His face was still black with coal. The whites of his eyes gleamed.

He threw himself into the dance, clapping his hands, leaping and pirouetting in the air, falling on to his knees, leaping again with his legs tucked up—it was as if he were made of rubber. He suddenly made tremendous bounds into the air, as if he wished to conquer the laws of nature and fly away. One felt that in this old body of his there was a soul struggling to carry away this flesh and cast itself like a meteor into the darkness. It shook the body which fell back to earth, since it could not stay very long in the air; it shook it again pitilessly, this time a little higher, but the poor body fell again, breathless.

Zorba puckered his brow; his face had assumed an alarming severity. He no longer uttered cries. With clenched teeth he was endeavoring to attain the impossible.

"Zorba! Zorba!" I shouted. "That's enough!"

I was afraid that his old body would not stand up to such violence and might be shattered into a thousand pieces and scattered to the four winds of heaven.

But what was the use of my shouting? How could Zorba hear my cries from the earth? His organs had become like those of a bird.

I anxiously followed the savage and desperate dance. When I was a child I used to let my imagination go and told my friends outrageous fibs which I came to believe myself.

"How did *your* grandfather die?" my little school-friend asked me one day.

And straight away I invented a myth, and the more I invented the more I believed.

"My grandfather had a white beard and used to wear rubber shoes. One day he leapt from the roof of our house, but when his feet touched the ground he bounced like a ball and bounced up higher than the house, and went higher and higher still till he disappeared in the clouds. That is how my grandfather died."

After inventing that myth, every time I went into the little church of St. Minas and saw at the bottom of the iconostasis the ascension of Christ, I would point to it and say to my comrades:

"Look, there's grandfather with his rubber shoes!"

Now, this evening, after so many years, seeing Zorba leaping into the air, I lived through my childish tale again with terror, fearing that Zorba might disappear in the clouds.

"Zorba! Zorba!" I shouted. "That's enough!"

At last Zorba crouched on the ground, out of breath. His face was shining and happy. His grey hairs were sticking to his forehead and the sweat, mixed with coal-dust, was running down his cheeks and chin.

I bent over him anxiously.

"I feel better for that," he said, after a minute, "as if I had been bled. Now I can talk."

He went back to the hut, sat in front of the brazier and looked at me with a radiant expression.

"What came over you to make you dance like that?"

"What could I do, boss? My joy was choking me. I had to find some outlet. And what sort of outlet? Words? Pff!"

"What joy?"

His face clouded over. His lip began to tremble.

"What joy? Well, what you said to me a moment ago, you said . . . just like that, in the air? You didn't understand it your-self? We didn't come here for the coal, you told me. That's what you said, didn't you? We came here to while away the time and lead them up the wrong track so that they shouldn't take us for lunatics and sling tomatoes at us! But when we're alone together and nobody can see us, we can laugh and enjoy ourselves! Isn't that right? I swear that's what I wanted, too, but I didn't realize it properly. Sometimes I thought of the coal, sometimes of old Bouboulina, sometimes of you . . . a regular muddle. When I was picking out a gallery, I said: It's coal I want! And from head to heel I became coal. But afterwards, when the work was finished, when I was sky-larking with that old sow—good luck to her!—I said, let all the sacks of lignite and all the bosses go hang—by the little ribbon round her neck—and Zorba with them! Then when I was alone and had noth-ing to do, I thought of you, boss, and my heart melted. It weighed on my conscience. 'It's disgraceful, Zorba,' I'd cry, 'disgraceful for you to go and fool that good man and eat up all his money. When'll you stop being a rotter, you Zorba, you? I've had enough of you!' I tell you, boss, I didn't know where I was. The devil was dragging me one way, God the other; and, between the two of them, they split me down the middle. Now, bless you, boss, you've said a great thing and I can see it all clearly now. I've seen, I've understood! We're agreed! Let's get cracking! How much money have you got left? Hand it over! Let's eat it up!"

Zorba mopped his brow and looked around. The remains of our dinner were still lying on the little table. He reached for them with his long arm.

"With your permission, boss," he said. "I'm hungry again."

He took a slice of bread, an onion and handful of olives.

He ate voraciously, tipped up the calabash, and the red wine gurgled down his throat without the calabash touching his lips. Zorba clicked his tongue; he was satisfied.

"That's better," he said.

He winked at me and asked:

"Why don't you laugh? Why d'you look at me like that? That's how I am. There's a devil in me who shouts, and I do what he says. Whenever I feel I'm choking with some emotion, he says: 'Dance!' and I dance. And I feel better! Once, when my little Dimitraki died, in Chalcidice, I got up as I did a moment ago and I danced. The relations and friends who saw me dancing in front of the body rushed up to stop me. 'Zorba has gone mad!' they cried, 'Zorba has gone mad!' But if at that moment I had not danced, I should really have gone mad—from grief. Because it was my first son and he was three years old and I could not bear to lose him. You understand what I'm saying, boss, don't you—or am I talking to myself?"

"I understand, Zorba, I understand; you're not talking to yourself."

"Another time. . . . I was in Russia then . . . yes, I've been there, too, for the mines again, copper this time, near Novo Rossisk . . . I had learnt five or six words of Russian, just enough for my work: no; yes; bread; water; I love you; come; how much? . . . But I got friendly with a Russian, a thorough-going Bolshevik. We went every evening to a tavern in the port. We knocked back a good number of bottles of vodka, and that put us into high spirits.

Once we began to feel good we wanted to talk. He wanted to tell me everything that had happened to him during the Russian revolution, and I wanted to let him know what I had been up to. . . . We had got drunk together, you see, and had become brothers.

"We had come to an arrangement as well as we could by gestures. He was to speak first. As soon as I couldn't follow him, I was to shout: 'Stop!' Then he'd get up and dance. D'you get me, boss? He danced what he wanted to tell me. And I did the same. Anything we couldn't say with our mouths we said with our feet, our hands, our belly or with wild cries: Hi! Hi! Hop-la! Ho-heigh!

"The Russian began. How he had taken a rifle; how war had spread; how they arrived in Novo Rossisk. When I couldn't follow any more, I cried: 'Stop!' The Russian straight away bounded up, and away he went dancing! He danced like a madman. And I watched his hands, his feet, his chest, his eyes, and I understood everything. How they had entered Novo Rossisk; how they had looted shops; how they had gone into houses and carried off the women. At first the hussies cried and scratched their own faces with their nails and scratched the men, too, but gradually they became tamed, they shut their eyes and yelped with pleasure. They were women, in fact. . . .

"And then, after that, it was my turn. I only managed to get out a few words—perhaps he was a bit dense and his brain didn't work properly—the Russian shouted: 'Stop!' That's all I was waiting for. I leapt up, pushed the chairs and tables away and began dancing. Ah, my poor friend, men have sunk very low, the devil take them! They've let their bodies become mute and they only speak with their mouths. But what d'you expect a mouth to say? What can it tell you? If only you could have seen how the Russian listened to me from head to foot, and how he followed everything! I danced my misfortunes; my travels; how many times I'd been married; the trades I'd learned—quarrier, miner, pedlar, potter, *comitadji, santuri*-player, *passa-tempo* hawker, blacksmith, smuggler—how I'd been shoved into prison; how I escaped; how I arrived in Russia. . . .

"Even he, dense as he was, could understand everything, everything. My feet and my hands spoke, so did my hair and my clothes. And a clasp-knife hanging from my waistband spoke, too. When I had finished, the great blockhead hugged me in his arms; we filled up our glasses with vodka once more; we wept and we laughed in each other's arms. At daybreak we were pulled apart and went staggering to our beds. And in the evening we met again.

"Are you laughing? Don't you believe me, boss? You're saying to yourself: Whatever are these yarns this Sinbad the Sailor is spinning? Is it possible to talk by dancing? And yet I dare swear that's how the gods and devils must talk to each other.

"But I can see you're sleepy. You're too delicate. You've no stamina. Go on, go to sleep, and tomorrow we'll speak about this again. I've a plan, a magnificent plan. I'll tell you about it tomorrow. I'm going to smoke one more cigarette. I may even take a dip in the sea. I'm on fire. I must put it out. Good night!"

I was a long time getting to sleep. My life is wasted, I thought. If only I could take a cloth and wipe out all I have learnt, all I have seen and heard, and go to Zorba's school and start the great, the real alphabet! What a different road I would choose. I should keep my five senses perfectly trained, and my whole body, too, so that it would enjoy and understand. I should learn to run, to wrestle, to swim, to ride horses, to row, to drive a car, to fire a rifle. I should fill my soul with flesh. I should fill my flesh with soul. In fact, I should reconcile at last within me the two eternal antagonists.

Sitting on my mattress, I thought of my life which was being completely wasted. Through the open door I could just discern Zorba by the light of the stars. He was crouching on a rock, like a night bird. I envied him. It is he who has discovered the truth, I thought. His is the right path.

In other, more primitive and creative ages, Zorba would have been the chief of a tribe. He would have gone before, opening up the path with a hatchet. Or else he would have been a renowned troubador visiting castles, and everybody would have hung on his words—lords and ladies and servants. . . . In our ungrateful age, Zorba wanders hungrily round the enclosures like a wolf, or else sinks into becoming some pen-pusher's buffoon.

I saw Zorba suddenly rise. He undressed, threw his clothes on to the pebbles and plunged into the sea. For a few moments, by the pale light of the moon, I could see his great head appearing and disappearing. From time to time he uttered a cry, barked, whinnied, crowed like a cock—his soul in this empty night found an affinity with animals.

Gently, without my realizing it, I fell asleep. The next day, at first light, I saw Zorba, smiling and rested, coming to pull me by the feet.

"Get up, boss," he said, "and let me confess my plan to you. Are you listening?"

"I'm listening."

He sat on the ground like a Turk and started explaining how he would set up an overhead cable from the top of the mountain to the coast; in this way we could bring down the wood which we needed for the pit props, and the rest we could sell as timber for building. We had decided to rent a pine forest belonging to the monastery, but transport was expensive and we could not find enough mules. So Zorba had imagined laying out a line with a heavy cable, pylons and pulleys.

"Agreed?" he asked me when he had finished explaining. "Will you sign?"

"I'll sign, Zorba. Agreed."

He lit the brazier, put the kettle on the fire, prepared my coffee, threw a rug over my feet so that I should not catch cold, and went out, content.

"We're going to open a new gallery today," he said. "I've found a beautiful seam! Real black diamonds!"

I opened the *Buddha* manuscript, and I, too, worked my way into my own galleries. I wrote all day, and the more I progressed, the freer I felt. My feelings were mixed: relief, pride, disgust. But I let myself be absorbed by the work, for I knew that as soon as I had finished this manuscript and had bound and sealed it I should be free.

I was hungry. I ate a few raisins, some almonds and a piece of bread. I was waiting for Zorba to return, and with him all the things which rejoice the heart of man: clear laughter, the kind word, tasty dishes.

He appeared in the evening, and prepared the meal. We ate, but his mind was elsewhere. He knelt down, stuck little bits of wood in the ground, hung a piece of string on them, hung a match from some minute pulleys, endeavoring to find the right slope, so that the whole contraption did not fall to pieces.

"If the slope is too steep," he explained to me, "we're dished. We must find the exact slope. And for that, boss, we need some brains and wine."

"We've plenty of wine," I said, laughing, "but, as for the brains. . . ."

Zorba burst out laughing.

"There are some things you get the hang of, boss," he said, looking at me affectionately.

He sat down to have a rest, and lit a cigarette.

He was in a good humor again and he became talkative.

"If this line worked," he said, "we could bring down the whole forest. We could open a factory, make planks, posts, scaffolding; why, we'd be rolling in money. We could lay down a three-master and then pack up, throw a stone behind us and sail round the world!"

Women in distant ports, towns, illuminations, gigantic buildings, machinery, ships came before Zorba's eyes.

"I'm white on top already, boss, and my teeth are getting loose. I've no time to lose. You're young, you can still afford to be patient. I can't. But I do declare, the older I get the wilder I become! Don't let anyone tell me old age steadies a man! Nor that when he sees death coming he stretches out his neck and says: Cut off my head, please, so that I can go to heaven! The longer I live, the more I rebel. I'm not going to give in; I want to conquer the world!"

He rose and unhooked the *santuri*.

"Come over here, you fiend," he said. "What the hell are you doing hanging on the wall without saying a word? Let's hear you sing!"

I never tired of seeing with what elaborate precautions, with what gentleness, Zorba removed the cloth in which he wrapped his *santuri*. He looked as if he was removing the skin from a purple fig, or undressing a woman.

He placed the *santuri* on his lap, bent over it, lightly touched the strings—as if he were consulting it to see what tune they should sing, as if he were begging it to wake, as if he were trying to coax it into keeping company with his wandering spirit which was tired of solitude. He tried a song. It somehow would not come out right; he abandoned it and began another; the strings grated as if in pain, as if they did not want to sing. Zorba leaned against the wall, mopped his brow, which had suddenly started to perspire.

"It doesn't want to. . . ." he muttered, looking with awe at the *santuri*, "it doesn't want to!"

He wrapped it up again with care, as if it were a wild animal and he was afraid it might bite. He rose slowly and hung it on the wall.

"It doesn't want to. . . ." he muttered again, "it doesn't want to . . . we mustn't force it!"

He sat down once more on the ground, poked some chestnuts amongst the embers and filled the glasses with wine. He drank, drank again, shelled a chestnut and gave it to me.

"Can you make it out, boss?" he asked me. "It's beyond me. Everything seems to have a soul—wood, stones, the wine we drink and the earth we tread on. Everything, boss, absolutely everything!"

He raised his glass: "Your health."

He emptied it and filled it afresh.

"What a jade life this is!" he murmured. "A jade! It's just like old Bouboulina!"

I started laughing.

"Listen to me, boss, don't laugh. Life is just like old Bouboulina. It's old, isn't it? All right, but it doesn't lack spice. She knows a trick or two to make you go off your rocker. If you close your eyes, you'd think you had a girl of twenty in your arms. She is twenty, I swear, when you're in the act and have put out the light.

"It's no use your telling me she's a bit overripe, she's led a pretty fast life and been on the spree with admirals, sailors, soldiers, peasants, travelling show men, priests, clergymen, policemen, schoolmasters and justices of the peace! So what? What of it? She soon forgets, does that old trollop. She can't remember any of her old lovers. Each time she becomes—I'm not joking—she becomes a sweet little pigeon, a pure white swan, a sucking dove, and she blushes—yes she does, she blushes and trembles all over, as if it were the first time! What a mystery woman is, boss! Even if she falls a thousand times, she rises a thousand times a virgin. But how's that? you'll say. Because she doesn't remember!"

"Well, the parrot remembers, Zorba," I said, to tease him. "He always squawks a name which isn't yours. Doesn't it annoy you, to hear that parrot screaming every time you reach the seventh heaven: 'Canavaro! Canavaro!' Don't you ever feel like taking him by the neck and wringing it? It's high time you taught him to shout: 'Zorba! Zorba!'"

"Oh, all that stuff and nonsense!" Zorba cried, stopping his ears with his great hands. "Wring his neck, you say? But I love to hear him shout the name! At night the old sinner hangs him up over the bed and the little devil's got an eye he can see with in the dark, and scarcely have you got started having it out together than he begins shouting: 'Canavaro! Canavaro!'

"And immediately, I swear, boss—but how could you understand that when you've been contaminated by those blasted books of yours?—I swear that I immediately feel patent-leather boots on my feet, plumes on my head and a silky beard smelling of patchouli on my chin. *Buon giorno! Buona sera! Mangiate macaroni!* I really become Canavaro. I clamber on to my flagship riddled with a thousand shots and away. . . . Fire the boilers! The cannonade begins!"

Zorba laughed heartily. He shut his left eye and looked at me with the other.

"You must forgive me, boss," he said, "but I'm like my grandfather Alexis—God sanctify his remains! He used to sit in the evening in front of his door when he was a hundred and ogle the young girls going to the well. His sight wasn't too good, he couldn't see very clearly, so he'd call the girls over to him. 'I say, which one are you?' 'Xenio, Mastrandoni's daughter.' 'Come closer then and let me touch you. Come along, don't be afraid!' She'd try and keep a solemn face, and go up to him. Then my grandad would raise his hand to her face and feel it slowly, sensually. And his tears would flow. 'Why d'you cry, Grandad?' I once asked him. 'Ah, don't you think I've something to cry about, my boy, when I'm slowly dying and leaving behind so many fine wenches?'"

Zorba sighed. "Ah, poor old Grandad!" he said. "How I feel for you! I often say myself: 'Ah, misery! If only all the pretty-looking women'd die at the same time as myself!' But the jades will go on living; they'll be having a high old time, men'll be taking them in their arms and kissing them, when I'm just dust for them to walk on!"

He pulled a few chestnuts out of the fire, shelled them, and we clinked glasses. We stayed a long time drinking and slowly munching like two great rabbits, and we could hear the roaring of the sea.

◇ 7 ◇

W<small>E STAYED</small> silent by the brazier until far into the night. I felt
once more how simple and frugal a thing is happiness: a
glass of wine, a roast chestnut, a wretched little brazier, the sound
of the sea. Nothing else. And all that is required to feel that here
and now is happiness is a simple, frugal heart.

"How many times have you been married, Zorba?" I asked.

We were both in a good humor, not so much for having drunk
a lot as on account of the indescribable happiness within us. We
were deeply aware, each of us in our own way, that we were two
ephemeral little insects, clinging tightly to the terrestrial bark, that
we had found a convenient corner near the sea, behind some bamboos, planks and empty petrol cans, where we hung together, and,
lastly, that we had before us some pleasant things and food, and
within us serenity, affection and security.

Zorba did not hear my question. Who knows on what oceans
beyond the reach of my voice his mind was sailing? I stretched out
my arm and touched him with the tip of my fingers.

"How many times have you been married, Zorba?" I asked again.

He started. He had heard this time. Waving his great hand, he
answered:

"What are you delving into now? D'you think I'm not a man?
Like everyone else, I've committed the Great Folly. That's what I
call marriage—may married folk forgive me! Yes, I've committed
the Great Folly, I've married!"

"Yes, but how many times?"

Zorba scratched his head vigorously.

"How many times?" he said, at last. "Honestly once, once and for all. Half-honestly twice. Dishonestly a thousand, two thousand, three thousand times. How d'you expect me to reckon it?"

"Tell me a little about your marriages, Zorba. Tomorrow's Sunday, we'll shave and put on our best clothes and go to old Bouboulina's 'for a good time and a bad girl!' Now, tell me!"

"Tell you what! Are those really things you talk about, boss? Honest marriages are tasteless; they're a dish without any pepper. Tell you what! When the saints ogle you from their icons and give you their blessing, d'you call that a kiss? In our village we say 'only stolen meat is tasty.' Your wife is no stolen meat. Now, as for the dishonest unions, how are you going to recall them? Does the cock keep a register? You bet! And why should he, anyhow? There was a time, when I was young, I kept a lock of hair of every woman I got familiar with. I always kept a pair of scissors on me. Even when I went to church, yes, there were my scissors in my pocket! We're men, after all; you never know what'll come along, do you?

"So, like that, I made a collection of locks of hair. There were dark ones, fair ones, ginger ones, even a few white ones. I collected such a lot, I stuffed a pillow with them. I stuffed the pillow I slept on—only in winter, though. In summer it made me too hot. Then, a bit later, I got fed up with that, too—you see, it began to stink, so I burned it."

Zorba started laughing.

"That was my register, boss," he said, "and it's burnt. But I was fed up to the teeth with it. I thought there wouldn't be so many, and then I saw there was no end to it. So I threw my scissors away."

"What about the half-honest marriages, Zorba?"

"Oh, those have a certain charm," he sighed. "O wonderful Slav, may you live a thousand years! What freedom! None of those: 'Where have you been?' 'Why're you late?' 'Where did you sleep?' She asks you no questions and you ask her none. Freedom!"

He reached for his glass, emptied it and shelled a chestnut. He munched as he spoke.

"One was called Sophinka, the other Noussa. I met Sophinka

in a tidy-sized village near Novo Rossisk. It was winter and snow-ing. I was going to look for work in a mine, and stopped in this village. It was market day and, from all the villages round about, men and women had come to buy and sell. A terrible famine and bitter cold. To buy bread people were selling all they had, even their icons!

"Well, I was going round the market when I saw a young peasant woman jumping down from her cart—a six-foot hussy with eyes as blue as the sea and such thighs and buttocks—I tell you, a real brood mare! . . . I stopped dead in my tracks. 'Poor Zorba, oh, my poor bloody Zorba!' I said.

"I started to follow her and look. . . . I couldn't keep my eyes off her! You should've seen her buttocks swinging like church-bells at Easter! 'Why go looking for mines, you poor mutt?' I said to myself. 'Why waste precious time there, you damned weather-cock? Here's the mine for you: get in it and open up the galleries!'

"The girl stopped, started to bargain, bought a load of wood, lifted it up—Jesus, what arms!—and threw it into her cart! She bought some bread and five or six smoked fish. 'How much is that?' she asked. 'So much. . . .' She took off her golden earrings to pay. As she'd no money, she was going to give her earrings. My heart leapt into my mouth. Me, let a woman give away her earrings, her trinkets, her scented cakes of soap, her little bottles of lavender-water? . . . If she gives away all that, it's all up with the world! It's as if you plucked a peacock's feathers. Would you have the heart to pluck a peacock? Never! No, as long as Zorba lives, I said to myself, that won't happen. I opened my purse and I paid. It was the time when roubles had become bits of paper. With a hundred drachmas you could buy a mule, with ten a woman.

"So I paid. The wench turned round and took a look at me out of the corner of her eyes. She took my hand to kiss it. But I pulled my hand away. What did she take me for? An old man? 'Spassiba! Spassiba!' she cried—that means: 'Thanks! Thanks!' And away she leaped into her cart. She took the reins and raised her whip. 'Zorba,' I said to myself, 'look out, my friend, she's going to slip through your fingers!' In one bound, I was at her side in the cart. She said nothing. She didn't even look round. A crack of the whip and off we went.

"On the way, she came to realize I wanted her to be mine. I could muster three words of Russian, but in these affairs there's no need to say much. We spoke to each other with our eyes, our hands, our knees. No need to beat about the bush. We arrived in the village and stopped in front of her *isba*. We got down. The girl thrust open the yard gate with her shoulder and we went in. We unloaded the wood in the yard, took the fish and bread and entered the room. A little old woman was sitting by the empty hearth. She was shivering. She was wrapped in sacks, rags, and sheepskins, but she was shivering. It was so cold, I tell you, your fingernails fairly fell out. I bent down, put an armful of wood in the fireplace and lit the fire. The little old woman looked at me and smiled. Her daughter had said something to her, but I hadn't understood. I made the fire go; the old woman warmed herself by it and recovered a little.

"Meanwhile, the girl was laying the table. She brought out some vodka; we drank it. She lit the samovar and made some tea. We ate and gave her share to the old woman. Then she quickly made the bed with clean sheets, lit the Holy Virgin's icon lamp and crossed herself three times. Then she signed to me; we knelt together in front of the old woman and kissed her hand. The old woman put her bony hands on our heads and muttered something. Probably her blessing on us. *'Spassiba! Spassiba!'* I cried, and in one bound, there I was in bed with the wench!"

Zorba became silent. He raised his head and gazed into the distance over the sea.

"Her name was Sophinka. . . ." he said after a while, and became silent again.

"Well?" I asked impatiently. "Well?"

"There's no well! What a mania you've got, boss, with your 'wells' and 'wherefores!' Now, does one talk about those things? Woman is a fresh spring. You lean over her, you see your reflection and you drink; you drink until your bones crack. Then there's another who comes, and he's thirsty, too; he bends over her, he sees his reflection and he drinks. Then a third. . . . A fresh spring, that's what she is, and she's a woman, too. . . ."

"Did you leave her after that?"

"What d'you expect? She's a spring, I told you, and I'm a passerby. I went back on the road. I'd stayed three months with her. God protect her, I've nothing to say against her! But after three months I remembered I was looking for a mine. 'Sophinka,' I said to her one morning, 'I've got some work to do. I must go.' 'Well,' Sophinka said, 'go along. I'll wait one month. If you're not back in one month's time, I'll be free. So will you. God bless you!' I went."

"And you came back after a month . . . ?"

"But you're stupid, boss, if you don't mind my saying so," Zorba exclaimed. "Came back! Do the jades ever leave you alone? Ten days later, in the Kuban, I met Noussa."

"Tell me about her! Tell me!"

"Another time, boss. We mustn't get them mixed up, the poor things! Your health, Sophinka!"

He quaffed the glass of wine. Then he leaned against the wall and said:

"All right! I'll tell you now about Noussa. I've got Russia on the brain tonight. Strike the flag! We'll empty the holds!"

He wiped his moustache and poked the embers.

"Well, as I said, I met this one in a Kuban village. It was summer. Mountains of melons and watermelons. I'd pick up one now and then and nobody'd say a thing. I'd cut it in two and stick my face into it.

"Everything's to be had in abundance in Russia, boss, everything in a heap. Roll up and take your choice! And not only melons and watermelons, I tell you, but fish and butter and women. You're passing by, you see a watermelon, you take it. Not like here in Greece, where if you ever pinch the tiniest bit of skin off a melon you're hauled up before the courts, and as soon as you touch a woman her brother rushes up and draws a knife to make sausage meat of you! Ugh! To hell with that measly crowd of beggars! You just go to Russia if you want to see how you can live like a lord.

"So, I was going through Kuban and I saw a woman in a kitchen garden. I liked the look of her. Let me tell you, boss, the Slav woman is not like those skinny, greedy little Greeks who sell you love a drop at a time, and do everything they can to palm you off with less than your due and swindle you over the weight. No, boss, the Slav gives you good measure. In sleep, in love, and in food. She's so nearly related to the beasts of the fields and the earth itself. She gives and gives bountifully, she's not niggardly about it like those haggling Greeks. I asked her: 'What's your name?' You see, through women, I'd picked up a bit of the language. 'Noussa! And yours?' 'Alexis. I like you very much, Noussa.' She looked me over carefully, like you look at a horse before buying it. 'You're no weed yourself,' she said. 'You've got sound teeth, a big moustache, a broad back, strong arms. I like you.' We didn't say much else, it wasn't necessary. We came to an understanding in a jiffy. I was to go to her place that evening in my glad rags. 'Have you got a fur-lined cloak?' Noussa asked me. 'Yes, but in this heat. . . .' 'Never mind. Bring it, it'll look smart.'

"That evening, then, I rigged myself out like a bridegroom, I put my cloak over my arm, I also took a silver-knobbed cane I had, and off I went. It was a big country house with out-buildings, cows, presses, two fires in the yard and cauldrons on the fires. 'What's boiling here?' I asked. 'Watermelon must.' 'And here?' 'Melon must.' 'What a country!' I said to myself. 'D'you hear that? Must of melons and watermelons! This is the Promised Land! Goodbye poverty! Here's to you, Zorba, you've fallen on your feet. Like a mouse in a pound of cheese!'

"I went up the staircase. An enormous wooden staircase which creaked. On the landing were Noussa's father and mother. They were wearing a sort of green breeches and red waistbands with big tassels—they were pretty well off, in fact. These monkey-faces opened their arms and enveloped you in huggings and kissings. I was soaked in slobber. They spoke to me at top speed; I didn't understand much, but what did that matter? It was obvious, by their expressions, they wished me no ill.

"I went into the room and what did I see? Tables groaning under food and drink, like great sailing ships. Everybody was standing —relations, women, men, and in front was Noussa, made-up, in evening dress, with her bosom showing, like a ship's figure head. She had dazzling youth and beauty. She was wearing a red kerchief over her hair, and over her heart was an embroidered hammer and sickle. 'Zorba, you double-dyed sinner, you,' I muttered to myself, 'is that your meat? Is that the body you're going to hold in your arms tonight? God forgive your father and mother who brought you into this world!'

"We all threw ourselves on the food with a will, the women as well as the men. We guzzled and swilled, we ate like pigs and drank like fish. 'What about the priest?' I asked Noussa's father, who was sitting beside me and whose body was steaming through eating so much. 'Where's the priest to bless us?' 'There's no priest,' he spluttered, 'there's no priest. Religion is opium for the masses.'

"On that he rose, puffed out his breast, loosened his red sash and raised his arm for silence. He was holding a glass filled to the brim and looking me straight in the eye. Then he began to talk and talk; he was making a speech to me. What was he saying? God knows! I was tired of standing. Besides, by this time I was a bit pissed. I sat down and pressed my knee against Noussa's. She was on my right.

"The old boy just wouldn't stop talking, the sweat was pouring off him. So they all rushed round him and hugged him to make him stop talking. He stopped. Noussa signed to me. 'Now you must speak!'

"So I got up in my turn and made a speech, half in Russian, half in Greek. What did I say? I'm damned if I know. I only remember that at the end I launched on some Klepht brigand songs. Without rhyme or reason, I began to bellow:

> From the hills the Klephts came down,
> Each a rustler!
> Of horses found they none,
> But they found Noussa!

"You see, boss, I changed the song to fit the circumstances.

> Away they go, away they go . . .
> (Away they go, mother!)
> Ah! My Noussa!
> Ah! My Noussa!
>   Vye!

"And, as I bellowed 'Vye!' I threw myself on Noussa and kissed her.

"That was just what was wanted. As if I had given the signal they were waiting for, and they were, in fact, only waiting for that, several great fellows with red beards rushed and put out the lights.

"The women, the jades, started yelping, screaming they were afraid. But almost at once, in the darkness, they giggled: 'Hee-hee-hee!' They liked being tickled and laughed.

"What happened, boss, God alone knows. But I don't think He knew either, because if He had known, He would have sent a thunderbolt to burn them up. There they were all mixed up, men and women, rolling on the ground. I started to search for Noussa, but where could I find her? I found another and did the job with her.

"At daybreak I rose to leave with my woman. It was still dark, I couldn't see clearly. I caught hold of a foot, I pulled it. No, it wasn't Noussa's. I caught hold of another foot—no! I pulled a third—no! I catch hold of a fourth, a fifth, and in the end, after no end of trouble, I found Noussa's foot, pulled it, and extricated her from two or three great devils who were sprawling over the poor girl, and I woke her up. 'Noussa,' I said, 'Let's go!' 'Don't forget your fur cape!' she replied. 'Let's go!' And we left."

"Well?" I asked again, seeing that Zorba remained silent.

"There you go again with your 'wells,'" said Zorba, impatient at these questions.

He sighed

"I lived six months with her. Since that day—God be my witness!—I need fear nothing. Nothing, I say. Nothing, except one thing: that the devil, or God, wipe out those six months from my memory. D'you understand? 'I understand,' you ought to say."

Zorba closed his eyes. He appeared very moved. It was the first time I had seen him so strongly gripped by a memory of long ago.

"Did you love that Noussa so much, then?" I asked a few moments later.

Zorba opened his eyes.

"You're young, boss," he said, "you're still young, you can't understand! When you've gone white on top like me, we'll talk again about this—this everlasting business."

"What everlasting business?"

"Why, women, of course! How many times must I tell you, woman is an everlasting business. Just now, you're like a young cock who covers the hens in two shakes of a lamb's tail and then puffs out his breast, gets on top of the dung hill and starts to crow and brag. He doesn't look at the hens, he looks at their combs! Well, what can he know of love? The devil take him!"

He spat on the ground in scorn. Then he turned his head away; he did not wish to look at me.

"Well, Zorba," I asked again, "what about Noussa?"

Zorba replied, gazing into the distance over the sea:

"When I came home one evening, I couldn't find her anywhere. She'd gone. A handsome soldier had just arrived in the village and she'd run off with him. It was all over! I tell you, my heart split in two. But the knave soon stuck itself together again. You must have seen those sails with red, yellow and black patches, sewn with thick twine, which never tear even in the roughest storms. Well, that's what my heart's like. Umpteen holes, and umpteen patches: it need fear nothing more!"

"And didn't you bear Noussa any grudge, Zorba?"

"Why? You can say what you like, woman is something different, boss . . . something different. She's not human! Why bear her any grudge? Woman's something incomprehensible, and all the laws of state and religion have got her all wrong. They shouldn't act like that towards a woman. They're too harsh, boss, too unjust. If I ever had to make laws, I shouldn't make the same laws for men and for women. Ten, a hundred, a thousand commandments for man. Man is a man, after all; he can stand up to it. But not a single law for woman. Because—how many times do I have to tell you this, boss?—woman is a creature with no strength. Let's drink to Noussa, boss! And to woman! . . . And may God give us men more sense!"

He drank, raised his arm and brought it down with force, as if he were using an axe.

"He must either give us men more sense," he said, "or else perform an operation on us. Otherwise, believe me, we're finished."

◇ 8 ◇

IT WAS raining again the next day. The sky mingled with the earth in infinite tenderness. I recalled a Hindu bas-relief in dark-grey stone. The man had thrown his arms around the woman and was united to her with such gentleness and resignation that one had the impression—the elements having worked over, and almost eaten into, the bodies—of seeing two copulating insects over which fine rain had started to fall and dampen their wings. Thus closely entwined, they were being slowly sucked back into the voracious maw of the earth.

I was sitting in front of the hut and watching the ground darken and the sea grow a phosphorescent green. Not a soul was to be seen from one end of the beach to the other, not a sail, not a bird. Only the smell of the earth entered through the window.

I rose and held out my hand to the rain like a beggar. I suddenly felt like weeping. Some sorrow, not my own but deeper and more obscure, was rising from the damp earth: the panic which a peaceful grazing animal feels when, all at once, without seeing anything, it rears its head and scents in the air about it that it is trapped and cannot escape.

I wanted to utter a cry, knowing that it would relieve my feelings, but I was ashamed to.

The clouds were coming lower and lower. I looked through the window; my heart was gently palpitating.

What a voluptuous enjoyment of sorrow those hours of soft rain can produce in you! All the bitter memories hidden in the depths of your mind come to the surface: separations from friends, women's smiles which have faded, hopes which have lost their wings like moths and of which only a grub remains—and that grub had crawled on to the leaf of my heart and was eating it away.

The image of my friend exiled in the Caucasus slowly appeared through the rain and sodden earth. I took my pen, bent over the paper, and began to speak to him in order to cut through the fine mesh of the rain and be able to breathe.

MY DEAR FRIEND,

I am writing to you from a lonely shore in Crete where destiny and I have agreed I should stay several months to play—to play at being a capitalist. If my game succeeds, I shall say it was not a game, but that I had made a great resolution and changed my mode of life.

You remember how, when you left, you called me a bookworm. That so vexed me I decided to abandon my scribbling on paper for a time—or forever?—and to throw myself into a life of action. I rented a hillside containing lignite; I engaged workmen and took picks and shovels, acetylene lamps, baskets, trucks. I opened up galleries and went into them. Just like that, to annoy you. And by dint of digging and making passages in the earth, the bookworm has become a mole. I hope you approve of the metamorphosis.

My joys here are great, because they are very simple and spring from the everlasting elements: the pure air, the sun, the sea and the wheaten loaf. In the evening an extraordinary Sinbad the Sailor squats before me, Turkish fashion, and speaks. He speaks and the world grows bigger. Occasionally, when words no longer suffice, he leaps up and dances. And when dancing no longer suffices he places his *santuri* on his knees and plays.

Sometimes he plays a savage air and you feel you are choking because you realize all at once that your life is colorless, miserable and unworthy of man. Sometimes he plays a dolorous air and you feel your life passing, running away like sand between your fingers, and that there is no salvation.

My heart is going to and fro in my breast like a weaver's shuttle.

It is weaving these few months which I am spending in Crete, and—God forgive me—I believe I am happy.

Confucius says: "Many seek happiness higher than man; others beneath him. But happiness is the same height as man." That is true. So there must be happiness to suit every man's stature. Such is, my dear pupil and master, my happiness of the day. I anxiously measure it and measure it again, to see what my stature of the moment is. For, you know this very well, man's stature is not always the same.

How the soul of man is transformed according to the climate, the silence, the solitude, or the company in which it lives!

Seen from my solitary state, men appear to me not like ants but, on the contrary, like enormous monsters—dinosaurs, pterodactyls living in an atmosphere saturated with carbonic acid and thick decaying vegetation from which creation is formed. An incomprehensible, absurd jungle. The notions of "nation" and "race" of which you are fond, the notions of a "super-nation" and "humanity" which seduced me, here acquire the same value under the all-powerful breath of destruction. We feel that we have risen to the surface to utter a few syllables and sometimes not even syllables, mere inarticulate sounds: an *Ah!*, a *yes!*—after which we are destroyed. And even the most elevated ideas, if they are dissected, are seen to be no more than puppets stuffed with bran, and hidden in the bran an iron spring is found.

You know me well enough to realize that these cruel meditations, far from making me flee, are, on the contrary, indispensable tinder for my inner flame. Because, as my master, Buddha, says: "I have seen." And as I have seen and, in the twinkling of an eye, have got on good terms with the jovial and whimsical, invisible producer, I can henceforward play my own part on earth to the end, that is to say coherently and without discouragement. For, having seen, I have also collaborated in the work in which I am acting on God's stage.

This is how it is that, scanning the universal stage, I can see you over there, in those legendary fastnesses of the Caucasus, also playing out your role; I can see you fighting to save thousands of souls of our race who are in danger of death. A pseudo-Prometheus who must, however, suffer very real tortures while he combats the dark forces of hunger, cold, sickness and death. But, being proud, you must sometimes rejoice that the dark forces of destruction are so numerous and invincible: for thus your aim to live almost without hope becomes more heroic and your soul acquires a more tragic greatness.

You certainly must consider the life you lead a happy one. And since you consider it such, such it is. You have also cut your happiness according to your stature; and your stature now—God be praised—is greater than mine. The good master desires no greater recompense than this: to form a pupil who surpasses him.

As for me, I often forget, I disparage myself, I lose my way, my faith is a mosaic of unbelief. Sometimes I feel I should like to make a bargain: to live one brief minute and give the rest of my life in exchange. But you keep a firm hold on the helm and you never forget, even in the sweetest moments of this life, towards which destination you have set your course.

Do you remember the day we both crossed Italy on our way to Greece? We had decided to make for the Pontus region, which was then in danger. We hastily alighted from the train in a little town— we had just one hour to catch the other train. We went into a large wooded garden near the station. There were broad-leaved trees, bananas growing, bamboos of dark metallic colors, bees were swarming over a flowering branch which trembled to see them suck.

We strolled on in mute ecstasy, as if in a dream. Suddenly, at a turn of the flower walk, two girls appeared, reading a book as they went along. I no longer remember whether they were pretty or plain. I remember only that one was fair, the other dark, and both were wearing spring blouses.

And with the boldness one has in dreams, we approached them and you said: "Whatever the book may be you are reading, we'll discuss it with you." They were reading Gorki. Then, going posthaste, for we had little time, we talked of life, of poverty, of the revolt of the mind, of love. . . .

I shall never forget our delight and our sorrow. We and these two unknown girls were already old friends, old lovers; we had become responsible for their souls and bodies, and we made haste, for a few minutes later we were going to leave them forever. In the vibrant air we could smell ravishment and death.

The train arrived and whistled. We started, as if awaking from a dream. We shook hands. How can I ever forget the tight and desperate grip of our hands, the ten fingers which did not wish to separate. One of the girls was very pale, the other was laughing and trembling.

And I said to you then, I remember: "What do Greece, Our Country, Duty mean? The truth is here!" And you replied: "Greece, Our Country, Duty mean nothing. And yet, for that nothing we willingly court destruction."

But why am I writing this to you? To let you see that I have forgotten none of the moments we have lived together. And also to have an opportunity of expressing what, because of our good (or bad) habit of curbing our feelings, I can never reveal to you when we are together.

Now that you are no longer before me and cannot see my face, and now that I run no risk of appearing soft or ridiculous, I can tell you I love you very deeply.

I had finished my letter. I had conversed with my friend, and I felt relieved. I called Zorba. Crouching beneath a rock, so as not to get wet, he was trying out his model line.

"Come along, Zorba," I cried. "Get up and let's go for a stroll to the village."

"You're in a good humor, boss. It's raining. Can't you go alone?"

"I don't want to lose my good humor. If we go together, there'll be no danger of that. Come along."

He laughed.

"I'm glad you need me," he said. "Come on, then."

He put on the little woolly Cretan coat with a pointed hood which I had given him and, splashing through the mud, we made for the road.

It was raining. The mountain peaks were hidden. There was not a breath of wind. The pebbles gleamed. The lignite hill was smothered by the mist. It was as if the woman's face of the hill were shrouded in sorrow, as if she had fainted beneath the rain.

"A man's heart suffers when it rains," Zorba said. "You mustn't bear it any ill will, boss. The poor wretch has a soul, too."

He stooped by a hedge and picked the first little wild narcissi. He looked at them a long while, as if he could not see enough of them, as if he were seeing narcissi for the first time. He closed his eyes and smelled them, sighed, then gave them to me.

"If only we knew, boss, what the stones and rain and flowers say. Maybe they call—call us—and we don't hear them. When will people's ears open, boss? When shall we have our eyes open to see? When shall we open our arms to embrace everything—stones, rain, flowers, and men? What d'you think about that, boss? And what do your books have to say about it?"

"The devil take them!" I said, using Zorba's favorite expression. "The devil take them! That's what they say, and nothing else!"

Zorba took me by the arm.

"I'm going to tell you of an idea of mine, boss, but you mustn't be angry. Make a heap of all your books and set light to them! After that, who knows, you're no fool, you're the right sort . . . we might make something of you!"

"He is right!" I exclaimed to myself. "He is right, but I can't."

Zorba hesitated and reflected. Then he said:

"There's one thing I can see. . . ."

"What? Out with it!"

"I don't know, but I think, just like that, I can see it. But if I try to tell you, I'll make a hash of it. One day, when I'm in good form, I'll dance it for you."

It started to rain harder. We came to the village. Little girls were bringing the sheep back from grazing; the ploughmen had unyoked the oxen and were abandoning the half-ploughed field; the women were running after their children in the narrow streets. A cheerful panic had broken out in the village when the shower started. Women uttered shrill cries and their eyes were laughing; from the men's stiff beards and curled-up moustaches hung large drops of rain. A pungent smell rose from the earth, the stones and the grass.

We dived into The Modesty Café-and-Butcher's-Shop like drowned rats. It was crowded. Some men were playing a game of *belote,* others arguing at the top of their voices as if they were calling to each other across the mountains. Round a little table at the far end the village elders were laying down the law: uncle Anagnosti with his broad-sleeved white shirt; Mavrandoni, severe and silent, smoking his hookah, with his eyes riveted on the floor; the gaunt, middle-aged and rather imposing schoolmaster leaning on his thick stick and listening with a condescending smile to a hairy giant who had just returned from Candia and was describing the marvels of that great town. The café proprietor, standing behind the counter, was listening and laughing as he kept an eye on the coffeepots which stood in a row on the stove.

As soon as he saw us, uncle Anagnosti got up.

"Do come and join us, countrymen," he said. "Sfakianonikoli is telling us about all he saw and heard in Candia. He's very funny. Do come!"

He turned to the café proprietor.

"Two rakis, Manolaki!" he said.

We sat down. The wild shepherd, seeing strangers present, withdrew into his shell and was silent.

"Well, chief Nikoli, didn't you go to the theater, too?" the schoolmaster said, to make him talk. "What did you think of it?"

Sfakianonikoli stretched out his great hand, seized his glass of wine, gulped it down and plucked up courage.

"Not go to the theater?" he shouted. "Of course I did! They all kept talking about Kotopouli this and Kotopouli that. So one evening I crossed myself and said: 'All right, why don't I go and see for myself? What the devil is *she* for them to make all this fuss about Kotopouli?' " *

"So what did you see, young fellow?" uncle Anagnosti asked. "What was it? Tell us, for God's sake."

"Well, upon my soul, not much of anything. You hear 'em all talking about this 'theater,' and you think to yourself, 'Now I'm going to see something.' But, I tell you, you're wasting your money. There's a great tavern of a place, but *round*, like a threshing floor, all full of chairs and lights and people. I didn't know where I was and the lights dazzled me and I couldn't see. 'The devil,' I said to myself, 'they'll be casting a spell on me next; I'll be off.' But just then a girl, as frisky as a wagtail, gets hold of me by the hand. 'Hi! Where are you taking me?' I called out, but she just pulls me along and at last she turns round and tells me to sit down. So I sat down. Just think of it. Nothing but people in front of me and behind and both sides, and right up to the ceiling. 'I'm going to stifle,' I told myself, 'I'll bust. There's no air at all.' Then I turn to my neighbor

* A celebrated Greek actress. *Pouli* means chicken.

95

and ask him, 'Can you tell me, friend, where do these permadonnas * come out from?'

" 'Why, from inside there,' he tells me, pointing to the curtain. And he was right, too, for the next thing a bell rings, and the curtain opens and there's this Kotopouli as they say, up in front of you on the stage. But don't ask me why they call her a chicken: she's a woman, all right, with all the bits and pieces. So she just turns around and wags her tail up and down, and when they've had enough of that, they start clapping their hands and she scuttles off."

The villagers rocked with laughter. Sfakianonikoli was annoyed and looked shamefaced. He turned to the door.

"Look at that rain coming down," he said, to change the subject.

Everyone's eyes followed his. At that very moment a woman ran by, with a mass of hair hanging over her shoulders and holding her black skirts up to her knees. She had a good, round figure, her clothes clung to her, revealing a firm, alluring body.

I started. What beast of prey is that? I thought. She appeared to me lithe and dangerous, a devourer of men.

The woman turned her head for an instant and gave a rapid, dazzling look into the café.

"Holy Virgin!" muttered a callow youth with a soft, downy beard, who was sitting near the window.

"A curse on that vamp!" roared Manolakas, the village constable. "A curse on you; you set a man on fire and then let him burn!"

The youth by the window began to hum, at first softly and hesitatingly. Gradually his voice became hoarse:

. . . *The widow's pillow has a fragrant smell of quince!*
I too have known that scent and never have slept since!

"Shut up!" Mavrandoni shouted, brandishing his hookah tube.

The young man kept quiet. An old man leaned over Manolakas, the constable.

"Now your uncle's getting angry," he whispered. "If she ever falls into his hands he'd hack the poor wretch to pieces. May God have mercy on her!"

"Ah, old Androulio," said Manolakas, "I do believe you are trail-

* A corruption of prima donna.

96

ing after the widow's skirts, too. And you a verger! Aren't you ashamed?"

"Listen to me. God have mercy on her! Maybe you haven't noticed the kind of children who are born in the village of late? . . . Blessed be the widow, I say! She's, as you might say, the mistress of the whole village: you put out the light and you imagine it's not the wife you take in your arms, but the widow. And, mark you, that's why our village brings into the world such fine children nowadays!"

After a moment's silence, old Androulio murmured:

"Good luck to the thighs that embrace her! Ah, my friend, if only I were twenty, like young Pavli, Mavrandoni's boy!"

"Now we'll see her double back home!" someone said, laughing.

They all turned towards the door. The rain was pelting down. The water was gurgling over the stones. Now and then lightning flashed across the sky. Zorba was breathless since the passing of the widow. He could not contain himself any longer, and he sighed to me:

"The rain's stopping, boss," he said. "Let's go!"

A young boy, barefoot, dishevelled and with great wild-looking eyes appeared at the door. That was just how the icon painters portray St. John the Baptist—with eyes enormously enlarged by hunger and prayer.

"Hello, Mimiko!" several shouted, laughing.

Every village has its simpleton, and if one does not exist they invent one to pass the time. Mimiko was the simpleton of this village.

"Friends," Mimiko stuttered in his effeminate voice. "Friends, the widow Sourmelina has lost her ewe. A reward of a gallon of wine for whoever finds it!"

"Get out!" shouted old Mavrandoni. "Get out!"

Terrified, Mimiko curled up in a corner near the door.

"Sit down, Mimiko, have a drink of raki, so you don't catch cold!" uncle Anagnosti said, feeling sorry for him. "What'd become of our village if we had no idiot?"

A weedy-looking young man, with watery blue eyes, appeared on the threshold. He was out of breath and his hair, which was flattened on his forehead, was dripping with water.

"Hello, Pavli!" Manolakas shouted. "Hello, cousin! Take a seat."

Mavrandoni looked round at his son and frowned.

"Is that my son?" he muttered to himself. "That little pip-squeak! Who the devil does he take after? I'd like to pick him up by the scruff of his neck and thump him on the ground like a young octopus!"

Zorba was like a cat on hot bricks. The widow had inflamed his senses, he could no longer stand being within these four walls.

"Let's go, boss, let's go," he whispered every second. "We'll burst in here!"

It looked to him as if the clouds had dispersed and the sun come out.

He turned to the café proprietor:

"Who is that widow?" he asked, feigning indifference.

"A brood mare," Kondomanolio replied.

He put his fingers to his lips and gave a meaning glance at Mavrandoni, who had once more riveted his eyes on the floor.

"A mare," he repeated. "Don't let's speak of her, lest we be damned!"

Mavrandoni rose and wound the smoking-tube round the neck of his nargileh.

"Excuse me," he said. "I'm going home. Pavli, follow me!"

He led his son away. They passed in front of us and immediately disappeared in the rain. Manolakas also rose and followed them.

Kondomanolio settled in Mavrandoni's chair.

"Poor old Mavrandoni!" he said, in a voice so low it could not be heard from the neighboring tables. "He'll die of rage. It's a great misfortune which has struck his house. Only yesterday I heard Pavli myself, with my own ears, saying to his father: 'If she won't be my wife, I'll kill myself!' But that jade doesn't want to have anything to do with him. She tells him to run along and wipe his nose."

"Let's go," Zorba repeated. At every word said about the widow he became more excited.

The cocks began to crow; the rain was not quite so heavy.

"Come on, then," I said, rising.

Mimiko leapt from his corner and slipped out after us.

The pebbles were gleaming; the doors running with water

looked black; the little old women were coming out with baskets to look for snails.

Mimiko came up to me and touched my arm.

"A cigarette, master," he said. "It'll bring you good luck in love."

I gave him the cigarette. He held out a skinny, sunburnt hand.

"Give me a light, too!"

I gave him a light; he drew the smoke in to his lungs and, with eyes half-closed, blew it out through his nostrils.

"As happy as a pasha!" he murmured.

"Where are you going?"

"To the widow's garden. She said she'd give me some food if I spread the news about her ewe."

We walked quickly. There were rifts in the clouds. The whole village was freshly washed and smiling.

"Do you like the widow, Mimiko?" Zorba asked, with a sigh.

Mimiko chuckled.

"Friend, why shouldn't I like her? And haven't I come out of a sewer, like everyone else?"

"Of a sewer?" I said, astounded. "What d'you mean, Mimiko?"

"Well, from a mother's innards."

I was amazed. Only a Shakespeare in his most creative moments, I thought, could have found an expression of such crude realism to portray the dark and repugnant mystery of birth.

I looked at Mimiko. His eyes were large and ecstatic and they had a slight squint.

"How do you spend your days, Mimiko?"

"How d'you think? I live like a lord! I wake in the morning, I eat a crust. Then I do odd jobs for people, anywhere, anything, I run errands, cart manure, collect horse-dung, and I've got a fishing rod. I live with my aunt, mother Lenio, the professional mourner. You're bound to know her, everybody does. She's even been photographed. In the evening I go back home, drink a bowl of soup and a drop of wine, if there is any. If there isn't, I drink enough of God's water to make my belly swell like a drum. Then, good night!"

"And won't you get married, Mimiko?"

"What, me? I'm not a loony! Whatever are you asking now,

99

friend? That I should saddle myself with trouble? A woman needs shoes! Where'd I find any? Look, I go barefoot!"

"Haven't you any boots?"

"What d'you take me for? Of course I have! A man died last year and my aunt Lenio pulled them off his feet. I wear them at Easter and when I go to church and stare at the priest. Then I pull them off, hang them round my neck, and come home."

"What do you like best of all, Mimiko?"

"First, bread. Ah, how I like that! All crisp and hot, 'specially if it's wheat bread. Then, wine. Then, sleep."

"What about women?"

"Fff! Eat, drink, and go to bed, I say. All the rest's just trouble!"

"And the widow?"

"Oh, leave her to the devil, I tell you, if you know what's good for you! Get thee behind me, Satan!"

He spat three times and crossed himself.

"Can you read?"

"Now, look here, I'm not such a fool! When I was little I was dragged to school, but I was lucky. I caught typhus and became an idiot. That's how I managed to get out of that!"

Zorba had had enough of my questionings. He could not think of anything save the widow.

"Boss . . ." he said, taking me by the arm. Then he turned to Mimiko and ordered him to walk on ahead. "We've got something to talk about.

"Boss," he said, "this is where I count on you. Now, don't dishonor the male species! The god-devil sends you this choice morsel. You've got teeth. All right, get 'em into it. Stretch out your arm and take her! What did the Creator give us hands for? To take things! So, take 'em! I've seen loads of women in my time. But that damned widow makes the steeples rock!"

"I don't want any trouble!" I replied angrily.

I was irritated because in my heart of hearts I also had desired that all-powerful body which had passed by me like a wild animal in heat, distilling musk.

"You don't want any trouble!" Zorba exclaimed in stupefaction. "And pray, what do you want, then?"

I did not answer.

"Life is trouble," Zorba continued. "Death, no. To live—do you know what that means? To undo your belt and look for trouble!"

I still said nothing. I knew Zorba was right, I knew it, but I did not dare. My life had got on the wrong track, and my contact with men had become now a mere soliloquy. I had fallen so low that, if I had had to choose between falling in love with a woman and reading a book about love, I should have chosen the book.

"Don't calculate, boss," Zorba continued. "Leave your figures alone, smash the blasted scales, shut up your grocer's shop, I tell you. Now's the time you're going to save or to lose your soul. Listen, boss, take a handkerchief, tie two or three pounds in it, make them gold ones, because the paper ones don't dazzle; and send them to the widow by Mimiko. Teach him what he is to say: 'The master of the mine sends you his best wishes and this little handkerchief. It's only a small thing, he said, but his love is big. He said, too, you weren't to worry about the ewe; if it's lost, don't bother, I'm here, don't be afraid! He says he saw you going by the café and he's fallen sick and only you can cure him!'

"There now! Then the same evening you knock on the door. Must beat the iron while it's hot. You've lost your way, you tell her. It's dark, will she lend you a lantern. Or else you've suddenly come over dizzy and would like a glass of water. Or, better still, you buy another ewe and take it to her: 'Look, my lady,' you say, 'here's the ewe you lost. It was I who found it for you!' And the widow—listen to this, boss—the widow gives you the reward and you enter into . . . God Almighty, if only I could ride your mare behind you—I tell you, boss, you'll enter into Paradise on horseback. If you're looking for any other paradise than that, my poor fellow, there is none! Don't listen to what the priests tell you, there's no other!"

We must have been approaching the widow's garden, for Mimiko sighed and began in his stammering voice to sing his sorrow:

> *Wine for the chestnut, honey for the walnut!*
> *A lass for the lad, and a lad for the lass!*

Zorba stepped out on his long shanks, his nostrils quivering. He stopped abruptly, drew in a long breath. He stared me straight in the eyes:

"Well? . . ." he said.
And he waited anxiously.
"That'll do!" I replied harshly.
And I quickened my pace.
Zorba shook his head and growled something I did not catch.

When we reached the hut, he sat on crossed legs, placed the *santuri* on his knees and lowered his head, lost in deep meditation. It was as if he were listening, with his head on his chest, to innumerable songs and trying to choose one, the most beautiful and most despairing of all. He at last made his choice and started a heart-rending air. From time to time he eyed me slantwise. I felt that what he could not or dare not tell me in words he was saying with the *santuri*. That I was wasting my life, that the widow and I were two insects who live but a second beneath the sun, then die for all eternity. Never more! Never more!

Zorba leapt up. He had suddenly realized that he was tiring himself in vain. He leaned against the wall, lit a cigarette, and, after a moment, spoke.

"I'm going to let you into a secret, boss, something a *hodja* * once told me in Salonica. . . . I'm going to tell it to you, even if it doesn't do any good.

"At that time I was a pedlar in Macedonia. I went into the villages to sell reels of thread, needles, the lives of the saints, benjamin and pepper. I had a rare voice, then, a real nightingale I was. You must know women also succumb to a voice. And what won't they succumb to—the jades! God only knows what goes on inside them! You may be as ugly as sin, lame or a hunchback, but if you've a soft voice and can sing the women completely lose their heads.

"I was also peddling in Salonica and even went into the Turkish districts. And, it appears, my voice had so charmed a rich Muslim woman, the daughter of a pasha, that she could not sleep. She called an old *hodja* and filled his hands with *mejidies*. '*Aman!*' † she said to him, 'go and tell the peddling Giaour to come. *Aman!* I must see him. I can't hold out any longer!'

* Turkish holy man.
† A Muslim interjection, expressing entreaty, deprecation or surrender. Compare: Alas! Mercy! C. W.

"The *hodja* came to find me. 'Listen, young Roumi,' he said to me. 'Come with me.' 'No,' I said. 'Where d'you want to take me to?' 'There's a pasha's daughter who's like spring water. She's waiting for you in her room. Come, little Roumi!' But I knew that at night they murdered Christian infidels in the Turkish districts. 'No, I'm not coming,' I said. 'Don't you fear God, Giaour?' 'Why should I?' 'Because, little Roumi, he who can sleep with a woman and does not, commits a great sin. My boy, if a woman calls you to share her bed and you don't go, your soul will be destroyed! That woman will sigh before God on judgment day, and that woman's sigh, whoever you may be and whatever your fine deeds, will cast you into Hell!' "

Zorba sighed.

"If Hell exists," he said, "I shall go to Hell, and that'll be the reason. Not because I've robbed, killed or committed adultery, no! All that's nothing. But I shall go to Hell because one night in Salonica a woman waited for me on her bed and I did not go to her. . . ."

He rose, lit the fire and started cooking our meal. He looked at me out of the corner of his eye and smiled scornfully.

"You can knock forever on a deaf man's door!" he muttered. And, bending down, he began to blow the damp wood angrily.

THE DAYS were growing shorter, the light was quickly failing, and towards the end of each afternoon the heart became uneasy. A primitive terror seized us—that of our ancestors who during the winter months watched the sun go out a little earlier each day. "Tomorrow it will go out forever," they must have thought in despair, and spent the entire night on the heights in fear and trembling.

Zorba felt this uneasiness more deeply, more primitively than I. To escape from it he would not leave the galleries of the mine until the stars were shining in the sky.

He had come across a seam of very good lignite, which did not produce much ash, was not very damp and was rich in calories. He was pleased. For in his mind our profits underwent marvellous transformations: they became travels, women and new adventures. He was waiting impatiently for the day when he would earn a fortune, when his wings would be sufficiently big—"wings" was the name he gave to money—for him to fly away. He therefore spent whole nights trying out his miniature cable railway, always seeking the right slope for the tree trunks to move down slowly—gently, gently, he said, as if borne by angels.

One day he took a large sheet of paper and some colored pencils and drew the mountain, the forest, the line, the trunks suspended from the cable and descending, each endowed with two sky-blue wings. In the little rounded bay he drew black boats and green sailors, like little parrots, and *mahones* loaded with yellow tree trunks. A monk was drawn in each of the four corners, and from their mouths came pink ribbons on which was printed in black capital letters: "Great is the Lord and wonderful are his works!"

For some days now Zorba had hastily lit the fire and prepared the evening meal. When we had eaten he would run off to the village. A little later he would return scowling.

"Where have you been again, Zorba?" I would ask him.

"Never you mind, boss," he would say, and change the subject.

When he returned one evening, he asked me anxiously:

"Is there a God—yes or no? What d'you think, boss? And if there is one—anything's possible—what d'you think he looks like?"

I shrugged my shoulders.

"I'm not joking, boss. I think of God as being exactly like me. Only bigger, stronger, crazier. And immortal, into the bargain. He's sitting on a pile of soft sheepskins and his hut's the sky. It isn't made out of old petrol-cans, like ours is, but clouds. In his right hand he's holding not a knife or a pair of scales—those damned instruments are meant for butchers and grocers—no, he's holding a large sponge full of water, like a rain-cloud. On his right is Paradise, on his left Hell. Here comes a soul; the poor little thing's quite naked, because it's lost its cloak—its body, I mean—and it's shivering. God looks at it, laughing up his sleeve, but he plays the bogy man: 'Come here,' he roars, 'come here, you miserable wretch!'

"And he begins his questioning. The naked soul throws itself at God's feet. 'Mercy!' it cries. 'I have sinned.' And away it goes reciting its sins. It recites a whole rigmarole and there's no end to it. God thinks this is too much of a good thing. He yawns. 'For heaven's sake stop!' he shouts. 'I've heard enough of all that!' Flap! Slap! a wipe of the sponge, and he washes out all the sins. 'Away with you, clear out, run off to Paradise!' he says to the soul. 'Peterkin, let this poor little creature in, too!'

"Because God, you know, is a great lord, and that's what being a lord means: to forgive!"

I remember I had to laugh that evening, while Zorba was pouring out his profound balderdash. But this "lordliness" of God was taking shape and maturing within me, compassionate, generous and all-powerful.

Another evening, when it was raining, and we were crouched over the brazier in the hut roasting chestnuts, Zorba turned round to me and looked at me a long while as if he were trying to unravel some great mystery. Finally, unable to contain himself any longer, he said:

"Boss, I'd like to know what the devil you can see in me; why you don't take me by the ear and pitch me out? I told you they called me Mildew, because everywhere I go I never leave one stone on another. . . . Your affairs will go to rack and ruin. Throw me out, I tell you!"

"I like you," I replied. "Leave it at that."

"But don't you realize, boss, that my brain's not the correct weight? Maybe it's a little overweight, maybe a little under, but the correct weight it certainly isn't! Look now, here's something you'll understand: I haven't been able to rest for days and nights because of that widow. No, I don't mean on my account; no, I swear that's not the case. The devil take her, that's what I say. I'll never touch her, that's one sure thing. I'm not her cup of tea. . . . But I don't want her to be lost for everybody. I don't want her to sleep alone. It wouldn't be right, boss; I can't bear that thought. So I wander at night round her garden—that's why you see me disappear and you ask me where I'm going. But d'you know why? To see if someone is going to sleep with her; then I can be easy in my mind."

I started laughing.

"Don't laugh, boss! If a woman sleeps all alone, it's the fault of us men. We'll all have to render our accounts on the day of the last judgment. God will forgive all sins, as we've said before—he'll have his sponge ready. But that sin he will not forgive. Woe betide the man who could sleep with a woman and who did not do so! Woe betide the woman who could sleep with a man and who did not do so! Remember the words of the *hodja*!"

He was silent for an instant.

"When a man dies, can he come to life again?" he asked abruptly.

"I don't think so, Zorba."

"Neither do I. But if he could, then those men I was referring to, those who've refused to serve, the deserters, will come back on earth, guess as what? As mules!"

He fell silent again and reflected. Suddenly his eyes sparkled.

"Who knows," he said, excited at his discovery, "maybe all the mules we see in the world today are those same people, the maimed, the deserters, who during their lifetime were men and women—and at the same time were not. And that's why they're always kicking. What d'you say, boss?"

"That your brain's underweight, Zorba," I replied, laughing. "Get your *santuri!*"

"No offence, boss, but there'll be no *santuri* tonight. If I go on talking, talking nonsense, d'you know why? Because I've got a load of worries on my mind. The new gallery—the devil take it—is going to play me up. And there you go talking to me about the *santuri*. . . ."

Thereupon he pulled the chestnuts out of the ashes, gave me a handful, and filled our glasses with raki.

"May God weight the scales on the right side!" I said, clinking glasses.

"On the left!" Zorba corrected. "On the left! Up to now, the right's produced nothing good."

He swallowed the liquid fire in one gulp and lay on his bed.

"Tomorrow," he said, "I'm going to need all my strength. I'll have to fight against a thousand demons. Good night!"

The next day, at first light, Zorba disappeared down into the mine. The men had made progress in cutting out the gallery along the good seam. The water was seeping through the roof and the men were splashing about in black mud.

Two days ago Zorba had called for tree trunks to strengthen the gallery. But he was uneasy. The props were not so big as they should have been, and, with his profound instinct which made him feel all that was going on in that subterranean labyrinth as if it were his own body, he sensed that the props were not safe. He could hear creakings, very slight ones, imperceptible as yet to the others—as if the supports of the roof were groaning under the weight.

Another thing had increased Zorba's uneasiness that day. Just as he was about to go down the shaft, the village priest, Pappa Stephanos, passed by on his mule, going posthaste to the neighboring convent to give the last sacrament to a dying nun. Fortunately Zorba had just enough time before the priest spoke to him to spit on the ground three times and pinch himself.

"Morning, father!" he replied glumly to the priest's greeting.

And then he added in a slightly lower voice:

"May your curse be upon me!"

He felt, however, that these exorcisms were insufficient, and he went nervously down the new gallery.

There was a heavy smell of lignite and acetylene. The men had already begun to strengthen the beams holding up the gallery roof. Zorba wished them good morning in a brusque, surly fashion. He rolled up his sleeves and set to work.

A dozen men were beginning to pick into the seam and heap the coal at their feet, others were shovelling it up and carting it out on little barrows.

Suddenly Zorba stopped, signed to the men to do likewise, and pricked up his ears. Just as the rider becomes one with his steed and the captain with his ship, so Zorba had become one with the mine. He could feel the ramifications of the galleries like veins in his flesh, and what the dark masses of coal could not feel, Zorba felt with a conscious, human lucidity.

After listening intently with his large, hairy ears, he peered into the gallery. It was at that moment I arrived. I had waked with a start, as if I had some presentiment, as if urged by some hand. I had dressed in haste and rushed out, without knowing why I was hurrying so, or where I was going. But my body had unhesitatingly taken the road to the mine. I had arrived at the moment when Zorba was anxiously listening and looking.

"Nothing . . ." he said after a while. "I thought for a moment . . . Never mind. To work, boys!"

He turned round, saw me and puckered up his lips.

"Boss, what are you doing here so early?"

He came up to me.

"Why don't you go up and get some fresh air, boss?" he whispered. "You can come and take a little turn here another day."

"What's the matter, Zorba?"

"Nothing . . . I was imagining things. A priest crossed my path first thing this morning. Go away."

"If there's any danger, wouldn't it be shameful if I left?"

"Yes," Zorba replied.

"Would you leave?"

"No."

"Well, then!"

"What Zorba has to do is one thing," he replied irritably, "what others have to do is another! But as you feel it's shameful to leave, don't. Stay here. It's your funeral!"

He took a heavy hammer and stood on tiptoe to hit some nails into the roof bracings. I took an acetylene lamp from a post and went up and down in the mud, looking at the dark, shining seam. Immense forests must have been swallowed up millions of years ago. The earth digested and transformed its children. The trees turned into lignite, the lignite into coal, Zorba came . . .

I hung the lamp up again on the nail and watched Zorba work. He was completely absorbed in his task; he thought of nothing else; he was one with the earth, the pick and the coal. He and the hammer and nails were united in the struggle with the wood. He suffered with the bulging roof of the gallery. He sparred with the mountainside to obtain its coal by cunning and force. Zorba could feel matter with a sure and infallible instinct, and he struck his blows shrewdly where it was weakest and could be conquered. And, as he appeared then, covered and plastered with dirt, with only the whites of his eyes gleaming, he seemed to me to be camouflaged as coal, to have become coal itself, in order to be able to approach his adversary unawares and penetrate its inner defences.

"Bravo, Zorba! Go to it!" I cried, carried away by a naïve admiration.

But he did not even look round. How could he possibly have talked at that moment to a bookworm who, instead of wielding a pick, held in his hand a miserable stump of pencil? He was busy, he did not wish to speak. "Don't speak to me when I'm working," he said one evening. "I might snap!" "Snap, Zorba? Why?" "There you go again with your 'whys' and 'wherefores'! Like a kid! How can I explain? I'm completely taken up by my work, stretched taut from head to foot, and riveted to the stone or the coal or the *santuri*. If you suddenly touched me or spoke to me and I tried to turn round, I might snap. Now, d'you see?"

I looked at my watch, it was ten o'clock.

"Time to break off for lunch, my friends!" I said. "You've gone past the time."

The workmen immediately threw their tools down in a corner, mopped the sweat off their faces and prepared to leave the gallery. Completely absorbed in his work, Zorba had not heard. Even if he had, he would not have budged from there. Once again he listened anxiously.

"One moment," I said to the men, "have a cigarette."

I was rummaging in my pockets, with the men standing round me.

Suddenly Zorba started up. He stuck his ear to the gallery partition. By the light of the acetylene lamps, I could see his gaping, contorted mouth.

"What's up, Zorba?" I shouted.

But at that moment the whole gallery roof seemed to shudder above us.

"Get out!" Zorba shouted in a hoarse voice, "Get out!"

We tore back towards the exit, but we had not reached the first wooden frame when a second, louder cracking noise burst out over our heads. Zorba, meanwhile, was lifting up a great tree-trunk to wedge it in as a buttress against the timbering which was giving way. If he managed it quickly enough, it might hold up the roof a few more seconds and give us time to escape.

"Get out!" Zorba yelled again, but this time his voice was muffled, as if it were coming from the bowels of the earth.

With the cowardice which often comes over men in critical moments, we all rushed out, completely forgetting Zorba. But after a few seconds I pulled myself together and ran back into the gallery.

"Zorba!" I shouted. "Zorba!"

At least, I thought I shouted. I realized afterwards that my cry had not left my throat. Fear had strangled my voice.

I was overcome with shame. I leapt towards him with arms outstretched. Zorba had just made firm the great prop and was running, slithering in the mire, towards the exit. Rushing headlong in the darkness, he ran into me and we accidentally fell into each other's arms.

"We must get out!" he yelled. "Get out!"

We ran and reached the light. The terror-stricken workmen had gathered at the entrance and were peering inside.

We heard a third and louder cracking noise, like a tree splitting in a storm. Then, suddenly, a fearful roar, like a clap of thunder. It shook the mountainside, and the gallery collapsed.

"God Almighty!" the men murmured, crossing themselves.

"You left your picks down there!" Zorba shouted angrily.

The men said nothing.

"Why didn't you take them with you?" he shouted again, furious. "You wet your pants, I bet! Too bad about the tools, eh?"

"Oh, Zorba, this is no time to bother about the picks," I said, coming between them. "Let's be grateful that all the men are safe and sound! Thanks to you, Zorba, for we all owe our lives to you."

"I'm hungry!" Zorba said. "That's made me feel empty."

He took his haversack, which he had left on a stone, opened it and pulled out some bread, olives, onions, a boiled potato and a little gourd of wine.

"Come on, boys, let's eat!" he said, with his mouth full.

He bolted his food quickly, as if he had suddenly lost a lot of strength and wanted to stoke up again.

He ate leaning forward, without speaking. He took his gourd, threw his head back and let the wine gurgle down his parched throat.

The workmen also took courage, opened their haversacks and started eating. They sat, cross-legged round Zorba, and ate, looking at him. They wanted to throw themselves at his feet and kiss his hands, but they knew he was brusque and strange, and none of them dared make a movement.

Finally Michelis, the eldest, who had a big, grey moustache, made up his mind and spoke:

"If you hadn't been there, good master Alexis," he said, "our children would be orphans by this time."

"Dry up!" Zorba said, with his mouth full; and no one else ventured a word.

◊ 10 ◊

"WHO THEN created this labyrinth of hesitation, this temple of presumption, this pitcher of sin, this field sown with a thousand deceptions, this gateway to Hell, this basket overflowing with artfulness, this poison which tastes like honey, this bond which chains mortals to the earth: woman?"

I was slowly, silently copying this Buddhist song, sitting on the ground near the brazier. I was trying exorcism upon exorcism, bent on casting out from my mind the image of a woman's body soaked by the rain, which every night that fall passed in the humid air to and fro before my eyes with swaying hips. Ever since the collapse of the gallery, when my life had nearly been cut short, I sensed the widow in my blood. She called to me like a wild animal, pressingly and reproachfully.

"Come! Come!" she cried. "Life passes in a flash. Come quickly, come, come, before it is too late!"

I was well aware that it was Mara, the spirit of the Evil One, in the shape of a woman with powerful thighs and buttocks. I fought against him. I applied myself to writing *Buddha* in the same way that savages in their caves engraved with a pointed stone or painted in red and white the famished and ferocious beasts who prowled around them. They, too, endeavored, by engraving and painting these beasts, to fix them fast on the rock. If they had not done so, the beasts would have leapt upon them.

From the day I had just missed being crushed to death, the widow passed ceaselessly in the fiery air of my solitude, beckoning to me and voluptuously swaying her hips. During the day I was strong, my mind was alert and I managed to cast her out. I wrote in what guise the Tempter appeared to Buddha, how he took on the shape of a woman, how he pressed his firm breasts against the knees of the ascetic, how Buddha saw the danger, mobilized all his powers and routed the Evil One.

Each sentence I wrote brought me fresh relief, I took courage, I felt the Evil One was withdrawing, cast out by the all-powerful exorcism of the word. I fought during the daytime with all my strength, but at night my mind laid down its arms, the inner doors opened and the widow entered.

In the morning I awoke exhausted and vanquished, and the struggle began afresh. When I raised my head from my paper, it was the end of the afternoon; the light was being chased away; darkness suddenly fell upon me. The days were shortening, Christmas was approaching. I threw myself with all my might into the struggle. I said to myself: I am not alone. A great force, the light of day, is also fighting. It, too, is sometimes vanquished, sometimes victorious. But it does not despair. I struggle and hope together with the light!

It seemed to me, and this thought gave me courage, that in fighting against the widow I, too, was obeying a great universal rhythm. Guileful matter has chosen this body, I thought, slowly to dampen and extinguish the free flame which flickers within me. I said to myself: The imperishable force which transforms matter into spirit is divine. Each man has within him an element of the divine whirlwind and that is how he can convert bread, water and meat into thought and action. Zorba was right: "Tell me what you do with what you eat and I will tell you who you are!"

And so I was painfully endeavoring to transform that violent desire of the flesh into *Buddha*.

"What are you thinking about, boss? You don't seem to be quite yourself," Zorba said to me on Christmas Eve. He had a shrewd idea as to what demon I was fighting.

I pretended not to hear. But Zorba did not give up so easily.

"You're young, boss," he said.

And suddenly his voice assumed a bitter and angry tone.

"You're young and pretty tough, eating well, drinking well, breathing exhilarating sea air, and storing up energy—but what are you doing with it all? You sleep alone, and it's just too bad for the energy! You get along there tonight—yes, lose no time! Boss, everything's simple in this world. How many times must I tell you? So don't go and complicate things!"

The manuscript of *Buddha* was open in front of me and I turned over its leaves as I listened to Zorba's words and realized that they showed me a sure, attractive and very human path to tread. It was again the spirit of Mara, the crafty pander, who was calling.

I listened without saying a word and continued slowly to turn the pages of the manuscript. I whistled to conceal my emotion. But Zorba, seeing I did not speak, suddenly burst out:

"This is Christmas Eve, my friend, hurry up, get to her before she goes to church. Christ will be born tonight, boss; you go and perform your miracle, too!"

I rose, irritated.

"That's enough, Zorba," I said. "Every one follows his own bent. Man is like a tree. You've never quarrelled with a fig tree because it doesn't bear cherries, have you? Well then, that'll do! It's nearly midnight. Let us go to the church and see Christ born ourselves."

Zorba pulled his thick winter cap over his head.

"All right, then!" he said unhappily. "Let's go! But I want you to know that God would have been much more pleased if you'd gone to the widow's tonight, like Archangel Gabriel. If God had followed the same path as you, boss, he'd never have gone to Mary's and Christ would never have been born. If you asked me what path God follows, I'd say: the one leading to Mary's. Mary is the widow."

He waited in silence and in vain for my reply. He thrust the door open, and he went out. He angrily struck at the pebbles with the end of his stick.

"Yes," he repeated persistently, "Mary is the widow!"

"Now, let's get along!" I said. "Don't shout!"

We strode along at a good pace in the winter night. The sky was perfectly clear, the stars looked big and hung low in the sky like balls of fire. The night, as we made our way along the shore, resembled a great black beast lying along the water's edge.

"From tonight," I said to myself, "the light which winter has forced back will begin to fight victoriously. As if it were born this night together with the infant god."

All the villagers had crowded into the warm and scented hive of the church. The men stood in front and the women, with clasped hands, behind. The tall priest, Stephanos, was in an exasperated state after his forty-days' fast. Clad in his heavy gold chasuble, he was running hither and thither in great strides, swinging his censer, singing at the top of his voice and in a great hurry to see Christ born and get home to a thick soup, savory sausages and smoked meats. . . .

If the scriptures had said: "Today, light is born," man's heart would not have leapt. The idea would not have become a legend and would not have conquered the world. They would merely have described a normal physical phenomenon and would not have fired our imagination—I mean our soul. But the light which is born in the dead of winter has become a child and the child has become God, and for twenty centuries our soul has suckled it. . . .

The mystic ceremony came to an end shortly after midnight. Christ had been born. The famished and happy villagers ran home, to have a feast and feel in the depths of their bowels the mystery of incarnation. The belly is the firm foundation; bread, wine and meat are the first essentials; it is only with bread, wine and meat that one can create God.

The stars were shining as large as angels above the white dome of the church. The milky way was flowing like a stream from one side of the heavens to the other. A green star was twinkling above us like an emerald. I sighed, a prey to my emotions.

Zorba turned to me.

"Boss, d'you believe that? That God became man and was born in a stable? Do you believe it, or are you just pulling our legs?"

"It's difficult to say, Zorba," I replied. "I can't say I believe it, nor that I don't. What about you?"

"I can't say I do either. I can't for the life of me. You see, when I was a kid and my grandma told me tales, I didn't believe a word of them. And yet I trembled with emotion, I laughed and I cried, just as if I did believe them. When I grew a beard on my chin, I just dropped them, and I even used to laugh at them; but now, in my old age—I suppose I'm getting soft, eh, boss?—in a kind of way I believe in them again. . . . Man's a mystery!"

We had taken the path leading to Dame Hortense's and we started galloping along like two hungry horses who can smell the stable.

"The holy fathers are pretty crafty, you know!" Zorba said. "They get at you through your belly, so how can you escape them? For forty days, they say, you shan't eat meat, you shan't drink wine; just fast. Why? So that you'll pine for meat and wine. Ah, the fat hogs, they know all the tricks of the game!"

He started going even faster.

"Let's get moving, boss," he said. "The turkey must be done to a turn!"

When we arrived in our good lady's room, with its great tempting bed, we found the table covered with a white cloth, and on it the steaming turkey lying on its back with its legs apart. The brazier was giving off a gentle heat.

Dame Hortense had curled her hair and was wearing a long dressing gown of faded pink color with enormous sleeves and frayed lacework. Round her wrinkled neck was a tight, canary-yellow ribbon, about the width of two fingers. She had sprayed herself generously with orange-blossom water.

How perfectly everything is matched on this earth, I thought. How well the earth is matched to the human heart! Here is this old cabaret singer who has led a thoroughly fast life, and now, cast up on this lonely coast, she concentrates in this miserable room all the sacred solicitude and warmth of womanhood.

The copious and carefully prepared repast, the burning brazier, the painted and pennanted body, the orange-blossom scent—with what rapidity and what simplicity all these very human, little, corporeal pleasures are transformed into a great spiritual joy!

My heart suddenly leaped in my breast. I felt, on that solemn evening, that I was not quite alone here on this deserted seashore. A creature full of feminine devotion, tenderness and patience was coming toward me: she was the mother, the sister, the wife. And I, who thought I needed nothing, suddenly felt I needed everything.

Zorba must have felt a like emotion, for scarcely had we entered the room than he rushed to the bedecked cabaret-singer and hugged her.

"Christ is born!" he cried. "Greetings to you, female of the species!"

He turned to me, laughing.

"See, boss, what a cunning creature is woman! She can even twist God round her little finger!"

We sat down at table; we hungrily devoured the dishes and drank the wine. Our bodies were satisfied and our souls thrilled with pleasure. Zorba became lively once more.

"Eat and drink," he continually shouted. "Eat and drink, boss, and get warmed up! You sing too, my boy, sing like the shepherds: 'Glory to the highest! . . . Glory to the lowest . . .' Christ is born, that's a terrific thing, you know. Pipe up with your song and let God hear you and rejoice."

He had quite recovered his spirits, and there was no stopping him.

"Christ is born, my wise Solomon, my wretched pen-pusher! Don't go picking things over with a needle! Is He born or isn't He? Of course He's born, don't be daft. If you take a magnifying-glass and look at your drinking water—an engineer told me this, one day —you'll see, he said, the water's full of little worms you couldn't see with your naked eye. You'll see the worms and you won't drink. You won't drink and you'll curl up with thirst. Smash your glass, boss, and the little worms'll vanish and you can drink and be refreshed!"

He turned towards our gaudy companion, raised his full glass and said:

"My very dear Bouboulina, my old comrade-in-arms, I'm going to drink to your health! I've seen many figureheads in my life; they're nailed to the ship's prow, they hold their breasts in their hands, and the cheeks and lips are painted a fiery red. They've sailed over all the seas, they've entered every port, and when the ship falls to bits they come on dry land and, till the end of their days, stay leaning against the wall of a fisherman's tavern where the captains go to drink. My Bouboulina, tonight, as I see you on this shore, now my belly's full of good things and my eyes are wide open, you look to me like the figurehead of a great ship. And I am your last port, I am the tavern where the sea captains come to drink. Come, lean on me, strike your sails! I drink this glass of Cretan wine to your health, my siren!"

Touched and overcome, Dame Hortense started to cry, and leaned on Zorba's shoulder.

"You just see, boss," Zorba whispered in my ear, "my fine speech is going to land me into some trouble. The jade won't want to let me go tonight. But, there you are, I'm sorry for the poor creatures, yes, I pity them!

"Christ is born!" he shouted loudly to his siren. "To our health!"

He slipped his arm under that of our lady and they quaffed their glasses together, arms entwined, and looking enraptured at each other.

Dawn could not have been far off when I left the two of them in the warm little bedroom with its great bed and took the road home. The villagers had eaten and drunk well, and now the village was sleeping with doors and windows closed, under the great winter stars.

It was cold, the sea was booming, Venus was dancing roguishly in the east. I walked along the water's edge playing a game with the waves. They ran up to try and wet me and I ran away. I was happy and said to myself: "This is true happiness: to have no ambition and to work like a horse as if you had every ambition. To live far from men, not to need them and yet to love them. To take part in the Christmas festivities and, after eating and drinking well, to escape on your own far from all the snares, to have the stars above, the land to your left and the sea to your right: and to realize of a sudden that, in your heart, life has accomplished its final miracle: it has become a fairy tale."

The days were passing by. I tried to put a brave face on it, I shouted and played the fool, but in my heart of hearts I knew I was sad. During all this week of festivities, memories had been aroused and filled my breast with distant music and loved ones. I was once more struck by the truth of the ancient saying: Man's heart is a ditch full of blood. The loved ones who have died throw themselves down on the bank of this ditch to drink the blood and so come to life again; the dearer they are to you, the more of your blood they drink.

New Year's Eve. A band of village children carrying a large paper boat came to our hut and started to sing *kalanda** in their shrill and merry voices:

> Saint Basil the Great arrived from Caesarea, his
> native city . . .

He was standing here on this little Cretan beach by the indigo-blue sea. He leaned on his staff and his staff was suddenly covered with leaves and flowers. The New Year's carol rang out:

> A happy new year to you, Christians!
> Master, may your house be filled with corn, olive-oil and wine;
> May your wife be a marble pillar to the roof of your house;
> May your daughter marry and beget nine sons and one daughter;
> May these sons liberate Constantinople, the city of our kings!

Zorba listened, entranced. He had seized the children's tambourine and was banging it frenziedly.

I watched and listened without saying anything. I could feel another leaf falling from my heart, the passing of another year. I was taking another step toward the black pit.

"What's come over you, boss?" Zorba asked, in between singing at the top of his voice, together with the children, and striking the tambourine. "What's come over you, man? You look years older, and your face is grey. This is when I turn into a little boy again; I'm reborn, like Christ. Isn't he born every year? So am I!"

I lay down on my bed and shut my eyes. My heart was in a wild mood that night; I did not wish to speak.

I could not sleep. I felt I had to account for my acts that very night. I went over my whole life, which appeared vapid, incoherent and hesitating, dreamlike. I contemplated it despairingly. Like a fleecy cloud attacked by the winds from the heights, my life constantly changed shape. It came to pieces, reformed, was metamorphosed—it was, by turns, a swan, a dog, a demon, a scorpion, a monkey—and the cloud was forever being frayed and torn. It was driven by the winds of heaven and shot with the rainbow.

Day broke. I did not open my eyes. I was trying to concentrate all my strength on my ardent desire to break through the crust of

* New Year carols.

the mind and penetrate to the dark and dangerous channel down which each human drop is carried to mingle with the ocean. I was eager to tear the veil and see what the New Year would bring me. . . .

"Morning, boss. Happy New Year!"

Zorba's voice brought me back brutally to earth. I opened my eyes just in time to see Zorba throw into the doorway of the hut a big pomegranate. Its seeds, like clear rubies, shot as far as my bed. I picked up a few and ate them, and my throat was refreshed.

"I hope we make a pile and are ravished by beautiful maidens!" Zorba cried good-humoredly. He washed, shaved and put on his best clothes—green cloth trousers and rough home-spun jacket, over which he threw a half-lined, goat-skin coatee. He put on his Russian astrakhan cap and twirled his moustaches.

"Boss," he said, "I'm going to put in an appearance at church as a representative of the Company. It wouldn't be in the interest of the mine for them to think we're freemasons. It'll cost me nothing and it'll pass the time."

He bent over and winked.

"Maybe I'll see the widow there, too," he whispered.

God, the interests of the Company and the widow blended harmoniously in Zorba's mind. I heard his light footsteps departing. I leaped up. The spell was broken, my soul was shut in the prison of the flesh anew.

I dressed and went down to the water's edge. I walked quickly. I was gay, as if I had escaped from a danger or a sin. My indiscreet desire of that morning to pry into and know the future before it was born suddenly appeared to me a sacrilege.

I remembered one morning when I discovered a cocoon in the bark of a tree, just as the butterfly was making a hole in its case and preparing to come out. I waited a while, but it was too long appearing and I was impatient. I bent over it and breathed on it to warm it. I warmed it as quickly as I could and the miracle began to happen before my eyes, faster than life. The case opened, the butterfly started slowly crawling out and I shall never forget my horror when I saw how its wings were folded back and crumpled; the wretched butterfly tried with its whole trembling body to unfold them.

Bending over it, I tried to help it with my breath. In vain. It needed to be hatched out patiently and the unfolding of the wings should be a gradual process in the sun. Now it was too late. My breath had forced the butterfly to appear, all crumpled, before its time. It struggled desperately and, a few seconds later, died in the palm of my hand.

That little body is, I do believe, the greatest weight I have on my conscience. For I realize today that it is a mortal sin to violate the great laws of nature. We should not hurry, we should not be impatient, but we should confidently obey the eternal rhythm.

I sat on a rock to absorb this New Year's thought. Ah, if only that little butterfly could always flutter before me to show me the way.

◊ 11 ◊

I ROSE as happy as if I had received my New Year presents. The
wind was cold, the sky clear, the sea gleaming.

I took the path to the village. Mass would have ended by now.
As I walked along, I wondered, with an absurd emotion, who would
be the first person—lucky or unlucky—I should meet this new year.
If only, I said to myself, it could be a small child with its arms loaded
with its New Year toys; or an active old man in a white shirt with
full, embroidered sleeves, content and proud that he had fulfilled his
duty on earth with courage. The further I went and the closer I
came to the village the more troubled I became.

Suddenly my knees gave way beneath me. Under the olive trees,
walking with a springing step along the village road, appeared in
red, with a black kerchief over her head, the graceful, slender-
waisted figure of the widow!

Her sinuous gait was really that of a black panther, and it seemed
to me that an acrid scent of musk was distilled in the air. If only I
could escape! I felt that when angry this beast would have no mercy
and that the only thing to do was to run away. But how? The widow
was steadily approaching. The gravel seemed to be crunching as if
an army were marching over it. She saw me, shook her head, her
kerchief slipped down and her hair appeared, black as jet and shining. She cast me a languorous look and smiled. Her eyes had a wild
sweetness. Hastily she adjusted her kerchief, as though she were

122

ashamed at having let me see one of woman's deepest secrets: her hair.

I wanted to speak to her, wish her a happy New Year, but my throat was too tight, as on the day when the gallery fell in and my life had been in danger. The reeds surrounding her garden stirred in the wind, the winter sun fell on the golden lemons and the oranges with their dark foliage. The entire garden was resplendent like a paradise.

The widow stopped, stretched out her arm and thrust the gate open. I was passing her just at that moment. She looked round and, raising her eyebrows, turned her gaze on me.

She left the gate open and I saw her disappear behind the orange trees, swaying her hips as she went.

To enter that gate and bolt it, to run after her, take her by the waist and, without a word, drag her to her large widow's bed, that was what you would call being a man! That was what my grandfather would have done, and what I hope my grandson will do! But I stood there like a post, weighing things up and reflecting. . . .

"In another life," I murmured, smiling bitterly, "in some other life I'll behave better than this!"

I plunged into the green defile, feeling a weight on my soul as if I had committed a mortal sin. I wandered up and down. It was cold and I was shivering. It was no use my chasing from my thoughts the widow's swaying hips, her smile, her eyes, her breasts, they always returned—I was suffocating.

The trees had no leaves as yet, but the buds were full of sap and already swelling and bursting. In every bud you could feel the concentrated presence of young shoots, flowers, fruits-to-be, lying in wait and ready to burst out to the light. Day and night in the middle of winter, the great miracle of spring was silently, secretly being prepared beneath the dry bark.

Suddenly I gave a cry of joy. A bold almond tree opposite me in a sheltered hollow had burst into flower in midwinter, leading the way to all the other trees and heralding the spring.

The oppression I felt left me. I took a deep breath of its somewhat peppery scent. I left the road and sat down beneath its flowering branches.

I stayed there a long time, thinking of nothing, care-free and happy. This was eternity and I was sitting beneath a tree in Paradise.

Suddenly a loud rough voice ejected me from this paradise.

"Now what might you be doing tucked away in there, boss? I've been looking high and low for you. It's close on twelve, come on!"

"Where?"

"Where? You ask me where? To old mother Sucking Pig, of course! Aren't you hungry? The sucking pig's out of the oven! What a smell . . . makes your mouth water! Come on!"

I rose, stroked the hard trunk of the almond tree containing so many mysteries and which had produced this miracle of blossom. Zorba went on ahead, light-footed, full of zest and hunger. The fundamental needs of man—food, drink, women and dance—were never exhausted or dulled in his robust and eager body.

He was holding in his hand a flat parcel wrapped in pink paper and tied with golden-colored string.

"A New Year's gift?" I asked with a smile.

Zorba laughed, trying to hide his emotion.

"Well, just so she's no room for complaint, poor woman!" he said, without turning round. "So she'll remember her past grandeur. . . . She's a woman—haven't we said so often enough?—and therefore a creature always mourning over her lot. . . ."

"A photograph?"

"You'll see . . . you'll see; don't be in so great a hurry! I made it myself. Come on, we'd better get a move on."

The midday sun was such as to gladden your very bones. The sea, too, was happily warming itself in the sun. In the distance the tiny uninhabited island, shrouded in light mist, looked as if it had raised itself out of the sea and was floating.

We approached the village, and Zorba came close to me and lowered his voice.

"You know, boss," he said, "the person in question was at church. I was standing in front by the cantor when I suddenly saw the sacred icons light up. Christ, the Holy Virgin, the Twelve Apostles, everything shone. . . . 'Whatever's happening?' I said, crossing myself. 'Is it the sun?' I turned round—it was the widow!"

"All right, Zorba. That'll do," I said, hurrying on.

But Zorba ran after me.

"I saw her close to, boss. She's got a beauty spot on her cheek that's enough to send you crazy. Another of those mysteries—beauty spots on women's cheeks!"

He opened wide his eyes with an air of stupefaction.

"Have you noticed, boss? The skin's all soft and smooth, and then, all of a sudden, a black spot! Well, that's all that's needed! It sends you crazy! D'you understand that, boss? What d'your books say about it?"

"The devil take them!"

Zorba laughed, pleased with himself.

"That's the stuff!" he exclaimed. "That's the stuff. You're beginning to realize. . . ."

We did not stop at the café; we pressed on.

Our good lady had cooked a sucking pig for us in the oven and was waiting for us on her doorstep.

She had put a canary-yellow ribbon round her neck once more, and, to see her like that—heavily powdered, lips plastered with a thick layer of crimson—was enough to dismay anyone. Was she, in fact, a ship's figurehead? As soon as she caught sight of us her whole flesh seemed to be gladdened and set in motion, her small eyes danced naughtily in her head and came to rest fixed on Zorba's curled-up moustache.

As soon as the outer door had closed behind us, Zorba took her by the waist.

"Happy New Year, my Bouboulina!" he said. "Look what I've brought you!" And he kissed her plump and wrinkled neck.

The old siren was tickled for a moment, but did not lose her head. Her eyes were clamped on the present. She seized it, undid the golden string, looked inside and uttered a cry of joy.

I leaned forward to see what it was: on a thick piece of cardboard that rascal Zorba had drawn in four colors—red, gold, grey and black—four huge battleships, decked with flags, sailing on an indigo-blue sea. In front of the battleships, floating on the waves, all naked and white, with hair flowing, breasts in the air, and a spiral fish-tail, was a siren—Dame Hortense, complete with yellow ribbon round her neck! She was holding four strings and pulling behind her the four battleships flying the flags of England, Russia, France and Italy. In each corner of the picture hung a beard, one fair, one red, one grey, and one black.

The old singer understood immediately.

"Me!" she said, pointing proudly to the siren.

She sighed.

"Ah! I used to be a Great Power, too, once upon a time!"

She moved a small round mirror from over her bed, near to the parrot's cage, and, in its place, hung Zorba's picture. Beneath her thick make-up she must have gone pale.

Zorba, meanwhile, had slipped into the kitchen. He was hungry. He brought in the dish with the sucking pig, placed a bottle of wine on the table in front of him and filled three glasses.

"Come! Eat, eat!" he cried, clapping his hands together. "Let's begin with the foundation—the belly. After that, my sweet, we'll take care of what's below!"

But the atmosphere was troubled by the old siren's sighs. Each New Year, she, too, had a little Doomsday of her own . . . she looked back on her life, weighed it up and found it wanting. Beneath this old woman's thinning hair, big cities, men, silk dresses, bottles of champagne and scented beards rose from the graves of her memory on all solemn occasions.

"I've no appetite," she murmured coyly. "None at all . . . none at all. . . ."

She kneeled down before the brazier and poked the hot coals. Her flabby cheeks reflected the light of the fire. A lock of hair slipped from her brow and was singed by a flame. The nauseating smell of burnt hair permeated the room.

"I won't eat . . . I won't eat . . ." she muttered once more, seeing we were taking no notice of her at all.

Zorba clenched his fists impatiently. He remained for a moment undecided. He could let her mutter to herself as much as she chose, while we got on with the roast pig—or he could throw himself on his knees, take her in his arms and calm her down with kind words. I watched his tanned face and saw, passing over his mobile features, waves of contradictory impulses.

Suddenly his expression set. He had come to a decision. He knelt beside her and seized the siren's knees.

"If you don't eat, my little charmer," he said in heart-rending tones, "it's the end of everything. Have pity on the poor pig, my lovely, and eat this sweet little trotter!" And he pushed into her mouth the crackling trotter covered with butter.

He took her in his arms, raised her from the ground, and placed her gently on her chair between the two of us.

"Eat," he said, "eat, my treasure, so that Saint Basil will come to our village! If you don't, you know, he won't come to us! He'll go back to his own country, to Caesarea. He'll pick up the inkhorn and paper, the Twelfth Cake, the New Year gifts, the children's toys, even this little sucking pig, and away with them all! So open your little mouth, my Bouboulina, and eat!"

He put out two fingers and tickled her under the arm. The old siren clucked with pleasure, wiped her small, reddened eyes and started busily to chew over the crackly trotter. . . .

Just at that moment two amorous cats began to howl on the roof over our heads. They howled in an indescribable tone of hatred, their voices rising and falling, threateningly. Suddenly we heard them scrambling wildly on the roof, tearing one another to pieces. . . .

"Miaow . . . miaow . . ." said Zorba, winking at the old siren.

She smiled and pressed his hand under the table. Her throat relaxed and she began to eat with appetite.

The sun moved round, came in through the small window and shone on the good lady's feet. The bottle was empty, Zorba had twisted up his moustaches like those of a wild cat and moved closed to the "female of the species." Dame Hortense, huddled up, her head sunk into her shoulders, shuddered as she felt his warm, vinous breath on her.

"Now, what's this other mystery, boss?" said Zorba, looking round at me. "Everything goes backwards with me. When I was a kid, so it seems, I looked like a little old man. I was dense, didn't talk much but had a big fellow's voice. They say I was like my grandad! But the older I grew, the more harum-scarum I became. I began doing wild things when I was twenty. Oh, nothing special, just the same as other fellows at that age. When I was forty I began to feel really young and went off on the maddest escapades. And now I'm over sixty—sixty-five, boss, but keep that dark—well, now I'm over sixty, how can I explain? Honestly, the world's grown too small for me!"

He raised his glass and turned with compunction to his lady.

"Your good health, Bouboulina," he said solemnly. "May God see to it that this year you grow some teeth and some neat eyebrows, and a new skin scented like a peach! And that you do away with all these beastly little ribbons! And that there's another revolution in Crete and the four Great Powers come back again. Bouboulina, my dear, with their fleets . . . and that each fleet has its admiral and each admiral his curled and scented beard. And may you rise from the waves once more, my siren, singing your lovely song. And may the fleets break to pieces on these two round and savage rocks!"

Whereupon he placed his big hands on the good lady's flabby, hanging breasts. . . .

Zorba was getting lively again, his voice was hoarse with desire. I laughed. One day, at the cinema, I had seen a Turkish pasha frolicking in a Paris cabaret. He was holding a fair-haired young midinette on his lap. The pasha was getting excited; the tassel on his fez began to rise slowly, stopped for a moment when it was horizontal, then suddenly stuck straight up in the air.

"What are you laughing at, boss?" Zorba asked.

The good lady, however, was still thinking of what Zorba had been saying.

"Oh," she said, "d'you think it's possible, Zorba? But when youth goes it never comes back. . . ."

Zorba moved closer still; the two chairs stuck together.

"Listen to me, ducky," he said, trying at the same time to undo the third, the decisive button of her bodice. "Listen, let me tell you about the fine present I'm going to get you. There's a new doctor —Voronoff—who performs miracles, they say. He gives you a medicine of some kind—drops or powder. I don't know which—and you become twenty again in a trice—twenty-five at the worst! Don't cry, my dear, I'll have some sent from Europe for you. . . ."

The old siren started. Her reddish scalp was gleaming between the thinning hair. She threw her fat, fleshy arms round Zorba's neck.

"If it's drops, my sweetie," she murmured, rubbing herself against Zorba like a cat, "you'll order a demijohn for me, won't you? And if it's powder . . ."

"A sackful!" said Zorba, undoing the third button.

The cats, who had been quiet for a time, started their howling again. One of the voices was plaintive and appealing, the other angry and threatening.

Our good lady yawned and her eyes became languorous.

"D'you hear those horrid cats?" she muttered. "They've no shame!" And she sat on Zorba's knee. She leaned her head back against his neck and heaved a great sigh. She had drunk a little too much and her eyes were growing misty.

"What are you thinking about, my Bouboulina?" Zorba asked, clutching hold of her breasts.

"Alexandria . . ." murmured the old siren, who had trundled about the world quite a bit. "Alexandria . . . Beirut . . . Constantinople . . . the Turks, the Arabs, sherbet, golden sandals, red fezes. . . ."

She heaved another sigh.

"When Ali Bey stayed the night with me—what a moustache, what eyebrows, what arms he had!—he'd call to the tambourine and flute players and throw them money through the window, so that they'd play in my courtyard until dawn. And the neighbors used to go green with envy: 'Ali Bey's there with her again!' they'd say in a rage.

"Afterwards, in Constantinople, Suleiman Pasha would never let me go out at all on Fridays. He was afraid the Sultan might see me on the way to the mosque and be so dazzled by my beauty he'd have me kidnapped. Every morning when he left the house he'd put three big negroes at the door to keep all males away from me. . . . Ah! my little Suleiman!"

She took a large, checked handkerchief from her bodice and bit it, hissing like a turtle.

Zorba got rid of her by placing her on the chair next to him, and stood up, annoyed. He walked up and down once or twice and he began hissing as well; the room was suddenly too cramped for him.

He picked up his stick and rushed out into the yard, and I saw
him lean the ladder against the wall and clamber up, two steps at
a time, in a fury.

"Who are you going to thrash, Zorba?" I shouted. "Suleiman
Pasha?"

"Those damned cats!" he shouted. "Can't they leave us for a
single moment?"

And in one bound he was on the roof.

Dame Hortense, quite drunk, her hair dishevelled, had now
closed her inflamed eyes, and a discreet snore came from her toothless mouth. Sleep had lifted her up and transported her to the great
cities of the East—into the closed gardens and dim harems of amorous pashas. Sleep let her pass through walls and sent her dreams.
She could see herself fishing; she had thrown out four lines and
caught up four great battleships.

Snoring and breathing heavily, the old siren smiled happily in
her sleep, and seemingly refreshed by her bathe in the sea.

Zorba came back, swinging his stick.

"Sleeping, eh?" he said as he saw her. "The jade's asleep, is she?"

"Yes, Zorba Pasha," I answered. "She's been carried off by the
Doctor Voronoff who makes old people young again—sleep. She's
only twenty, and she's strolling about Alexandria and Beirut. . . ."

"Let her go to the devil, the old slut!" Zorba growled, and spat
on the floor. "Just look at the way she's grinning! I wonder who
she's grinning at, the brazen bitch? Come on, boss, let's go!"

He slapped on his cap and opened the door.

"She's not all on her own," cried Zorba; "she's with Suleiman
Pasha. Can't you see? She's in her seventh heaven, the dirty cow!
. . . Come on. Let's beat it!"

We went out into the cold air. The moon was sailing across a
calm sky.

"Women!" said Zorba in disgust. "Ugh! Still, it's not your
fault, it's the fault of hare-brained harum-scarums like Suleiman
and Zorba!"

And after a moment's pause:

"No, it's not even our fault," he went on furiously. "There's
one being who's the cause of it all, and one alone—the Grand

Hare-brained Harum-scarum, the Grand Suleiman Pasha . . . you know who!"

"If he exists," I answered. "What if he doesn't?"

"God Almighty, then we're done for!"

For some time we strode along without a word. Zorba was certainly going over some wild ideas in his mind, because every second or so he would lash out at the pebbles with his stick and spit on the ground.

Suddenly he turned to me.

"May God sanctify my grandad's bones!" he said. "He knew a thing or two about women. He liked them a lot, poor wretch, and they led him a regular dance in his lifetime. 'By all the good things I wish you, Alexis, my boy,' he'd say, 'beware of women! When God took Adam's rib out to create woman—curse that minute!—the devil turned into a serpent, and pff! he snatched the rib and ran off with it. . . . God dashed after him and caught him, but he slipped out of his fingers and God was left with just the devil's horns in his hands. "A good housekeeper," said God, "can sew even with a spoon. Well, I'll create a woman with the devil's horns!" And he did; and that's how the devil got us all, Alexis my boy. No matter where you touch a woman, you touch the devil's horns. Beware of her, my boy! She also stole the apples in the garden of Eden; she shoved them down her bodice, and now she goes out and about, strutting all over the place. A plague on her! Eat any of those apples and you're lost; don't eat any and you'll still be lost! What advice can I give you, then, my boy? Do as you please!' That's what my old grandad said to me. But how could you expect me to grow up sensible? I went the same way as he did —I went to the devil!"

We hurried through the village. The moonlight was disturbing. Imagine how it would be if you had been drinking and came out for a walk and found the world suddenly transformed. The roads had turned into rivers of milk, the holes in the road and the ruts overflowed with chalk, the hills were covered with snow. Your hands, face and neck were phosphorescent, like a glowworm's tail. And the moon hung on your chest like an exotic round medal.

We were walking along briskly, in silence. Intoxicated by the moonlight as well as by the wine, we hardly felt our feet touch the ground. Behind us, in the sleeping village, the dogs had got up on the roofs and were howling at the moon. And we, for no reason at all, also felt a desire to stretch our necks towards the moon and begin to howl. . . .

We came to the widow's garden. Zorba stopped. Wine, good food and the moon had turned his head. He craned his neck and, in his big ass's voice, began to bray a bawdy couplet which, in his excited state, he composed on the spur of the moment.

"She's another of the devil's horns!" he said. "Let's go, boss!"

Dawn was about to break when we arrived at the hut. I threw myself on my bed, worn out. Zorba washed, lit the stove and made some coffee. He crouched on the floor by the door, lit a cigarette and began to smoke placidly, his body straight and motionless as he looked out at the sea. His face was grave and thoughtful. He reminded me of a Japanese painting I like: an ascetic sitting on his crossed legs and wrapped in a long orange-colored robe; his face shining like a carving in hard wood, blackened by the rain; his neck erect, smiling as he gazes, without fear, into the dark night. . . .

I looked at Zorba in the light of the moon and admired the jauntiness and simplicity with which he adapted himself to the world around him, the way his body and soul formed one harmonious whole, and all things—women, bread, water, meat, sleep—blended happily with his flesh and became Zorba. I had never seen such a friendly accord between a man and the universe.

The moon would soon be setting now. It was round and of a pale green. An indescribable peacefulness spread across the sea.

Zorba threw away his cigarette and reached out for a basket. He fumbled in it and pulled out some string, pulleys and little pieces of wood; he lit the oil-lamp and once more started to experiment with his overhead railway. Stooping over his primitive toy, he began to make calculations which must have been extremely complicated and difficult, for every other second he scratched his head furiously and swore.

Suddenly he had had enough of it. He aimed one kick at the model and it crashed to the ground.

◇ 12 ◇

S LEEP OVERCAME ME, and when I awoke Zorba had gone. It was
cold and I did not have the slightest desire to rise. I reached
up to some bookshelves above my head and took down a book
which I had brought with me and of which I was fond: the poems
of Mallarmé. I read slowly and at random. I closed the book,
opened it again, and finally threw it down. For the first time in my
life it all seemed bloodless, odorless, void of any human substance.
Pale-blue, hollow words in a vacuum. Perfectly clear distilled water without any bacteria, but also without any nutritive substances.
Without life.

In religions which have lost their creative spark, the gods even-
tually become no more than poetic motifs or ornaments for deco-
rating human solitude and walls. Something similar had happened
to this poetry. The ardent aspirations of the heart, laden with earth
and seed, had become a flawless intellectual game, a clever, aerial
and intricate architecture.

I reopened the book and began reading again. Why had these
poems gripped me for so many years? Pure poetry! Life had turned
into a lucid, transparent game, unencumbered by even a single
drop of blood. The human element is brutish, uncouth, impure—
it is composed of love, the flesh and a cry of distress. Let it be
sublimated into an abstract idea, and, in the crucible of the spirit,
by various processes of alchemy, let it be rarefied and evaporate.

All these things which had formerly so fascinated me appeared this morning to be no more than cerebral acrobatics and refined charlatanism! That is how it always is at the decline of a civilization. That is how man's anguish ends—in masterly conjuring tricks: pure poetry, pure music, pure thought. The last man—who has freed himself from all belief, from all illusions and has nothing more to expect or to fear—sees the clay of which he is made reduced to spirit, and this spirit has no soil left for its roots, from which to draw its sap. The last man has emptied himself; no more seed, no more excrement, no more blood. Everything having turned into words, every set of words into musical jugglery, the last man goes even further: he sits in his utter solitude and decomposes the music into mute, mathematical equations.

I started. "Buddha is that last man!" I cried. That is his secret and terrible significance. Buddha is the "pure" soul which has emptied itself; in him is the void, he is the Void. "Empty your body, empty your spirit, empty your heart!" he cries. Wherever he sets his foot, water no longer flows, no grass can grow, no child be born.

I must mobilize words and their necromantic power, I thought, invoke magic rhythms; lay siege to him, cast a spell over him and drive him out of my entrails! I must throw over him the net of images, catch him and free myself!

Writing *Buddha* was, in fact, ceasing to be a literary exercise. It was a life-and-death struggle against a tremendous force of destruction lurking within me, a duel with a great NO which was consuming my heart, and on the result of this duel depended the salvation of my soul.

With briskness and determination I seized the manuscript. I had discovered my goal, I knew now where to strike! Buddha was the last man. We are only at the beginning; we have neither eaten, drunk, nor loved enough; we have not yet lived. This delicate old man, scant of breath, has come to us too soon. We must oust him as quickly as possible!

So I spoke to myself and I began to write. But no, this was not writing: it was a real war, a merciless hunt, a siege, a spell to bring the monster out of its hiding place. Art is, in fact, a magic incantation. Obscure homicidal forces lurk in our entrails, deadly impulses to kill, destroy, hate, dishonor. Then art appears with its sweet piping and delivers us.

I wrote, pursued, struggled the whole day through. In the evening I was exhausted. But I felt I had made progress, had mastered a few advance posts of the enemy. I was now anxious for Zorba to return, so that I could eat, sleep and build up my strength to resume the fight at dawn.

It was already dark when Zorba came in. He had a radiant expression on his face. He has found the answer to something, too, I thought. And I waited.

I had begun to grow impatient with him and, only a few days before, I had said angrily:

"Zorba, our funds are getting low. Whatever has to be done, do it quickly! Let's get this railway going; if we're not successful with the coal, let's go all out for the timber. Otherwise we've had it!"

Zorba had scratched his head.

"Funds getting low, are they, boss? That's bad!" he said.

"They're gone, Zorba. We've swallowed up the lot. Do something! How are your experiments going? No luck yet?"

Zorba had hung his head and made no reply. He had felt ashamed that evening. "That damned slope!" he said furiously. "I'll get the better of it yet!" And now he had come in, his face lit up with success.

"I've done it, boss!" he shouted. "I've found the right angle! It was slipping through my hands, trying to get away from me, but I held on and pinned it down, boss!"

"Well, hurry up and get the thing working! Fire away, Zorba! What else do you need?"

"Early tomorrow morning I must go to town and buy the tackle: a thick steel cable, pulleys, bearings, nails, hooks. . . . Don't worry, I'll be back almost before you've seen me go!"

He lit the fire shortly afterwards, prepared our meal and we ate and drank with excellent appetites. We had both worked well that day.

The next morning I went with Zorba as far as the village. We talked like serious and practical-minded people about the working of the lignite. While going down a slope, Zorba kicked against a stone, which went rolling downhill. He stopped for a moment in amazement, as if he were seeing this astounding spectacle for the first time in his life. He looked round at me, and in his look I discerned faint consternation.

"Boss, did you see that?" he said at last. "On slopes, stones come to life again."

I said nothing, but I felt a deep joy. This, I thought, is how great visionaries and poets see everything—as if for the first time. Each morning they see a new world before their eyes; they do not really see it, they create it.

The universe for Zorba, as for the first men on earth, was a weighty, intense vision; the stars glided over him, the sea broke against his temples. He lived the earth, water, the animals and God, without the distorting intervention of reason.

Dame Hortense had been informed and she was waiting for us on her doorstep. She was painted, caulked with powder, and uneasy. She had got herself up like a fun fair on a Saturday night. The mule was in front of her gate; Zorba jumped on its back and seized the reins.

The old siren came up timidly and placed her plump little hand on the animal's breast, as if she wanted to prevent her beloved from leaving.

"Zorba. . . ." she cooed, raising herself on tiptoe. "Zorba. . . ."

Zorba turned his head away. He hated having to listen to lovers' nonsense like this in the middle of the road. The poor woman saw his look and was terrified. But her hand still pressed on the mule's breast, full of tender entreaty.

"What do you want?" Zorba asked angrily.

"Zorba," she pleaded, "be good. . . . Don't forget me, Zorba. . . . Be good. . . ."

Zorba shook the reins without replying. The mule started off.

"Good luck, Zorba!" I cried. "Three days, do you hear? No more!"

He turned round, waving his big hand. The old siren was weeping and her tears washed furrows in the powder on her face.

"I gave you my word, boss!" Zorba shouted. "Goodbye!"

And he disappeared beneath the olive trees. Dame Hortense

went on crying, but she kept her eyes on the splash of color made by the gay red rug which she had placed so carefully for her beloved so that he should be comfortably seated. It was constantly being hidden by the silver foliage of the trees. Soon even that had disappeared. Dame Hortense looked round her. The world was empty.

I did not go back to the beach. I felt sad and walked towards the mountains. As I reached the mountain track, I heard a trumpet sound. The country postman was announcing his arrival in the village.

"Master!" he called to me, waving his hand.

He came over and gave me a packet of newspapers, some literary reviews and two letters: one I immediately put away in my pocket to read in the evening, when day is done and the spirit is calm. I knew who had written it and I wanted to defer my joy so that it should last longer.

The other letter I recognized from its sharp, jerky writing and the exotic stamps: it came from one of my old fellow students, Karayannis. It was from a wild African mountainside, near Tanganyika.

He was a strange, impulsive, dark man with very white teeth. One of his canines stuck out like a wild boar's. He never talked, he shouted. He never discussed, he quarrelled. He had left his own country, Crete, where he had been a young theology teacher and a monk. He had flirted with one of his students, and they had been surprised one day kissing out in the fields. They had been booed. The same day the young teacher threw off the cowl and took a boat. He went to an uncle in Africa and started to work with a will. He opened a rope factory and made a lot of money. From time to time he wrote to me and invited me to go and stay with him for six months. Whenever I opened one of his letters, even before I read it, I could feel, arising from the crowded pages, which were always sewn together with string, a violent breath which made my hair stand on end. I was always deciding I would go and see him in Africa, but never went.

I left the track, sat on a stone, opened and began reading this letter:

When are you going to make up your mind to come here to me, you damned limpet clamped to the rocks of Greece? You, too, have turned into a typical lousy Greek, a tavern-loafer, a wallower in café-life. Because you need not think only cafés are cafés; books are, too, and habits, and your precious ideologies. They are all cafés. It is Sunday today and I have nothing to do: I am on my estate and I'm thinking of you. The sun is like a furnace, and there has not been a drop of rain. Here, when the rain does fall, in April, May and June, it's an absolute deluge.

I'm all alone, and I like that. There are quite a lot of lousy Greeks here (Is there anywhere this vermin doesn't get to?) but I don't want to mix with them. They disgust me. Even here, you damned tavern-loafers—may the Devil take you—you've sent us your leprosy, your miserable back-biting. That's what is ruining Greece—politics! There's card-playing, too, of course, and ignorance, and the sins of the flesh.

I detest Europeans; that's why I am wandering about here in the mountains of Usumbara. I hate Europeans, but most of all I hate the lousy Greeks and everything Greek. I'll never set foot in Greece again. This is where I'll finish up. I've had my tomb made already, in front of my hut, here on the wild mountainside. I've even put up the stone and myself carved these words in large capitals:

HERE LIES A GREEK WHO HATES THE GREEKS

I burst out laughing, spit, swear and weep whenever I think of Greece. So as to see no Greeks and nothing Greek, I left the country forever. I came here, brought my destiny with me—it was not my destiny which brought me: man does what he chooses!—I brought my destiny here and I've worked and still am working like a slave. I've been sweating and will continue to sweat by the bucketful. I am fighting with the earth, the wind, the rain, and with the workmen, my red and black slaves.

I have no pleasures. Yes, one: work. Physical and mental, but preferably physical. I like to exhaust myself, sweat, hear my bones crack. Half my money I throw away, waste it however and wherever I feel inclined. I'm not a slave to money: money is my slave. I am a slave to work, and I'm proud of it. I fell trees; I have a contract with the British. I make rope; and now I've started planting cotton, too. Last

night, among my negroes, two tribes—the Wa'yao and the Wa'ngoni
—began fighting over a woman—over a whore. Just hurt pride, you
know. Just the same as in Greece. Insults, brawls, and then out come
the clubs. They broke one another's heads over her. The women ran
to fetch me in the middle of the night, and woke me with their yap-
ping, to go and arbitrate. I was angry, told them all to go to the devil,
then to the British police. But they stayed there howling in front of
my door the whole night. At dawn I went out and arbitrated.

Tomorrow, early, I am going to scale the Usumbara mountains,
with their dense forest, fresh waters and everlasting greenness. Well,
you lousy Babylonian Greek, when will you cut adrift from Europe?
". . . that great whore that sitteth upon many waters, with whom the
kings of the earth have committed fornication . . . !" When will
you come, so that we can climb these pure and wild mountains together?

I have a child by a black woman: a girl. I've sent her mother away:
she cuckolded me in public in the full glare of the midday sun, under
every green tree in the neighborhood. I had enough of her, and threw
her out. But I kept the girl; she's two. She can walk, and she's beginning to talk. I'm teaching her Greek; the first sentence I taught her
was: "I spit on you, you lousy Greeks, I spit on you, you lousy Greeks!"

She looks like me, the little scamp; she's only got her mother's broad,
flat nose. I love her, but just as you love a dog or a cat. Come out here
and get a boy by a Usumbara woman. We'll marry the two of them
one day, just to amuse ourselves, and to amuse them, too!

Goodbye! May the devil go with you, and with me, dear friend!

KARAYANNIS, *Servus diabolicus Dei.*

I left the letter open on my knees. An ardent desire to go took
possession of me once more. Not because I wanted to leave—I was
quite all right on this Cretan coast, and I felt happy and free here
and I needed nothing—but because I have always been consumed
with one desire: to touch and see as much as possible of the earth
and the sea before I die.

I stood up, changed my mind, and instead of climbing the hill
went hurriedly towards the beach. I felt the other letter in the upper pocket of my coat, and could not wait any more. That sweet,
unbearable foretaste of joy had lasted long enough.

I reached the hut, lit the fire, made some tea, ate some bread and honey and oranges. I undressed, stretched out on my bed and opened the letter:

MASTER AND NEOPHYTE—GREETINGS!

I have a tremendous and difficult job here, thank "God"—I enclose the dangerous word in inverted commas (like a wild beast behind bars) so that you do not get excited as soon as you open my letter. Well, a very difficult job, "God" be praised! Half a million Greeks are in danger in the south of Russia and the Caucasus. Many of them speak only Turkish or Russian, but their hearts speak Greek fanatically. They are of our race. Just to look at them—the way their eyes flash, rapacious, ferrety, the cunning and sensuality of their lips when they smile, the way they have managed to become bosses and have moujiks working for them in this immense territory of Russia—it's quite enough to convince you that they are descendants of your beloved Odysseus. So one comes to love them and cannot let them perish.

For they *are* in danger of perishing. They have lost all they had, are hungry and naked. From one side they are harried by the Bolsheviks; from the other by the Kurds. Refugees have swarmed in from every direction to settle in one town or another in Georgia and Armenia. There's no food, medicine, or clothing. They gather in the ports, scan the horizon anxiously for Greek ships coming to take them back to their Mother—Greece. One part of our race—that means one part of our soul—is panic-stricken.

If we leave them to their fate, they will perish. We need a lot of love and understanding, enthusiasm and practical sense—those qualities which you like so much to see united—if we are going to save them and get them back to the part of our own free land where they will be of most use—that is, on the frontiers of Macedonia, and, further afield, on the frontiers of Thrace. That is the only way we shall save hundreds of thousands of Greeks, and save ourselves with them. For as soon as I arrived here I drew a circle, in the way you taught me, and called that circle "my duty." I said: "If I save this entire circle, I am saved; if I do not save it, I am lost!" Well, inside that circle there are five hundred thousand Greeks!

I go to towns and villages, collect all the Greeks together, write reports, send telegrams, try to make our officials in Athens send boats, food, clothes, and medicine, and transport these poor creatures to Greece. If to struggle with zeal and obstinacy is to be happy, then I am happy. I do not know whether I have cut my happiness to my stature, to use your phrase. Please heaven I have, because then I would be a great person. I would like to increase my stature to what I think would make me happy; that is, to the farthest frontiers of Greece! But that's enough theory! You are lying on your Cretan beach, listening to the sound of the sea and the *santuri*—you have time, I have not. I am swallowed up by activity and I am glad of it. Action, dear inactive master, action; there is no other salvation.

The subject of my meditations is, in fact, very simple and all of a piece. I say: These inhabitants of the Pontus and the Caucasus, peasants of Kars, big and small merchants of Tiflis, Batum, Novo Rossisk, Rostov, Odessa and the Crimea, are ours, they are of our blood; for them, as for us, the capital of Greece is Constantinople. We all have the same chief. You call him Odysseus, others Constantinos Palaeologos *—not the one who was killed beneath the walls of Byzantium, but the other, the legendary one, who was changed into marble and still stands erect waiting for the Angel of Liberty. With your permission, I call this chief of our race Acritas. † I like that name better; it is more austere and warlike. As soon as you hear it, there rises within you the image of the eternal Hellene, fully armed, fighting without cease or respite on the boundaries and frontiers. On every frontier: national, intellectual, and spiritual. And if you add Digenes, † you describe even more completely that marvellous synthesis of East and West which is our race.

I am in Kars now; I came to assemble all the Greeks of the neighboring villages. On the day of my arrival the Kurds had seized a Greek teacher and priest in the district and nailed horse-shoes to their feet. The notables were horrified and took refuge in the house where I am staying. We can hear the Kurds' guns coming closer all the time. All these Greeks have their eyes fixed on me, as if I were the only one with the strength to save them.

I was counting on leaving tomorrow for Tiflis, but now, in the face

* The last of the East Roman Emperors (1448–53).
† Basilius Digenes Acritas: tenth-century Byzantine hero. Digenes: of double birth (Moslem father and Christian mother). Acritas: frontier-guard of the Empire. C. W.

of this danger, I am ashamed to leave. So I am staying. I don't say I am not afraid; I am afraid, but I'm ashamed. Wouldn't Rembrandt's Warrior, my Warrior, have done the same thing? He would have stayed; so I am staying, too. If the Kurds come into the town it is only natural and just that I should be the first to be shoed. I am sure, master, you never thought your pupil would end like this!

After one of those interminable Greek discussions we decided that everyone should assemble this evening with mules, horses, cattle, women and children, and at dawn we will all start out together for the north. I shall walk in front, the ram guiding the flock.

A patriarchal emigration of a people over chains of mountains and plains with legendary names! And I shall be a sort of Moses—an imitation Moses—leading the chosen race to the Promised Land, as these naive people are calling Greece. Of course, to be really worthy of this Mosaic mission and not disgrace you, I should have done away with my elegant leggings which you tease me about and wrapped my legs in sheepskin. I should also have a long, greasy, wavy beard, and, above all, a large pair of horns. But I'm sorry, I can't give you that pleasure. It's easier to get me to change my soul than my costume. I wear leggings; I am as smooth shaven as a cabbage stump; and I'm not married.

Master, I hope you get this letter, for it may be the last. No one can say. I have no confidence in the secret forces which are said to protect men. I believe in the blind forces which hit out right and left, without malice, without purpose, killing whoever happens to be in their way. If I leave this earth (I say "leave" so as not to frighten you or myself with the proper word), if I leave this earth, I say, I hope you keep well and happy, dear master! I am embarrassed at having to say it, but I must, so please excuse me: I, too, have loved you very dearly.

Then underneath, written hurriedly in pencil, was this postscriptum:

ps. I haven't forgotten the agreement we made on the boat the day I left. If I have to "leave" this earth, I shall warn you, remember, wherever you are; don't let it scare you.

◊ 13 ◊

THREE DAYS, four days, five days went by, and still no Zorba. On the sixth day I received from Candia a letter several pages long, a whole lot of rigmarole. It was written on scented pink paper and, in the corner of the page, was a heart pierced by an arrow.

I kept it carefully and am copying it faithfully, retaining the labored expressions to be found here and there. I have merely corrected the charming spelling. Zorba held a pen like a pickaxe; he attacked the paper violently with it, and that is why the paper had a number of holes in it and was covered with blots.

DEAR BOSS! MISTER CAPITALIST!

I take up the pen to ask if your health is favorable. We are quite well, too, God be praised!

I have realized for some time I didn't come into this world to be a horse, or an ox. Only animals live to eat. To escape the above accusation, I invent jobs for myself day and night. I risk my daily bread for an idea, I turn the proverb round and say: "Better be a lean moorhen on a pond than a fat sparrow in a cage."

Lots of people are patriots without it costing them anything. I am not a patriot, and will not be, whatever it costs me. Lots of people believe in paradise and they keep an ass tethered there. I have no ass, I am free! I am not afraid of hell where my ass would die. I don't long for paradise either, where he would stuff himself with clover. I am an ignorant blockhead, I don't know how to put things, but you understand me, boss.

Lots of people have been afraid of the vanity of things! I've overcome it. Lots reflect hard; I have no need to reflect. I don't rejoice over the good and don't despair over the bad. If I hear that the Greeks have taken Constantinople, it's just the same to me as if the Turks were taking Athens.

If you think from the balderdash I talk I'm going soft in the head, write to me. I go into the shops here in Candia, trying to buy cable, and I laugh.

"What are you laughing at, brother?" they keep asking. But how can I tell them? I laugh because, just when I hold out my hand to see if the steel cable is good, I think about what mankind is and why he ever came onto this earth and what good he is. . . . No good at all, if you ask me. It makes no difference whether I have a woman or whether I don't, whether I'm honest or not, whether I'm a pasha or a street-porter. The only thing that makes any difference is whether I'm alive or dead. Whether the devil or God calls me (and do you know what, boss? I think the devil and God are the same), I shall die, turn into a reeking corpse, and stink people out. They'll be obliged to shove me at least four feet down in the earth, so that they won't get choked!

By the way, I'm going to ask you about something that rather scares me—the only thing, mind—and it leaves me no peace, night or day What scares me, boss, is old age. Heaven preserve us from that! Death is nothing—just pff! and the candle is snuffed out. But old age is a disgrace.

I consider it a deep disgrace to admit I'm getting on, and I do all I can to stop people seeing I've grown old: I hop about, dance, my back aches but I keep dancing. I drink, get dizzy, everything spins round, but I don't sit down, I just act as if everything's hunky-dory. I sweat, so I plunge into the sea, catch cold and want to cough—gooh! gooh!— to relieve myself but I feel ashamed, boss, and force back the cough. Have you ever heard me cough? Never! And not, as you might think, just when there are other people about, but when I'm by myself, too! I feel ashamed in front of Zorba—what do you think of that, boss? I'm ashamed in front of him!

One day on Mount Athos—because I've been there, and I'd have done better to cut off my right hand!—I met a monk, Father Lavrentio, a native of Chios. He, poor fellow, believed he had a devil inside him and he'd even given him a name: he called him *Hodja*. "Hodja wants to eat meat on Good Friday!" poor Lavrentio used to roar, beating his head on the church wall. "Hodja wants to sleep with a woman. Hodja wants to kill the Abbot. It's Hodja, Hodja, it isn't me!" And he'd bang his head on the stone.

I've a kind of devil inside me, too, boss, and I call him Zorba! The inner Zorba doesn't want to grow old, not at all, and he hasn't grown old, he never will grow old. He's an ogre, he's got hair as black as jet, thirty-two (figures: 32) teeth, and a red carnation behind his ear. But the outer Zorba, poor devil, has got a bit of a corporation and quite a few white hairs. He's shrivelled and gone wrinkled; his teeth fall out and his big ear is full of the white hair of old age, long ass's hair!

What can he do, boss? How long will these two Zorbas fight each other? Which one will win? If I kick the bucket soon, it'll be all right, I don't care. But if I go on living for a long time yet, I'm done. Done, boss! The day will come when I'll be disgraced. I'll lose my liberty: my daughter-in-law and daughter will order me to keep watch on some infant, a fearful little monster of theirs, so that he doesn't burn himself, or fall over, or dirty himself. And if he does dirty himself, pooh! they'll make me clean him up!

You'll have to go through the same sort of shame, boss, although you're young. You watch out. Listen to what I tell you, follow the same road as me, there's no other salvation: let's go up into the mountains, mine them for coal, copper, iron and calamine; let's make our pile so that relatives respect us and friends lick our boots and all the well-to-do raise their hats to us. If we don't succeed, boss, we might as well pack up, be killed by wolves, or bears, or any wild beast we can find—and much good may it do them! That's why God sent wild beasts on earth: to finish off a few people like us, so they don't fall too low.

Here Zorba had drawn with colored pencils a tall, lean man, fleeing under some green trees, with seven red wolves at his heels, and at the top of the picture, in big letters, was written: "Zorba and the Seven Deadly Sins."

Then he went on:

You must see from this letter what an unhappy man I am. It's only when I'm with you that I have any chance, through talking to you, of getting some relief from my morbid state of mind. Because you're like me, too, only you don't know it. You've got a devil inside you, as well, but you don't know his name yet, and, since you don't know that, you can breathe. Baptize him, boss, and you'll feel better!

I was saying how unhappy I am. I can see clearly that all my intelligence is stupidity and nothing more. There are times, though, when for whole days great thoughts occur to me, and if only I could do what that inside Zorba tells me to do the world would be amazed!

Seeing as how I have no time-limit clause in my contract with life, I let the brakes off when I get to the most dangerous slopes. The life of man is a road with steep rises and dips. All sensible people use their brakes. But—and this is where, boss, maybe I show what I'm made of—I did away with my brakes altogether a long time ago, because I'm not at all scared of a jolt. When a machine goes off the rails we mechanics call that "a jolt!" And the devil knows if I take any notice of the jolts I get. Day and night, I go full steam ahead, doing just what I like; so much the worse if I fold up and get smashed to pieces. What have I got to lose? Nothing. Even if I do take it easy, won't I end up just the same? Of course I will! So let's scorch along!

I'm sure I'm making you laugh now, boss, but I'm writing down my blather, or, if you like, my reflections, or my weaknesses—what's the difference between the three?—I really couldn't say—I'm writing to you, and you have a good laugh if you're not bored. I'm laughing at the thought of you laughing, and that's how laughing never stops on this earth. Every man has his folly, but the greatest folly of all, in my view, is not to have one.

So you can see I'm sorting out my own brand of folly here in Candia, and I'm giving you the whole shoot, boss, because I want to ask your advice. You're still young, of course, but you have read the old books of wisdom and you've become, if you don't mind my saying so, a bit old fashioned; so I'd like your advice.

Well, I think every man has his own smell. We don't notice it much because smells mingle all together and we can't tell which is yours and which is mine, really. . . . All we know is that there's a foul smell and that's what we call "humanity" . . . I mean "the human stench." There are people who sniff at it as if it was lavender. It makes me want to spew. Anyway, let's get on, that's another story. . . .

I wanted to say—I was just going to let off the brake again—that women, the jades, have wet noses, like bitches, and straight away smell out a man who desires them and one who doesn't. That's why in every town I've ever set foot in, even now when I'm old, ugly as an ape and got no smart clothes, I've always had one or two women running after me. They sniff me out, the bitches! God bless 'em!

Anyway, the first day I arrived safely in Candia, it was dusk. I rushed straight to the shops, but they were all closed. I went to an inn, gave the mule some fodder, ate myself and had a clean-up. I lit a cigarette and went out for a look-around. I didn't know a soul in the town and no one knew me; I was absolutely free. I could whistle in the street, laugh, talk to myself. I bought some *passa-tempo*,* nibbled, spat and wandered to my heart's content. The street-lamps were lit, men were having their aperitifs, women were going home, the air was scented with powder, toilet-soap, anisette, and *souvlakia*.† I said to myself: "Listen, Zorba, how long do you expect to live with those quivering nostrils? You haven't got very long left, to sniff the air. Go on, old chap, breathe it in as deep as you can!"

That's what I was saying as I walked up and down the big square —you know the one. Suddenly—praise be to God—I heard shouts, dancing, a tambourine playing and some oriental songs. I pricked up my ears and ran to where the noise was coming from. It was a café with a cabaret. That was just what I wanted. I went in. I sat down at a little table, well to the front. Why shouldn't I be bold? As I say, nobody knew me, I was absolutely free.

A big gawk of a woman was dancing on the platform, lifting her skirts up, but I didn't pay any attention. I ordered a bottle of beer, and then a sweet, dusky little creature came and sat down at my table. She'd plastered on her paint with a trowel.

"Do you mind, grandad?" she asked, laughing.

The blood rushed up to my head at this. I felt a terrible urge to

* Salted roast pumpkin seeds.
† Grilled meat on a skewer.

wring her neck, the hussy! But I held myself back, I was sorry for the "female of the species" so I called a waiter.

"Two bottles of champagne!"

Forgive me, boss! I've spent some of your money, but it was such a terrible insult, I had to save our honor, yours as well as mine, I had to bring that little brat to her knees before us, I really had to. I know you would never have left me defenseless, like that, at a difficult moment! So, "Two bottles of champagne, waiter!"

The champagne arrived, and I ordered cakes as well, then some more champagne. A man with some jasmine came up and I bought the basketful and emptied it into the lap of the little bit of fluff who'd dared insult us.

We drank and drank, but on my oath, boss, I didn't even pinch her. I know my stuff. When I was young the first thing I did was to pinch and play with them. Now I'm old, the first thing I do is to spend money, be gallant, open-fisted. Women adore being treated like that. The jades go crazy about you; and you can be hump-backed, an old ruin, as ugly as a louse, and they'll forget all that. They can't see anything else, the bitches, but the hand that brings out the money and lets it flow away like a basket with a hole in it. So, as I was saying, I spent a fortune—may God bless you, boss, and return it to you a hundred-fold—and the above-mentioned girl stuck tight to me. She came closer and closer; she pressed her little knee up against my big bony stumps. But I was just like a block of ice, although inside I was hot and bothered. That's what makes women lose their heads; you'd better learn that, in case you find yourself in the same situation, it might stand you in good stead: let 'em feel you're burning inside and yet you don't touch 'em!

Well, midnight came and went. The lights began going out, the café was closing. I took out a roll of thousand-drachma notes, paid the bill and left a generous tip for the waiter. The girl clung to me.

"What's your name?" she asked me in a love-sick tone.

"Grandad!" I replied, vexed.

The brazen little bitch pinched me hard, and whispered: "Come with me . . . come with me!"

I took her little hand, squeezed it with a knowing air and answered: "Come, then, little one. . . ." My voice was hoarse.

You can imagine the rest, boss. We did our stuff. Then we went to sleep. When I woke up it must have been at least midday. I looked round, and what do I see? A charming little room, spick and span, easychairs, a washbasin, soaps, scent bottles, mirrors of all sizes, gaily-colored dresses hanging on the wall, a crowd of photographs: sailors, officers, captains, policemen, dancing-women, women with only one thing on—a pair of sandals. And next to me in the bed—warm, scented, and with ruffled hair, the female of the species!

"Ah, Zorba," I said to myself, closing my eyes, "you've entered Paradise while you're still alive! This is a good place to be; don't budge!"

I told you once before, boss, that each man has his own particular paradise. For you, Paradise will be stocked full of books and big demijohns of ink. For someone else it'll be full of casks of wine, of rum and brandy, for another piles of money. For me Paradise is this: a little perfumed room with gay-colored dresses on the wall, scented soaps, a big bed with good springs, and at my side the female of the species.

A fault confessed is half redressed. I didn't stick my nose outside the door that day. Where would I have gone? What should I have done? No fear! I was fine where I was. I sent an order to the best inn of the town and they brought us a tray of food—nothing but good, strength-giving food: black caviar, chops, fish, lemon-juice, *cadaif*.*
We looked after our little affairs again and had another nap. We woke up in the evening, dressed and went off arm-in-arm to the café once more.

To cut a long story short and not drown you in words, that program is still in operation. But don't you worry yourself, boss, I'm looking after your little affairs, too. Now and then I go and look round the shops. I'll buy the cable and all we need, don't you worry. A day sooner, or a day or a week later, even a month later, what does it matter? As we say, if the cat's in too much of a hurry, she has peculiar kittens. In your interest, I'm waiting for my ears to pick up everything and my mind to clear, so I'm not swindled. The cable must be first-class, or we shall be dished. So be patient, boss, and trust in me.

Above all, don't worry about my health. Adventures are good for me. In the matter of a few days I've become a young man of twenty

* A sweet Turkish pastry, containing nuts, etc.

again. I'm so strong, I tell you, I shall be growing a new set o' teeth. My back was hurting me a bit when I arrived, now I'm as fit as a fiddle. Every morning I look at myself in the mirror and I'm amazed my hair hasn't turned as black as boot polish overnight.

But you'll be asking why I'm writing to you like this? Well . . . you're a sort of confessor to me, boss, and I'm not ashamed to admit all my sins to you. Do you know why? So far as I can see, whether I do right or wrong, you don't care a rap. You hold a damp sponge, like God, and flap! slap! you just wipe it all out. That's what prompts me to tell you everything like this. So listen!

I'm all topsy-turvy and on the point of going completely off my head. Please, boss, take your pen and write to me as soon as you get this letter. Until I have your answer, I'll be on tenterhooks. I think that for years now my name's been scratched off God's register. And off the devil's, too. Yours is the only register I think I'm still on, so I've got nobody but your worshipful self to turn to; so listen to what I've got to say. This is what it's about:

Yesterday there was a fête on in a village near Candia—devil take me if I know what saint it was in aid of! Lola—ah! true enough, I'd forgotten to introduce her to you; her name's Lola—she says to me:

"Grandad!" She calls me grandad once more, but now it's a pet name, boss. "Grandad," she says, "I'd like to go to the fête!"

"Go on, then, Granma," I say to her.

"But I want to go with you."

"I'm not going. I don't like saints. You go by yourself."

"All right, I shan't go either."

I stared at her.

"You won't? Why not? Don't you want to?"

"If you come with me, I do. If not, I don't."

"Why not? You're a free person, aren't you?"

"No, I'm not."

"You don't want to be free?"

"No, I don't."

I thought I must be hearing voices. I really did.

"You don't want to be free?" I cried.

"No, I don't! I don't! I don't!"

Boss, I'm writing this in Lola's room, on Lola's paper; for God's sake, listen carefully. I think only people who want to be free are human beings. Women don't want to be free. Well, is woman a human being?

For heaven's sake, answer as soon as possible.

All the best to the best of bosses.

ME, ALEXIS ZORBA.

When I had finished reading Zorba's letter I was for a while in two minds—no, three. I did not know whether to be angry, or laugh, or just admire this primitive man who simply cracked life's shell—logic, morality, honesty—and went straight to its very substance. All the little virtues which are so useful are lacking in him. All he has is an uncomfortable, dangerous virtue which is hard to satisfy and which urges him continually and irresistibly towards the utmost limits, towards the abyss.

When he writes, this ignorant workman breaks his pens in his impetuosity. Like the first men to cast off their monkey skins, or like the great philosophers, he is dominated by the basic problems of mankind. He lives them as if they were immediate and urgent necessities. Like the child, he sees everything for the first time. He is forever astonished and wonders why and wherefore. Everything seems miraculous to him, and each morning when he opens his eyes he sees trees, sea, stones and birds, and is amazed.

"What is this miracle?" he cries. "What are these mysteries called: trees, sea, stones, birds?"

One day, I remember, when we were making our way to the village, we met a little old man astride a mule. Zorba opened his eyes wide as he looked at the beast. And his look was so intense that the peasant cried out in terror:

"For God's sake, brother, don't give him the evil eye!" And he crossed himself.

I turned to Zorba.

"What did you do to the old chap to make him cry out like that?" I asked him.

"Me? What d'you think I did? I was looking at his mule, that's all! Didn't it strike you, boss?"

"What?"

"Well . . . that there are such things as mules in this world!"

Another day, I was reading, stretched out on the shore, and Zorba came and sat down opposite me, placed his *santuri* on his knees and began to play. I raised my eyes to look at him. Gradually his expression changed and a wild joy took possession of him. He shook his long, creased neck and began to sing.

Macedonian songs, Klepht songs, savage cries; the human throat became as it was in prehistoric times, when the cry was a great synthesis which bore within it all we call today by the names of poetry, music and thought. "Akh! Akh!" The cry came from the depth of Zorba's being and the whole thin crust of what we call civilization cracked and let out the immortal beast, the hairy god, the terrifying gorilla.

Lignite, profits and losses, Dame Hortense and plans for the future, all vanished. That cry carried everything before it; we had no need of anything else. Immobile, on that solitary coast of Crete, we both held in our breasts all the bitterness and sweetness of life. Bitterness and sweetness no longer existed. The sun went down, night came, the Great Bear danced round the immovable axis of the sky, the moon rose and gazed in horror at two tiny beasts who were singing on the sands and fearing no one.

"Ha! Man is a wild beast," Zorba said suddenly, overexcited with his singing. "Leave your books alone. Aren't you ashamed? Man is a wild beast, and wild beasts don't read."

He was silent a moment, then started to laugh.

"D'you know," he said, "how God made man? Do you know the first words this animal, man, addressed to God?"

"No. How should I know? I wasn't there."

"I was!" cried Zorba, his eyes sparkling.

"Well, tell me."

Half in ecstasy, half in mockery, he began inventing the fabulous story of the creation of man.

"Well, listen, boss! One morning God woke up feeling down in the dumps. 'What a devil of a God I am! I haven't even any men to burn incense to me and swear by my name to help pass the time away! I've had enough of living all alone like an old screech-owl. Ftt!' He spat on his hands, pulled up his sleeves, put on his glasses, took a piece of earth, spat on it, made mud of it, kneaded it well and made it into a little man which he stuck in the sun.

"Seven days later he pulled it out of the sun. It was baked. God looked at it and began to split his sides with laughter.

"'Devil take me,' he says, 'it's a pig standing up on its hind legs! That's not what I wanted at all! There's no mistake, I've made a mess of things!'

"So he picks him up by the scruff of his neck and kicks his backside.

"'Go on, clear off! All you've got to do now is to make other little pigs; the earth's yours! Now, jump to it. Left, right, left, right. . . . Quick march! . . .'

"But, you see, it wasn't a pig at all! It was wearing a felt hat, a jacket thrown carelessly across its shoulders, well-creased trousers, and Turkish slippers with red tassels. And in its belt—it must have been the devil who'd given it that—was a pointed dagger with the words: 'I'll get you!' engraved on it.

"It was man! God held out his hand for the other to kiss, but man twirled up his moustache and said:

"'Come on, old 'un, out of the way! Let me pass!'"

Here Zorba stopped as he saw me bursting with laughter. He frowned.

"Don't laugh!" he said. "That's exactly what happened!"

"How do you know?"

"That's how I feel it happened, and that's what I'd have done if I'd been in Adam's place. I'd wager my head being chopped off if Adam acted any different. And don't you believe all the books tell you; I'm the one you should trust!"

He stretched out his big hand without waiting for an answer and started playing the *santuri* once more.

I was still holding Zorba's scented letter with its heart pierced by an arrow, and was living through those days, filled with his human presence, which I had spent at his side. Time had taken on a new savour in Zorba's company. It was no longer an arithmetical succession of events without, nor an insoluble philosophical problem within. It was warm sand, finely sieved, and I felt it running gently through my fingers.

"Blessed be Zorba!" I murmured. "He has given a warm, beloved, living body to all the abstract ideas which were shivering inside me. When he is not there, I start shivering again."

I took a sheet of paper, called a workman and sent an urgent telegram:

"Come back immediately."

◊ 14 ◊

SATURDAY AFTERNOON, the first of March. I was leaning against a rock facing the sea, writing. That day I had seen the first swallow and I was happy. The exorcism of Buddha was flowing without hindrance onto the paper, and my struggle with him had become calmer; I was no longer in a desperate hurry, and I was sure of my deliverance.

Suddenly I heard steps on the pebbles. I raised my eyes and saw our old siren rolling along the shore, decked out like a frigate. She was hot and short of breath. She seemed to be worried about something.

"Is there a letter?" she asked anxiously.

"Yes!" I answered with a laugh, and rose to welcome her. "He sends you lots of greetings; says he's thinking about you day and night. He can hardly eat or drink, he finds the separation so unbearable."

"Is that all he says?" the unhappy woman asked, gasping for breath.

I was sorry for her. I took his letter from my pocket and pretended that I was reading it. The old siren opened her toothless mouth, her little eyes blinked and she listened breathlessly.

I made believe I was reading, but, as I got rather involved, I pretended I had difficulty in making out the writing: "Yesterday, boss,

I went into a cheap eating-house for a meal. I was hungry. . . .
When I saw an absolutely beautiful young girl come in, a real goddess. . . . My God! She looked just like my Bouboulina! And
straight away my eyes began spouting water like a fountain, I had a
lump in my throat. . . . I couldn't swallow! I got up, paid my bill
and left. And I who only think of the saints once in a blue moon,
I was so deeply moved, boss, I ran to Saint Minas's church and lit a
candle to him. 'Saint Minas,' I said in my prayer, 'let me have good
news of the angel I love. May our wings be united very soon!'"

"Ha! Ha! Ha!" went Dame Hortense, her face beaming with joy.

"What are you laughing at, my good woman?" I asked stopping
to get my breath and concoct some more lies. "What are you laughing at? This makes me feel more like weeping."

"If only you knew . . . if only you knew. . . ." she chuckled
and burst into laughter.

"What?"

"Wings. . . . That's what he calls feet, the rascal. That's the
name he gives them when we're alone. May our wings be united,
he says. . . . Ha! Ha! Ha!"

"Listen to what comes next, then. You'll be really astounded. . . ."

I turned over the page and made believe I was reading again:

"And today, as I was passing a barber's shop, the barber emptied
outside his bowl of soapy water. The whole street was filled with the
scent. And I thought of Bouboulina again and began to cry. I can't
stay away from her any longer, boss. . . . I shall go off my head.
. . . Look, I've even written poetry. I couldn't sleep two nights ago
and I began writing a little poem for her. . . . I hope you'll read it
to her so that she'll see how I'm suffering. . . .

> "Ah! if only on some footpath you and I could meet,
> And it were wide enough to hold our rue!
> Let me be ground to crumbs or pie-meat,
> My shattered bones would still have strength to run to you!"

Dame Hortense, her eyes languid and half-closed, was listening
happily, all attention. She even took the little ribbon from her neck,
where it was nearly strangling her, and set her wrinkles free for a
moment. She was silent and smiling. Happy and contented, her
mind seemed to be drifting far away.

The month of March, fresh grass, little red, yellow and purple flowers, limpid water where groups of white and black swans were mating as they sang. The females white, the males black and with half-open, crimson beaks. Great blue Moray eels rose gleaming from the water and twined themselves round big yellow serpents. Dame Hortense was fourteen again, dancing on oriental carpets in Alexandria, Beirut, Smyrna, Constantinople, then off Crete on the polished decks of ships. . . . She could not remember very clearly now. It was becoming confused, her breast was heaving, the shores were splitting. And suddenly, while she was dancing, the sea was covered with vessels with golden prows. On their decks, multicolored tents and silken oriflames. A whole procession of pashas came from the tents with golden tassels upright on their fezes, wealthy old beys on pilgrimages with hands full of rich offerings, and their melancholy, beardless sons. Admirals came, too, with their shining three-cornered hats, and sailors with their dazzling white collars and broad, flapping trousers. Young Cretans followed, in their billowing breeches of light-blue cloth, yellow boots, and black kerchiefs knotted over their hair. A good last came Zorba, huge, grown lean from love-making, with a massive engagement ring on his finger, a crown of orange-blossom on his greying hair. . . .

From the ships came all the men she had known in her adventurous lifetime, not one was missing, not even the old gap-toothed and hunchbacked boatman who had taken her out on the water one evening at Constantinople. Night had fallen and no one could see them. They all came out, all of them, and in the background, mating away, oho! the Morays, the Serpents, the Swans!

The men came and joined her; they formed clusters, like amorous snakes in the spring, who rise hissing in a sheaf. And in the center, all white and naked, and glistening with sweat, lips parted to show her little pointed teeth, rigid, insatiable, her breasts erect, hissed a Dame Hortense of fourteen, twenty, thirty, forty, sixty summers.

Nothing was lost, no lover had died! In her wilted breast they were all resuscitated, in full parade dress. As if Dame Hortense were a noble three-masted frigate and all her lovers—she had seen forty-five working years—were boarding her, climbing into the holds, onto the gunwale, into the rigging, while she sailed along, much-battered and much-caulked, towards the last great haven she had longed for so ardently: marriage. And Zorba assumed a thousand faces: Turkish, European, Armenian, Arab, Greek, and, as she hugged him, Dame Hortense hugged the entire, blessed and interminable procession. . . .

The old siren, all at once, realized that I had ceased reading; her vision suddenly stopped and she raised her heavy lids:

"Doesn't he say anything else?" she asked in a tone of reproach, licking her lips greedily.

"What more do you want, Madame Hortense? Don't you see? The whole letter talks about you and nothing else. Look, four sheets of it! And there's a heart here in the corner, too. Zorba says he drew it himself, with his own hand. Look, love has pierced it through, and underneath, look, two doves embracing, and on their wings, in small microscopic letters in red ink, two names intertwined: Hortense—Zorba!"

There were neither doves nor names, but the old siren's small eyes had filled with tears and could see anything they wished.

"Nothing else? Nothing else?" she asked again, still not satisfied.

Wings, the barber's soapy water, the little doves—that was all very well, a lot of fine words all that, nothing but air. Her practical woman's mind wanted something else, something more tangible, solid. How many times in her life had she heard this sort of nonsense! And what good had it done her? After years of hard work, she had been left all alone, high and dry.

"Nothing else?" she murmured again reproachfully. "Nothing else?"

She looked at me with eyes like those of a hind at bay. I took pity on her.

"He says something else very, very important, Madame Hortense," I said. "That's why I kept it till the end."

"What is it. . . . ?" she said with a sigh.

"He writes that, as soon as he gets back, he'll go on his knees to implore you, with tears in his eyes, to marry him. He can't wait any longer. He wants to make you, he says, his own little wife, Madame Hortense Zorba, so that you need never be separated again."

This time the tears really began to flow. This was the supreme joy, the ardently desired haven; this was what she had hitherto regretted not having in her life! Tranquillity and lying in an honest bed, nothing more!

She covered her eyes with her hands.

"All right," she said, with the condescension of a great lady, "I accept. But please write to him; say that here in the village there are no orange-blossom wreaths. He'll have to bring them from Candia. He must bring two white candles as well, with pink ribbons and some good sugared almonds. Then he must buy me a wedding dress, a white one, and silk stockings and satin court shoes. We've got sheets, tell him, so he needn't bring any. We've also got a bed."

She arranged her list of orders, already making an errand boy of her husband. She stood up. She had suddenly taken on the look of a dignified married woman.

"I've something to ask you," she said. "Something serious." Then she waited, moved.

"Go on, Madame Hortense, I'm at your service."

"Zorba and I are very fond of you. You are very kind, and you'll not disgrace us. Would you care to be our witness?"

I shuddered. Formerly, at my parents' house, we had had an old serving-woman named Diamandoula, who was over sixty, an old maid with a moustache, half-crazed by virginity, nervous, shrivelled up and flat-chested. She fell in love with Mitso, the local grocer's boy, a dirty, well-fed and beardless young peasant lad.

"When is it you be going to marry me?" she used to ask him every Sunday. "Marry me now! How can you wait so long? I can't bear it!"

"I can't either!" said the cunning grocer's boy, who was getting round her for her custom. "I can't hold out any longer, Diamandoula; but all the same, we can't get married till I've a moustache as well as you. . . ."

The years went past like that, and old Diamandoula waited. Her nerves became calmer, she had fewer headaches, her bitter lips that had never been kissed learned to smile. She washed the clothes more carefully now, broke fewer dishes, and never burned the food.

"Will you come and be our witness, young master?" she asked me one evening on the sly.

"Certainly I will, Diamandoula," I answered, a lump forming in my throat, out of pity for her.

The very suggestion had wrung my heart; that is why I shuddered when I heard Dame Hortense ask the same thing.

"Certainly I would," I replied. "It will be an honor, Madame Hortense."

She rose, patted the little ringlets that hung from beneath her little hat and licked her lips.

"Good night," she said. "Good night, and may he soon come back to us!"

I watched her waddling away, swaying her old body with all the affected airs of a young girl. Joy gave her wings, and her twisted old court shoes made deep impressions in the sand.

She had hardly rounded the headland than shrill cries and wailing came from along the shore.

I leaped up and ran in the direction from which the noise was coming. On the opposite headland women were howling as though they were singing a funeral dirge. I climbed a rock and looked. Men and women were running up from the village; behind them dogs were barking. Two or three were on horseback and going on ahead. A thick cloud of dust was rising from the ground.

"There's been an accident," I thought, and ran round the bay.

The hubbub was growing more intense. Two or three spring clouds stood still in the light of the setting sun. The Fig Tree of Our Young Lady was covered with fresh green leaves.

Suddenly Dame Hortense staggered up to me. She was running back again, dishevelled, out of breath, and one of her shoes had come off. She was holding it in her hand and was crying as she ran.

"My God . . . my God. . . ." she sobbed as she saw me. She stumbled and nearly fell.

I caught her.

"What are you crying for? What's happened?" And I helped her put on her worn shoe.

"I'm frightened. . . . I'm frightened. . . ."

"Of what?"

"Of death."

She had scented with terror the smell of death in the air.

I took her limp arm to lead her to the place, but her ageing body resisted and trembled.

"I don't want to. . . . I don't want to. . . ." she cried.

The poor wretch was terrified of going close to a place where death had appeared. Charon must not see her and remember her. . . . Like all old people our poor siren tried to hide herself by taking on the green color of grass, or by taking on an earthly color, so that Charon could not distinguish her from earth or grass. She had tucked her head into her fat, rounded shoulders, and was trembling.

She dragged herself to an olive tree, spread out her patched coat and sank to the ground.

"Put this over me, will you? Put this over me and you go and have a look."

"Are you feeling cold?"

"I am. Cover me up."

I covered her up as well as I could, so that she was indistinguishable from the earth, then I went off.

I came up to the headland and now clearly heard the songs of lamentation. Mimiko came running past me.

"What is it, Mimiko?" I asked.

"He's drowned himself! Drowned himself!" he shouted without stopping.

"Who?"

"Pavli, Mavrandoni's son."

"Why?"

"The widow. . . ."

The word hung in the evening air and conjured up the dangerous, supple body of that woman.

I reached the rocks and there found the whole village assembled. The men were silent, bare-headed; the women, with their kerchiefs thrown back over their shoulders, were tearing their hair and uttering piercing cries. A swollen, livid corpse lay on the pebbled beach. Old Mavrandoni was standing motionless over it, gazing at it. With his right hand he was leaning on his staff. With his left he was holding his curly grey beard.

"A curse on you, widow!" a shrill voice said suddenly. "God shall make you pay for this!"

A woman leaped up and turned to the men.

"Isn't there a single man in the village to throw her across his knees and cut her throat like a sheep? Bah! you cowards!"

And she spat at the men, who looked at her without a word.

Kondomanolio, the café proprietor, answered her:

"Don't humiliate us, crazy Katerina," he shouted, "don't humiliate us, there are still some men, some *Palikaria*, in our village, you'll see!"

I could not contain myself.

"Shame on you all!" I cried. "In what way is that woman responsible? It was fated. Don't you fear God?"

But no one replied.

Manolakas, the drowned man's cousin, bent his huge body, lifted the corpse in his arms and took the first path back to the village.

The women were screaming, scratching their faces and tearing their hair. When they saw the body was being carried away, they ran to clasp it. But old Mavrandoni, brandishing his staff, drove them off and took the head of the procession, followed by the women singing dirges. Lastly, in silence, came the men.

They disappeared into the twilight. You could hear the peaceful breathing of the sea once more. I looked around me. I was alone.

"I'll go back home," I said. "Another day, O God, which has had its measure of sorrow!"

Deep in thought, I followed the pathway. I admired these people, so closely and warmly involved in human sufferings: Dame Hortense, Zorba, the widow, and the pale Pavli who had so bravely thrown himself in the sea to drown his sorrow, and Deli-Katerina shouting for them to cut the widow's throat like a sheep, and Mavrandoni refusing to weep or even to speak in front of the others. I alone was impotent and rational, my blood did not boil, nor did I love or hate with passion. I still wanted to put things right, in cowardly fashion, by laying everything at destiny's door.

In the twilight I could just see uncle Anagnosti still sitting there on a stone. He had propped his chin on his long stick and was gazing at the sea.

I called to him, but he did not hear. I went up to him; he saw me and shook his head.

"Poor humanity!" he murmured. "The waste of a young life! The poor boy couldn't bear his sorrow, so he threw himself in the sea and was drowned. Now he's saved."

"Saved?"

"Saved, my son, yes, saved. What could he have done with his life? If he'd married the widow, there would very soon have been quarrels, perhaps even dishonor. She's just like a brood mare, that shameless woman! As soon as she sees a man, she starts to whinny. And if he hadn't married her, it would have been the torment of his life, because the idea would have been fixed in his head that he'd missed a great happiness! A yawning abyss in front, a precipice behind!"

"Don't talk like that, uncle Anagnosti; you'd bring despair to anyone who heard you!"

"Come on, don't be so frightened. No one can hear me, except you. And even if they could, would they believe me? Look, has there ever been a luckier man than me? I've had fields, vineyards, olive groves, and a two-storied house. I've been rich and a village elder. I lighted on a good, docile woman who gave me only sons. I've never seen her raise her eyes to me in defiance, and all my children are good fathers. I've nothing to complain about. I've had grandchildren, too. What more could I want? My roots go deep. And yet if I had to start my life all over again I'd put a stone round my neck, like Pavli, and throw myself in the sea. Life is hard, my God it is; even the luckiest life is hard, a curse on it!"

"But what is there you lack, uncle Anagnosti? What are you complaining of?"

"I lack nothing, I tell you! But you go and question men's hearts!"

He was silent a moment, and looked again at the darkening sea.

"Well, Pavli, you did the right thing!" he cried, waving his stick. "Let the women scream; they're women and have no brains. You're saved now, Pavli—your father knows it and that's why he didn't make a sound!"

He scanned the sky and the mountains which were already growing indistinct.

"Here's the night," he said. "Better get back."

He stopped all of a sudden, seeming to regret the words he had let drop, as if he had betrayed a great secret and now wanted to recover it.

He placed his shrivelled hand on my shoulder.

"You're young," he said, smiling at me; "don't listen to the old. If the world did heed them, it would rush headlong to its destruction. If a widow crosses your path, get hold of her! Get married, have children, don't hesitate! Troubles were made for young men!"

I reached my beach, lit the fire and made my evening tea. I was tired and hungry, and I ate ravenously, giving myself up entirely to animal pleasure.

Suddenly Mimiko pushed his little flattened head through the window, looked at me crouching by the fire and eating. He smiled cunningly.

"What have you come for, Mimiko?"

"I've brought you something, boss . . . from the widow. . . . A basket of oranges. She says they're the last from her garden. . . ."

"From the widow?" I said with a start. "Why did she send me them?"

"Because of the good word you put in for her to the villagers this afternoon, so she says."

"What good word?"

"How do I know? I'm just telling you what she said, that's all!"

He emptied the oranges on the bed. The whole hut became redolent with their smell.

"Tell her I thank her very much for her present, and I advise her to be careful. She must watch her step and not show herself in the village on any account, do you hear? She must stay indoors for a time, until this unhappy business has been forgotten. Do you understand, Mimiko?"

"Is that all, boss?"

"That's all. You can go now."

Mimiko winked at me.

"Is that all?"

"Get away!"

He went. I peeled one of the juicy oranges; it was as sweet as honey. I lay down, fell asleep, and the whole night through I wandered in orange groves. A warm wind was blowing; I had bared my chest to the wind and had a sprig of sweet basil behind my ear. I was a young peasant of twenty, and I roamed about the orange grove whistling and waiting. For whom was I waiting?—I do not know. But my heart was ready to burst for joy. I twirled up my moustache and listened, the whole night through, to the sea sighing like a woman behind the orange trees.

◇ 15 ◇

THAT DAY there was a strong south wind, which came burning from the sands of Africa across the Mediterranean. Clouds of fine sand twisted and turned in the air and got into throat and lungs. Teeth were gritty and eyes inflamed; doors and windows had to be locked tight if one wanted to make sure of eating a single piece of bread that was not sprinkled with sand.

It was close. During those oppressive days when the sap was rising I was myself a prey to the prevailing springtime unrest. A feeling of lassitude, an emotional tension in the breast, a tingling sensation throughout my body, a desire—or was it memory—of a vast and simple happiness.

I took the pebbly mountain track. I had a sudden impulse to visit the small Minoan city which had risen from the ground after three or four thousand years and was warming itself once more under its beloved Cretan sun. I thought that perhaps after three or four hours' walk fatigue would calm the unrest that spring had brought.

Bare grey stones, a luminous nakedness, the harsh and deserted mountain that I love. An owl, its round yellow eyes staring, blinded by the bright light, had perched on a stone. It was grave, beautiful, full of mystery. I was walking lightly, but its hearing was keen; it took fright, flew up silently among the stones and disappeared. There was a scent of thyme in the air. The first tender flowers of the yellow gorse were already showing amongst its thorns.

When I came in sight of the small ruined city I stood spell-bound. It must have been about noon, the sun's rays were falling perpendicularly and drenching the stones with light. In old ruined cities this is a dangerous time of day, for the air is filled with cries and the noise of spirits. If a branch cracks, if a lizard darts, if a cloud throws a shadow as it passes overhead, panic seizes you. Every inch of ground you tread is a grave, and you hear the dead groaning.

Gradually my eyes grew accustomed to the bright light. I could now see traces of the hand of man in the ruins: two broad roads paved with shining stones. To the left and right of them, narrow tortuous alleys. In the center the circular agora, or public meeting place, and next to it, with a totally democratic condescension, had been placed the king's palace with its double columns, large stone stairways and numerous outbuildings.

In the heart of the city the stones were most heavily trodden by the foot of man and that was where the inner shrine must have been: the Great Goddess was there, with her huge breasts, set wide apart, and her arms wreathed in snakes.

Everywhere were small shops, oil presses, forges, and the workshops of joiners and potters. A cleverly designed anthill, well-built in a sheltered position, and whence the ants had disappeared thousands of years ago. In one place a craftsman had been carving a jar out of veined stone but had not had the time to finish it; the chisel had fallen from his hand, to be discovered thousands of years later, lying next to the unfinished work of art.

The eternal, vain, stupid questions: why? what for? come to poison your heart. The unfinished jar, where the artist's happy and confident inspiration had suddenly been defeated, fills you with bitterness.

All at once a little shepherd, tanned by the sun and wearing a fringed handkerchief round his curly hair, stood up on a stone beside the crumbling palace and showed his black knees.

"You there, brother!" he shouted.

I wanted to be alone, and made believe I had not heard. But the little shepherd began to laugh mockingly.

"Ha! Playing deaf, eh? Any cigarettes? Give me one! In this empty hole I get so fed up with life."

He dragged out the last words and there was such misery in them that I felt sorry for him.

I had no cigarettes, so I offered him money. But the little shepherd was annoyed:

"To hell with money!" he shouted. "What would I do with it? I tell you I'm fed up with everything. I want a cigarette!"

"I haven't any," I said in despair. "I haven't any."

"No cigarettes?" He was beside himself and struck the ground with his crook. "No cigarettes! Well, what have you got in your pockets? They're bulging with something."

"A book, a handkerchief, paper, a pencil, a penknife," I answered, pulling out one by one the things in my pocket. "Would you like this penknife?"

"I've got one. I've got everything I want: bread, cheese, olives, my knife, leather for my boots and an awl, and water in my bottle, everything . . . except a cigarette! And it's as though I'd got nothing at all! And what might you be after in the ruins?"

"I'm studying antiquity."

"What good do you get out of that?"

"None."

"None. Nor do I. This is all dead, and we're alive. You'd do better to go, quick. God be with you!"

"I'm going," I said obediently.

I went back along the little track with some anxiety in my mind.

I turned for a moment and could see the little shepherd who was so tired of his solitude still standing on his stone. His curly hair, escaping from under his black handkerchief, was waving in the south wind. The light streamed over him from head to foot. I felt I was looking at a bronze statue of a youth. He had placed his crook across his shoulders and was whistling.

I took another track and went down towards the coast. Now and then, warm breezes laden with perfume reached me from nearby gardens. The earth had a rich smell, the sea was rippling with laughter, the sky was blue and gleaming like steel.

Winter shrivels up the mind and body of man, but then there comes the warmth which swells the breast. As I walked I suddenly heard loud trumpetings in the air. I raised my eyes and saw a marvellous spectacle which had always moved me deeply ever since my childhood: cranes deploying across the sky in battle order, returning from wintering in a warmer country, and, as legend has it, carrying swallows on their wings and in the deep hollows of their bony bodies.

The unfailing rhythm of the seasons, the ever-turning wheel of life, the four facets of the earth which are lit in turn by the sun, the passing of life—all these filled me once more with a feeling of oppression. Once more there sounded within me, together with the cranes' cry, the terrible warning that there is only one life for all men, that there is no other, and that all that can be enjoyed must be enjoyed here. In eternity no other chance will be given to us.

A mind hearing this pitiless warning—a warning which, at the same time, is so compassionate—would decide to conquer its weakness and meanness, its laziness and vain hopes and cling with all its power to every second which flies away forever.

Great examples come to your mind and you see clearly that you are a lost soul, your life is being frittered away on petty pleasures and pains and trifling talk. "Shame! Shame!" you cry, and bite your lips.

The cranes had crossed the sky and disappeared to the north, but in my head they continued to fly from one temple to another, uttering their hollow cries.

I came to the sea. I was walking rapidly along the edge of the water. How disquieting it is to walk alone by the sea! Each wave, each bird in the sky calls to you and reminds you of your duty. When walking with company you laugh and talk, and cannot hear what the waves and birds are saying. It may be, of course, that they are saying nothing. They watch you passing in a cloud of chatter and they stop calling.

I stretched out on the pebbles and closed my eyes. "What is the soul, then?" I wondered. "And what is this secret connection between the soul, and sea, clouds and perfumes? The soul itself appears to be sea, cloud and perfume. . . ."

I rose and started walking again, as if I had come to a decision. What decision? I did not know.

Suddenly I heard a voice behind me.

"Where are you going, sir, by the grace of God? To the convent?"

I turned round. A stocky, robust old man, with a handkerchief twisted round his white hair, was waving his hand and smiling at me. An old woman walked behind him, and behind her their daughter, a dark-skinned girl with fierce eyes, wearing a white scarf over her head.

"The convent?" asked the old man a second time.

And suddenly I realized that I had decided to go that way. For months I had wanted to go to the little convent built for the nuns near the sea, but I had never managed to make up my mind. My body had abruptly made the decision for me that afternoon.

"Yes," I answered. "I'm going to the convent to hear the chants to the Holy Virgin."

"May Her blessing be upon you."

He quickened his pace and caught me up.

"Are you what they call the Coal Company?"

"That's right."

"Well, may the Blessed Virgin send you good profits! You are doing a lot of good for the village, bringing a means of livelihood to many a poor father with a family to keep. May you be blessed!"

And a moment or two later the cunning old fellow, who must have known that we were not doing very well, added these words of consolation:

"And even if you get no profit out of it, my son, don't worry. You'll not be the loser. Your soul will go direct to paradise . . ."

"That's what I'm hoping, grandad."

"I never had any education, but one day at church I heard something Christ had said. It stuck in my head and I never forget it: 'Sell,' he said, 'everything you possess to obtain the Great Pearl.' And what is that Great Pearl? The salvation of your soul. You are well on the way to getting the Great Pearl, sir."

The Great Pearl! How many times it had gleamed in the darkness of my mind like a huge tear!

We began walking, the two men in front, the two women behind with clasped hands. From time to time we made a remark. Would the olive blossom last on the trees? Would it rain and swell the barley? We must both have been hungry because we constantly led the conversation round to food.

"What is your favorite dish, grandad?"

"All of them, my son. It's a great sin to say this is good and that is bad."

"Why? Can't we make a choice?"

"No, of course we can't."

"Why not?"

"Because there are people who are hungry."

I was silent, ashamed. My heart had never been able to reach that height of nobility and compassion.

The little convent bell rang out merrily and playfully, like a woman's laugh.

The old man made the sign of the cross.

"May the Martyred Virgin come to our help!" he murmured. "She has a knife wound in the neck and bleeds. In the time of the corsairs . . ."

And the old man began embroidering on the sufferings of the Virgin, as though it were the story of a real woman, a young persecuted refugee who had come in tears with her child from the East and had been stabbed by the unfaithful.

"Once a year real warm blood runs from her wound," the old man went on. "I remember a long time ago, on her anniversary—I hadn't yet grown a moustache—people had come down from all the villages in the hills to worship the Virgin. It was the fifteenth of August. We men slept outside, in the yard; the women were inside. And in my sleep I heard the Virgin cry out. I got up in a hurry, ran to her icon and put my hand on her throat. And what do you think I saw? My fingers were red with blood. . . ."

The old man crossed himself and looked round at the women.

"Come on, you women! We're nearly there!" he cried.

He lowered his voice.

"I wasn't married then. I prostrated myself to Her Holiness, and decided to leave this world of lies and be a monk. . . ."

He laughed.

"Why are you laughing, grandad?"

"Isn't it enough to make you laugh, my son? The very same day, during the festival, the devil, dressed up as a woman, stood before me. It was she!"

Without turning his head, he jerked his thumb backwards and

indicated the old woman behind him, who was following us in silence.

"She doesn't bear looking at now," he said; "the thought of touching her disgusts you. But in those days she was a regular flirt; she quivered with life like a fish. 'The long-lashed beauty,' they used to call her, and she well deserved the name, the little minx! But now . . . God rest my soul, where are her lashes now? Gone to blazes! Not a single one left!"

At that moment, just behind us, the old woman made a muffled growl like a churlish dog on a chain. But she did not say a word.

"There, that's the convent," said the old man.

At the edge of the sea, wedged between two great rocks, was the white, sparkling convent. In the middle the chapel dome, freshly whitewashed, small and round like a woman's breast. About the chapel were half a dozen cells with blue doors, three large cypress trees in the courtyard, and along the wall some sturdy prickly pears in flower.

We went faster. Melodious chanting floated down from the open door of the sanctuary, the salt air was perfumed with benjamin. The entrance door in the middle of the arch stood wide open and gave on to the clean, scented courtyard strewn with black and white pebbles. Along the walls, to the right and to the left, were rows of pots, with rosemary, marjoram and basil.

What serenity! What sweetness! The sun was going down now and the whitewashed walls were turning pink.

The little chapel, warm and rather dark inside, smelled of wax. Men and women were moving in clouds of incense, and five or six nuns, tightly wrapped in their long black dresses, were singing: "O, Almighty God . . ." in their sweet, high-pitched voices. They were constantly kneeling as they sang and the rustling of their dresses sounded like birds on the wing.

I had not heard hymns sung to the Virgin Mary for many years past. During the revolt of my early youth I had passed by every church with anger and contempt in my heart. As time went on I grew less violent. Now and again, in fact, I went to religious festivals—Christmas, the Vigils, the Resurrection—and I was happy to see the child in me come to life again. The mystic fervor of my early years had degenerated into an aesthetic pleasure. Savages believe that when a musical instrument is no longer used for religious rites it loses its divine power and begins to give out harmonious sounds. Religion, in the same way, had become degraded in me: it had become art.

I went into a corner, leaned on the gleaming stall that the hands of the faithful had polished as smooth as ivory, and listened in enchantment as the Byzantine hymns came from the distant past: "Hail! heights inaccessible to the human mind! Hail! depths impenetrable even to the eyes of angels! Hail! immaculate bride, O never-fading Rose . . ."

The nuns once more dropped on their knees with head bowed and their dresses rustled like wings.

Minutes went by—angels with benjamin-scented wings, bearing closed lilies in their hands and singing the beauties of Mary. The sun went down, leaving us in a downy blue twilight. I do not remember how we came to be in the courtyard, but I was alone there with the old Mother Superior and two young nuns, beneath the largest of the cypress trees. A young novice came out to offer me a spoonful of jam, fresh water and coffee, and a peaceful conversation began.

We talked of the miracles wrought by the Virgin Mary, of lignite, of the hens beginning to lay now that it was spring, of sister Eudoxia who was epileptic and continually falling down on the floor of the chapel and quivering like a fish, foaming at the mouth and tearing her clothes.

"She is thirty-five," added the Mother Superior with a sigh. "An unhappy age—very difficult! May the Holy Martyred Virgin come to her aid and cure her! In ten or fifteen years she will be cured."

"Ten or fifteen years," I murmured, aghast.

"What are ten or fifteen years?" asked the Mother Superior severely. "Think of eternity!"

I made no answer. I knew that eternity is each minute that passes. I kissed the Mother Superior's hand—a plump, white hand, smelling of incense—and departed.

Night had fallen. Two or three crows were hurrying back to their nests; owls were coming out of the hollow trees to hunt. Snails, caterpillars, worms, field-mice were coming out of the earth to be eaten by the owls.

The mysterious snake that devours its own tail enclosed me in its circle: the earth brings to life and devours her own children, then bears more and devours them in their turn.

I looked about me. It was quite dark. The last of the villagers had gone, no one could see me, I was absolutely alone. I bared my feet and dipped them in the sea. I rolled on the sand. I felt an urge to touch the stones, the water, and the air with my bare body. The Mother Superior had exasperated me with her "eternity," and I felt the word fall about me, like a lasso catching a wild horse. I made a leap to try to escape. I felt a desire to press my naked body against the earth and the sea, to feel with certainty that these beloved ephemeral things really existed.

"You exist, and you alone!" I cried in my innermost self. "O Earth! I am your last-born, I am sucking at your breast and will not let go. You do not let me live for more than one minute, but that minute turns into a breast and I suck."

I shuddered as if I felt I was running the risk of being hurled in to that anthropophagous word "eternity." I remembered how formerly—when? only a year ago—I had eagerly pondered it with closed eyes and arms apart, wanting to throw myself into it.

When I was in the first form at the state school there was a story in the reading book we used for the second half of the alphabet:

A little child had fallen into a well, said the story. There it found a marvellous city, flower gardens, a lake of pure honey, a mountain of rice pudding and multi-colored toys. As I spelled it out, each syllable seemed to take me further into that magic city. Once, at midday, when I had come home from school, I ran into the garden, rushed to the rim of the well beneath the vine arbor and stood fascinated, staring at the smooth black surface of the water. I soon thought I could see the marvellous city, houses and streets, the children and the vine arbor loaded with grapes. I could hold out no longer; I hung my head down, held out my arms and kicked against the ground to push myself over the edge. But at that moment my mother noticed me. She screamed, rushed out and caught me by my waistband, just in time. . . .

As a child, then, I had almost fallen into the well. When grown up, I nearly fell into the word "eternity," and into quite a number of other words too—"love," "hope," "country," "God." As each word was conquered and left behind, I had the feeling that I had escaped a danger and made some progress. But no, I was only changing words and calling it deliverance. And there I had been, for the last two years, hanging over the edge of the word "Buddha."

But I now feel sure—Zorba be praised—that Buddha will be the last well of all, the last word precipice, and then I shall be delivered forever. Forever? That is what we say each time.

I jumped up. I was happy from head to foot. I undressed and plunged into the sea; the joyful waves were frolicking and I frolicked with them. Tired at last, I came out of the water, let the night wind dry me, and set out again with long easy strides, feeling I had escaped a great danger and that I had a still tighter grip on the Great Mother's breast.

◊ 16 ◊

As soon as I came within sight of the lignite beach I stopped abruptly: there was a light in the hut.

"Zorba must be back!" I thought happily.

I felt like running, but restrained myself. I must hide my joy, I thought. I must look annoyed and first give him a good talking-to. I sent him there on urgent business, and he'd just gone through my money, lived with some cabaret tart, and now comes back twelve days late. I must look as if I'm in a furious temper . . . I must!

I walked slower to give me time to work up a temper. I tried hard to be angry—frowned and clenched my fists, did everything an angry man usually does—but could not manage it. On the contrary, the nearer I came the happier I grew.

I crept up to the hut and looked through the small lighted window. Zorba was on his knees by the tiny stove which he had lit and was making coffee.

My heart melted and I shouted: "Zorba!"

In a trice the door swung open and Zorba, barefoot, rushed out. He craned his neck, peering in the dark, discovered me, opened his arms to embrace me, then stopped and let them fall to his sides.

"Glad to see you again, boss," he said hesitantly, standing long-faced and motionless before me.

I tried to raise my voice angrily:

176

"Glad to see you've taken the trouble to come back," I mocked. "Don't come any nearer—you reek of toilet soap."

"Ah, if only you knew what a scrubbing I've given myself, boss," he said. "Have I cleaned myself up! I scraped my blasted skin to bits before seeing you, boss! I've sandstoned myself for an hour. But this hellish smell . . . Anyway, what of it? It'll pass off sooner or later. It isn't the first time—it's bound to go."

"Let's get inside," I said, nearly bursting with laughter.

We went in. The hut smelled of perfume, powder, soap and women.

"What in God's name is all that, may I ask?" I said, pointing to a case filled with handbags, bars of toilet soap, stockings, a small red parasol and two minute bottles of scent.

"Presents . . ." muttered Zorba, hanging his head.

"Presents?" I said, trying to sound furious. "Presents?"

"Presents, boss . . . for little Bouboulina. Don't be angry, boss. Easter's coming soon, and she's a human being too, you know."

I managed to restrain my laughter once again.

"You haven't brought her the most important thing," I said.

"What?"

"The marriage wreaths, of course."

"What? What d'you mean? I don't understand."

I then told him the way I had pulled the lovesick siren's leg.

Zorba scratched his head a second, reflected and then said:

"You shouldn't do things like that, boss, if you don't mind my saying so. That sort of joke, you know, is . . . women are weak, delicate creatures—how many times have I got to tell you that? Like porcelain vases, they are, and you have to handle them very carefully, boss."

I felt ashamed. I had regretted it, too, but it was too late. I changed the subject.

"And the cable?" I asked. "And the tools?"

"I've brought everything; don't get worked up! 'You can't have your cake and eat it!' as they say! The cable railway, Lola, Bouboulina—everything's well in hand."

He took the *briki** off the flame, filled my cup, gave me some

* A small pyramidal vessel for making coffee.

jumbals * with sesame which he had brought and honey *halva*†
which he knew was my favorite sweet.

"I've brought you a present of a large box of *halva!*" he said
fondly. "I didn't forget you, you see."

"Look, I've brought a little bag of peanuts for the parrot. I've
forgotten no one. You know, my brain's overweight." Zorba was
sipping his coffee, smoking and watching me. His eyes fascinated
me like those of a serpent.

"Have you solved the problem which was tormenting you, you
old rogue?" I asked him, my voice gentler now.

"What problem, boss?"

"If women are human beings or not?"

"Oh! That's settled!" answered Zorba, waving his hand. "A
woman's human, too, a human like us—only worse! The minute she
sees your purse she loses her head. She clings to you, gives up her
freedom and is glad to give it up because, at the back of her mind,
the purse is glittering. But she soon . . . Ah, to hell with all that,
boss!"

He stood up and threw his cigarette out of the window.

"Now, man to man," he went on. "Holy Week's coming, we've
got the cable, it's high time we went up to the monastery and got
those fat pigs to sign the documents for that forest land . . . before
they see the line and become excited—see what I mean? Time's
going by, boss, and we'll never get anywhere being so lackadaisical;
we must get down to it; we've got to start raking in . . . we must
start loading the ships to make up for what we've spent. . . . That
trip to Candia cost a packet. You see, the devil . . ."

He stopped. I was sorry for him. He was just like a child who has
done something silly and, not knowing how he can put things right
again, just trembles all over.

"Shame on you!" I said to myself. "How can you let a soul like
that tremble with fright? Where will you ever find another Zorba?
Come on, sponge it all out!"

"Zorba!" I cried. "Leave the devil alone; we have no use for him!
What's done is done . . . and forgotten! Take down your *santuri!*"

* Pastries or sweets made of fruit paste, in a ring.
† A sweet containing sesame oil and sugar.

C. W.

He opened his arms again as if he wanted to embrace me. But he closed them slowly, still hesitant.

In one bound he was at the wall. He stood up on his toes and took down the *santuri*. As he came back into the light of the lamp I saw his hair: it was as black as pitch.

"You old dog," I shouted, "what on earth have you done to your hair? Where did you get that?"

Zorba began to laugh.

"I've dyed it, boss. Don't get upset . . . I dyed it because I had no luck with it. . . ."

"What for?"

"Vanity, by God! One day I was out walking with Lola, holding her arm. Not even holding . . . look, like that, just the end of my fingers! And some bloody little urchin, no bigger than this hand, started shouting after us: 'I say, old 'un!' the whoreson kid shouted. 'You there! Where are you taking her, baby-snatcher?'

"Lola was ashamed, you can imagine, and so was I. So I went the same night to the barber's and had my wig dyed black."

I began to laugh. Zorba watched me gravely.

"Does that sound comic to you, boss? Well, just wait and see what a strange animal man is, though! From the day I had it done, I've been another man altogether. You'd think I had black hair for good; I've begun to believe it myself—a man easily forgets what doesn't suit him, you know—and I swear I've got stronger. Lola's noticed it, too. D'you remember that pain I used to have in my back here? Well, it's gone! Haven't had it since! You don't believe me, of course, your books don't tell you things like that."

He laughed ironically, then repented.

"If I may say so, boss . . . the only book I've ever read in my life is *Sinbad the Sailor,* and for all the good that did me . . ."

He undid the *santuri* slowly and affectionately.

"Come outside," he said. "The *santuri* isn't at home between four walls. It's wild and needs the open spaces."

We went out. The stars sparkled. The Milky Way flowed from one side of the sky to the other. The sea was frothing. We sat down on the pebbles and the waves licked our feet.

"When you're broke, you have to have a good time," said Zorba. "What, us give up? Come here, *santuri!*"

"A Macedonian song of your own country, Zorba," I said.

"A Cretan song of your country!" said Zorba. "I'll sing you something I was taught at Candia; it changed my life."

He reflected for a moment.

"No, it hasn't changed really," he said, "only now I know I was right."

He placed his big fingers on the *santuri* and craned his neck. He sang in a wild, harsh, dolorous voice:

> *When you've made up your mind, no use lagging behind, go ahead and no relenting*
> *Let your youth have free reign, it won't come again, so be bold and no repenting.*

Our cares were scattered, petty troubles vanished, the soul reached its peak. Lola, lignite, the line, "eternity," big and small worries, all became blue smoke that faded into the air, and there remained only a bird of steel, the human soul which sang.

"I make you a present of everything, Zorba!" I cried, when the proud song was done. "All you've done—the woman, your dyed hair, the money you spent—all of it's yours! Just go on singing!"

He craned out his scraggy neck once more:

> *Courage! In God's name! Venture, come what may!*
> *If you don't lose, you're bound to win the day!*

A number of workmen sleeping near the mine heard the songs; they got up, crept down to us and squatted round. They listened to their favorite songs and felt their legs tingling. At last, unable to restrain themselves longer, they loomed out of the darkness, half-naked, their hair ruffled and their breeches baggy. They made a circle round Zorba and the *santuri* and began dancing on the pebbled shore.

Thrilled, I watched them in silence.

This is, I thought, the real vein I have been looking for! I want no other.

The next day, before dawn, the galleries of the mine were echoing with Zorba's cries and the sounds of the picks. The men were working frenziedly. Zorba alone could lead them on like that. With him work became wine, women and song, and the men were intoxicated. The earth came to life in his hands, the stones, coal, wood and workers adopted his rhythm, a sort of war was declared in the galleries in the white light of the acetylene lamps and Zorba was in the forefront, fighting hand to hand. He gave a name to each gallery and seam, and a face to all invisible forces, and after that it became difficult for them to escape him.

"When I know that that is the 'Canavaro' gallery," he used to say about the first gallery he had christened, "where the hell do you think it can hide? I know its name, it wouldn't have the cheek to do the dirty on me. No more than 'Mother Superior,' or 'Knock-knees,' or 'The Piddler.' I know them all, I tell you, each one by its own name."

That day I slipped into the gallery without his noticing me.

"Come on! Put some life into it!" he was shouting to the workmen, as he always did when he was in good form. "Come on! We'll eat up the whole mountain, yet! We're men, aren't we? Creatures to be reckoned with! God himself must tremble when he sees us! You Cretans and me, a Macedonian, we'll have this mountain; it takes more than a mountain to beat us! We beat the Turks, didn't we? So why should a little mountain like this put us off? Come on, then!"

Someone ran up to Zorba. In the acetylene light I could just make out Mimiko's thin face.

"Zorba," he said in his mumbling voice, "Zorba . . ."

Zorba turned round, and saw at a glance what it was about. He lifted his big hand:

"Beat it!" he shouted. "Clear out!"

"I've come for her . . ." faltered the simpleton.

"Clear out, I tell you! We've got work to do!"

Mimiko made off as fast as his legs would carry him. Zorba spat in exasperation.

"The day's for working," he said. "Daytime is a man. The night-time's for enjoying yourself. Night is a woman. You mustn't mix them up!"

I came up at that moment.

"It's twelve o'clock," I said. "Time you stopped work and had a meal."

Zorba turned round, saw me and scowled.

"Don't wait for us, boss, d'you mind. You go and have your lunch. We've lost twelve days, remember, and we've got to catch up. I hope you eat well."

I left the gallery and walked down towards the sea. I opened the book I was carrying. I was hungry, but I forgot my hunger. Meditation is also a mine, I thought, so go ahead! And I plunged into the great galleries of the mind.

A disturbing book: it described the snow-covered mountains of Tibet, the mysterious monasteries, the silent monks in their saffron robes who concentrate their will and oblige the ether to take what shape they desire.

High mountain tops, the air full of spirits. The vain murmur of human life never reaches so high. The great ascetic takes his pupils, boys of sixteen to eighteen, and leads them at midnight up to an icy lake in the mountain. They undress, break the ice, plunge their clothes into the freezing water, put them on again and leave them to dry on their backs. Then they plunge them in afresh, and leave them to dry once more on their bodies. They do this seven times in succession. Then they return to the monastery for morning service.

They climb a mountain peak, fifteen to eighteen thousand feet high. They sit down quietly, breathe deeply and regularly. They are naked to the waist but feel no cold. They hold a goblet of icy water in their hands, look at it, concentrate with all their power on it, and the water boils. Then they make their tea.

The great ascetic collects his students round him and says:

"Woe to him who has not within himself the source of happiness!

"Woe to him who wants to please others!

"Woe to him who does not feel that this life and the next are but one!"

Night had fallen and I could not see to read. I closed the book and looked at the sea. I must free myself of all these phantoms, I thought, Buddhas, Gods, Motherlands, Ideas. . . . Woe to him who cannot free himself from Buddhas, Gods, Motherlands and Ideas.

The sea had suddenly turned black. The young moon was rapidly setting. In the gardens in the distance, dogs were howling sadly, and the whole ravine howled back.

Zorba appeared, covered with dirt; his shirt was hanging in shreds.

He crouched by me.

"It went very well today," he said happily; "plenty of good work done."

I heard Zorba's words without grasping their meaning. My mind was still far away on distant and dangerous slopes.

"What are you thinking of, boss?" he asked me. "Is your mind out at sea?"

I brought my mind back, looked round at Zorba and shook my head.

"Zorba," I said, "you think you're a wonderful Sinbad the Sailor, and you talk big because you've knocked about the world a bit. But you've seen nothing, nothing at all. Not a thing, you poor fool! Nor have I, mind you. The world's much vaster than we think. We travel, crossing whole countries and seas and yet we've never pushed our noses past the doorstep of our own home."

Zorba pursed his lips and said nothing. He just grunted like a faithful dog when he is hit.

"There are mountains in the world," I said, "which are huge, immense and dotted all over with monasteries. And in those monasteries live monks in saffron robes. They stay seated, with crossed legs, for one, two, six months at a time, thinking of one thing and one thing only. One thing, do you hear? Not two—one! They don't think of women and lignite or books and lignite, as we do; they concentrate their minds on one and the same thing, and they achieve miracles. You have seen what happens when you hold a glass out to the sun and concentrate all the rays onto one spot, Zorba? That spot soon catches fire, doesn't it? Why? Because the sun's power has not been dispersed but concentrated on that one spot. It is the same with men's minds. You do miracles, if you concentrate your mind on one thing and only one. Do you understand, Zorba?"

Zorba was breathing heavily. For a moment he shook himself as though he wanted to run away, but he controlled himself.

"Go on," he grunted, in a strangled voice.

Then he straightway leaped up.

"Shut up! Shut up!" he shouted. "Why are you saying this to me, boss? Why are you poisoning my mind? I was all right here, why are you upsetting me? I was hungry, and God and the devil (I'm damned if I can see the difference) threw me a bone and I was licking it. I was wagging my tail and shouting: 'Thank you! Thank you!' And now . . ."

He stamped his foot, turned his back, made a move as if he were going over to the hut, but he was still boiling inside. He stopped.

"Pff! A fine bone it was he threw me, that god-devil!" he roared. "A dirty old cabaret tart! An old tub that isn't even seaworthy!"

He seized a handful of pebbles and threw them into the sea.

"But who is he? Who is it who throws these bones to us? Eh?"

He waited a little, then when he felt no reply was coming he became excited.

"Can't you say anything, boss?" he cried. "If you know, tell me, so that I know his name. Then, don't you worry, I'll look after him! But if it's just on the off-chance, like that, which way must I go? I'll come to grief."

"I'm hungry," I said. "Go and get some food. Let's eat first!"

"Can't we last an evening without eating, boss? One of my uncles was a monk, and weekdays he took nothing but salt and water. On Sundays and feast days he added a bit of bran. He lived to be a hundred and twenty."

"He lived to be a hundred and twenty, Zorba, because he had faith. He had found his God and he had no worries. But we have no God to nourish us, Zorba, so light the fire, will you, and we'll cook those chads. Make a thick, hot soup with plenty of onions and pepper, the sort we like. Then we'll see."

"See what?" asked Zorba in a rage. "As soon as our bellies are full we shall forget all that!"

"Exactly! That's what food's really for, Zorba. Now then, off you go and make a good fish soup so that our heads don't burst!"

But Zorba didn't budge. He stayed where he was, motionless, looking at me.

"Listen, boss, I want to tell you something. I know what you're up to. Just now when you were talking to me I suddenly had an inkling; I saw it all in a flash."

"What am I up to, Zorba?" I asked, intrigued.

"You want to build a monastery. That's it! Instead of monks you'd stick a few quill drivers like your honored self inside and they'd pass the time scribbling day and night. Then, like the saints in the old pictures, printed ribbons would come rolling out of your mouths. I've guessed right, haven't I?"

I hung my head, saddened. Old dreams of my youth, huge wings that have lost their feathers, naïve, noble, generous impulses. . . . Build an intellectual community and bury ourselves there; a dozen friends—musicians, poets, painters. . . . Work all day, meet only at night, eat, sing, read together, discuss the great problems of humanity, demolish the traditional answers. I had worked out the rules of the community already. I had even found the building in one of the passes of Mount Hymettus, at St. John the Hunter.

"I've guessed it right enough," said Zorba happily, when he saw I remained silent.

"Well, I'm going to ask you a favor, holy abbot: I want you to appoint me doorkeeper to your monastery so that I can do some smuggling and, now and then, let some very strange things through into the holy precincts: women, mandolins, demijohns of raki, roast sucking pigs. . . . All so that you don't fritter away your life with a lot of nonsense!"

He laughed and went quickly towards the hut. I ran after him. He cleaned the fish, without opening his mouth, while I fetched wood and lit the fire. As soon as the soup was ready, we took our spoons and began eating straight out of the pot.

Neither of us spoke. We had not had a bite all day and we both ate ravenously. We drank some wine and our spirits improved. Zorba opened his mouth at last.

"It would be fun to see Dame Bouboulina turn up now, boss. It would be a good moment for her to come, but God preserve us! She'd be the last straw. And yet you know, boss, I've missed her, devil take her!"

"You aren't asking me who threw you that particular little bone, are you?"

"What do you care, boss? It's like a flea in a haystack. . . . Take the bone and don't worry about who threw it down to you. Is it tasty? Is there any flesh on it? Those are the questions to ask. All the rest is. . . ."

"Food has worked its wondrous miracle!" I said, slapping him on the back. "The famished body is calmed . . . and so the soul that was asking questions has calmed down, too. Get your *santuri!*"

But just as Zorba stood up we heard quick, heavy steps on the pebbles. Zorba's hairy nostrils quivered.

"Speak of the devil. . . ." he said in a low voice, slapping his thighs. "Here she is! The bitch has scented a Zorba smell in the air, and here she comes."

"I'm off," I said, rising. "I don't want anything to do with this. I'll go out for a bit. I leave this to you."

"Good night, boss."

"And don't forget, Zorba. You promised to marry her. . . . Don't make me a liar."

Zorba sighed.

"Marry again, boss? I've had my bellyful!"

The scent of toilet soap was coming nearer.

"Courage, Zorba!"

I left quickly. Outside, I could already hear the panting breath of the old siren.

◊ 17 ◊

THE NEXT DAY at dawn Zorba's voice woke me from sleep. "What's got into you so early in the morning? Why all this shouting?"

"We have to take things seriously, boss," he answered, filling his haversack with food. "I've brought two mules; get up and we'll go to the monastery and have the papers signed for the cable railway. There's only one thing makes a lion afraid and that's a louse. The lice will eat us all up, boss."

"Why call that poor Bouboulina a louse?" I asked him with a laugh.

But Zorba pretended he had not heard.

"Come on," he said, "before the sun is too high."

I was really very glad to go up into the mountains and enjoy the smell of the pine trees. We mounted our beasts and began the ascent, halting for a moment at the mine where Zorba gave some instructions to the workmen. He told them to work at the "Mother Superior," to dig out the trench in "The Piddler" and clean out the "Canavaro."

The day shone like a diamond of the first water. The higher we went, the more our spirits seemed to become purged and exalted. Once again I felt the influence on the soul of pure air, easy breathing and a vast horizon. Anyone would think the soul, too, was an animal with lungs and nostrils, and that it needed oxygen, was stifled in the dust or in the midst of too much stale breath.

The sun was already high when we entered the pine forest. The air there smelled of honey, the wind was blowing above us and soughed like the sea.

During the trek Zorba studied the slope of the mountainside. In his imagination he was driving in piles every so many yards, and when he raised his eyes he could already see the cable shining in the sun and running right down to the shore. Attached to the cable the felled tree trunks descended, whistling along like arrows from a bow.

He rubbed his hands together:

"Capital!" he said. "This'll be a gold mine! We'll soon be rolling in money, and we can do all we said."

I looked at him in astonishment.

"Hm! Don't tell me you've forgotten already! Before we built your monastery, we were going up the great mountain. What's its name?"

"Tibet, Zorba, Tibet. But only the two of us. You can't take women there."

"Who mentioned taking women? The poor creatures are very useful, anyway, so don't say anything against them; very useful, when a man hasn't got any man's work to do, such as cutting coal, taking towns by assault or talking to God. What else is there for him to do, then, if he isn't going to burst? He drinks wine, plays dice, or puts his arms round a woman . . . and he waits . . . waits for his hour to come—if it is coming."

He was silent for a moment.

"If it is coming," he repeated, in an irritated tone, "because it might never come at all."

And a moment later:

"It can't just go on like this, boss; either the world will have to get smaller or I shall have to get bigger. Otherwise I'm done for!"

A monk appeared between the pines, redhaired and yellow complexioned, his sleeves rolled up, a round homespun cap on his head. He was carrying an iron rod with which he struck the ground as he strode along. When he saw us he stopped and raised his stick in the air.

"Where are you going?" he asked.

"To the monastery," Zorba replied; "we're going to say our prayers."

"Turn back, Christians!" cried the monk, his clear blue eyes growing inflamed as he spoke. "Turn back, if you'll take my advice! It is not the Virgin's orchard you'll find there, but the garden of Satan! Poverty, humility, chastity . . . the monk's crown, as they say! Very likely. Go back, I tell you. Money, pride, and young boys! That's their Holy Trinity!"

"He's a comic, this chap," whispered Zorba, enchanted. He leaned towards him.

"What's your name, brother?" he asked the monk. "And where do you come from?"

"My name is Zaharia. I've packed up my things and I'm off! Right away. I can't bear it any longer! Kindly tell me your name, countryman."

"Canavaro."

"I can't endure it any longer, brother Canavaro. All night long Christ moans and prevents me sleeping. And I moan with him. Then the abbot—may he roast in hell-fire forever—sent for me early this morning."

" 'Well, Zaharia,' he said. 'So, you won't let your brother monks sleep. I'm going to throw you out.'

" 'I won't let them sleep?' I said. 'I won't? Or Christ won't? He's the one who keeps moaning.'

"Then he raised his cross, that anti-Christ, and, well . . . look!"

He took off his monk's cap and revealed a patch of congealed blood in his hair.

"So I shook the dust of the place from my shoes and left."

"Come back to the monastery with us," said Zorba. "I'll get round the abbot. Come on, you can keep us company and show us the way. You've been sent by heaven itself."

The monk thought for a moment. His eyes shone.

"What will you give me?" he asked.

"What do you want?"

"Two pounds of salt cod and a bottle of brandy."

Zorba leaned forward and looked at him.

"You wouldn't by any chance have a sort of devil inside you, would you, Zaharia?"

The monk started.

"How did you guess?" he asked in amazement.

"I come from Mount Athos myself," answered Zorba. "I know something about it."

The monk hung his head. We could scarcely hear his reply.

"Yes, I have a devil inside me."

"And he'd like some salt cod and brandy, would he?"

"Yes, thrice damned as he is!"

"All right! Done! Does he smoke as well?"

Zorba threw him a cigarette and the monk seized it eagerly.

"He smokes, yes, he smokes, plague on him!" he said.

And he took a small flint and a piece of wick from his pocket, lit the cigarette and inhaled deeply.

"In Christ's name!" he said.

He raised his iron rod, turned about face and started off.

"What's your devil's name?" asked Zorba, winking at me.

"Joseph!" answered Zaharia, without turning his head.

This half-crazed monk's company was not at all to my taste. A sick mind, like a sick body, makes me feel compassion, and at the same time disgust. But I said nothing; I left it to Zorba to do what he liked.

The clear pure air made us hungry and we sat down beneath a giant pine tree and opened the haversack. The monk leaned forward and hungrily peered into it to see what it contained.

"Not so fast!" cried Zorba. "Don't lick your chops too soon, Zaharia! It's Holy Monday today. We are freemasons, so we shall eat some meat and chicken, God forgive us! But look, there's some *halva* and a few olives for your own saintly stomach!"

The monk stroked his filthy beard.

"I will have olives and bread and fresh water," he said with contrition. "But Joseph's a devil, he will eat meat with you, brothers; he likes chicken—oh, he's a lost soul—and he'll drink wine from your gourd!"

He made the sign of the cross, swallowed the bread, olives and *halva*, wiped his mouth with the back of his hand, drank the water, and then crossed himself again as if he had finished his meal.

"Now," he said, "it's Joseph's turn, the poor thrice-damned soul.'

And he threw himself on the chicken.

"Eat, you lost soul!" he mumbled furiously as he rammed great lumps of chicken into his mouth. "Eat!"

"Hoorah! Good for you, monk!" shouted Zorba enthusiastically. "You've got two strings to your bow, I can see."

He turned to me.

"What do you think of him, boss?"

"He's very like you," I said with a laugh.

Zorba gave the monk the wine gourd.

"Joseph! Have a drink!"

"Drink! You lost soul!" said the monk, seizing the bottle and clapping it to his mouth.

The sun was very hot and we moved further into the shade. The monk reeked of sour sweat and incense. He almost ran liquid in the sun and Zorba dragged him to the shadiest spot to reduce the stench.

"How did you become a monk?" asked Zorba, who had eaten well and wanted to gossip.

The monk grinned.

"I suppose you think it was because I'm so saintly? You bet! It was through poverty, brother, poverty! I had nothing left to eat, so I said to myself: if I go into a monastery, I can't starve!"

"And are you satisfied?"

"God be praised! I sigh and complain often enough but don't you pay any attention to that. I don't sigh for earthly things; as far as I'm concerned they can go and be . . . forgive me . . . and I tell them every day to go and be. . . . But I long for heaven! I tell jokes and cut capers about the place and make the monks laugh. They all say I'm possessed by the devil and insult me. But I say to myself: 'It can't be true; God must like fun and laughter. "Come inside, my little buffoon, come inside," he'll say to me one day, I know. "Come and make me laugh!"' That's the way I'll get into Paradise, as a buffoon!"

"You've got your head screwed on the right way, old fellow!" said Zorba, standing up. "Come on, we must make a move, so that we don't get caught by the dark."

The monk went ahead again. As we climbed the mountain I felt we were clambering over ranges of the mind within me, passing from base and petty cares to nobler ones, from the comfortable truths of the plains to precipitous conceptions.

Suddenly the monk stopped.

"Our Lady of Revenge!" he cried, pointing to a small chapel with a graceful dome. He sank to his knees and made the sign of the cross. I dismounted and entered the cool oratory. In one corner was an old icon, black with smoke and covered with votive offerings: thin sheets of silver on which had been crudely engraved figures of feet, hands, eyes, hearts. . . . A silver candlestick stood before the icon holding an ever-burning light.

I approached in silence: a fierce, warlike madonna with a strong neck and the austere, uneasy look of a virgin, held in her hand, not the holy babe, but a long straight spear.

"Woe to him who attacks the monastery!" said the monk in terror. "She hurls herself at him and sticks him through with her spear. In ancient times the Algerians came here and burnt the monastery. But see what it cost these heathens: as they passed this chapel the Holy Virgin, all of a sudden, threw herself from the icon, rushed outside and started thrusting with her spear, this way and that, in all directions. . . . And she killed them all to a man. My grandfather remembered seeing their bones; they littered the whole of the forest. Since then, we call her Our Lady of Revenge. Before that she was called Our Lady of Mercy."

"Why didn't she perform her miracle before they burnt the monastery, Father Zaharia?" asked Zorba.

"That was the will of the All-High!" answered the monk, crossing himself three times.

"Good for the All-High!" muttered Zorba, climbing back into the saddle. "On we go!"

Soon a plateau appeared on which we could see the outline of the Holy Virgin's monastery surrounded by rocks and pine trees. Serene, smiling, cut off from the rest of the world in the hollow of this high green gorge, uniting in deep harmony the nobility of the peak and the gentleness of the plain, this monastery appeared to me a marvellously chosen retreat for human meditation.

"Here," I thought, "a gentle, sober spirit could cultivate a religious exaltation that would match the stature of men. Neither a precipitous, superhuman peak, nor a lazy, voluptuous plain, but what is needed, and no more, for the soul to be elevated without losing its human tenderness. A site like this will fashion neither heroes nor swine. It will fashion men."

Here a graceful ancient Greek temple or a gay Mohammedan mosque would be in keeping. God must come down here in simple human form, walk barefoot across the spring grass, and converse quietly with men.

"What a marvel! What solitude! What felicity!" I murmured.

We dismounted, went through the central door, climbed to the visiting room, where we were offered the traditional tray of raki, jam and coffee. The guest master, or hospitaller, came to see us, and in a moment we were surrounded by monks who began to talk. Cunning eyes, insatiable lips, beards, moustaches, and the odor of so many he-goats.

"Haven't you brought a newspaper?" one monk asked anxiously.

"A newspaper?" I said in astonishment. "What would you do with a newspaper here?"

"A newspaper, brother, would tell us what is happening in the world below!" cried two or three indignant voices.

Leaning on the rails of the balcony, they croaked like a lot of ravens. They were talking excitedly of England, Russia, Venizelos, the king. The world had banished them, but they had not banished the world. Their eyes were full of the great cities, shops, women, newspapers. . . .

A big, fat hairy monk stood up and sniffed.

"I have something to show you," he said to me. "You can tell me what you think of it. I'll go and fetch it."

He went off, his short hairy hands clasped together over his stomach, his cloth slippers dragging along the floor. He disappeared through the door.

The monks all grinned nastily.

"Father Demetrios is going to fetch his clay nun again," said the hospitaller. "The devil buried it in the ground especially for him and one day Demetrios found it when he was digging in the garden. He took it to his cell and has lost his sleep ever since. He's nearly lost his senses, too."

Zorba stood up. He was suffocating.

"We came to see the Abbot and to sign some papers," he said.

"The holy abbot isn't here," said the hospitaller. "He went to the village this morning. Have patience."

Father Demetrios reappeared, his two clasped hands outstretched as though he were carrying the holy chalice.

"There!" he said, opening his hands cautiously.

I went up to him. A tiny Tanagra figurine, half-naked and coy, smiled up at me from the monk's fat fingers. She was holding her head with the one hand that still remained to her.

"For her to show her head like that," said Demetrios, "means that she has a precious stone inside it, maybe a diamond or a pearl. What do you think?"

"I think," came one monk's acid comment, "that she's got a headache."

But big Demetrios, his lips hanging down like a goat's, watched me and waited impatiently.

"I think I ought to break her and see," he said. "I can't get any sleep at night for it. . . . If there were a diamond inside. . . ."

I looked at the graceful young girl with her tiny, firm breasts, exiled here in the smell of incense and among crucified gods that lay their curse on the flesh, on laughter and kisses.

Ah! if only I could save her!

Zorba took the terra-cotta figurine, felt the thin womanly body, and his fingers stayed, trembling on the firm, pointed breasts.

"But can't you see, my good monk," he said, "that this is the devil? It's the devil himself, and no mistake. Don't you worry, I know him well enough, accursed as he is. Look at her breasts here, Father Demetrios—cool, round and firm. That's just what the devil's breast is like, and I know plenty about that!"

A young monk appeared in the doorway. The sun shone on his golden hair and round, downy face.

The venomous-tongued monk who had spoken before winked to the hospitaller. They both smiled cunningly.

"Father Demetrios," they said. "Here is your novice, Gavrili."

The monk seized his tiny clay woman immediately and went rolling like a barrel towards the door. The handsome novice walked silently in front of him with a swinging step. They disappeared down the long, dilapidated corridor.

I signed to Zorba and we went out into the courtyard. It was agreeably hot outside. In the middle of the courtyard an orange tree in blossom scented the air. Close by, water ran murmuring from an ancient ram's head in marble. I put my head underneath and felt refreshed.

"What in God's name are these people?" Zorba asked with some disgust. "They're neither men nor women; they're mules. Pooh! let them go hang!"

He too plunged his head beneath the fresh water and began to laugh.

"Pooh! let them go hang!" he said again. "They've all got a devil of some sort in them. One wants a woman, another salt cod, another money, another newspapers . . . bunch of noodles! Why don't they come down into the world, stuff themselves full of all that and purge their brains?"

He lit a cigarette and sat on the bench beneath the blossoming orange tree.

"When I have a longing for something myself," he said, "do you know what I do? I cram myself chockful of it, and so I get rid of it and don't think about it any longer. Or, if I do, it makes me retch. Once when I was a kid—this'll show you—I was mad on cherries. I had no money, so I couldn't buy many at a time, and when I'd eaten all I could buy I still wanted more. Day and night I thought of nothing but cherries. I foamed at the mouth; it was torture! But one day I got mad, or ashamed, I don't know which. Anyway, I just felt cherries were doing what they liked with me and it was ludicrous. So what did I do? I got up one night, searched my father's pockets and found a silver *mejidie* and pinched it. I was up early the next morning, went to a market gardener and bought a basket o' cherries. I settled down in a ditch and began eating. I stuffed and stuffed till I was all swollen out. My stomach began to ache and I was sick. Yes, boss, I was thoroughly sick, and from that day to this I've never wanted a cherry. I couldn't bear the sight of them. I was saved. I could say to any cherry: I don't need you any more. And I did the same thing later with wine and tobacco. I still drink and smoke, but at any second, if I want to, whoop! I can cut it out. I'm not ruled by passion. It's the same with my country. I thought too much about it, so I stuffed myself up to the neck with it, spewed it up, and it's never troubled me since."

"What about women?" I asked.

"Their turn will come, damn them! It'll come! When I'm about seventy!"

He thought for a moment, and it seemed too imminent.

"Eighty," he said, correcting himself. "That makes you laugh, boss, I can see, but you needn't. That's how men free themselves! Listen to me; there's no other way except by stuffing themselves till they burst. Not by turning ascetic. How do you expect to get the better of a devil, boss, if you don't turn into a devil-and-a-half yourself?"

Demetrios came panting into the courtyard, followed by the fair young monk.

"Anybody'd think he was an angel in a temper," muttered Zorba, admiring his shyness and youthful grace.

They went towards the stone staircase leading to the upper cells. Demetrios turned round, looked at the young monk, and said a few words. The monk shook his head as in refusal. But immediately afterwards he nodded in submission, put his arm round the old monk and they mounted the steps together.

"Get it?" asked Zorba. "D'you see? Sodom and Gomorrah!"

Two monks peeped out, winked at one another and began to laugh.

"Spiteful bunch!" grunted Zorba. "Wolves don't tear one another to pieces, but look at these monks! Have you ever seen women go for one another like this?"

"They're all men," I said, laughing.

"There's not much difference here, boss, you take it from me! Mules, all of them. You can call them Gavrilis, or Gavrila, Demetrios, or Demetria, according to how you feel. Come on, boss, let's be off. Get the papers signed as quick as we can and let's go. We'll soon get disgusted with men and women altogether if we stay here."

He lowered his voice.

"Besides, I've got a scheme. . . ."

"Another mad idea, I know. Don't you think you've done enough foolish things in your time, you old goat? Tell me what your scheme is."

196

Zorba shrugged his shoulders.

"How can I tell you a thing like that, boss? You're a nice chap, if you'll allow me to say so! You do your utmost for everybody, whoever they are. If you found a flea on your eiderdown in the winter you'd put it underneath so that it wouldn't catch cold. How should you understand an old scoundrel like me? If I find a flea, crack! I crush him. If I find a sheep, swish! I cut its throat, slap it onto the spit and invite my friends to a feast! But you'd say: the sheep isn't yours! No, I admit that. But, boss, let's finish eating it first, afterwards we'll talk it over quietly and discuss what's 'yours' and 'mine' as much as you like. You could talk to your heart's content about it, while I cleaned my teeth with a matchstick."

The courtyard resounded with his peals of laughter. Zaharia appeared, terrified. He placed a finger on his lips and crept up to us on tiptoe.

"Sh!" he said. "You mustn't laugh! Look up there, that little window . . . that's where the bishop is working; it's the library. He's writing, the holy man is. He writes all day long, so don't make a noise."

"Ha, you're just the person I wanted to see, Father Joseph!" said Zorba, taking the monk's arm. "Come, take me to your cell, I want a chat with you."

Then he turned to me:

"While we're away, you go and have a look round the chapel and all the old icons," he said. "I'll wait for the abbot, he won't be long. But don't start anything yourself, you'll only make a mess of it. Leave it to me, I've got a scheme."

He bent down and spoke in my ear.

"We'll have that forest at half price. . . . Don't say a word."
And he went off quickly, holding the mad monk's arm.

◊ 18 ◊

I CROSSED the threshold of the chapel and plunged into the
shadowy interior, which was cool and fragrant.

The building was deserted. The bronze chandeliers shed a faint
light. A finely worked iconostasis filled the far end of the chapel.
It represented a golden vine arbor laden with grapes. The walls
were covered from top to bottom with half-obliterated frescoes:
terrifying pictures of skeleton-like ascetics, the Fathers of the
Church, Christ's prolonged Passion, huge fierce-looking angels with
their hair tied in broad blue and pink ribbons which had faded
with the damp.

High up in the vault was the Virgin, with arms imploringly outstretched. A heavy silver lamp stood before her and the soft light
flickered round her, caressing her long, contorted face. I shall never
forget her dolorous eyes, her puckered, rounded mouth and strong
wilful chin. Here, I thought, is the completely happy and satisfied
Mother, even in the most agonizing pain, because she feels that
from her mortal loins has issued something that will not die.

When I recrossed the threshrold the sun was sinking. I sat down
under the orange tree in a state of happiness. The dome of the
chapel was turning pink as though it were dawn. The monks had
gone to their cells and were resting. They would not sleep at all;
they had to muster all their strength. Christ would begin to climb
Golgotha that night, and they had to go with him. Two black sows

with pink teats were lying fast asleep beneath a carob tree. Pigeons were strutting on the roofs and cooing.

How long, I thought, shall I live to enjoy the sweetness of the earth, the air, the silence and the scent of the orange tree in blossom? An icon of Saint Bacchus, which I had looked at in the chapel, had made my heart overflow with happiness. The things that move me most deeply—unity, firmness of purpose and constancy of desire —were once again revealed to me. Blessed be that charming little icon of a Christian youth with curly hair falling over his forehead like bunches of grapes. Dionysus, the handsome god of wine and ecstasy, and Saint Bacchus fused in my mind and took on the same appearance. Under the vine leaves and the monk's habit there quivered with life the same body, burnt by the sun—Greece.

Zorba returned and hurriedly gave the news:

"The abbot did come. We had a little talk; he needs a lot of coaxing; he says he's not going to give the forest away for a song; he's asking a lot more than we said, the old rogue, but I haven't finished with him yet."

"Why does he need coaxing? I thought we were agreed?"

"Don't you meddle in this, for heaven's sake, boss," Zorba pleaded. "You'd only spoil things. There you are, after all this, talking about the old agreement; that's buried long ago. Don't frown; it's buried, I tell you. We'll have that forest at half price!"

"What mischief are you up to now, Zorba?"

"Never you mind. That's my business. I'm going to oil the works and make them turn, do you get it?"

"But why? I don't get it at all."

"Because I spent more than I should have done at Candia, that's why! Because Lola swallowed quite a heap of my—that is to say, your money. You don't think I've forgotten, do you? There is such a thing as self-respect. No blots on my copybook! I've spent so much, so I pay so much. I've reckoned it up; Lola cost me seven thousand drachmas. I'll knock them off the price of the forest. It's the abbot, the monastery and the Holy Virgin who'll pay for Lola. That's my scheme. How d'you like it?"

"Not at all. Why should the Holy Virgin be responsible for your excesses?"

"She is responsible and more than responsible! Look, she had her son: God. God made me, Zorba, and he gave me some instruments—you know what I mean. And these damned instruments, no matter where I meet the female of the species, make me lose my head and open my purse. See? Therefore, Her Holiness is responsible and more than responsible. Let her pay."

"I don't like it, Zorba."

"That's another question altogether. Let's save the seven little banknotes first; we'll discuss it later! 'Make love to me first, darling, I'll be your aunt again afterwards. . . .' You know how the song goes. . . ."

The fat hospitaller appeared: "Come inside," he said, in a suave ecclesiastical tone; "dinner is served."

We went down to the refectory, a large hall with benches and long narrow tables. The smell of sour, rancid oil filled the air. At the far end was an old fresco of the Last Supper. The eleven faithful disciples crowded around Christ like a flock of sheep, and on the other side, standing quite alone, was the redhaired Judas, the black sheep. He had a bulging forehead and aquiline nose. And Christ could not take his eyes off him.

The hospitaller sat down, placing me on his right and Zorba on his left.

"We are fasting," he said, "so I hope you will excuse us—no oil or wine, even for visitors. But you are welcome!"

We made the sign of the cross; then we served ourselves in silence to olives, spring onions, fresh beans and *halva*. We all three munched slowly, like rabbits.

"Such is life here below," said the hospitaller. "A crucifixion and a fast. But patience, brothers, patience, the Resurrection and the Lamb are coming, and the Kingdom of Heaven."

I coughed. Zorba trod on my foot as though to say: "Shut up!"

"I've seen Father Zaharia . . ." said Zorba, to change the subject.

The hospitaller started:

"What did that madman say to you?" he asked anxiously. "He has all seven demons in him, don't listen to a word he says. His soul is impure and he sees impurity all around him."

The bell for the monks rang lugubriously. The hospitaller crossed himself and stood up.

"I shall have to go," he said. "Christ's Passion is beginning; we must carry the cross with him. You can rest tonight, you must be tired after your journey. But at matins tomorrow. . . ."

"Those swine!" Zorba muttered between his teeth as soon as the monk had gone. "Swine! Liars! Mules!"

"What's wrong, Zorba? Has Zaharia told you something?"

"Never mind, boss, to hell with it! If they don't want to sign, I'll show them what I'm made of!"

We went to the cell which had been assigned to us. In the corner was an icon representing the Virgin pressing her cheek against her son's, her big eyes full of tears.

Zorba shook his big head.

"Do you know why she's crying, boss?"

"No."

"Because she can see what's going on. If I was a painter of icons, I'd draw the Virgin without eyes, ears or nose. Because I'd be sorry for her."

We stretched out on the hard beds. The wooden beams smelled of cypress; through the open window was wafted the gentle breath of spring, laden with the perfume of flowers. Occasionally the mournful tunes surged from the courtyard like gusts of wind. A nightingale began to sing close to the window, then another a short distance away, and still another. The night was overflowing with love.

I could not sleep. The nightingale's song mingled with the lamentations of Christ, and I tried to climb Golgotha myself through the flowering orange trees, guiding myself by the huge spots of blood. In the blue spring night I could see the cold sweat glistening all over Christ's pale, faltering body. I could see his hands outstretched and trembling, as though he were a beggar imploring the bystanders to listen. The poor people of Galilee hurried after him, crying: "Hosannah! Hosannah!" They had palm leaves in their hands and spread their mantles before his feet. He looked at the ones he loved, though none could divine the depths of his despair. He alone knew he was going to his death. Beneath the stars, weeping and silent, he consoled his poor human heart that was full of fear:

"Like unto a grain of wheat, my heart, you, too, must fall into the ground and die. Be not afraid. If you do not, how can you bring forth fruit? How can you nourish men who die of hunger?"

But, within him, his man's heart was fainting and trembling, and did not want to die. . . .

The wood round the monastery was full of the song of night-ingales. Their song rose amidst the damp foliage and spoke entirely of love and passion. And with it trembled, swelled and wept the poor heart of mankind.

Gradually, imperceptibly, together with Christ's Passion and the nightingale's song, I entered the realm of sleep, just as the soul must enter Paradise.

I had been sleeping less than an hour when I awoke with a start, terror-stricken.

"Zorba!" I cried. "Did you hear? A revolver shot!"

But Zorba was sitting on his bed smoking a cigarette.

"Don't be alarmed, boss," he said, still trying to control his anger, "let them settle their own accounts, the swine!"

Cries came from the corridor; we could hear heavy slippers drag-ging along, doors opening and closing, and a moaning in the dis-tance as though someone were wounded.

I leaped from my bed and opened the door. A wizened old man appeared before me and spread out his arms, barring my passage. He was wearing a white pointed bonnet and a white shirt down to his knees.

"Who are you?"

"The bishop . . ." he replied, his voice trembling.

I almost burst out laughing. A bishop? Where were his orna-ments, the gold chasuble, mitre and cross, the many-colored false stones . . . It was the first time I had seen a bishop in his night attire.

"What was that revolver shot, Your Lordship?"

"I don't know, I don't know . . ." he stammered, pushing me gently back into the room.

Zorba burst out laughing from his bed.

"Are you scared, little Father?" he said. "Come in, then, old fellow, and stay with us. We are no monks, so you needn't worry."

"Zorba," I said in an undertone, "show more respect, can't you? It's the bishop."

"H'm! in a shirt nobody's a bishop! Come in, old chap!"

He stood up, took the bishop by the arm and led him into the cell, closing the door behind him. He took a bottle of rum out of his haversack and filled a small glass.

"Drink, my friend," he said. "That'll buck you up."

The little old man drained the glass and soon came round. He sat down on my bed and leaned against the wall.

"Very Reverend Father," I said, "what was that revolver shot?"

"I don't know, my son. . . . I had worked till midnight and gone to bed, when next door in Father Demetrios's cell I heard. . . ."

"Ah! ah!" said Zorba with a laugh. "You were right, then, Zaharia! Those dirty swine!"

The bishop bowed his head.

"It must have been a thief of some sort," he murmured.

In the corridor the uproar had ceased and the monastery sank into silence once more. The bishop looked at me with his kind, frightened eyes, as if in supplication.

"Are you sleepy, my son?" he asked.

I felt clearly that he did not want to leave and go back to be alone in his cell. He was afraid.

"No," I answered, "I'm not at all sleepy; stay here a while."

We began to talk. Zorba was leaning on his pillow and rolling a cigarette.

"You appear to be a cultured young man," the bishop said to me. "Here I can't find anyone to talk to. I have three theories that help to make my life agreeable; I would like to tell you about them, my child."

He didn't wait for my reply but began straight away:

"My first theory is this: the shape of flowers influences their color; their color influences their properties. Thus it is that each flower has a different effect on a man's body, and therefore on his soul. That is why we must be extremely careful in passing through a field when the flowers are in bloom."

He stopped as though waiting for my opinion. I could see the little old man wandering through a field, searching the ground, with secret excitement, for the shapes and colors of the flowers. The poor old man must tremble with mystic awe; in the spring the fields must be peopled for him with many-colored devils and angels.

"This is my second theory: every idea that has a real influence has also a real existence. It is really there, it does not float invisibly in the atmosphere—it has a real body—eyes, a mouth, feet, a stomach. It is male or female and therefore runs after men or women, as the case may be. That is why the Gospel says: 'The Word became flesh . . .'"

He looked anxiously at me again.

"My third theory," he went on hurriedly, as he could not bear my silence, "is this: there is some Eternity even in our ephemeral lives, only it is very difficult for us to discover it alone. Our daily cares lead us astray. A few people only, the flower of humanity, manage to live an eternity even in their transitory lives on this earth. Since all the others would therefore be lost, God had mercy on them and sent them religion—thus the crowd is able to live in eternity, too."

He had finished and was visibly relieved for having spoken. He raised his small eyes, which had no lashes, and smiled at me. It was as though he were saying: "There, I am giving you all I have, take it!" I was very moved at the sight of this little old man thus offering me outright, when he hardly knew me, the fruits of a lifetime's work.

He had tears in his eyes.

"What do you think of my theories?" he asked, taking my hand between his own and looking into my eyes. I felt that he depended on my reply to tell him whether his life had been of any use or not.

I knew that, over and above the truth, there exists another duty which is much more important and much more human.

"Those theories may save many souls," I answered.

The bishop's face lit up. That was the justification of his entire life.

"Thank you, my son," he whispered, squeezing my hand affectionately.

Zorba leaped from his corner.

"I've got a fourth theory!" he cried.

I looked anxiously at him. The bishop turned to him.

"Speak, my son, and may your theory be blessed! What is it?"

"That two and two make four!" said Zorba gravely.

The bishop looked at him, flabbergasted.

"And a fifth theory, old man," Zorba went on. "That two and two don't make four. Go on, my friend, take a chance! Make your choice!"

"I don't understand," stammered the old man, casting a questioning glance at me.

"Neither do I!" said Zorba, bursting into laughter.

I turned to the poor old man, who was abashed, and changed the subject.

"What are your special studies here in the monastery, Reverend Father?" I asked.

"I am making copies of the ancient manuscripts of the monastery, my son, and recently I have been collecting all the sacred epithets used by the Church in connection with the Virgin Mother."

He sighed.

"I am old," he said, "and I can't do anything else. I find relief in listing all the verbal adornments of the Virgin, and thus I forget the miseries of this world."

He leaned his elbow on the pillow, closed his eyes and began murmuring as though in delirium:

"Imperishable Rose, Fruitful Earth, Vine, Fountain, Source of Miracles, Ladder to Heaven, Bridge, Rescuing Frigate for the Shipwrecked, Haven of Rest, Key to Paradise, Dawn, Eternal Light, Lightning, Pillar of Fire, Invincible General, Immovable Tower, Impregnable Fortress, Consolation, Joy, Staff for the Blind, Mother for the Orphan, Table, Food, Peace, Serenity, Perfume, Banquet, Milk and Honey . . ."

"The old boy's delirious . . ." said Zorba in an undertone. "I'll cover him over so that he doesn't catch cold."

He stood up, threw a blanket over the bishop and put his pillow straight.

"There are seventy-seven kinds of madness, so I've heard," he said. "This one must be the seventy-eighth."

Day was dawning. We could hear the ringing of the semantron.

I leaned my head out of the window. In the first rays of dawn I saw a gaunt monk, a long black hood over his head, walk slowly round the courtyard striking with a small hammer on a long piece of wood which had marvellously musical properties. The sound of the semantron echoed through the morning air, full of sweetness, harmony and appeal. The nightingales had stopped singing and other birds were beginning to chirp in the trees.

I listened, charmed with the sweet evocative notes of the semantron. I thought how, even in decay, an elevated rhythm in life preserves all its outward form, is impressive and full of nobility. The spirit departs, but it leaves its vast dwelling which it has slowly evolved and which is as intricate as a sea shell.

The wonderful cathedrals you see in noisy, godless cities are just such empty shells, I thought. Prehistoric monsters of which only a skeleton, worn by sun and rain, is left.

There was a knock at the door of our cell. The unctuous voice of the hospitaller came to our ears.

"Come, rise now, brothers, it's time for matins."

Zorba leaped up:

"What was the revolver shot in the night?" he shouted, beside himself.

He waited a moment. Silence. The monk must have heard him through the door, because we could hear his noisy breathing. Zorba stamped with rage.

"What was that revolver shot?" he asked again, in a fury.

We heard steps going rapidly away. With one bound Zorba was at the door. He opened it:

"Filthy scoundrels! Blackguards!" he shouted, spitting in the direction of the retreating monk. "Priests, nuns, monks, church-wardens, sacristans, the whole lot of you, that's all you're worth!" And he spat again.

"Let's go!" I said. "There's a smell of blood in the air."

"If it were only blood!" grunted Zorba. "You go to matins, boss, if you want to. I'll have a look round to see what I can find out."

"Let's go!" I said again, nauseated. "And will you be good enough not to go poking your nose where it's none of your business?"

"That's just where I always want to poke it!" said Zorba.

He thought for a moment, then smiled cunningly:

"The devil is doing us a favor," he said. "I think he's bringing things to a head. Do you realize what that might cost the monastery, boss, a revolver shot like that? A cool seven thousand!"

He went down into the courtyard. The scent of blossom, morning sweetness, heavenly felicity. Zaharia was waiting for us. He ran up and seized Zorba's arm.

"Brother Canavaro," he whispered with a trembling voice. "Come, we must go!"

"What was that revolver shot? They killed somebody, didn't they? Come on, talk or I'll wring your neck!"

The monk's chin quivered. He looked round him. The courtyard was deserted, the cells closed; through the open chapel door came waves of music.

"Follow me, both of you," he muttered. "Sodom and Gomorrah!"

We slipped along the side of the wall, gained the other side of the courtyard and went out of the garden. A hundred yards or so from the monastery was a cemetery. We went inside.

We stepped over the graves, Zaharia pushed the little door of the chapel and we entered behind him. In the center, on a rush mat, lay a body covered over with a monk's habit. There was a candle burning at both head and foot of the corpse.

I stooped to look at the body.

"The young monk!" I murmured with a shudder. "Father Demetrios's fair-haired young novice!"

On the door of the sanctuary, with widespread wings and unsheathed sword, and wearing red sandals, glittered the figure of the archangel Michael.

"Archangel Michael!" cried the monk, "send fire and brimstone and burn them all! Archangel Michael, do something. Leave your icon! Raise your sword and smite them! Did you not hear that revolver shot?"

"Who killed him? Who was it? Demetrios? Speak, old goatbeard!"

The monk slipped out of Zorba's grasp and threw himself flat on the floor before the archangel. He remained motionless for a few moments, face upraised, eyes starting from his head, mouth wide open, watching the icon intently.

Suddenly he jumped for joy.

"I will burn them!" he declared in a resolute voice. "The arch-angel moved, I saw him, he made a sign to me!"

He went close to the icon and glued his thick lips to the arch-angel's sword.

"God be praised!" he said. "I am relieved!"

Zorba seized the monk again.

"Come here, Zaharia," he said. "Now, you'll do what I tell you." Then he turned to me.

"Give me the money, boss, I'll sign the papers myself. They're all wolves in there, and you're a lamb, they'll eat you. Leave it to me. Don't you worry, I've got the fat hogs where I want them. We'll leave here at midday with the forest in our pockets. Come on, Zaharia."

They slipped away furtively towards the monastery. I went for a stroll under the pine trees.

The sun was high already and the dew was sparkling on the leaves. A blackbird in front of me flew on to the branch of a wild pear tree, flicked his tail, opened his beak, looked at me and whis-tled two or three mocking notes.

Through the pines I could see the courtyard and the monks coming out in a long file, their heads bowed and black cowls hang-ing over their shoulders. The service was over; they were on their way to the refectory.

"What a pity," I thought, "that such austerity and nobility should be without a soul."

I was tired, I had not slept well, and I stretched out on the grass. The wild violets, broom, rosemary and sage made the air redolent. Insects buzzed continually as in their hunger they plunged into the flowers like pirates and sucked the honey. In the distance the moun-tains sparkled, transparent, serene, like a moving haze in the burn-ing light of the sun.

I closed my eyes, soothed. A quiet, mysterious pleasure took pos-session of me—as if all that green miracle around me were paradise itself, as if all the freshness, airiness and sober rapture which I was feeling were God. God changes his appearance every second. Blessed is the man who can recognize him in all his disguises. At one moment he is a glass of fresh water, the next your son bouncing on your knees or an enchanting woman, or perhaps merely a morning walk.

Little by little, everything around me, without changing shape, became a dream. I was happy. Earth and paradise were one. A flower in the fields with a large drop of honey in its center: that was how life appeared to me. And my soul, a wild bee plundering.

I was brutally awakened from this state of beatitude. I heard steps behind me and whispers. At the same instant a happy voice cried:

"Boss, we're off!"

Zorba stood in front of me and his small eyes shone with a diabolical gleam.

"Off?" I said with relief. "Is it all settled?"

"Everything!" said Zorba, tapping the upper part of his jacket. "Here's the forest. I hope it brings us luck! And here are the seven thousand Lola cost us!"

He took a roll of banknotes from his inside pocket.

"Take 'em!" he said. "I pay my debts; I'm not ashamed to look you in the face any more. The stockings, and handbags, and perfume and Dame Bouboulina's parasol are all included in that. Even the parrot's nuts! And the *halva* I brought you, as well!"

"Keep it yourself, Zorba; it's a present from me," I said. "Go and burn a candle to the Virgin you've sinned against."

Zorba turned round. Father Zaharia was coming towards us in his filthy gown, which was turning green, and his down-at-heel shoes. He was leading our two mules.

Zorba showed him the roll of notes.

"We'll split, Father Joseph," he said. "You can buy two hundred pounds of salt cod and stuff yourself with it till you burst your belly. Till you spew it up and deliver yourself from cod for ever and ever! Come on, hold out your paw!"

The monk took the dirty notes and hid them.

"I shall buy some paraffin!" he said.

Zorba lowered his voice and whispered in the old monk's ear.

"In the dark when they're all asleep, the bearded old goats; and there must be a good wind," he recommended. "Sprinkle the walls on all sides. You only need soak some rags or cotton waste, anything, then put a light to it. Got the idea?"

The monk was trembling.

"Don't tremble like that! The archangel ordered you to do it, didn't he? Put your trust in paraffin and the grace of God! Good luck to you!"

We mounted, and I took a last look at the monastery.

"Have you learned anything, Zorba?" I asked.

"About the revolver shot? Don't worry your head about that, boss; old Zaharia's right: Sodom and Gomorrah! Demetrios killed the nice little monk. There you have it."

"Demetrios? Why?"

"Don't try to ferret it out, boss, it's all filth and foulness."

He turned towards the monastery. The monks were filing out of the refectory, heads bent, hands clasped, on their way to lock themselves in their cells.

"Give me your curses, holy Fathers!" he cried.

◇ 19 ◇

The first person we met as we dismounted on our beach that night was Bouboulina, who was sitting huddled up in front of the hut. When the lamp was lit and I saw her face I was alarmed.

"What's wrong, Madame Hortense? Are you ill?"

From the moment the great hope—marriage—had gleamed in her mind, our old siren had lost all her indefinable and dubious charms. She tried to wipe out the past and cast off the gaudy feathers with which she had adorned herself out of the spoils from her pashas, beys and admirals. She had no aspiration beyond that of becoming a serious and respectable commoner, a good, virtuous woman. She no longer made up, nor decked herself out; she showed herself just as she was: a poor creature who wanted to get married.

Zorba did not open his mouth. He kept nervously pulling at his newly dyed moustache. He bent down, lit the stove and put on some water for making coffee.

"You're cruel!" the old cabaret singer said all of a sudden in a hoarse voice.

Zorba raised his head and looked at her. His eyes softened. He could never hear a woman say anything to him in a harrowing tone without being completely overwhelmed. One tear from a woman could drown him.

He said nothing, put the coffee and sugar in the pot, and stirred.

"Why do you keep me pining so long before marrying me?" said the old siren. "I daren't show myself in the village any more. I'm disgraced! Disgraced! I shall kill myself."

I was resting on the bed. Leaning with my elbow on the pillow, I enjoyed this comically moving scene.

"Why didn't you bring the marriage wreaths?"

Zorba felt Bouboulina's plump little hand trembling on his knee. That knee was the last inch of solid ground to which this poor creature of a thousand and one shipwrecks could cling.

Zorba seemed to understand this and his heart relented. But once more he said nothing. He poured the coffee into three cups.

"Why didn't you bring the marriage wreaths, darling?" she repeated in a quavering voice.

"They haven't got any good ones in Candia," Zorba replied curtly.

He handed the cups round and squatted in a corner.

"I've written to Athens for them to send some," he went on. "I've ordered some white candles, too, and sugared almonds with chocolate flavor."

As he spoke his imagination kindled. His eyes sparkled, and like a poet in the burning second of creation, Zorba soared to heights where fiction and truth mingle and resemble each other, like sisters. He was squatting, and, resting thus, noisily drank his coffee. He lit a second cigarette; it had been a good day—he had the forest settlement in his pocket, he had paid off his debts, he was happy. He let himself go.

"Our marriage, my sweet Bouboulina," he said, "must make a stir. You wait till you see the bridal gown I've ordered for you. That's why I stayed so long in Candia, my love. I sent for two big fashion designers from Athens and I told them: 'Look! The woman I'm going to marry has no equal in the East or West! She was the acknowledged queen of four great Powers; now she's a widow, the great Powers are dead and she's consented to take me as her husband. So I want her bridal gown to have no equal either: it must be all in silk, pearls and gold stars!' The two designers protested: 'But that will be too beautiful!' they said. 'All the guests will be blinded by such magnificence!' 'Never mind about that!' I said. 'What does it matter? As long as my beloved is satisfied!'"

Dame Hortense listened to him, leaning against the wall. A wide, fleshy smile spread across her creased and flabby face, and the red ribbon round her neck was well nigh splitting.

"I want to whisper in your ear," she said to Zorba, making great sheep's eyes at him.

Zorba winked at me and leaned forward.

"I've brought you something tonight," whispered his future wife, almost poking her little tongue into his big hairy ear.

She pulled out of her bodice a handkerchief with one corner knotted, and proffered it to Zorba.

He took the little handkerchief between two fingers and placed it on his right knee, then, turning to the door, looked out at the sea.

"Aren't you going to undo the knot, Zorba?" she asked. "You don't seem to be in a hurry!"

"Let me drink my coffee and smoke my cigarette first," he answered. "I don't have to undo it, I know what there is inside."

"Undo it, undo it!" the old siren begged him.

"I'm going to finish my smoke first, I tell you!"

And he cast a glance of accusation at me, as if to say: "This is your fault!"

He was smoking slowly, expelling the smoke from his nostrils as he looked at the sea.

"We'll have a sirocco tomorrow," he said. "The weather's changed. The tree'll swell, and so will young girls' breasts—they'll be bursting out of their bodices! Ah! spring's a rogue! An invention of the devil!"

He stopped speaking. A few moments later he added:

"Have you noticed, boss, everything good in this world is an invention of the devil? Pretty women, spring, roast suckling, wine—the devil made them all! God made monks, fasting, camomile-tea and ugly women . . . pooh!"

As he said that he threw a fierce glance at poor Dame Hortense, who was curled up in a corner, listening to him.

"Zorba! Zorba!" she implored him every second.

But he lit another cigarette and started contemplating the sea afresh.

"In the spring," he said, "Satan reigns supreme. Belts are

slackened, blouses unbuttoned, old ladies sigh. . . . Hands off, Bouboulina!"

"Zorba! Zorba!" the poor old creature implored. She stooped to pick up the handkerchief and thrust it into his hand.

He threw away his cigarette, took hold of the knot and undid it. He held his hand open and looked.

"Whatever's this, Dame Bouboulina?" he asked with disgust.

"Rings, little rings, my treasure. Wedding rings," muttered the old siren, all of a tremble. "Here is a witness, God bless him, the night is beautiful, it's sirocco weather, God is watching, let's get engaged, Zorba!"

Zorba looked now at me, now at Dame Hortense, now at the rings. A host of demons were fighting inside him and for the moment none was on top. The wretched woman looked at him in terror.

"Zorba! . . . My Zorba!" she cooed.

I had sat up on my bed and was watching. Of all courses open to him, which was Zorba going to choose?

Suddenly he shook his head. He had made his decision. His face cleared, he clapped his hands and leaped up.

"Let's go outside!" he cried. "Beneath the stars, so that God himself can see us! You carry the rings, boss; can you chant?"

"No," I replied, amused. "But that doesn't matter!" I had already jumped down from the bed and was helping the good lady to get up.

"Well, I can. I forgot to tell you I was once a choirboy; I used to follow the priest at weddings, baptisms, funerals and so on; I learned all the church songs by heart. Come, my Bouboulina, come, hoist your sail, my little French frigate, and come on my right!"

Of all Zorba's demons it was the kind-hearted clown who had won. Zorba had been sorry for the old siren, his heart had been torn when he saw her faded eyes fixed on him so anxiously.

"Devil take me," he muttered as he made his decision, "I can still give some joy to the female of the species! Come on!"

He rushed out onto the beach, took Dame Hortense's arm, gave me the rings, turned to the sea and began to chant:

"Blessed be our Lord in the world without end, amen!"

He turned to me and said:

"Do your stuff, boss!"

"There is no such thing as 'boss' tonight," I said. "I'm your best man."

"Well, keep your wits about you, then. When I cry out: 'Bravo!' you put the rings on."

He started chanting again in his deep ass's bray:

"For the servant of God, Alexis, and the servant of God, Hortense, now affianced to each other, we beg salvation, O Lord."

"*Kyrie eleison! Kyrie eleison!*" I quavered, with difficulty controlling laughter and tears.

"There's a lot more business, yet," said Zorba, "damned if I can remember it all! Anyway, let's get the ticklish part over!"

He leaped in the air like a carp and cried:

"Bravo! Bravo!" holding out his big hands towards me.

"Now you hold out your little hand," he said to his fiancée.

The fat hand, lined with washing and housework, was held out trembling towards me.

I put their rings on while Zorba, quite beside himself, roared out like a Dervish:

"The servant of God, Alexis is affianced to the servant of God, Hortense, in the name of God the Father, the Son and the Holy Ghost, amen! The servant of God, Hortense is affianced to the servant of God, Alexis!"

"Good. Now, that's done till next year! Come here, my sweet, let me give you the first respectable and legitimate kiss you've ever had!"

But Dame Hortense had collapsed to the ground; she was clasping Zorba's legs and weeping. Zorba shook his head with compassion.

"Poor women! What fools they are!" he murmured.

Dame Hortense stood up, shook her skirt and opened her arms.

"Eh, now!" shouted Zorba. "It's Shrove Tuesday today, keep your hands off! It's Lent!"

"My Zorba. . . ." she faltered faintly.

"Patience, my dear. Wait till Easter; we'll eat some meat then, and crack red eggs together. Now it's time you were getting home. What will folks say if they see you hanging about here till this time of night?"

Bouboulina's look was imploring.

"No! No! It's Lent!" said Zorba. "Not before Easter! Come along with us."

He leaned over and said in my ear:

"Don't leave us alone, for God's sake! I'm not in the mood!"

We took the road to the village. The sky was bright, the tang of the sea enveloped us, the birds of night hooted about us. The old siren, hanging on to Zorba's arm, dragged along happy but disappointed.

She had at last entered the harbor she had yearned for so much. All her life she had sung and danced, had a high old time, made fun of decent women . . . but her heart had been torn to shreds. When she went by, perfumed and heavily plastered with paint, wearing loud and garish clothes, in the streets of Alexandria, Beirut, Constantinople, and saw women giving the breast to their babies, her own breasts tingled and swelled, her nipples stood out, asking for a tiny childlike mouth as well. "Get a husband, get a husband, have a child. . . ." that had been her dream throughout her long life. But she never revealed these painful longings to a living soul. Now, God be praised, a little late but better than never, she was entering the longed-for haven, though crippled and buffeted by the waves.

From time to time she raised her eyes and peeped sideways at the great gawk of a fellow who was striding beside her. "He isn't a rich pasha with a gold-tasselled fez," she was thinking, "and he's not the handsome son of a bey, but, God be praised, he's better than nothing! He will be my husband! My husband forever, God be praised!"

Zorba felt her weighing on his arm and dragged her on eager to reach the village and be rid of her. And the poor woman kept tripping over the stones in the road; her toenails were almost torn out, her corns were hurting, but she said not a word. Why speak? Why complain? Everything was splendid, praise be to God!

We passed the Fig Tree of Our Young Lady and the widow's garden, and when the first village houses appeared we stopped.

"Good night, my treasure," said the old siren fondly, standing up on tiptoe to reach her fiancé's lips.

But Zorba did not bend.

"Let me kiss your feet, my love!" said Bouboulina, making ready to drop to the ground.

"No! No!" protested Zorba. He was moved and took her in his arms. "I ought to kiss *your* feet, my love! I ought to . . . but I don't feel up to it! Good night!"

We left her and went in silence along the road, breathing in the scented air. Zorba suddenly turned to me.

"What ought we to do, boss? Laugh? Or cry? Give me some advice."

I made no answer. I was tight about the throat, too, and could not say why: was it from laughing or crying?

"Boss," said Zorba suddenly, "who was that rascally god who would never let a single woman have room for complaint? I've heard something about him, I know. It seems he used to dye his beard, too, and tattooed hearts and arrows and sirens on his arms; he used to disguise himself, they say: turned into a bull, a swan, a ram, and, saving his reverence, an ass; in fact, whatever the jades desired. What was his name?"

"You must be talking about Zeus. What made you think of him?"

"God preserve his soul!" said Zorba, raising his arms to heaven. "He had some rough times, he did! What he must have gone through! A great martyr, believe me, boss! You swallow everything your books say, but just think a moment what the people who write books are like! Pff! a lot of schoolmasters. What do they know about women, or men who run after women? Not the first thing!"

"Why don't you write a book yourself, Zorba? And explain all the mysteries of the world to us?" I sneered.

"Why not? For the simple reason that I live all those mysteries, as you call them, and I haven't the time to write. Sometimes it's war, sometimes women, sometimes wine, sometimes the *santuri*: where would I find time to drive a miserable pen? That's how the business falls into the hands of the pen-pushers! All those who actually live the mysteries of life haven't the time to write, and all those who have the time don't live them! D'you see?"

"Let's get back to our subject! What about Zeus?"

"Ah! the poor chap!" sighed Zorba. "I'm the only one to know what he suffered. He loved women, of course, but not the way you think, you pen-pushers! Not at all! He was sorry for them! He understood what they all suffered and he sacrificed himself for their sakes! When, in some god-forsaken country hole, he saw an old maid wasting away with desire and regret, or a pretty young wife—or even if she wasn't at all pretty, even if she was a monster—and her husband away and she couldn't get to sleep, he used to cross himself, this good fellow, change his clothes, take on whatever shape the woman had in mind and go to her room.

"He never bothered about women who just wanted petting. No! Often enough even he was dead-beat: you can understand that. How could anybody satisfy all those she-goats? Ah! Zeus! the poor old goat. More than once he couldn't be bothered, he didn't feel too good. Have you never seen a billy after he's covered several she-goats? He slobbers at the mouth, his eyes are all misty and rheumy, he coughs a bit and can hardly stand on his feet. Well, poor old Zeus must have been in that sad state quite often.

"At dawn he'd come home, saying: 'Ah! my God! whenever shall I be able to have a good night's rest? I'm dropping!' And he'd keep wiping the saliva from his mouth.

"But suddenly he'd hear a sigh: down there on earth some woman had thrown off her bedclothes, gone out onto the balcony, almost stark naked, and was sighing enough to turn the sails of a mill! And my old Zeus would be quite overcome. 'Oh, hell! I'll have to go down again!' he'd groan. 'There's a woman bemoaning her lot! I'll have to go and console her!'

"And it went on like that to such an extent that the women emptied him completely. He couldn't move his back, he started vomiting, became paralyzed and died. That's when his heir, Christ, arrived. He saw the wretched state the old man was in: 'Beware of women!' he cried."

I admired Zorba's freshness of mind and rocked with laughter.

"You can laugh, boss! But if the god-devil makes our little venture here successful—it seems impossible to me, but still—do you know what sort of shop I'll open? A marriage bureau. Yes . . . that's right. 'The Zeus Marriage Agency'! Then the poor women who haven't managed to pick up a husband can all have another chance: old maids, plain women, the knock-kneed, the cross-eyed, the hump-backed, the lame, and I shall receive them all in a small lounge with a crowd of photographs on the walls of fine young fellows, and I'll say to them: 'Take your pick, ladies, choose the one you want, and I'll set about making him your husband.' Then I'll find any fellow who looks a bit like the photo, dress him up the same, give him some money and tell him: 'So-and-so Street, such-and-such a number, go and see Miss What's-it and make violent love to her. Don't be disgusted; I'll pay for it. Sleep with her. Tell her all the nice things a man ever tells a woman; she's never heard any of them, poor creature. Swear you'll marry her. Give the poor wretch a bit of pleasure, the sort of pleasure nanny-goats have, and even tortoises and centipedes.'

"And if some old nanny turned up on the lines of our old Bouboulina—God bless her!—and nobody would agree to console her, no matter how much I paid him, well . . . I'd cross myself, and I, director of the marriage bureau, would do it in person! Then you'd hear all the old fools of the neighborhood saying: 'Look at that! What an old rake! Hasn't he any eyes to see or nose to smell with?' 'Yes, you bunch of donkeys, I have got eyes! Yes, you pack of flint-hearted gossips, I have got a nose! But I've got a heart, too, and I'm sorry for her! And if you've got a heart, it's no use having all the eyes and noses in the world. When the time comes, they don't count a jot!'

"Then, when I'm absolutely impotent myself, through sowing wild oats, and I peg out, Saint Peter the Porter will open the gate of Paradise to me: 'Come in, Zorba, poor fellow,' he'll say; 'come in, Zorba the martyr. Go and lie down beside your comrade, Zeus! Rest, old chap, you did your bit on earth! My blessing on you!' "

Zorba went on talking. His imagination laid traps for him and he fell right into them. He began to believe in his own stories. As we were passing the Fig Tree of Our Young Lady, he sighed. Then holding out his arms as though swearing an oath, he said:

"Don't fret, Bouboulina, poor ill-treated, rotting old hulk. Don't fret! I won't leave you without consolation! You may have been abandoned by the four great Powers, by youth, and even by God himself, but I, Zorba, will not abandon you!"

It was after midnight when we got back to the beach, and the wind was rising. From yonder, from Africa, came the Notus, the warm south wind which swells out the trees, the vines, and the breasts of Crete. The whole island, as it lay by the water, came to life beneath the warm breath of this wind which makes the sap begin to rise. Zeus, Zorba and the south wind mingled together, and in the night I distinctly saw a great male face, with black beard and oily hair, bending down and pressing hot red lips on Dame Hortense, the Earth.

◊ 20 ◊

As soon as we arrived, we went to bed. Zorba rubbed his hands together in satisfaction.

"This has been a good day, boss. I suppose you'll ask me what I mean by 'good'? I mean full. Just think: this morning we were miles away at the monastery, settling the abbot's hash—he must have cursed us! Afterwards we came down here to our hut, found Dame Bouboulina and I got engaged. By the way, look at the ring. Mint gold. . . . She said she still had two English sovereigns the English admiral gave her towards the end of last century. She was keeping them, she said, for her funeral; and now—may the hour be kind to her—she goes and gives them to the goldsmith to have rings made of them. What a damned mystery mankind is!"

"Go to sleep, Zorba!" I said. "Calm down! That's enough for one day. Tomorrow we have a solemn ceremony to perform: the setting up of the first pylon for our cable. I've asked Pappa Stephanos to come."

"You did well, boss; that's not a bad idea. Let him come, that old goat-bearded priest, and let all the village notables come as well; we'll even give out little candles and they can light them. That's the sort of thing to make an impression; it'll be good for our business. Don't take any notice of what I do; I've got my own God and my own devil. But other people. . . ."

He began to laugh. He could not sleep; his brain was in a turmoil. "Ah, Grandad, may God sanctify your bones!" he said after a time. "He was a rake, too; just like me. And yet the old rascal went to the Holy Sepulcher and became a *hadji*,* God knows why! When he got back to the village, one of his cronies, a goat thief, who had never done a decent thing in his life, said: 'Well, my friend, didn't you bring me back a piece of the Holy Cross from the Holy Sepulcher?' 'What do you mean, didn't I bring you any back?' said my cunning old grandad, 'Do you think I'd forget you? Come to my house tonight and bring the priest with you to give his blessing and I'll hand it over to you. Bring a roast sucking pig, too, and some wine, to bring us luck!'

"That evening grandad went home and cut out of the doorpost, which was all worm-eaten, a small piece of wood, no bigger than a grain of rice; he wrapped it in some wadding, poured a drop or two of oil over it and waited. After a time, up comes the fellow in question with the priest, the sucking pig and the wine. The priest brings out his stole and gives the blessing. Grandad performs the ceremony of handing over the precious piece of wood, and then they start devouring the sucking pig. Well, believe me, boss, the fellow bowed and prostrated himself before that little piece of wood, hung it round his neck, and from that day forth was another man altogether. He changed completely. He went up into the mountains, joined the Armatoles and Klephts, and helped to burn Turkish villages. He'd run fearlessly through showers of bullets. Why should he be afraid? He was carrying a piece of the Holy Cross from the Holy Sepulcher—the bullets couldn't hit him."

Zorba burst out laughing.

"The idea's everything," he said. "Have you faith? Then a splinter from an old door becomes a sacred relic. Have you no faith? Then the whole Holy Cross itself becomes an old doorpost to you."

I admired this man whose brain functioned with so much confidence and daring and whose soul, wherever you touched it, struck out fire.

"Have you ever been to war, Zorba?"

* A person who has been on a pilgrimage to Mecca or Jerusalem, and, by extension, a person having made any pilgrimage, or related to such a person. C. W.

"How do I know?" he asked with a frown. "I can't remember. What war?"

"I mean, have you ever fought for your country?"

"Couldn't you talk about something else? All that nonsense is over and done with and best forgotten."

"Do you call that nonsense, Zorba? Aren't you ashamed? Is that how you speak of your country?"

Zorba raised his head and looked at me. I was lying on my bed, too, and the oil lamp was burning above my head. He looked at me severely for a time, then, taking a firm hold of his moustache, said:

"That's a half-baked thing to say; it's what I expect from a school-master. I might as well be singing, boss, for all the good it is my talking to you, if you'll pardon my saying so."

"What?" I protested. "I understand things, Zorba, don't forget."

"Yes, you understand with your brain. You say: 'This is right, and that's wrong; this is true, and that isn't; he's right, the other one's wrong. . . .' But where does that lead us? While you are talking I watch your arms and chest. Well, what are they doing? They're silent. They don't say a word. As though they hadn't a drop of blood between them. Well, what do you think you under-stand with? With your head? Bah!"

"Come, give me an answer, Zorba; don't try to dodge the ques-tion!" I said, to excite him. "I'm pretty sure you don't bother yourself overmuch about your country, do you?"

He was angry and banged his fist on the wall of petrol cans.

"The man you see here in front of you," he cried, "once embroi-dered the Church of Saint Sophia in hairs from his own head, and carried it round with him, hanging on his chest like a charm. Yes, boss, that's what I did, and I embroidered it with these great paws of mine, and with these hairs, too, which were as black as jet at the time. I used to wander about the mountains of Macedonia with Pavlos Melas *—I was a strapping fellow then, taller than this hut, with my kilt, red fez, silver charms, amulets, yataghan, cartridge cases and pistols. I was covered with steel, silver and studs. When I

* A Greek officer who distinguished himself in the war against the Bulgarian Comitadjis.

marched, there was a clatter and clank as if a regiment were passing down the street! Look here! Here! And look there!"

He opened his shirt and lowered his trousers.

"Bring the light over!" he ordered.

I held the lamp close to the thin, tanned body. What with deep scars, bullet and sword marks, his body was like a collander.

"Now look at the other side!"

He turned round and showed me his back.

"Not a scratch on the back, you see. Do you understand? Now take the lamp back."

"Nonsense!" he cried in a rage. "It's disgusting! When will men really be men, d'you think? We put trousers on, and shirts and collars and hats, and yet we're still a lot of mules, foxes, wolves and pigs. We say we're made in the image of God! Who, us? I spit on our idiotic mugs!"

Terrifying memories seemed to be coming to his mind and he was getting more and more exasperated. Incomprehensible words issued from between his shaking, hollow teeth.

He rose, picked up the water jug, took a long drink and seemed refreshed and calmer.

"No matter where you touch me, I yell," he said. "I'm all wounds and scars and lumps. What d'you mean by all that rot about women? When I discovered I was really a man, I didn't even turn round to look at them. I touched them for a minute, like that, in passing, like a cock, then went on. 'The dirty ferrets,' I said to myself. 'They'd like to suck me dry of all my strength. Bah! To hell with women!'

"Then I picked up my rifle and off I went! I went into the mountains as a *comitadji*. One day, at dusk, I came into a Bulgarian village and hid in a stable. It was the very house of a priest, a ferocious, pitiless Bulgarian *comitadji*. At night he'd take off his cassock, put on shepherd's clothes, pick up his rifle and go over into the neighboring Greek villages. He came back before dawn, trickling with mud and blood, and hurried to church to conduct mass for the faithful. A few days before this, he had killed a Greek schoolmaster asleep in his bed. So I went into this priest's stable and waited. Towards nightfall the priest came into the stable to feed the animals. I threw myself on him and cut his throat like a sheep. I lopped off his ears and stuck them in my pocket. I was making a collection of Bulgar ears, you see; so I took the priest's ears and made off.

"A few days later, there I was in the village again. It was midday. I was peddling. I'd left my arms in the mountains and had come down to buy bread, salt and boots for the others. Then I met five little kids in front of one of the houses—they were all dressed in black, barefoot, holding one another by the hand and begging. Three girls and two boys. The eldest couldn't have been more than ten, the youngest was still a baby. The eldest girl was carrying the youngster in her arms, kissing him and caressing him so that he shouldn't cry. I don't know why, divine inspiration I suppose, but I went up to them.

" 'Whose children are you?' I asked them in Bulgarian.

"The eldest boy raised his little head.

" 'The priest's. Father's throat was cut the other day in the stable,' he answered.

"The tears came to my eyes and the earth began turning round like a millstone. I leaned against the wall, and it stopped.

" 'Come here, children,' I said, 'come near to me.'

"I took out my purse; it was full of Turkish pounds and *mejidies*. I knelt down and poured them all out on the floor.

" 'There, take them!' I cried. 'Take them! Take them!'

"The children threw themselves on the ground and gathered up the money.

" 'It's for you! It's for you!' I cried. 'Take it all!'

"Then I left them my basket with all I had bought.

" 'All that's for you, too; take it all!'

"And I cleared out. I left the village, opened my shirt, seized the Saint Sophia I had embroidered and tore it to shreds, threw it away and ran for all I was worth.

"And I'm still running . . ."

Zorba leaned against the wall, and turned towards me.

"That was how I was rescued," he said.

"Rescued from your country?"

"Yes, from my country," he said in a firm, calm voice.

Then after a moment:

"Rescued from my country, from priests, and from money. I be-

225

gan sifting things, sifting more and more things out. I lighten my burden that way. I—how shall I put it?—I find my own deliverance, I become a man."

Zorba's eyes glowed, his large mouth laughed contentedly.

After staying silent a moment or two he started off again. His heart was overflowing, he couldn't control it.

"There was a time when I used to say: that man's a Turk, or a Bulgar, or a Greek. I've done things for my country that would make your hair stand on end, boss. I've cut people's throats, burned villages, robbed and raped women, wiped out entire families. Why? Because they were Bulgars, or Turks. 'Bah! To hell with you, you swine!' I say to myself sometimes. 'To hell with you right away, you ass.' Nowadays I say this man is a good fellow, that one's a bastard. They can be Greeks or Bulgars or Turks, it doesn't matter. Is he good? Or is he bad? That's the only thing I ask nowadays. And as I grow older—I'd swear this on the last crust I eat—I feel I shan't even go on asking that! Whether a man's good or bad, I'm sorry for him, for all of 'em. The sight of a man just rends my insides, even if I act as though I don't care a damn! There he is, poor devil, I think; he also eats and drinks and makes love and is frightened, whoever he is: he has his God and his devil just the same, and he'll peg out and lie as stiff as a board beneath the ground and be food for worms, just the same. Poor devil! We're all brothers! All worm meat!

"And if it's a woman. . . . Ah! then I just want to cry my eyes out! Your honored self, boss, keeps teasing me and saying I'm too fond of the women. Why shouldn't I be fond of 'em, when they're all weak creatures who don't know what they're doing and surrender on the spot if you just catch hold of their breasts . . .

"Once I went into another Bulgarian village. And one old brute who'd spotted me—he was a village elder—told the others and they surrounded the house I was lodging in. I slipped out onto the balcony and crept from one roof to the next; the moon was up and I jumped from balcony to balcony like a cat. But they saw my shadow, climbed up on to the roofs and started shooting. So what do I do? I dropped down into the yard, and there I found a Bulgarian woman in bed. She stood up in her nightdress, saw me and opened her mouth to shout, but I held out my arms and whispered: 'Mercy!

Mercy! Don't shout!' and seized her breasts. She went pale and half swooned.

" 'Come inside,' she said in a low voice. 'Come in so that we can't be seen. . . .'

"I went inside, she gripped my hand: 'Are you a Greek?' she said. 'Yes, Greek. Don't betray me.' I took her by the waist. She said not a word. I went to bed with her, and my heart trembled with pleasure. 'There, Zorba, you dog,' I said to myself, 'there's a woman for you; that's what humanity means! What is she? Bulgar? Greek? Papuan? That's the last thing that matters! She's human, and a human being with a mouth, and breasts, and she can love. Aren't you ashamed of killing? Bah! Swine!'

"That's the way I thought while I was with her, sharing her warmth. But did that mad bitch, my country, leave me in peace for that, do you think? I disappeared next morning in the clothes the Bulgar woman gave me. She was a widow. She took her late husband's clothes out of a chest, gave them to me, and she hugged my knees and begged me to come back to her.

"Yes, yes, I did go back . . . the following night. I was a patriot then, of course—a wild beast; I went back with a can of paraffin and set fire to the village. She must have been burnt along with the others, poor wretch. Her name was Ludmilla."

Zorba sighed. He lit a cigarette, took one or two puffs and then threw it away.

"My country, you say? . . . You believe all the rubbish your books tell you . . . ? Well, I'm the one you should believe. So long as there are countries, man will stay like an animal, a ferocious animal. . . . But I am delivered from all that, God be praised! It's finished for me! What about you?"

I didn't answer. I was envious of the man. He had lived with his flesh and blood—fighting, killing, kissing—all that I had tried to learn through pen and ink alone. All the problems I was trying to solve point by point in my solitude and glued to my chair, this man had solved up in the pure air of the mountains with his sword.

I closed my eyes, inconsolable.

"Are you asleep, boss?" said Zorba, vexed. "Here I am, like a fool, talking to you!"

He lay down grumbling, and very soon I heard him snoring.

I was not able to sleep all night. A nightingale we heard for the first time that night filled our solitude with an unbearable sadness and suddenly I felt the tears on my cheeks.

I was choking. I rose at dawn and gazed at the earth and the sea from the doorway of our hut. It seemed to me that the world had been transformed overnight. Opposite me on the sand, a small clump of thorny bushes, which had been a miserable dull color the day before, was now covered with tiny white blossoms. In the air hung a sweet, haunting perfume of lemon and orange trees in flower. I walked out a few steps. I could never see too much of this ever-recurring miracle.

Suddenly I heard a happy cry behind me. Zorba had risen and rushed to the door, half-naked. He, too, was thrilled by this sight of spring.

"What is that?" he asked stupefied. "That miracle over there, boss, that moving blue, what do they call it? Sea? Sea? And what's that wearing a flowered green apron? Earth? Who was the artist who did it? It's the first time I've seen that, boss, I swear!"

His eyes were brimming over.

"Zorba!" I cried. "Have you gone off your head?"

"What are you laughing at? Don't you see? There's magic behind all that, boss."

He rushed outside, began dancing and rolling in the grass like a foal in spring.

The sun appeared and I held out my palms to the warmth. Rising sap . . . the swelling breast . . . and the soul also blossoming like a tree; you could feel that body and soul were kneaded from the same material.

Zorba had stood up again, his hair full of dew and earth.

"Quick, boss!" he shouted. "We'll dress and make ourselves smart! Today we are to be blessed. It won't be long before the priest and the village notables are here. If they find us grovelling in the grass like this it will be a disgrace to the firm! So on with the collars and ties! Out with the serious faces! It doesn't matter a damn if you have no head, you must wear the right sort of hat . . . ! It's a crazy world!"

We dressed, the workmen arrived, and soon after them the notables.

"Make your mind up, boss, no fooling today! We mustn't make ourselves look ridiculous."

Pappa Stephanos walked in front in his dirty cassock with its deep pockets. At consecration ceremonies, funerals, marriages, baptisms, he would throw into these abysmal pockets anything he was offered: raisins, rolls, cheese pies, cucumbers, bits of meat, sugared sweets, everything . . . and at night, his wife, old Pappadia, would put on her spectacles and sort it all out, nibbling all the time.

Behind Pappa Stephanos came the elders: Kondomanolio, the café proprietor, who fancied he knew the world because he had been as far as Canea and had seen Prince George himself; uncle Anagnosti, calm and smiling, wearing a wide-sleeved, dazzling white shirt; the schoolmaster, grave and solemn with his stick, and, last of all, Mavrandoni, with his slow, heavy tread. He wore a black kerchief on his head, a black shirt and black shoes; he acknowledged us with a forced air. He was bitter and aloof. He stood a little apart, his back to the sea.

"In the name of Our Lord Jesus Christ!" said Zorba in a solemn voice. He went to the head of the procession and all followed him in pious self-communion.

Century-old memories of magic ceremonies were awakened in those peasant breasts. They all had their eyes riveted on the priest as though they expected him to confront and exorcise invisible forces. Thousands of years ago the sorcerer raised his arms, sprinkled the air with his holy water, muttered mysterious and allpowerful words, and the evil demons fled while the good spirits came from water, earth and air, to the aid of mankind.

We arrived at the pit we had dug by the sea to take the first pylon of the line. The men raised a huge pine trunk and set it up erect in the hole. Pappa Stephanos put on his stole, took his censer and, gazing at the trunk all the time, began intoning the exorcism: "May it be founded on solid rock, that neither wind nor water may shake it. Amen."

"Amen!" thundered Zorba, crossing himself.

"Amen!" murmured the elders.

"Amen!" said the workmen, last.

"May God bless your work and give you the wealth of Abraham

and Isaac!" the village priest continued, and Zorba pushed a hundred drachma note into his hand.

"My blessing on you!" said the priest, well content.

We returned to the hut, where Zorba offered them all wine and lenten hors d'œuvres—grilled octopus, fried squid, soaked beans and olives. When they had devoured the lot, the officials went off home. The magic ceremony was over.

"We managed to get through that all right!" said Zorba, rubbing his hands.

He undressed, put on his work clothes and took a pick.

"Come on!" he shouted to the men. "Cross yourselves and get on with the work!"

Zorba didn't raise his head again for the rest of the day.

Every fifty yards the workmen dug a hole, put in a post, and went on, making a beeline for the summit of the hill. Zorba measured, calculated and gave orders; he did not eat, smoke, or take a rest the whole day long. He was completely absorbed in the job.

"It's all because of doing things by halves," he would often say to me, and "saying things by halves, being good by halves, that the world is in the mess it's in today. Do things properly by God! One good knock for each nail and you'll win through! God hates a half-devil ten times more than an archdevil!"

That evening, when he came in from work, he lay down on the sand, exhausted.

"I'm going to sleep here," he said. "I'll wait for dawn, then we'll begin work again. I'm going to start night shifts."

"Why all the hurry, Zorba?"

He hesitated a moment.

"Why? Well, I want to see whether I've found the right slope or not. If I haven't, we're done for. Don't you see, boss? The sooner I see if we're dished, the better it'll be for us."

He ate quickly, gluttonously, and soon afterwards the beach echoed to his snores. I, for my part, stayed awake a long time, watching the stars travel across the sky. I saw the whole sky change its position—and the shell of my skull, like an observatory dome, changed position, too, together with the constellations. "Watch the movement of the stars as if you were turning with them. . . ." This sentence of Marcus Aurelius filled my heart with harmony.

◇ 21 ◇

IT WAS Easter Day. Zorba had dressed himself up. He had put on some thick, dark-purple, woollen socks which he said had been knitted for him by one of his women friends in Macedonia. He anxiously ran up and down a hillock near our beach. Putting his hand up over his thick eyebrows to shield his eyes, he watched the village road.

"She's late, the old seal; she's late, the trollop; she's late, the old tattered banner!"

A butterfly, fresh from the chrysalis, flew up and tried to light on Zorba's moustache, but it tickled him, he snorted and the butterfly flew calmly away and disappeared in the rays of the sun.

We were expecting Dame Hortense that day to celebrate Easter. We had roasted a lamb on the spit, laid a white cloth on the sand and painted some eggs. Half in fun, half in earnest, we had decided to prepare a grand reception for her. On that isolated beach, this dumpy, perfumed, slightly rotting siren always exercised a strange charm upon us. When she wasn't there we missed something—a scent like eau-de-Cologne, a jerky waddling gait like that of a duck, a slightly husky voice, and two pale, acidulous eyes.

So we had cut myrtle and laurel branches and made a triumphal arch under which she would have to pass. And on the arch itself we had stuck four flags—English, French, Italian, Russian—and in the center, on high, a long white sheet striped with blue. Not being admirals we had no cannon, but we had borrowed two rifles and had decided to wait on the hillock, and as soon as we saw our seal rolling and bouncing along the road to fire a salvo. We wanted to revive on this solitary coast something of her past grandeur, so that she, too, could enjoy a momentary illusion, poor wretch, and think herself once more a ruby-lipped young woman with firm breasts, patent-leather court shoes and silk stockings. What was the use of the Resurrection of Christ, if it was not a sign for the rekindling of youth and joy in us as well? If it could not make an old *cocotte* feel one-and-twenty again?

"She's late, the old seal; she's late, the trollop; she's late, the old tattered banner!" Zorba grumbled every minute, pulling up his aubergine-colored socks, which kept falling down.

"Come and sit down, Zorba! Come and have a smoke in the shade here. She won't be long!"

He cast a last glance down the village road and then came over to sit under the carob tree. It was nearly midday and it was hot. In the distance we could hear the lively, joyous bells of Easter. From time to time the wind brought us the sound of the Cretan lyre.* The whole village was buzzing with life, like a hive in springtime.

Zorba shook his head.

"It's finished. I used to feel my soul rise again every Easter, at the same time as Christ, but that's all finished!" he said. "Now, only my body is reborn—because when somebody stands you a meal, and then a second and a third, and they say: 'Just have this little mouthful, and just this one more' . . . well, you just fill yourself up with more heaps of luscious food, which doesn't all turn into dung. There's something which stays, something that's saved and turns into good humor, dancing, singing, wrangling even—that's what I call Resurrection."

He stood up, looked at the horizon and frowned.

"There's a youngster running this way," he said, and hurried to meet him.

The boy stood on tiptoe and whispered something in Zorba's ear, who started back, furious.

* A kind of *viola da braccio* with three strings and bells attached to the bow. It shows Venetian influence. C. W.

"Ill?" he shouted. "Ill? Shoot off or I'll beat you up!" Then he turned to me.

"Boss, I'm running down to the village to see what's happened to the old seal. . . . Just a minute. . . . Give me two red eggs so that I can crack them with her. I'll be back."

He put the two eggs in his pocket, pulled up his aubergine socks and went off.

I came down from the hillock and lay on the cool pebbles. There was a light breeze, the sea was faintly ruffled; two seagulls bobbed up and down on the tiny waves, with necks fluffed out, voluptuously enjoying the movement of the water.

I could well imagine their delight in the freshness of the water under their bellies. As I watched the seagulls, I thought: "That's the road to take; find the absolute rhythm and follow it with absolute trust."

An hour later Zorba reappeared, stroking his moustache with an air of satisfaction.

"She's caught cold, poor sweet," he said. "Nothing really. The last few days—in fact the whole of Holy Week—she's been going to the midnight service, even though she's a Frank.* She went on my account, she says. And she caught cold at it. So I cupped her, rubbed her with oil from the lamp and gave her a glass of rum. Tomorrow she'll be hale and hearty again. Ha! the old crock, she's amusing in her way; you should have heard her cooing like a dove while I massaged her—she said it tickled!"

We sat down to eat, and Zorba filled the glasses.

"To her health! May the devil not think of taking her off for a long while yet!"

We ate and drank for some time in silence. The wind carried up to us, like the droning of bees, the distant, passionate notes of the lyre. Christ was being reborn again on the village terraces. The paschal lamb and the Easter cakes were being transformed into love songs.

When Zorba had eaten and drunk quite copiously, he put his hand to his big hairy ear.

"The lyre . . ." he murmured. "They're dancing in the village."

* In the Levant, Europeans are referred to as "Franks." C. W.

He stood up suddenly. The wine had gone to his head.

"What ever are we doing here, all alone, like a pair of cuckoos? Let's go and dance! Aren't you sorry for the lamb we've been eating? Are you going to let it fizzle out into nothing, like that? Come on! Turn it into song and dance! Zorba is reborn!"

"Wait a minute, Zorba, you idiot, are you crazy?"

"Honestly, boss, I don't care! But I'm sorry for the lamb, and I'm sorry for the red eggs, the Easter cakes and the cream cheese! If I'd just scoffed a few bits of bread and some olives, I'd say: 'Oh, let's go to sleep; I don't need to go celebrating!' Olives and bread are nothing, are they? What can you expect from them? But, let me tell you, it's a sin to waste food like that! Come on, let's celebrate the Resurrection, boss!"

"I don't feel like it today. You go—you can dance for me as well."

Zorba took my arm and pulled me up.

"Christ is reborn, my friend! Ah! if only I was as young as you! I'd throw myself headlong into everything! Headlong into work, wine, love—everything, and I'd fear neither God nor devil! That's youth for you!"

"It's the lamb talking, Zorba! It's turned wild inside you, changed into a wolf!"

"The lamb's changed into Zorba, that's all, and Zorba's talking to you! Listen, you can swear at me afterwards! I'm a Sinbad the Sailor . . . I don't mean I've wandered all over the world; not at all! But I've robbed, killed, lied, slept with heaps of women and broken all the commandments. How many are there? Ten? Why aren't there twenty, fifty, a hundred? So I could break them all? Yet, if there is a God, I shan't be afraid to appear before him when the time comes. I don't know how to put it to make you understand. I don't think any of that's important, do you see? Would God bother to sit over the earthworms and keep count of everything they do? And get angry and storm and fret himself silly because one went astray with the female earthworm next door or swallowed a mouthful of meat on Good Friday? Bah! Get away with you, all you soup-swilling priests! Bah!"

"Well, Zorba," I said, to make him wild, "God may not ask you what you ate, but he'll certainly ask you what you did."

"And I say he won't ask that either! 'And how do you know that,

Zorba, you ignoramus?' you'll ask me. I just know! I'm sure of it! If I had two sons, one quiet, careful, moderate and pious, and the other rascally, greedy, lawless and a woman-chaser, my heart would go out to the second one. Perhaps because he'd be like me? But who's to say I'm not more like God himself than old Pappa Stephanos, who spends his days and nights going down on his knees, and collecting money?

"God enjoys himself, kills, commits injustice, makes love, works, likes impossible things, just the same as I do. He eats what he pleases; takes the woman he chooses. If you see a lovely woman going by, as fresh as clear water, your heart leaps at the sight. Suddenly the ground opens and she disappears. Where does she go? Who takes her? If she's a good woman, they say: 'God has taken her.' If she's a harlot, they say: 'The devil's carried her off.' But, boss, I've said so before, and I say it again, God and the devil are one and the same thing!"

Zorba picked up his stick, pushed his cap to one side, perkily, looked at me with pity and his lips moved for a moment as if he wanted to add something to what he had just said. But he said nothing and went off with his head in the air towards the village.

In the evening light I could see his giant shadow and his swinging stick. The whole beach came alive as Zorba passed by. I listened for some time, picking out his steps as they grew fainter and fainter. As soon as I felt myself to be absolutely alone, I leaped up. Why? To go where? I did not know. My mind had made no decision. was my body that had leaped up. My body alone was deciding aı was not consulting me.

"Go on! Forward!" it commanded.

I went towards the village with quick determined steps, stopping here and there to enjoy a deep breath of spring. The earth smelled of camomile, and as I approached the gardens I ran into wave upon wave of perfume from the blossom on the lemon and orange trees and the laurels. In the west the evening star began to dance merrily in the sky.

"Sea, women, wine and hard work!" I was murmuring Zorba's words in spite of myself as I walked. "Sea, women, wine and hard work! Throwing yourself headlong into your work, into wine, and love, and never being afraid of either God or devil . . . that's what youth is!" I kept saying it to myself and repeating it as if to give myself courage, and I walked on.

Suddenly I stopped dead. As though I had come to my destination. Where? I looked round: I was in front of the widow's garden. Behind the hedge of reeds and prickly pear I could hear someone humming in a soft, feminine voice. I went near and parted the reeds. Beneath the orange tree was a woman, dressed in black, with a great swelling bosom. She was cutting branches of blossom and singing as she did so. In the dusk I could see the white globes of her half-naked breasts.

It took my breath away. She's a wild beast, I thought, and she knows it. What poor, vain, absurd, defenceless creatures men are to her! She is fat and voracious, just like some female insects—the praying mantis, the grasshopper, the spider—and she too must devour the males at dawn.

Had the widow become aware of my gaze? She suddenly ceased her song and turned round. Our eyes met. I felt my knees give way, as though I had seen a tigress behind the reeds.

"Who is it?" she said in a strangled voice. She pulled her neckerchief over her bosom. Her face darkened.

I was on the point of leaving, but Zorba's words suddenly filled my heart. I gathered strength. "Sea, women, wine . . ."

"It's me," I answered. "It's me. Let me in."

I had hardly said these words when a feeling of terror gripped me and I was just about to run away again. But I controlled myself, though filled with shame.

"Who d'you mean, you?"

She took a slow, cautious step forward, leaning in my direction. She half-closed her eyes to see more clearly, advanced another step, with head forward, on the alert.

Suddenly her face lit up. She put the tip of her tongue out and licked her lips.

"The boss!" she said in a softer voice.

She came forward again, crouching as if ready to leap.

"You, boss?" she asked hoarsely.

"Yes."

"Come!"

Dawn was breaking. Zorba was home already, sitting before the hut on the beach. He was smoking, looking out to sea. He seemed to be waiting for me.

As soon as I appeared he raised his head and fixed me with his gaze. His nostrils were quivering, like those of a greyhound. He craned his neck and took a long sniff . . . he was scenting me. In a second his face lit up with joy; he had scented the widow.

He stood up slowly, smiled with his whole being and stretched out his arms to me.

"My blessing on you!" he said.

I went to bed, closed my eyes. I heard the sea quietly, rhythmically breathing, and I felt myself rise and fall on it like a seagull. Thus, gently rocked, I fell asleep and dreamed: I saw, as it were, a giant negress crouching on the ground, and she looked to me like a gigantic old temple in granite. I was going round and round her desperately trying to find the entrance. I was scarcely as big as her little toe. Suddenly, as I rounded her heel, I saw a dark opening, rather like a cave. A great voice commanded: "Enter!"

And I entered.

I woke towards midday. The sun was coming in through the window, bathing the bedclothes in light; its rays were beating with such force on the small mirror hanging on the wall that they seemed to be shattering it into a thousand fragments.

The dream about the giant negress came back to my mind, I could hear the sea murmuring, I closed my eyes again and I was deeply happy. My body was light and contented, like an animal after the hunt, when it has caught and eaten its prey and is lying in the sun, licking its lips. My mind, a body too in its way, was resting, contented. It seemed to have found a marvellously simple answer to the vital, complicated problems which tormented it.

All of the joy of the previous night flowed back from the inner-most depths of my being, spread out into fresh courses and abundantly watered the earth of which I was made. As I lay, with my eyes closed, I seemed to hear my being bursting its shell and growing larger. That night, for the first time, I felt clearly that the soul is flesh as well, perhaps more volatile, more diaphanous, perhaps freer, but flesh all the same. And the flesh is soul, somewhat turgid perhaps, somewhat exhausted by its long journeys, and bowed under the burden it has inherited.

I felt a shadow fall across me and opened my eyes; Zorba was standing in the doorway looking at me happily.

"Don't wake, don't wake, old chap! . . ." he said gently with an almost maternal solicitude. "It's a holiday today, too. Sleep on!"

"I've slept enough," I said, sitting up.

"I'll beat up an egg for you," said Zorba, smiling. "It builds you up!"

I made no answer but ran down to the sea, dived into the water, then dried in the sun. But I could still feel a sweet, persistent odor in my nostrils, on my lips and fingers. The scent of orange water and of the laurel oil with which Cretan women dress their hair.

Last night she had cut an armful of orange blossom which she was going to take to Christ that evening when the villagers were dancing beneath the white poplars in the square and the church was empty. The iconostasis above her bed was loaded with lemon flowers, and through the petals could be seen the mourning Virgin, with large almond eyes.

Zorba brought the egg in a cup down to the beach for me, with two oranges and a small Easter bun. He served me quietly and happily, as a mother would her son when he returns from the wars. He looked at me fondly and then went away.

"I'm going to put a few pylons in," he said.

I calmly chewed my food in the sun and felt a deep physical happiness as if I was floating on the cool, green waters of the sea. I did not allow my mind to take possession of this carnal joy, to press it into its own moulds, and make thoughts of it. I let my whole body rejoice from head to foot, like an animal. Now and then, nevertheless, in ecstasy, I gazed about me and within me, at the miracle of this life: What is happening? I said to myself. How did it come about that the world is so perfectly adapted to our feet and hands and bellies? And once again I closed my eyes and was silent.

Suddenly I stood up and went into the hut; there I picked up the Buddha manuscript and opened it. I had finished it. At the end, Buddha was lying beneath the flowering tree. He had raised his hand and ordered the five elements he was made of—earth, water, fire, air, spirit—to dissolve.

I had no more need of this image of my torment; I had gone beyond it, I had completed my service with Buddha—I, too, raised my hand, and ordered the Buddha within me to dissolve.

In great haste, with the help of words and their great exorcising power, I devastated his body, mind and spirit. Pitilessly I scratched the final words onto the paper, uttered the ultimate cry and wrote my name with a big red pencil. It was finished.

I took a thick piece of string and tied up the manuscript. I felt a strange sort of pleasure, as though I were tying up the hands and feet of a redoubtable enemy, or as savages must feel as they bind the bodies of their loved ones when they die, so that they shall not climb out of their graves and turn into ghosts.

A little girl suddenly ran up to me, barefoot. She was wearing a yellow dress and clasping a red egg tightly in her hand. She stopped and looked at me, terror-stricken.

"Well," I asked her, smiling to encourage her, "did you want something?"

She sniffed and answered in a small, breathless voice.

"The lady has sent me to ask you to come. She is in bed. Are you the one they call Zorba?"

"All right. I'll come."

I slipped another red egg into her other tiny hand and she ran off.

I rose and started along the road. The village noises grew louder: the sweet sounds of the lyre, shouts, gunshots, joyous songs. When I came to the square, youths and girls had gathered beneath the fresh foliage of the poplars and were about to begin dancing. Sitting on the benches round the trees, the old men were watching, with their chins resting on their sticks. The old women were standing behind. The brilliant lyre player, Fanurio, an April rose stuck behind his ear, was lording it amidst the dancers. With his left hand he held the lyre upright on his knee and with the right he was trying his bow with its noisy bells.

"Christ is reborn!" I shouted as I passed.

"He is, indeed!" came the answer in a joyful murmur from them all.

I looked round quickly. Well-built youths, with slim waists, wearing puffed-out breeches and, on their heads, kerchiefs with fringes which fell over their foreheads and temples like curly locks. And young girls, with sequins round their necks, embroidered white fichus, and lowered eyes, were trembling with expectation.

"Wouldn't you care to stay with us, sir?" asked a few voices.

But I had already passed.

Madame Hortense was lying in her big bed, the only piece of furniture she had always managed to hold on to. Her cheeks were burning with fever, and she was coughing.

As soon as she saw me she sighed complainingly.

"And Zorba? Where is Zorba?"

"He's not very well. Since the day you fell ill, he's been sick, too. He keeps holding your photograph in his hand and sighing as he gazes at it."

"Tell me more, tell me more . . ." murmured the poor old siren, closing her eyes in happiness.

"He's sent me to ask you if you want anything. He'll come himself this evening, he said, although he can't get about very well himself. He can't bear being away from you any longer. . . ."

"Go on, please, go on. . . ."

"He's had a telegram from Athens. The wedding clothes are ready, and the wreaths. They are on the boat and should be here soon . . . with the white candles and their pink ribbons. . . ."

"Go on, go on. . . ."

Sleep had won, her breathing changed; she began to talk deliriously. The room smelled of eau-de-Cologne, ammonia and sweat. Through the open window came the pungent odor of the excrement from the hens and rabbits in the yard.

I rose and slipped out of the room. At the door I ran across Mimiko. He was wearing new breeches and boots, and he had pushed a sprig of sweet basil behind his ear.

"Mimiko," I said to him, "run to Kalo village, will you, and bring the doctor!"

Mimiko had his boots off before I had finished speaking—he did not mean to spoil them on the way. He tucked them under his arm.

"Find the doctor, give him my respects and tell him to mount his old mare and come over here without fail. Tell him the lady's

240

dangerously ill. She's caught cold, poor thing, she's feverish and she's dying, say. Don't forget to tell him that. Now be off!"

"Right away!"

He spat into his hands, clapped them joyously against one another, but didn't move. He looked at me with a gay twinkle in his eye.

"Get going! Didn't I say?"

He still did not budge. He winked at me and smiled satanically.

"Sir," he said, "I've taken a bottle of orange water up to your place as a present."

He stopped for a second. He was waiting for me to ask him who had sent it, but I did not do so.

"Don't you want to know who sent it, sir?" he chuckled. "It's for you to put in your hair, she said, to make you smell good."

"Get along! Quick! And keep your mouth shut!"

He laughed, spitting on his hands once more.

"Right away!" he cried again. "Christ is reborn!"

And he disappeared.

◊ 22 ◊

Beneath the poplar trees the paschal dance was at its height. It was led by a tall, handsome, dark youth of about twenty, whose cheeks were covered with a thick down which had never known a razor. In the opening of his shirt his chest made a splash of dark color—it was covered with curly hair. His head was thrown back, his feet beating against the earth like wings; from time to time he cast a glance at some girl, and the whites of his eyes gleamed steadily, disturbingly from a visage blackened by the sun.

I was enchanted and at the same time frightened. I was returning from Dame Hortense's house; I had called a woman in to look after her. This relieved me, and I had come to watch the Cretans dance. So I went up to uncle Anagnosti and sat down on a bench next to him.

"Who is that young man leading the dance?" I asked.

Uncle Anagnosti laughed:

"He's like the archangel who bears your soul away, the rascal," he said with admiration. "It's Sifakas, the shepherd. All the year round he keeps his flock on the mountains, then comes down at Easter to see people and to dance."

He sighed.

"Ah, if only I had his youth!" he muttered. "If I had his youth, by God! I'd take Constantinople by storm!"

The young man shook his head and gave a cry, bleating inhumanly, like a rutting ram.

"Play, play, Fanurio!" he shouted. "Play until Charon himself is dead."

Every minute death was dying and being reborn, just like life. For thousands of years young girls and boys have danced beneath the tender foliage of the trees in spring—beneath the poplars, firs, oaks, planes and slender palms—and they will go on dancing for thousands more years, their faces consumed with desire. Faces change, crumble, return to earth; but others rise to take their place. There is only one dancer, but he has a thousand masks. He is always twenty. He is immortal.

The young man raised his hand to stroke his moustache, but he had none.

"Play!" he cried again. "Play, Fanurio, or I shall burst!"

The lyre player shook his hand, the lyre responded, the bells began to tinkle in rhythm and the young man took one leap, striking his feet together three times on the air, as high as a man stands, and with his boots caught the white kerchief from round the head of his neighbor, Manolakas, the constable.

"Bravo, Sifakas!" they cried, and the young girls trembled and lowered their eyes.

But the young man was silent and not looking at anyone at all. Wild and yet self-disciplined, he rested his left hand, palm outwards on his slim and powerful thighs, as he danced with his eyes fixed timidly on the ground. The dance ceased abruptly as the old verger, Androulio, came rushing into the square, his arms raised to heaven.

"The widow! The widow!" he shouted breathlessly.

Manolakas, the constable, was the first to run to him, breaking off the dance. From the square you could see the church, which was still adorned with myrtle and laurel branches. The dancers stopped, the blood coursing through their heads, and the old men rose from their seats. Fanurio put the lyre down on his lap, took the April rose from behind his ear and smelled it.

"Where, Androulio?" they cried, boiling with rage. "Where is she?"

"In the church; the wretch has just gone in; she was carrying an armful of lemon blossom!"

"Come on! At her!" cried the constable, rushing ahead.

At that moment the widow appeared on the doorstep of the church, a black kerchief over her head. She crossed herself.

"Wretch! Slut! Murderess!" the voices cried. "And she's got the cheek to show herself here! After her! She's disgraced the village!"

Some followed the constable who was running towards the church, others, from above, threw stones at her. One stone hit her on the shoulder; she screamed, covered her face with her hands, and rushed forward. But the young men had already reached the church door and Manolakas had pulled out his knife.

The widow drew back uttering little cries of terror, bent herself double to protect her face and ran back stumbling to shelter in the church. But on the threshold was planted old Mavrandoni. With a hand on each side of the door he blocked the way.

The widow jumped to the left and clung to the big cypress tree in the courtyard. A stone whistled through the air, hit her head and tore off her kerchief. Her hair came undone and tumbled down over her shoulders.

"In Christ's name! In Christ's name!" the widow screamed, clinging tightly to the cypress tree.

Standing in a row on the square the young girls of the village were biting their white kerchiefs, eagerly watching the scene. The old women, leaning on the walls, were yelping: "Kill her! Kill her!"

Two young men threw themselves at her, caught her. Her black blouse was torn open and her breasts gleamed, white as marble. The blood was running from the top of her head down her forehead, cheeks and neck.

"In Christ's name! In Christ's name!" she panted.

The flowing blood and the gleaming breasts had excited the young men. Knives appeared from their belts.

"Stop!" shouted Mavrandoni. "She's mine!"

Mavrandoni, still standing on the threshold of the church, raised his hand. They all stopped.

"Manolakas," he said in a deep voice, "your cousin's blood is crying out to you. Give him peace."

I leaped from the wall on which I had climbed and ran towards the church; my foot hit a stone and I fell to the ground.

Just at that moment Sifakas was passing. He bent down, picked me up by the scruff of the neck like a cat and put me on my feet.

"This is no place for the likes of you!" he said. "Clear off!"

"Have you no feeling for her, Sifakas?" I asked. "Have pity on her!"

The savage mountaineer laughed in my face.

"D'you take me for a woman? Asking me to have pity! I'm a man!"

And in a second he was in the churchyard.

I followed him closely but was out of breath. They were all round the widow now. There was a heavy silence. You could hear only the victim's strangled breathing.

Manolakas crossed himself, stepped forward, raised the knife; the old women, up on the walls, yelped with joy. The young girls pulled down their kerchiefs and hid their faces.

The widow raised her eyes, saw the knife above her, and bellowed like a heifer. She collapsed at the foot of the cypress and her head sank between her shoulders. Her hair covered the ground, her throbbing neck glistened in the half-light.

"I call on God's justice!" cried old Mavrandoni, and he also crossed himself.

But just at that second a loud voice was heard behind us:

"Lower your knife, you murderer!"

Everyone turned round in stupefaction. Manolakas raised his head: Zorba was standing before him, swinging his arms with rage. He shouted:

"Aren't you ashamed? Fine lot of men you are! A whole village to kill a single woman! Take care or you'll disgrace the whole of Crete!"

"Mind your own business, Zorba! And keep your nose out of ours!" roared Mavrandoni.

Then he turned to his nephew.

"Manolakas," he said, "in the name of Christ and the Holy Virgin, strike!"

Manolakas leaped up. He seized the widow, threw her to the ground, placed his knee on her stomach and raised his knife. But in a flash Zorba had seized his arm and, with his big handkerchief

245

wrapped round his hand, strained to pull the knife from the constable's hand.

The widow got onto her knees and looked about her for a way of escape, but the villagers had barred the way. They were in a circle round the churchyard and standing on the benches; when they saw her looking for an opening they stepped forward and closed the circle.

Meanwhile Zorba, agile, resolute and calm, was struggling silently. From my place near the church door, I watched anxiously. Manolakas's face had gone purple with fury. Sifakas and another giant of a man came up to help him. But Manolakas indignantly rolled his eyes:

"Keep away! Keep away! Nobody's to come near!" he shouted.

He attacked Zorba again fiercely. He charged him with his head like a bull.

Zorba bit his lips without saying a word. He got a hold like a vise on the constable's right arm, and dodged to right and left to avoid the blows from the constable's head. Mad with rage, Manolakas lunged forward and seized Zorba's ear between his teeth, and tore at it with all his might. The blood spurted.

"Zorba!" I cried, terrified, rushing forward to save him.

"Get away, boss!" he cried. "Keep out of it!"

He clenched his fist and hit Manolakas a terrible blow in the lower part of the abdomen. The wild beast let go immediately. His teeth parted and set free the half-torn ear. His purple face turned ghastly white. Zorba thrust him to the ground, snatched away his knife and threw it over the church wall.

He stemmed the flow of blood from his ear with his handkerchief. He then wiped his face, which was streaming with sweat and his face became all smeared with blood. He straightened up, glanced around him. His eyes were swollen and red. He shouted to the widow:

"Get up! Come with me!"

And he walked towards the churchyard door.

The widow stood up; she gathered all her strength together in order to rush forward. But she did not have the time. Like a falcon, old Mavrandoni threw himself on her, knocked her over, wound her long black hair three times round his arm and with a single blow of his knife cut off her head.

"I take the responsibility for this sin!" he cried, and threw the victim's head on the doorstep of the church. Then he crossed himself.

Zorba looked round and saw the terrible sight. He gripped his moustache and pulled out a number of hairs in horror. I went up to him and took his arm. He leaned forward and looked at me. Two big tears were hanging on his lashes.

"Let's get away, boss," he said in a choking voice.

That evening Zorba would have nothing to eat or drink. "My throat's too tight," he said; "nothing will go down." He washed his ear in cold water, dipped a piece of cotton wool in some raki and made a bandage. Seated on his mattress, his head between his hands, he remained pensive.

I too was leaning on my elbows as I lay on the floor along by the wall, and I felt warm tears run slowly down my cheeks. My brain was not working at all, I was thinking of nothing. I wept, like a child overcome by deep sorrow.

Suddenly Zorba raised his head and gave vent to his feelings. Pursuing his savage thoughts, he began to shout aloud:

"I tell you, boss, everything that happens in this world is unjust, unjust, unjust! I won't be a party to it! I, Zorba, the worm, the slug! Why must the young die and the old wrecks go on living? Why do little children die? I had a boy once—Dimitri he was called—and I lost him when he was three years old. Well . . . I shall never, never forgive God for that, do you hear? I tell you, the day I die, if He has the cheek to appear in front of me, and if He is really and truly a God, He'll be ashamed! Yes, yes, He'll be ashamed to show himself to Zorba, the slug!"

He grimaced as though he was in pain. The blood started flowing again from his wound. He bit his lips so that he should not cry out.

"Wait, Zorba!" I said. "I'll change your dressing!"

I washed his ear once again in raki, then I took the orange-water which the widow had sent me and which I had found on my bed, and I dipped the cotton wool in it.

"Orange water?" said Zorba, eagerly sniffing at it. "Orange water? Put some on my hair, like that, will you? That's it! And on my hands, pour it all out, go on!"

He had come back to life. I looked at him astounded.

"I feel as though I'm entering the widow's garden," he said.

And he began his lamentations again.

"How many years it's taken," he muttered, "how many long years for the earth to succeed in making a body like that! You looked at her and said: Ah! if only I were twenty and the whole race of men disappeared from the earth and only that woman remained, and I gave her children! No, not children, real gods they'd be. . . . Whereas now . . ."

He leaped to his feet. His eyes filled with tears.

"I can't stand it, boss," he said. "I've got to walk, I shall have to go up and down the mountainside two or three times tonight to tire myself, calm myself a bit. . . . Ah! that widow! I feel I must chant a *mirologue* * for you!"

He rushed out, went towards the mountain and disappeared into the darkness.

I lay down on my bed, turned out the lamp and once more began, in my wretched, inhuman way, to transpose reality, removing blood, flesh and bones and reduce it to the abstract, link it with universal laws, until I came to the awful conclusion that what had happened was necessary. And, what is more, that it contributed to the universal harmony. I arrived at this final and abominable consolation: it was right that all that had happened should have happened.

The widow's murder entered my brain—the hive in which for years all poisons had been changed into honey—and threw it into confusion. But my philosophy immediately seized upon the dreadful warning, surrounded it with images and artifice and quickly made it harmless. In the same way, bees encase the starving drone in wax when it comes to steal their honey.

A few hours later the widow was at rest in my memory, calm and serene, changed into a symbol. She was encased in wax in my heart; she could no longer spread panic inside me and paralyze

* A mourning song, or dirge, chanted by modern Greeks. C. W.

my brain. The terrible events of that one day broadened, extended into time and space, and became one with great past civilizations; the civilizations became one with the earth's destiny; the earth with the destiny of the universe—and thus, returning to the widow, I found her subject to the great laws of existence, reconciled with her murderers, immobile and serene.

For me time had found its real meaning: the widow had died thousands of years before, in the epoch of the Aegean civilization, and the young girls of Cnossos with their curly hair had died that very morning on the shores of this pleasant sea.

Sleep took possession of me, just as one day—nothing is more certain—death will do, and I slipped gently into darkness. I did not hear when Zorba returned, or even if he returned. The next morning I found him on the mountainside shouting and cursing at the workers.

Nothing they did was to his liking. He dismissed three workers who were obstinate, took the pick himself and began clearing through the rocks and brush the path which he had marked out for the posts. He climbed the mountain, met some woodcutters who were cutting down the pines and began to thunder abuse. One of them laughed and muttered; Zorba hurled himself at him.

That evening he came down to the hut worn out and in rags. He sat beside me on the beach. He could hardly open his mouth; when he did speak at last, it was about timber, cables and lignite; he was like a grasping contractor, in a hurry to devastate the place, make as much profit out of it as he could and leave.

In the stage of self-consolation which I had reached, I was once on the point of speaking about the widow; Zorba stretched out his long arm and put his big hand over my mouth.

"Shut up!" he said in a muffled voice.

I stopped, ashamed. That is what a real man is like, I thought, envying Zorba's sorrow. A man with warm blood and solid bones, who lets real tears run down his cheeks when he is suffering; and when he is happy he does not spoil the freshness of his joy by running it through the fine sieve of metaphysics.

Three or four days went by in this way. Zorba worked steadily, not stopping to eat, or drink, or rest. He was laying the foundations.

One evening I mentioned that Dame Bouboulina was still in bed, that the doctor had not come and that she was continually calling for him in her delirium.

He clenched his fists.

"All right," he answered.

The next morning at dawn he went to the village and almost immediately afterwards returned to the hut.

"Did you see her?" I asked. "How is she?"

"Nothing wrong with her," he answered, "she's going to die." And he strode off to his work.

That evening, without eating, he took his thick stick and went out.

"Where are you going?" I asked. "To the village?"

"No. I'm going for a walk. I'll soon be back."

He strode towards the village with fast determined steps.

I was tired and went to bed. My mind again set itself to passing the whole world in review; memories came, and sorrows; my thoughts flitted around the most remote ideas but came back and settled on Zorba.

If he ever runs across Manolakas while he's out, I thought, that Cretan giant will hurl himself on him in a savage fury. They say that for these last few days he has been staying indoors. He is ashamed to show himself in the village and keeps saying that if he catches Zorba he will "tear him to bits with his teeth, like a sardine." One of the workmen said he had seen him in the middle of the night prowling about the hut fully armed. If they meet tonight there will be murder.

I leaped up, dressed and hurried down the road to the village. The calm, humid night air smelled of wild violets. After a time I saw Zorba walking slowly, as if very tired, towards the village. From time to time he stopped, stared at the stars, listened; then he started off again, a little faster, and I could hear his stick on the stones.

He was approaching the widow's garden. The air was full of the scent of lemon blossom and honeysuckle. At that moment, from the orange trees in the garden, the nightingale began to pour out its heart-rending song in notes as clear as spring water. It sang and sang in the darkness with breath-taking beauty. Zorba stopped, gasping at the sweetness of the song.

Suddenly the reeds of the hedge moved; their sharp leaves clashed like blades of steel.

"You, there!" shouted a loud and furious voice. "You doting old fool! So I've found you at last!"

My blood ran cold. I recognized the voice.

Zorba stepped forward, raised his stick and stopped. I could see every one of his movements by the light of the stars.

A huge man leaped out from the reed hedge.

"Who is it?" cried Zorba, craning his neck.

"Me, Manolakas."

"Go your way! Beat it!"

"Why did you disgrace me?"

"I didn't disgrace you, Manolakas! Beat it, I say. You're a big, strong fellow, yes, but luck was against you . . . and luck is blind, didn't you know that?"

"Luck or no luck, blind or not," said Manolakas, and I heard his teeth grinding, "I'm going to wipe out the disgrace. And tonight, too. Got a knife?"

"No," answered Zorba. "Just a stick."

"Go and fetch your knife. I'll wait here. Go on!"

Zorba did not move.

"Afraid?" hissed Manolakas, in a sneer. "Go on, I tell you!"

"And what would I do with a knife?" asked Zorba, who was beginning to get excited. "What would I do with it? What happened at the church? I seem to remember you had a knife then, and I didn't . . . but I came out on top, didn't I?"

Manolakas roared in fury.

"Trying to get a rise out of me as well, eh? You've picked the wrong moment to sneer; don't forget I'm armed and you're not! Fetch your knife, you lousy Macedonian, then we'll see who's best."

Zorba raised his arm, threw away his stick; I heard it fall among the reeds.

"Throw your knife away!" he cried.

I had gone up to them on tiptoe, and in the light of the stars I could just see the glitter of the knife as it too fell among the reeds.

Zorba spat upon his hands.

"Come on!" he shouted, making a preliminary leap into the air. But before they had time to come to grips I ran in between them.

"Stop!" I cried. "Here, Manolakas! And you, Zorba! Come here! Shame on you!"

The two adversaries came slowly towards me. I took each by the right hand.

"Shake hands!" I said. "You are both good, stout fellows, you must patch up this quarrel."

"He's dishonored me!" said Manolakas, trying to withdraw his hand.

"No one can dishonor you as easily as that," I said. "The whole village knows you're a brave man. Forget what happened at the church the other day. It was an unlucky hour! What's happened is over and done with! And don't forget, Zorba is a foreigner, a Macedonian, and it's the greatest disgrace we Cretans can bring on ourselves to raise a hand against a guest in our country. . . . Come now, give him your hand, that's real gallantry—and come to the hut, Manolakas. We'll drink together and roast a yard of sausage to seal our friendship!"

I took Manolakas by the waist and led him a little apart.

"The poor fellow's old, remember," I whispered. "A strong, young fellow like you shouldn't attack a man of his age."

Manolakas softened a little.

"All right," he said. "Just to please you."

He stepped towards Zorba and held out his huge hand.

"Come, friend Zorba," he said. "It's all over and forgotten; give me your hand."

"You chewed my ear," said Zorba, "much good may it do you! Here's my hand!"

They shook hands forcefully, more and more vigorously, looking each other in the eyes. I was afraid they were going to start fighting again.

"You've got a strong grip, Manolakas," said Zorba. "You're a stout fellow and pretty tough!"

"You've a strong hand, too; see if you can grip me tighter still."

"That's enough!" I cried. "Let's go and seal our friendship with a drink!"

On the way back to the beach I walked in between them, Zorba on my right and Manolakas on my left.

"There'll be a very good harvest this year . . ." I said, to change the subject. "There's been a lot of rain."

Neither of them answered. They were still tight about the chest. My hope lay in the wine. We reached the hut.

"Welcome to our humble home," I said. "Zorba, roast the sausage and find something to drink."

Manolakas sat down on a stone in front of the hut. Zorba took a handful of twigs, roasted the sausage and filled three glasses.

"Good health!" I said, raising my glass. "Good health, Manolakas! Good health, Zorba! Clink glasses!"

They clinked glasses, and Manolakas spilled a few drops on the ground.

"May my blood run like this wine," he said in a solemn voice, "if ever I raise my hand against you, Zorba."

"May my blood, too, run like this wine," said Zorba, following suit and pouring a few spots on the ground, "if I haven't already forgotten the way you chewed my ear!"

◊ 23 ◊

As DAWN BROKE Zorba sat up in bed and spoke to me, waking me.

"Are you asleep, boss?"

"What is it, Zorba?"

"I've been dreaming. A funny dream. I think we shan't be long before we go on some journey or other. Listen, this'll make you laugh. There was a ship as big as a town here in the harbor. Its siren was going, it was preparing to leave. Then I came running up from the village to catch it, and I was carrying a parrot in my hands. I reached the ship and went aboard. The captain came running up. 'Ticket!' he shouted. 'How much is it?' I asked, pulling a roll of notes out of my pocket. 'A thousand drachmas.' 'Look here, take it easy, won't eight hundred do?' I said. 'No, a thousand.' 'I've only got eight hundred; you can take them!' 'A thousand,' he said, 'nothing less! If you haven't got them, get off the boat quick!' I was annoyed. 'Listen, captain,' I said, 'for your own sake take the eight hundred I'm offering you, because if you don't I'll wake up and then, my friend, you'll lose the lot!'"

Zorba burst out laughing.

"What a strange machine man is!" he said, with astonishment. "You fill him with bread, wine, fish, radishes, and out of him come sighs, laughter and dreams. Like a factory. I'm sure there's a sort of talking-film cinema in our heads."

He suddenly leaped out of bed.

"But why the parrot?" he cried anxiously. "What does that mean, taking a parrot off with me? Ha! I'm afraid. . . ."

He had no time to finish his sentence. In rushed a stumpy, red-haired messenger, looking like the devil in person. He was gasping for breath.

"For God's sake! the poor woman's screaming her head off for the doctor! She says she's dying, for sure . . . and you'll have it on your conscience, she says!"

I felt ashamed. In the distress the widow had caused us, we had completely forgotten our old friend.

"She's going through it, poor woman," the red haired man went on talkatively. "She coughs so, her whole hotel's shaking with it. Yes, it's a proper ass's cough! Whoof! Whoof! It shakes the whole village!"

"Be quiet!" I said. "Don't joke about it!"

I took a piece of paper and wrote a message.

"Go and take this letter to the doctor and don't come away till you've seen him, with your own eyes, ride off on his mare! Do you understand? Now, go!"

He seized the letter, stuck it in his belt and ran off.

Zorba was up already. He dressed hurriedly without a word.

"Wait a moment, I'll come with you," I said.

"I'm in a hurry," he replied, and started out.

A little later I also set out for the village. The widow's deserted garden perfumed the air. Mimiko was sitting huddled up before the house and glowering like a beaten dog. He looked very thin; his eyes were red and sunken in their sockets. He turned round, saw me and picked up a stone.

"What are you doing here, Mimiko?" I asked, glancing regretfully at the garden. I could feel two warm, all-powerful arms twined round my neck . . . a scent of lemon blossom and laurel oil. We said nothing. I could see in the dusk her burning, black eyes and her gleaming, pointed, white teeth which she had rubbed with walnut leaf.

"Why d'you ask me that?" he growled. "Go away. Go about your business."

"Like a cigarette?"

"I'm not smoking any more. You're all a lot of swine! All of you! All of you!"

He stopped, panting, seeming to search for a word he could not find.

"Swine . . . scoundrels . . . liars . . . murderers . . ."

He seemed at last to have found the word he wanted and be relieved. He clapped his hands.

"Murderers! murderers! murderers!" he shouted in a shrill voice. He started laughing. It wrung my heart to see him.

"You're quite right, Mimiko," I said. "You're right." And I hurried away.

As I entered the village I saw old Anagnosti, leaning on his stick, smiling as he watched two yellow butterflies chasing each other over the spring grass. Now that he was old and no longer worried about his fields and his wife and children, he had time to look disinterestedly on the world around him. He noticed my shadow on the ground and looked up.

"What lucky chance brings you here so early in the morning?" he asked.

But he must have read my anxious face, and went on without waiting for an answer.

"Do something quickly, my son," he said. "I'm not sure whether you'll find her alive or not. . . . Ah, the poor wretch!"

The large bed which had seen so much use, her most faithful companion, had been put in the middle of her little room and nearly filled it. Above her head there bent over the singer her devoted privy councillor, the parrot—with his green crown, yellow bonnet and round, evil eye. He was gazing down at his mistress as she lay groaning. And he leaned his almost human head to one side to listen.

No, these were not the choking sighs of joy he knew so well, that she would utter in the act of love-making, nor the tender cooing of the dove, nor the little shrieks of laughter. The beads of ice-cold sweat running down his mistress's face, her hair like tow —unwashed, uncombed—sticking to her temples, the convulsive movements in the bed, these the parrot saw for the first time, and he was uneasy. He wanted to shout: "Canavaro! Canavaro!" but his voice stuck in his throat.

256

His poor mistress was groaning; she kept lifting up the sheets with her wilting, flabby arms; she was suffocating. She had no make-up on her face and her cheeks were swollen; she smelled of stale sweat and of flesh which is beginning to decompose. Her down-at-heel, out-of-shape court shoes were poking out from under the bed. It wrung your heart to see them. Those shoes were more moving than the sight of their owner herself.

Zorba sat at her bedside, looking at the shoes. He could not take his eyes off them. He was biting his lips to keep back the tears. I went in and sat behind Zorba, but he did not hear me.

The poor woman was finding it difficult to breathe; she was choking. Zorba took down a hat decorated with artificial roses and fanned her with it. He waved his big hand up and down very quickly and clumsily as though he were trying to light some damp coal.

She opened her eyes in terror and looked around her. It was dark and she could see no one, not even Zorba fanning her with the flowered hat.

Everything was dark and disturbing about her; blue vapors were rising from the ground and changing shape. They formed sneering mouths, claw-like feet, black wings.

She dug her nails into her pillow, which was stained with tears, saliva and sweat, and she cried out.

"I don't want to die! I don't want to!"

But the two mourners from the village had heard of the condition she was in and had just arrived. They slipped into the room, sat on the floor and leaned against the wall.

The parrot saw them, with his round staring eyes, and was angry. He stretched out his head and cried: "Canav . . ." but Zorba savagely shot his hand out at the cage and silenced the bird.

Again the cry of despair rang out.

"I don't want to die! I don't want to!"

Two beardless youths, tanned by the sun, poked their heads round the door, looked carefully at the sick woman. Satisfied, they winked at each other and disappeared.

Soon afterwards we heard a terrified clucking and beating of wings coming from the yard; someone was chasing the hens.

The first dirge singer, old Malamatenia, turned to her companion.

"Did you see them, auntie Lenio, did you see them? They're in a hurry, the hungry wretches; they're going to wring the hens' necks and eat them. All the good-for-nothings of the village have collected in the yard; it'll not be long before they plunder the place!"

Then, turning to the dying woman's bed:

"Hurry up and die, my friend," she muttered impatiently; "give up the ghost as quick as you can so that we get a chance as well as the others."

"To tell you God's own truth," said aunt Lenio, creasing her little toothless mouth, "mother Malamatenia, they're doing right, those boys. 'If you want to eat something, pilfer; if you want to own something, steal. . . .' That's what my old mother used to say to me. We've only got to rattle off our *mirologues* as fast as we can, lay our hands on a couple of handfuls of rice, some sugar, and a saucepan, and then we can bless her memory. She had neither parents nor children, did she, so who's going to eat her hens and her rabbits? Who'll drink her wine? Who'll inherit all those cottons and combs and sweets and things? Ha, what d'you expect, mother Malamatenia? God forgive me, but that's the way the world is . . . and I'd like to pick up a few things myself!"

"Wait a bit, dear, don't be in too much of a hurry," said mother Malamatenia, seizing her arm. "I had the same idea myself, I don't mind admitting, but just wait till she's given up the ghost."

Meanwhile the dying woman was fumbling frantically beneath her pillow. As soon as she thought she was in danger she had taken out of her trunk a crucifix in gleaming white bone and thrust it under her pillow. For years she had entirely forgotten it and it had lain among her tattered chemises and bits of velvet and rags at the bottom of the trunk. As if Christ were a medicine to be taken only when gravely ill, and of no use so long as you can have a good time, eat, drink and make love.

At last her groping hand found the crucifix and she pressed it to her bosom, which was damp with sweat.

"Dear Jesus, my dear Jesus . . ." she uttered passionately, clasping her last lover to her breast.

Her words, which were half-French, half-Greek, but full of tenderness and passion, were very confused. The parrot heard her.

He sensed that the tone of voice had changed, remembered the former long sleepless nights and livened up immediately.

"Canavaro! Canavaro!" he shouted hoarsely, like a cock crowing at the sun.

Zorba this time did not try to silence him. He looked at the woman as she wept and kissed the crucified image whilst an unexpected sweetness spread over her ravaged face.

The door opened, old Anagnosti came in quietly, cap in hand. He came up to the sick woman, bowed and knelt down.

"Forgive me, dear lady," he said to her, "forgive me, and may God forgive you. If sometimes I spoke a harsh word, we're only men . . . Forgive me."

But the dear soul was now lying quietly, sunk in an unspeakable felicity, and she did not hear what old Anagnosti said. All her torments were gone—unhappy old age, all the sneers and hard words she had endured, the sad evenings she had spent alone in her doorway, knitting thick woollen socks. This elegant Parisienne, this tantalizing woman men could not resist and who, in her time, had bounced the four great Powers on her knee, and had been saluted by four naval squadrons!

The sea was azure blue, the waves were flecked with foam, the sea-going fortresses were dancing in the harbor, and flags of many colors were flapping from every mast. You could smell the partridges roasting and the red mullet on the grill, glacé fruits were carried to the table in bowls of cut crystal and the champagne corks flew up to the ceiling.

Black and fair beards, red and grey beards, four sorts of perfume —violet, eau-de-Cologne, musk, patchouli; the doors of the metal cabin were closed, the heavy curtains drawn to, the lights were lit. Madame Hortense closed her eyes. All her life of love, all her life of torment—ah, almighty God! it had lasted no more than a second. . . .

She goes from knee to knee, clasps in her arms gold-braided uniforms, buries her fingers in thick-scented beards. She cannot remember their names, any more than her parrot can. She can only remember Canavaro, because he was the youngest of them all and his name was the only one the parrot could pronounce. The others were complicated and difficult to pronounce, and so were forgotten.

Madame Hortense sighed deeply and hugged the crucifix passionately to her.

"My Canavaro, my little Canavaro . . ." she murmured in her delirium, pressing it to her flabby breasts.

"She's beginning not to know what she's saying," murmured aunt Lenio. "She must have seen her guardian angel and had a scare. . . . We'll loosen our kerchiefs and go nearer."

"What! Haven't you any fear of God, then?" said mother Malamatenia. "D'you want us to begin singing while she's still alive?"

"Ha, mother Malamatenia," grumbled aunt Lenio under her breath, "instead of thinking about her trunk and her clothes and all the things she has outside in the shop, and the hens and rabbits in the yard, there are you telling me we ought to wait till she's breathed her last! No! First come first served, I say!"

And as she spoke she stood up, and the other followed her angrily. They undid their black kerchiefs, let down their thin white hair and gripped the edges of the bed.

Aunt Lenio gave the signal by letting out a long piercing cry enough to make a cold shiver go down your spine.

"Eeeee!"

Zorba leaped up, seized the two old women by the hair and dragged them back.

"Shut your traps, you old magpies!" he shouted. "Can't you see she's still alive? Go to hell!"

"Doddering old idiot!" grumbled mother Malamatenia, fastening her kerchief again. "Where's he sprung from, I'd like to know, the interfering fool!"

Dame Hortense, the sorely tried old siren, heard the strident cry beside her bed. Her sweet vision faded; the admiral's vessel sank, the roast pheasants, champagne and perfumed beards disappeared and she fell back on to that stinking deathbed, at the end of the world. She made an effort to raise herself, as though trying to escape, but she fell back again and cried softly and plaintively.

"I don't want to die! I don't want to. . . ."

Zorba leaned forward and touched her forehead with his great horny hand, and brushed away the hair which was sticking to her face; his bird-like eyes filled with tears.

"Quiet, my dear, quiet," he murmured. "I'm here; this is Zorba. Don't be afraid."

And suddenly the vision returned, like an enormous sea-green butterfly and spread its wings over the whole bed. The dying woman seized Zorba's big hand, slowly stretched out her arm and put it round his neck as he bent over her. Her lips moved . . .

"My Canavaro, my little Canavaro. . . ."

The crucifix slipped off the pillow, fell to the floor and broke into little pieces. A man's voice rang out in the yard:

"Come on! Pop the hen in now, the water's boiling!"

I was sitting in a corner of the room and from time to time my eyes filled with tears. That is life, I thought—checkered, incoherent, indifferent, perverse . . . pitiless. These primitive Cretan peasants surround this old cabaret singer come from the other end of the earth and with inhuman joy watch her die, as if she were not also a human being. As though a huge exotic bird had fallen from the sky, its wings broken, and they had gathered on the seashore by their village to watch it die. An old pea fowl, an old angora cat, a sick old seal. . . .

Zorba gently removed Dame Hortense's arm from round his neck and stood up, white-faced. He wiped his eyes with the back of his hand, looked at the sick woman but could see nothing. He wiped his eyes again and could just see her moving her swollen helpless feet in the bed and twisting her mouth in terror. She shook herself once, twice, the bedclothes slipped to the floor and she appeared, half-naked, covered with sweat, swollen, a greenish-yellow color. She uttered a strident, piercing cry like a fowl when its throat is cut, then she remained motionless, her eyes wide open, terrified, glassy.

The parrot jumped down to the bottom of its cage, clutched the bars and watched as Zorba reached out his huge hand and, with indescribable tenderness, closed his mistress's eyelids.

"Quick, all of you! She's gone!" yelped the dirge singers, rushing to the bed. They uttered a prolonged cry, rocking backwards and forwards, clenching their fists and beating their breasts. Little by little the monotony of this lugubrious oscillation produced in them a slight state of hypnosis, old griefs of their own invaded their minds like poison, their hearts were opened and the *mirologue* burst forth.

"It was not meet for thee, to lie beneath the earth. . . ."

Zorba went out into the yard. He wanted to weep, but he was ashamed to do so in front of the women. I remember he said to me once: "I'm not ashamed to cry, if it's in front of men. Between men there's some unity, isn't there? It's no disgrace. But in front of women a man always has to prove that he's courageous. Because if we started crying our eyes out, too, what'd happen to these poor creatures? It would be the end!"

They washed her with wine; the old woman who was laying her out opened the trunk, took out clean clothes and changed her, pouring over her a bottle of eau-de-Cologne. From the nearby gardens came the blow flies and laid their eggs in her nostrils, round her eyes and in the corners of her lips.

Night was falling. The sky to the west was beautifully serene. Small, fleecy red clouds edged with gold were sailing slowly across the dark-purple evening sky, looking one moment like ships, the next like swans, then like fantastic monsters made of cotton wool and frayed silk. Between the reeds in the yard could be seen the gleaming waves of the choppy sea.

Two well-fed crows flew from a fig tree close by and walked up and down the yard. Zorba angrily picked up a pebble and made them fly away.

In the other corner of the yard the village marauders had prepared a tremendous feast. They had brought out the large kitchen table, searched out bread, plates, knives and forks. They had brought from the cellar a demijohn of wine, and cooked a few hens in the pot. Now, hungry and happy, they were eating and drinking with a fine relish and clinking glasses.

"God save her soul! And for all she's done let her off the forfeits!"

"May all her lovers turn into angels and carry her soul to heaven!"

"Just take a look at old Zorba," said Manolakas. "He's throwing stones at the crows! He's a widower now; let's ask him to drink to the memory of his woman! Hullo, Zorba! Come and join us, countryman."

Zorba turned round. He saw the full table, the steaming hens in the dishes, the wine glistening in the glasses, the stout sun-tanned fellows sitting jauntily with their scarves tied round their heads, all instinct with youth.

"Zorba, Zorba!" he murmured. "Hold on! This is where you'll have to show what you're made of!"

He went over to them, drank a glass at one gulp, then a second, then a third, and ate a leg of chicken. They spoke to him, but he made no reply. He ate and drank fast, greedily, in huge mouthfuls, lengthy draughts, and in silence. He kept looking towards the room where Bouboulina was lying and listening to the *mirologues* coming through the open window. From time to time the funereal chants broke off and they could hear some shouts, as though a quarrel had started, and the sounds of cupboards and trunks being opened and shut, and heavy, rapid tramplings as if people were fighting. Then, the *mirologue* would begin again, monotonous, despairing, a soft murmur like that of a bee.

The two women were running to and fro in the death chamber, chanting their *mirologues* while they feverishly rummaged in every little corner. They opened a cupboard and found several little spoons, some sugar, a tin of coffee and a box of *loukoums*.* Aunt Lenio pounced on them and seized the coffee and *loukoums*. Old mother Malamatenia seized the sugar and spoons. She picked up two *loukoums* as well, thrust them into her mouth, and for a while the *mirologue* came out in muffled and choking fashion through the sugary paste.

"May flowers rain on thee and apples fall in thy lap. . . ."

Two other old women crept into the room, rushed to the trunk, plunged their hands inside, picked up a few little handkerchiefs, two or three towels, three pairs of silk stockings, a garter, and thrust them down their bodices, then turned to the dead woman on the bed and crossed themselves.

Mother Malamatenia saw the old women rob the trunk and that put her into a fury.

"You go on; keep going, dear, I shan't be a second!" she cried to aunt Lenio, and dived head first into the trunk herself.

Bits of old satin, an old-fashioned mauve dress, antique red

* A variety of Turkish Delight. C. W.

sandals, a broken fan, a new scarlet sunshade, and, right at the bottom, an admiral's three-cornered hat. A present someone had made Bouboulina long ago. When she was alone in the house sometimes she used to put it on and sadly and gravely admire herself in the mirror.

Someone approached the door. The old women went out, while aunt Lenio gripped the deathbed once more and started beating her breast as she chanted:

". . . and crimson carnations round thy neck. . . ."

Zorba entered, looked at the dead woman, still and peaceful now, quite yellow and covered with flies, as she lay with her arms folded, and a tiny velvet ribbon round her neck.

"A bit of earth," he thought, "a bit of earth that was hungry . . . and laughed, and kissed. A lump of mud that wept human tears. And now? . . . Who the devil brings us onto this earth and who the devil takes us away?"

He spat and sat down.

Outside in the yard the young people were taking their places for the dance. The clever lyre player, Fanurio, came at last and they pulled the tables aside, and cleared away the paraffin cans, the washtub and the clothesbasket, to make room for the dance.

The village worthies appeared: uncle Anagnosti, with his long crooked stick and full, white shirt; Kondomanolio, plump and dirty; the schoolmaster, with a large brass inkhorn in his belt and a green penholder stuck behind his ear. Old Mavrandoni was not there; he had gone into the mountains as an outlaw.

"Glad to see you!" said uncle Anagnosti, raising his hand in greeting. "Glad to see you're enjoying yourselves! God bless you all! But don't shout . . . you mustn't. The dead can hear, remember, the dead can hear."

Kondomanolio explained:

"We've come to make an inventory of the dead woman's belongings, so that they can be divided among the poor. You've all eaten and drunk your fill, now that's enough. Don't strip the whole place! Look!" he waved his stick threateningly in the air.

Behind the three elders appeared a dozen ragged women, with untidy hair and bare feet. Each one carried an empty sack under her arm and a basket on her back. They came in furtively, step by step, without a word.

Uncle Anagnosti turned round, saw them and burst out: "You get back, there, you pack of gipsies. What? Come to rush the place? We're going to write everything down, item by item, and then it'll all be divided properly and fairly between the poor. Get back, will you!"

The schoolmaster took the long inkhorn from his belt, opened a large sheet of paper and went to the little shop to begin the inventory.

But at that very moment a deafening noise was heard—as if someone was banging on tins, as if cases of cotton reels were falling, and cups were knocking together and breaking. And in the kitchen was heard a tremendous din among saucepans, plates and cutlery.

Old Kondomanolio rushed there, brandishing his stick. But what could he do? Old women, men, children went rushing through the doors, jumped through the open windows, over the fences and off the balcony, each carrying whatever he had been able to snatch—saucepans, frying pans, mattresses, rabbits. . . . Some of them had taken doors or windows off their hinges and had put them on their backs. Mimiko had seized the two court shoes, tied on a piece of string and hung them round his neck—it looked as though Dame Hortense were going off astraddle on his shoulders and only her shoes were visible. . . .

The schoolmaster frowned, put the inkhorn back in his belt, folded up the virgin-white sheet of paper, then, without a word and with an air of deeply offended dignity, crossed the threshold and walked away.

Poor old uncle Anagnosti went about shouting, begging the people to stop, waving his stick at them.

"It's a disgrace! It's a disgrace! The dead can hear you, remember!"

"Shall I go and call the priest?" said Mimiko.

"What priest, you fool?" said Kondomanolio furiously. "She was a Frank; didn't you ever notice how she crossed herself? With four fingers—like that—the infidel! Come on, let's get her underground, so that she doesn't stink us all out and infect the whole village!"

"She's beginning to fill with worms, by the Holy Cross itself!" said Mimiko, crossing himself.

Uncle Anagnosti, the grand old man of the village, shook his fine head.

"What's strange in that, you idiot? The truth is that man is full of worms from the day he's born, but you can't see them. When they find that you're beginning to stink they come out of their holes—white they are, all white like cheese maggots!"

The first stars appeared and hung in the air, trembling, like little silver bells. All the darkness was filled with tinkling bells.

Zorba took down the parrot and his cage from over the dead woman's head. The orphan bird was crouching in one corner, terrified; he was gazing with staring eyes but could understand nothing. He pushed his head under his wings and crumpled up with fear.

When Zorba took down the cage the parrot raised himself. He was going to speak but Zorba held out his hand to stop him.

"Quiet," he murmured in a soothing tone, "quiet! Come with me."

Zorba leaned forward and looked at the dead woman's face. He looked a long time, his throat tight and dry.

He stooped, as if to kiss her, but refrained.

"Let's go, for God's sake!" he muttered. He picked up the cage and went out into the yard. There he saw me and came over to me.

"Let's leave now. . . ." he said in a low voice, taking my arm.

He seemed calm, but his lips were trembling.

"We all have to go the same way. . . ." I said to him.

"That's a great consolation!" he said sarcastically. "Let's be off."

"One moment," I said. "They're just beginning to take her away. We ought to wait and see that. . . . Can't you stick it one more minute?"

"All right. . . ." he answered in a choking voice. He put the cage down and folded his arms.

From the death chamber uncle Anagnosti and Kondomanolio came bareheaded and crossed themselves. Behind them came four of the dancers, with April roses still stuck behind their ears. They were gay, half-drunk. Each was holding a corner of the door on which they had placed the dead woman's body. There followed the lyre player with his instrument, a dozen more men who were rather tipsy, still marching, and five or six women, each carrying a saucepan or chair. Mimiko came last, with the down-at-heel court shoes tied round his neck.

"Murderers! Murderers! Murderers!" he shouted gaily.

A warm, humid wind was blowing and the sea was choppy. The lyre player raised his bow—his fresh voice rang out merrily and sarcastically in the warm night:

"O sun, how hurriedly hast thou set in the west. . . ."

"Come on," said Zorba, "it's over now. . . ."

◇ 24 ◇

WE WENT in silence through the narrow streets of the village. There were no lights in the houses and they cast black shadows in the night. Somewhere a dog was barking, and a bullock sighed. From afar the wind carried to us the joyful tinkling of the lyre bells, dancing like the playful waters of a fountain.

"Zorba," I said, to break our heavy silence, "what is this wind, the Notus?"

But Zorba marched on in front, holding the parrot's cage like a lantern, and made no reply. When we came to the beach he turned round.

"Are you hungry, boss?" he asked

"No, I'm not hungry, Zorba."

"Are you sleepy?"

"No."

"Neither am I. Shall we sit down on the pebbles for a bit? I've got something to ask you."

We were both tired, but neither of us wanted to sleep. We were unwilling to lose the bitterness of those last few hours, and sleep seemed to us like running away in the hour of danger. We were ashamed of going to bed.

We sat down by the sea. Zorba put the cage between his knees and remained silent for a time. A disturbing constellation appeared in the sky from behind the mountain, a monster with countless eyes and a spiral tail. From time to time a star detached itself and fell away.

Zorba looked at the sky with open mouth in a sort of ecstasy, as though he were seeing it for the first time.

"What can be happening up there?" he murmured.

A moment later he decided to speak.

"Can you tell me, boss," he said, and his voice sounded deep and earnest in the warm night, "what all these things mean? Who made them all? And why? And, above all"—here Zorba's voice trembled with anger and fear—"why do people die?"

"I don't know, Zorba," I replied, ashamed, as if I had been asked the simplest thing, the most essential thing, and was unable to explain it.

"You don't know!" said Zorba in round-eyed astonishment, just like his expression the night I had confessed I could not dance.

He was silent a moment and then suddenly broke out.

"Well, all those damned books you read—what good are they? Why do you read them? If they don't tell you that, what *do* they tell you?"

"They tell me about the perplexity of mankind, who can give no answer to the question you've just put me, Zorba."

"Oh, damn their perplexity!" he cried, tapping his foot on the ground in exasperation.

The parrot started up at these noises.

"Canavaro! Canavaro!" he called, as if for help.

"Shut up! You, too!" shouted Zorba, banging on the cage with his fist.

He turned back to me.

"I want you to tell me where we come from and where we are going to. During all those years you've been burning yourself up consuming their black books of magic, you must have chewed over about fifty tons of paper! What did you get out of them?"

There was so much anguish in his voice that my heart was wrung with distress. Ah! how I would have liked to be able to answer him!

I felt deep within me that the highest point a man can attain is not Knowledge, or Virtue, or Goodness, or Victory, but something even greater, more heroic and more despairing: Sacred Awe!

"Can't you answer?" asked Zorba anxiously.

I tried to make my companion understand what I meant by Sacred Awe.

"We are little grubs, Zorba, minute grubs on the small leaf of a tremendous tree. This small leaf is the earth. The other leaves are the stars that you see moving at night. We make our way on this little leaf examining it anxiously and carefully. We smell it; it smells good or bad to us. We taste it and find it eatable. We beat on it and it cries out like a living thing.

"Some men—the more intrepid ones—reach the edge of the leaf. From there we stretch out, gazing into chaos. We tremble. We guess what a frightening abyss lies beneath us. In the distance we can hear the noise of the other leaves of the tremendous tree, we feel the sap rising from the roots to our leaf and our hearts swell. Bent thus over the awe-inspiring abyss, with all our bodies and all our souls, we tremble with terror. From that moment begins . . ."

I stopped. I wanted to say "from that moment begins poetry," but Zorba would not have understood. I stopped.

"What begins?" asked Zorba's anxious voice. "Why did you stop?"

". . . begins the great danger, Zorba. Some grow dizzy and delirious, others are afraid; they try to find an answer to strengthen their hearts, and they say: 'God!' Others again, from the edge of the leaf, look over the precipice calmly and bravely and say: 'I like it.'"

Zorba reflected for a long time. He was straining to understand.

"You know," he said at last, "I think of death every second. I look at it and I'm not frightened. But never, never, do I say I like it. No, I don't like it at all! I don't agree!"

He was silent, but soon broke out again.

"No, I'm not the sort to hold out my neck to Charon like a sheep and say: 'Cut my throat, Mr. Charon, please: I want to go straight to Paradise!'"

I listened to Zorba in perplexity. Who was the sage who tried to teach his disciples to do voluntarily what the law ordered should be done? To say "yes" to necessity and change the inevitable into something done of their own free will? That is perhaps the only human way to deliverance. It is a pitiable way, but there is no other.

But what of revolt? The proud, quixotic reaction of mankind to conquer Necessity and make external laws conform to the internal laws of the soul, to deny all that is and create a new world according to the laws of one's own heart, which are contrary to the inhuman laws of nature—to create a new world which is purer, better and more moral than the one that exists?

Zorba looked at me, saw that I had no more to say to him, took up the cage carefully so that he should not wake the parrot, placed it by his head and stretched out on the pebbles.

"Good night, boss!" he said. "That's enough."

A strong south wind was blowing from Africa. It was making the vegetables and fruits and Cretan breasts all swell and grow. I felt it on my forehead, lips and neck; and like a fruit my brain cracked and swelled.

I could not and would not sleep. I thought of nothing. I just felt something, someone growing to maturity inside me in the warm night. I lived lucidly through a most surprising experience: I saw myself change. A thing that usually happens only in the most obscure depths of our bowels was this time occurring in the open, before my eyes. Crouched by the sea, I watched this miracle take place.

The stars grew dim, the sky grew light and against this luminous background appeared, as if delicately traced in ink, the mountains, trees and gulls.

Dawn was breaking.

Several days went by. The corn had ripened and the heavy ears were hanging down with the weight of the grain. On the olive trees the cicadas sawed the air, and brilliant insects hummed in the burning light. Vapor was rising from the sea.

Zorba went off silently at dawn every day to the mountain. The work of installing the overhead line was nearing an end. The pylons were all in place, the cable was stretched ready and the pulleys fixed. Zorba came back from work at dusk, worn out. He lit the fire, made the evening meal, and we ate. We took care not to arouse the demons that were sleeping within us—death and fear; we never talked of the widow, or Dame Hortense, or God. Silently we gazed out over the sea.

Because of Zorba's silence, the eternal but vain questions rose up once more within me. Once more my breast was filled with anguish. What is this world? I wondered. What is its aim and in what way can we help to attain it during our ephemeral lives? The aim of man and matter is to create joy, according to Zorba—others would say "to create spirit," but that comes to the same thing on another plane. But why? With what object? And when the body dissolves, does anything at all remain of what we have called the soul? Or does nothing remain, and does our unquenchable desire for immortality spring, not from the fact that we are immortal, but from the fact that during the short span of our life we are in the service of something immortal?

One day I rose and washed, and the earth, it seemed, had also just risen and finished its ablutions. It shone as if it were a new creation. I went down to the village. On my left the indigo-blue sea was motionless, on my right in the distance glistened the fields of wheat, like an army flourishing a host of golden lances. I passed the Fig Tree of Our Young Lady, covered with green leaves and tiny little figs, hastened by the widow's garden without so much as turning my head, and entered the village. The small hotel was deserted now, abandoned. Doors and windows were missing, dogs walked in and out of the yard as they pleased, the rooms were empty. In the death chamber, the bed, trunk and chairs had all gone; there remained only a tattered slipper with a worn heel and red pompon, in one corner of the room. It still faithfully preserved the shape of its owner's foot. That wretched slipper, more compassionate than the human mind, had not yet forgotten the beloved but maltreated foot.

I was late returning. Zorba had already lit the fire and was preparing to cook. As he raised his eyes to greet me, he knew immediately where I had been. He frowned. After so many days of silence he unlocked his heart that evening and spoke.

"Every time I suffer, boss," he said, as though to justify himself, "it just cracks my heart in two. But it's all scarred and riddled with wounds already, and it sticks itself together again in a trice and the wound can't be seen. I'm covered with healed wounds, that's why I can stand so much."

272

"You've soon forgotten poor Bouboulina, Zorba," I said, in a tone which was somewhat brutal for me.

Zorba was piqued and raised his voice.

"A fresh road, and fresh plans!" he cried. "I've stopped thinking all the time of what happened yesterday. And stopped asking myself what's going to happen tomorrow. What's happening today, this minute, that's what I care about. I say: 'What are you doing at this moment, Zorba?' 'I'm sleeping.' 'Well, sleep well.' 'What are you doing at this moment, Zorba?' 'I'm working.' 'Well, work well.' 'What are you doing at this moment, Zorba?' 'I'm kissing a woman.' 'Well, kiss her well, Zorba! And forget all the rest while you're doing it; there's nothing else on earth, only you and her! Get on with it!'"

A few moments later he continued.

"When she, Bouboulina, was alive, you know, no kind of Canavaro had ever given her so much pleasure as I did—old rag-and-bone Zorba. Do you want to know why? Because all the Canavaros in the world, while they were kissing her, kept thinking about their fleets, or the king, or Crete, or their stripes and decorations, or their wives. But I used to forget everything else, and she knew that, the old trollop. And let me tell you this, my learned friend—there's no greater pleasure for a woman than that. A real woman—now listen to this and I hope it helps you—gets more out of the pleasure she gives than the pleasure she takes from a man."

He bent down to put some wood on the fire and was silent.

I looked at him and was very happy. I felt these minutes on that deserted shore to be simple but rich in deep human value. And our meal every evening was like the stews that sailors make when they land on some deserted beach—with fish, oysters, onions, and plenty of pepper; they are more tasty than any other dish and have no equal for nourishing a man's spirit. There, at the edge of the world, we were like two shipwrecked men.

"The day after tomorrow we get our line started," said Zorba, pursuing his train of thought. "I'm not walking on the ground any more; I'm a creature of the air. I can feel the pulleys on my shoulders!"

"Do you remember the bait you threw me in the Piraeus Restau-

rant to land me on the hook?" I asked. "You said you could cook
wonderful soups—and it happens to be the dish I like best. How
did you know?"

Zorba shook his head with slight scorn.

"I can't say, boss. It just came into my head like that. The way
you were sitting there in the corner of the café, quiet, reserved,
bent over that little gilt-edged book—I don't know, I just felt you
liked soup, that's all. It just came to me like that; there's no understanding it!"

He suddenly stopped and leaned forward, listening.

"Quiet!" he said. "There's someone coming!"

We heard rapid footsteps and the heavy breathing of someone
running. Suddenly there appeared in the flickering light of the
flames a monk in a torn habit, bare headed, red bearded and with
a small moustache. He brought with him a strong smell of paraffin.

"Ha! welcome, Father Zaharia!" cried Zorba. "What's put you
in such a state?"

The monk sank to the floor near the fire. His chin was trembling.
Zorba leaned towards him and winked.

"Yes," said the monk.

"Bravo, monk!" cried Zorba. "Now you're sure to go to Paradise;
you can't miss it! And you'll have a can of paraffin in your hand
as you enter!"

"Amen!" murmured the monk, crossing himself.

"How did it work out? When? Come on, tell us!"

"I saw the archangel Michael, brother Canavaro. He gave me an
order. Listen how it came: I was in the kitchen stringing some
beans. I was all alone. The door was closed, the monks were at
vespers; it was absolutely quiet. I could hear the birds singing outside, and it sounded like angels. I had prepared everything, and I
was waiting. I'd bought a can of paraffin and hidden it in the chapel
in the cemetery, beneath the holy table itself, so that the archangel
Michael would bless it.

"So yesterday afternoon I was stringing beans and Paradise was
running in my head. I was saying to myself: 'Lord Jesus, I deserve
the Kingdom of Heaven, too, and I'm quite prepared to string
beans for all eternity in the kitchens of Paradise!' That's what I was

thinking, and the tears were running down my face. Suddenly I heard the beating of wings above me. I understood, and bent my head, trembling with fear. Then I heard a voice: 'Zaharia, look up and be not afraid.' But I was quaking so much I fell to the floor. 'Look up, Zaharia!' said the voice again. I looked up and saw. The door was open and on the threshold stood the archangel Michael, just as he is depicted on the doors of the sanctuary of the monastery, just the same; with black wings, red sandals and a golden halo; only instead of a sword he was holding a lighted torch. 'Hail, Zaharia!' he said. 'I'm the servant of God,' I answered. 'What do you command?' 'Take the flaming torch, and may the Lord be with you.' I held out my hand and felt my palms burn. But the archangel had disappeared. All I saw was a line of fire in the sky, like a shooting star."

The monk wiped the sweat off his face. He had gone quite white. His teeth were chattering as if he were feverish.

"Well?" said Zorba. "Bear up, Zaharia! What next?"

"Just at that moment the monks were coming away from vespers and going into the refectory. As he went by, the abbot kicked me like a dog, and all the monks laughed. I didn't say anything. After the visit of the archangel there was still a smell of sulphur in the air, but no one noticed it. 'Zaharia!' said the perceptor. 'Aren't you going to eat?' I kept my mouth shut.

" 'Angels' food is enough for him!' said Demetrios, the Sodomite. The monks all laughed again. So I got up and walked away to the cemetery. I prostrated myself before the archangel . . . for hours I felt his foot heavy on my neck. The time passed like lightning. That is how the hours and the centuries will pass in Paradise. Midnight came. Everything was quiet. The monks had gone to bed. I stood up, crossed myself and kissed the archangel's foot. 'Thy will be done,' I said. I took the can of paraffin, opened it and went. I had stuffed my robe with rags.

"The night was as black as ink. The moon had not risen. The monastery was dark, as dark as hell. I went into the courtyard, climbed the steps and came to the abbot's quarters. I threw paraffin on the door, windows and walls. I ran to Demetrios's cell. There I started pouring paraffin all over the cells and along the big wooden gallery—just as you told me. Then I went into the chapel, lit a candle from the lamp before the statue of Christ and started the fire."

The monk was breathless now, and stopped. His eyes burned with an inner flame.

"God be praised!" he roared, crossing himself. "God be praised! In a moment the whole monastery was in flames. 'The flames of Hell!' I shouted at the top of my voice and then ran away as fast as I could. I ran and ran, and I could hear the bells ringing, the monks shouting . . . and I ran and ran. . . .

"Day came. I hid in the wood. I was shivering. The sun rose and I heard the monks searching the woods for me. But God sent a mist to cover me and they did not see me. Towards dusk, I heard a voice say: 'Go down to the sea! Away!' 'Guide me, guide me, archangel!' I cried, and started out. I didn't know which way I was going, but the archangel guided me, sometimes by means of a flash of lightning, at others by a dark bird in the trees, or by a path coming down the mountain. And I ran after him as hard as I could, trusting him completely. And his bounty is great, as you see! I've found you, my dear Canavaro! I'm saved!"

Zorba did not say a word, but there was a broad, sensual smile across his face, from the corners of his mouth to his hairy ass's ears.

Dinner was ready and he took the pot off the fire.

"Zaharia," he asked, "what is angels' food?"

"The spirit," answered the monk, crossing himself.

"The spirit? In other words, wind? That doesn't nourish a man; come and eat some bread and have some fish soup and a scrap or two of meat, then you'll feel yourself again. You've done a good job! Eat!"

"I'm not hungry," said the monk.

"Zaharia isn't hungry, but what about Joseph? Isn't he hungry either?"

"Joseph," said the monk in a low voice, as if he were revealing a deep mystery, "was burnt, curse his soul, burnt, God be praised!"

"Burnt!" cried Zorba with a laugh. "How? When? Did you see him burnt?"

"Brother Canavaro, he burnt the second I lit the candle at the lamp of Christ. I saw him with my own eyes come out of my mouth

276

like a black ribbon with letters of fire. The flame from the candle fell on him and he writhed like a snake, but was burnt to ashes. What a relief! God be praised! I feel I've entered Paradise already!"

He rose from beside the fire, where he had curled up.

"I shall go and sleep on the sea shore; that was what I was ordered to do."

He walked away along the edge of the water and disappeared into the blackness of the night.

"You are responsible for him, Zorba," I said. "If the monks find him he's done for."

"They won't find him, don't you worry, boss. I know this sort of game too well: early tomorrow morning—I'll shave him, give him some really human clothes and put him on a ship. Don't bother yourself about him, it isn't worth it. Is the stew good? Eat a man's bread and enjoy it, and don't worry your head about all the rest!"

Zorba ate with a very good appetite, drank and wiped his moustache. Now he wanted to talk.

"Did you notice, boss?" he said. "His devil's dead. And now he's empty, poor fellow, completely empty, finished! He will be just like everybody else from now on!"

He thought for a moment or two.

"Do you think, boss, that this devil of his was . . . ?"

"Of course," I replied. "The idea of burning the monastery had possessed him; now he's burnt it he's calmed. That idea wanted to eat meat, drink wine, ripen and turn into action. The other Zaharia had no need of wine or meat. He matured by fasting."

Zorba turned this over and over in his head.

"Why, I think you're right, boss! I think I must have five or six demons inside me!"

"We've all got some, Zorba, don't you worry. And the more we have, the better. The main thing is that they should all aim at the same end, even if they do go different ways about it."

These words seemed to move Zorba deeply. He lodged his big head between his knees and thought.

"What end?" he asked at last, raising his eyes to me.

"How should I know, Zorba? You ask difficult questions. How can I explain that?"

"Just say it simply, so that I understand. Up till now I've always

277

let my demons do just what they liked, and go any way they liked about it—and that's why some people call me dishonest and others honest, and some think I'm crazy and others say I'm as wise as Solomon. I'm all those things and a lot more—a real Russian salad. So help me to get it clearer, will you, boss . . . what end?"

"I think, Zorba—but I may be wrong—that there are three kinds of men: those who make it their aim, as they say, to live their lives, eat, drink, make love, grow rich, and famous; then come those who make it their aim not to live their own lives but to concern themselves with the lives of all men—they feel that all men are one and they try to enlighten them, to love them as much as they can and do good to them; finally there are those who aim at living the life of the entire universe—everything, men, animals, trees, stars, we are all one, we are all one substance involved in the same terrible struggle. What struggle? . . . Turning matter into spirit."

Zorba scratched his head.

"I've got a thick skull, boss, I don't grasp these things easily. . . . Ah, if only you could dance all that you've just said, then I'd understand."

I bit my lip in consternation. All those desperate thoughts, if only I could have danced them! But I was incapable of it; my life was wasted.

"Or if you could tell me all that in a story, boss. Like Hussein Aga did. He was an old Turk, a neighbor of ours. Very old, very poor, no wife, no children, completely alone. His clothes were worn, but shining with cleanliness. He washed them himself, did his own cooking, scrubbed and polished the floor, and at night used to come in to see us. He used to sit in the yard with my grandmother and a few other old women and knit socks.

"Well, as I was saying, this Hussein Aga was a saintly man. One day he took me on his knee and placed his hand on my head as though he were giving me his blessing. 'Alexis,' he said, 'I'm going to tell you a secret. You're too small to understand now, but you'll understand when you are bigger. Listen, little one: neither the seven stories of heaven nor the seven stories of the earth are enough to contain God; but a man's heart can contain him. So be very careful, Alexis—and may my blessing go with you—never to wound a man's heart!'"

I listened to Zorba in silence. If only I could never open my mouth, I thought, until the abstract idea had reached its highest point—and had become a story! But only the great poets reach a point like that, or a people, after centuries of silent effort.

Zorba stood up.

"I'm going to see what our firebrand's up to, and spread a blanket over him so that he doesn't catch cold. I'll take some scissors, too; it won't be a very first-class job."

He went off laughing along the edge of the sea, carrying the scissors and blanket. The moon had just come up and was spreading a livid, sickly light over the earth.

Alone by the dying fire, I weighed Zorba's words—they were rich in meaning and had a warm earthy smell. You felt they came up from the depths of his being and that they still had a human warmth. My words were made of paper. They came down from my head, scarcely splashed by a spot of blood. If they had any value at all it was to that mere spot of blood they owed it.

Lying on my stomach, I was rummaging about in the warm cinders when Zorba returned, his arms hanging loosely by his side, and a look of amazement on his face.

"Boss, don't take it too hard. . . ."

I leaped up.

"The monk is dead," he said.

"Dead?"

"I found him lying on a rock. He was in the full light of the moon. I went down on my knees and began cutting his beard off and the remains of his moustache. I kept cutting and cutting, and he didn't budge. I got excited and started cutting his thatch clean off; I must have taken at least a pound of hair off his face. Then when I saw him like that, shorn like a sheep, I just laughed, hysterically! 'I say, Signor Zaharia!' I cried, shaking him as I laughed. 'Wake up and see the miracle the Holy Virgin's performed!' Wake be damned! He didn't budge! I shook him again. Nothing happened! 'He can't have packed it in, poor fellow!' I said to myself. I opened his robe, bared his chest and put my hand over his heart. Tick-tick-tick? Nothing at all! The engine had stopped!"

As he talked Zorba regained his spirits. Death had made him speechless for an instant, but he had soon put it in its proper place.

"Now, what shall we do, boss? I think we ought to burn him. He who kills others by paraffin shall perish by paraffin himself. Isn't there something like that in the Gospel? And with his clothes stiff with dirt and paraffin already, he'd flame up like Judas himself on Maundy Thursday!"

"Do what you like," I said, ill at ease.

Zorba became absorbed in profound meditation.

"It is a nuisance," he said at last, "a hell of a nuisance. If I set light to him, his clothes will flame like a torch, but he's all skin and bone himself, poor chap! Thin like he is, he'll take a devil of a time to burn to ashes. There's not an ounce of fat on him to help the fire."

Shaking his head, he added:

"If God existed, don't you think he would have known all this in advance and made him fat and fleshy to help us out? What do you think?"

"Don't mix me up with this business at all. You do just what you like, but do it quickly."

"The best thing would be if some sort of miracle occurred! The monks would have to believe that God himself had turned barber, shaved him and then did him in to punish him for the damage he did to the monastery."

He scratched his head.

"But what miracle? What miracle? This is where we've got you, Zorba!"

The crescent of the moon was on the point of disappearing below the horizon and was the color of burnished copper.

Tired, I went to bed. When I awoke at dawn, I saw Zorba making coffee close to me. He was white-faced and his eyes were all red and swollen from not sleeping. But his big goat-like lips wore a malicious smile.

"I haven't been to sleep, boss, I had some work to do."

"What work, you rascal?"

"I was doing the miracle."

He laughed and placed his finger across his lips. "I'm not going to tell you! Tomorrow is the inauguration ceremony for our cable railway. All those fat hogs will be here to give their blessing; then they'll learn about the new miracle performed by the Virgin of Revenge—great is her power!"

He served the coffee.

"You know, I'd make a good abbot, I think," he said. "If I started a monastery, I bet you I'd close all the others down and pinch all their customers. How would you like some tears? A tiny wet sponge behind the icons and the saints would weep at will. Thunder claps? I'd have a machine under the holy table which would make a deafening row. Ghosts? Two of the most trusty monks would roam about at night on the roof of the monastery wrapped in sheets. And every year I'd gather a crowd of cripples and blind and paralytics for her feast day and see that they all saw the light of day again and stood up straight on their legs to dance to her glory!

"What is there to laugh at, boss? I had an uncle once who found an old mule on the point of death. He'd been left in the mountains to die. My uncle took him home. Every morning he took him out to pasture and at night back home. 'You there, Haralambos!' the people from the village shouted at him as he went past, 'what do you think you're doing with that old crock?' 'He's my dung factory!' answered my uncle. Well, boss, in my hands the monastery would be a miracle factory!"

◇ 25 ◇

THE EVE of that first of May I shall never forget as long as I live. The cable railway was ready; the pylons, cable and pulleys gleamed in the morning sun. Huge pine trunks lay heaped at the top of the mountain, and workmen stood there waiting for the signal to attach them to the cable and send them down to the sea.

A large Greek flag was flapping at the top of the pole up at the point of departure on the mountainside and a similar one down below by the sea. In front of the hut Zorba had set up a small barrel of wine. Next to it was a workman roasting a good fat sheep on a spit. After the benediction ceremony and the inauguration, the guests were to have wine and wish us success.

Zorba had taken the parrot's cage, too, and placed it on a high rock near the first pylon.

"It's as if I could see his mistress," he murmured, looking fondly at the bird. He took a handful of peanuts from his pocket and gave them to the parrot.

Zorba was wearing his best clothes: unbuttoned white shirt, green jacket, grey trousers and good elastic-sided shoes. Moreover, he had waxed his moustache, which was beginning to lose its dye.

Like a great noble doing the honors to his peers, he hastened to welcome the village worthies as they arrived, and explained to them what a cable railway was, and what a benefit it would be to the countryside, and that the Holy Virgin—in her infinite grace—had helped him with her wisdom in the perfect execution of this project.

"It is a great piece of engineering," he said. "You've got to find the exact slope, and that takes some working out! I racked my brains for months, but to no purpose. It's obvious that for great works like this the mind of man is inadequate; we need God's aid. . . . Well, the Holy Virgin saw me hard at it, and she had pity on me: 'Poor Zorba,' she said, 'he's not a bad fellow, he's doing all that for the good of the village, I think I'll go and give him a hand.' And then, O miracle of God! . . ."

Zorba stopped to cross himself three times in succession.

"O miracle! One night in my sleep a woman in black came to me—it was the Holy Virgin. In her hand she held a small model line, no bigger than that. 'Zorba,' she said, 'I've brought you your plans; they come from heaven. Here is the slope you need, and here is my blessing!' And she disappeared! I woke up with a start, ran to the place where I was testing at the time and what did I see? The wire was set at the right angle, all by itself. And it smelled of benjamin, too, which proved that the hand of the Holy Virgin had touched it!"

Kondomanolio was opening his mouth to ask a question when five monks mounted on mules appeared along the stony mountain pathway. A sixth, carrying a large wooden cross on his shoulders, ran shouting in front of them. We strained to know what he was shouting but we could not make it out.

We could hear chanting. The monks were waving their arms in the air, crossing themselves, and the hooves of their mules struck sparks from the stones.

The monk who was on foot came up to us, his face streaming with sweat. He raised the cross on high.

"Christians! A miracle!" he cried. "Christians! A miracle! The fathers are bringing the Most Holy Virgin herself! On your knees and worship her!"

The villagers, notables and workmen ran up excitedly, surrounded the monk and crossed themselves. I stood apart. Zorba glanced at me, his eyes twinkling.

"You go closer, too, boss," he said. "Go and hear about the Most Holy Virgin's miracle!"

The monk, breathless and in haste, began his story.

"Down on your knees, Christians, and listen to the divine miracle! Listen, Christians! The devil had seized upon the soul of the accursed Zaharia and two days ago led him to sprinkle the holy monastery with paraffin. We noticed the fire at midnight. We got out of bed in all haste; the priory, the galleries and the cells were all in flames. We rang the monastery bell and cried: 'Help! Help! Holy Virgin of Revenge!' And we rushed to the fire with pitchers and buckets of water! By early morning the flames were out, praise be to her Holy Grace!

"We went to the chapel and sank to our knees before her miraculous icon, crying: 'Holy Virgin of Revenge! Take up your lance and strike the culprit!' Then we gathered together in the courtyard and noticed that Zaharia, our Judas, was absent. 'He is the one who set us on fire! He *must* be the one!' we cried and rushed after him. We searched the whole day long but found nothing; then the whole night, but still nothing. But today at dawn, we went once more to the chapel and what did we see, brothers? A terrible miracle! Zaharia was lying dead at the foot of the sacred icon and the virgin's lance had a large spot of blood on its point!"

"*Kyrie eleison! Kyrie eleison!*" murmured the villagers in terror.

"That's not all," added the monk, swallowing his spittle. "When we bent down to lift up the accursed Zaharia we stood aghast: for the Virgin had shaved off his hair, moustache and beard—like a Catholic priest!"

Controlling my laughter with the greatest difficulty, I turned to Zorba.

"Scoundrel!" I said in a low voice.

But he was watching the monk, his eyes wide open in surprise, and was crossing himself with deep emotion all the time, to show his utter amazement.

"You are great, O Lord! You are great, O Lord! And your works are wonderful!" he murmured.

At this moment the other monks arrived and dismounted. The hospitaller held the icon in his arms; he climbed up a rock, and all rushed and scrambled to prostrate themselves before the miraculous

Virgin. Last came the fat Demetrios, carrying a plate, making the collection and sprinkling the peasants' hard heads with rose water. Three monks stood round him chanting hymns, with their hands folded together over their stomachs, their faces covered with great beads of sweat.

"We are going to take her in procession round the villages of Crete," said the fat Demetrios, "so that the believers can kneel to Her Holiness and bring their offerings. We need money, lots of money, to restore the holy monastery. . . ."

"The fat hogs!" grumbled Zorba. "They're even going to make something out of this!"

He went up to the abbot.

"Holy father, everything is ready for the ceremony. May the Holy Virgin bless our work!"

The sun was already high, it was very hot, and there was not a breath of wind. The monks placed themselves round the pylon bearing the flag. They wiped their foreheads with their broad sleeves and began chanting the prayer for "the foundations of buildings."

"Lord, O Lord, found this contrivance on solid rock that neither wind nor water may shake it. . . ." They dipped the aspergillum in the copper bowl and sprinkled objects and people—the pylon, the cable, the pulleys, Zorba and me, and, finally, the peasants, workmen and the sea itself.

Then, with great care, as if they were handling a sick woman, they lifted the icon, set it close to the parrot, and surrounded it. On the other side were the elders, in the center Zorba. I myself had withdrawn slightly towards the sea and was waiting.

The line was to be given a trial with three trees: a holy trinity. Nevertheless a fourth was added as a sign of recognition towards the Holy Virgin of Revenge.

Monks, villagers, and workmen crossed themselves.

"In the name of the Holy Trinity and the Holy Virgin!" they murmured.

In a single bound Zorba was at the first pylon, pulled the cord and down came the flag. It was the signal for which the men at the top of the mountain had been waiting. All the spectators stepped back and looked towards the summit.

"In the name of the Father!" cried the abbot.

Impossible to describe what happened then. The catastrophe burst upon us like a thunderbolt. We had scarcely time to run away. The entire structure swayed. The pine tree, which the workmen had attached to the cable, assumed a demoniac impetus. Sparks flew, large splinters of wood shot through the air, and when the tree arrived at the bottom a few seconds later it was no more than a charred log.

Zorba gave me a hang-dog look. The monks and villagers retreated prudently and the tethered mules began rearing. Big Demetrios collapsed, panting.

"Lord have mercy on me!" he murmured, terror-stricken.

Zorba raised his hand.

"It's nothing," he said with assurance. "It's always the same with the first trunk. Now the machine will be run in . . . Look!"

He sent the flag up, gave the signal again, and then ran away.

"And the Son!" cried the abbot in a rather trembling voice.

The second tree trunk was released. The pylons shivered, the trunk gained speed, leaping about like a porpoise, and rushed headlong towards us. But it did not get far, it was pulverized half-way down the slope.

"The devil take it!" muttered Zorba, biting into his moustache. "The blasted slope isn't right yet!"

He leaped to the pylon and signalled with the flag once more, furiously, for the third attempt. The monks were by now standing behind their mules, and they crossed themselves. The village worthies waited with one foot raised, ready to take flight.

"And the Holy Ghost!" the abbot stammered, holding up his robe in readiness.

The third tree trunk was enormous. It had hardly been released from the summit when a tremendous noise was heard.

"Lie flat, for God's sake!" shouted Zorba, as he scurried away.

The monks threw themselves to the ground and the villagers ran away as fast as their legs would carry them.

The trunk made one leap, fell back on the cable, threw out a shower of sparks and, before we could see what was happening, sped down the mountainside, over the beach and dived far into the sea, throwing up a great spout of foam.

The pylons were vibrating in a most terrifying fashion, several of them were leaning over already. The mules broke their tethers and ran off.

"That's nothing! Nothing to worry about!" cried Zorba, beside himself. "Now the machine's really run in, so we can make a proper start!"

He sent the flag up once again. We felt how desperate he was, and anxious to see the end of it all.

"And the Holy Virgin of Revenge!" stammered out the abbot as he raced towards the rocks.

The fourth trunk was released. A tremendous splintering noise resounded twice through the air and all the pylons fell down, one after the other, like a pack of cards.

"Kyrie eleison! Kyrie eleison!" yelped the villagers, workmen and monks, as they stampeded.

A flying splinter wounded Demetrios in the thigh and another was within a hair's breadth of taking out the abbot's eye. The villagers had disappeared. The Virgin alone was erect on her rock, lance in hand, looking at the men below with a cold and severe eye. Next to her, more dead than alive, was a trembling parrot, his green feathers standing out from his body.

The monks seized the Virgin, clasped her in their arms, helped up Demetrios, who was groaning with pain, collected their mules together, mounted them and beat a retreat. Scared to death, the workmen who had been turning the spit had abandoned the sheep and the meat was beginning to burn.

"The sheep will be burnt to a cinder!" shouted Zorba anxiously, as he ran to the spit.

I sat down beside him. There was no one else left on the beach, we were quite alone. He turned to me and cast me a dubious, hesitant glance. He did not know how I was going to take the catastrophe, or how this adventure was likely to end.

He took a knife, bent over the sheep once more, tasted it and immediately took the beast off the fire and stood it up on the spit against a tree.

"Just right," he said, "just right, boss! Would you like a piece, as well?"

"Bring the bread and the wine, too," I said. "I'm hungry."

Zorba hurried to the barrel, rolled it close to the sheep, brought a loaf of white bread and two glasses. We each took a knife, carved off two slices of meat, cut some bread and began to eat.

"See how good it is, boss? It melts in your mouth! Here there are no rich pastures, the animals eat dry grass all the time, that's why their meat's so tasty. I can only remember once in my life eating meat as succulent as this. It was that time I embroidered the Saint Sophia with some of my hair and wore it as a charm . . . an old story. . . ."

"Go on, tell me!"

"An old story, I tell you, boss! A crazy Greek's idea!"

"Go on, Zorba, I'd like to hear you spin the yarn."

"Well, it was like this. The Bulgars had surrounded us, it was evening, we could see them all round us lighting fires on the slopes of the mountains. To frighten us they'd start banging cymbals and howling like a lot of wolves. There must have been a good three hundred of 'em. We were twenty-eight, and Rouvas was our chief—God save his soul if he's dead, he was a fine fellow! 'Come on, Zorba,' he said, 'put the sheep on the spit!' 'It's much more tasty cooked in a hole in the ground, captain,' I said. 'Do it any way you like, but get on with it, we're ravenous,' he said. So we dug a hole, stuffed the sheep in it, piled a layer of coal on top and lit it; then we took the bread from our packs and sat down round the fire. 'It may well be the last one we eat!' said our chief. 'Any of you got cold feet?' We all laughed. No one deigned to answer him. We took our gourds and said: 'Your health, chief. They'd better be good shots if they want to hit us!' We drank, drank again, then pulled the sheep out of the hole. Oh, boss, what mutton! When I think of it my mouth still waters! It melted, like *loukoum*! We all sank our teeth in it without delay. 'I've never had tastier meat in my life!' said the chief. 'God save us all!' And though he'd never drunk before, he quaffed his glass of wine in one go. 'Sing a Klepht song!' he commanded. 'Those chaps over there are howling like wolves: we'll sing like men. Let's begin with Old Dimos.' We drank up quickly, filled and drank again. Then we started the song. It grew louder and louder, resounding and echoing through the ravines: *And I've been a Klepht brigand for forty years, boys!* . . . We sang loud and with a will. 'Well, God help us!' said the captain. 'That's the spirit! Now, Alexis, look at the sheep's back there. . . . What does it say?' I bent over the fire and began scraping the sheep's back with my knife.

" 'I can't see any graves, captain,' I cried. 'Nor any dead. We shall get away with it once again, boys!' 'May God have heard you!' said our chief, who had not long been married. 'Just let me have a son! I don't care what happens after that.' "

Zorba cut himself a large piece from round the kidneys.

"That sheep was wondefrul," he said, "but this one doesn't give a point away; it's a little beauty!"

"Pour out some wine, Zorba," I said. "Fill the glasses to the brim and we'll drain them."

We clinked glasses and tasted the wine, an exquisite Cretan wine, a rich red color, like hare's blood. When you drank it, you felt as if you were in communion with the blood of the earth itself and you became a sort of ogre. Your veins overflowed with strength, your heart with goodness! If you were a lamb you turned into a lion. You forgot the pettiness of life, constraints all fell away. United to man, beast and God, you felt that you were one with the universe.

"Look at this sheep's back and read what it says," I cried. "Go on, Zorba."

He very carefully sucked the pieces off the back, scraped it with his knife, held it up to the light and gazed at it attentively.

"Everything's fine," he said. "We shall live a thousand years, boss; we've hearts of steel!"

He bent down, examining the back again in the light from the fire.

"I see a journey," he said, "a long journey. At the end of it a large house with a lot of doors. It must be the capital of some kingdom, boss . . . or the monastery where I shall be doorkeeper, and where I'll do the smuggling, as we said?"

"Pour some wine, Zorba, and leave your prophecies. I'll tell you what the large house with all those doors really is: it's the earth and all its graves, Zorba. That's the end of the long voyage. Good health, you rascal!"

"Good health, boss! Luck is blind, they say. It can't see where it's going and keeps running into people . . . and the people it knocks into we call lucky! Well, to hell with luck if it's like that, I say! We don't want it, do we, boss?"

"We don't, Zorba! Good health!"

We drank, finished off the sheep, and the world was somehow lighter—the sea looked happy, the earth swayed like the deck of a ship, two gulls walked across the pebbles chattering together like human beings.

I stood up.

"Come on, Zorba," I cried, "teach me to dance!"

Zorba leaped to his feet, his face sparkling.

"To dance, boss? To dance? Fine! Come on!"

"Off we go, then, Zorba! My life has changed! Let's have it!"

"To start with I'll teach you the *Zéimbékiko*. It's a wild, military dance; we always danced it when I was a *comitadji*, before going into battle."

He took off his shoes and purple socks and kept on only his shirt. But he was still too hot and removed that as well.

"Watch my feet, boss," he enjoined me. "Watch!"

He put out his foot, touched the ground lightly with his toes, then pointed the other foot; the steps were mingled violently, joyously, the ground reverberated like a drum.

He shook me by the shoulder.

"Now then, my boy," he said. "Both together!"

We threw ourselves into the dance. Zorba instructed me, corrected me gravely, patiently, and with great gentleness. I grew bold and felt my heart on the wing like a bird.

"Bravo! You're a wonder!" cried Zorba, clapping his hands to mark the beat. "Bravo, youngster! To hell with paper and ink! To hell with goods and profits! To hell with mines and workmen and monasteries! And now that you, my boy, can dance as well and have learnt my language, what shan't we be able to tell each other!"

He pounded on the pebbles with his bare feet and clapped his hands.

"Boss," he said, "I've dozens of things to say to you. I've never loved anyone as much before. I've hundreds of things to say, but my tongue just can't manage them. So I'll dance them for you! Here goes!"

He leaped into the air and his feet and arms seemed to sprout wings. As he threw himself straight in the air against that background of sea and sky, he looked like an old archangel in rebellion. For Zorba's dance was full of defiance and obstinacy. He seemed to be shouting to the sky: "What can you do to me, Almighty? You can do nothing to me except kill me. Well, kill me, I don't care! I've vented my spleen, I've said all I want to say; I've had time to dance . . . and I don't need you any more!"

Watching Zorba dance, I understood for the first time the fantastic efforts of man to overcome his weight. I admired Zorba's endurance, his agility and proud bearing. His clever and impetuous steps were writing on the sand the demoniac history of mankind.

He stopped, contemplated the shattered cable line and its series of heaps. The sun was declining, shadows were growing longer. Zorba turned to me and with a gesture common to him, covered his mouth with his palm.

"I say, boss," he said, "did you see the showers of sparks the thing threw out?"

We burst out laughing.

Zorba threw himself on me, embraced and kissed me.

"Does it make you laugh, too?" he said tenderly. "Are you laughing, too? Eh, boss? Good!"

Rocking with laughter, we wrestled playfully with one another for some time. Then, falling to the ground, we stretched out on the pebbles and fell asleep in one another's arms.

I woke at dawn and walked rapidly along the beach towards the village; my heart was leaping in my breast. I had rarely felt so full of joy in my life. It was no ordinary joy, it was a sublime, absurd and unjustifiable gladness. Not only unjustifiable, contrary to all justification. This time I had lost everything—my money, my men, the line, the trucks; we had constructed a small port and now we had nothing to export. It was all lost.

Well, it was precisely at that moment that I felt an unexpected sense of deliverance. As if in the hard, somber labyrinth of necessity I had discovered liberty herself playing happily in a corner. And I played with her.

When everything goes wrong, what a joy to test your soul and see if it has endurance and courage! An invisible and all-powerful enemy—some call him God, others the Devil, seems to rush upon us to destroy us; but we are not destroyed.

Each time that within ourselves we are the conquerors, although externally utterly defeated, we human beings feel an indescribable pride and joy. Outward calamity is transformed into a supreme and unshakable felicity.

I remember something Zorba told me once:

"One night on a snow-covered Macedonian mountain a terrible wind arose. It shook the little hut where I had sheltered and tried to tip it over. But I had shored it up and strengthened it. I was sitting alone by the fire, laughing at and taunting the wind. 'You won't get into my little hut, brother! I shan't open the door to you. You won't put my fire out; you won't tip my hut over!'"

In these few words of Zorba's I had understood how men should behave and what tone they should adopt when addressing powerful but blind necessity.

I walked rapidly along the beach, talking with the invisible enemy. I cried: "You won't get into my soul! I shan't open the door to you! You won't put my fire out; you won't tip me over!"

The sun had not yet peeped over the mountain. Colors played in the sky over the water—blues, greens, pinks, and mother-of-pearl; inland, among the olive trees, small birds were waking and chirping, intoxicated by the morning light.

I walked along the edge of the water to say goodbye to this solitary beach, to engrave it upon my mind and carry it away with me.

I had known much joy and many pleasures on that beach. My life with Zorba had enlarged my heart; some of his words had calmed my soul. This man with his infallible instinct and his primitive eagle-like look had taken confident short cuts and, without even losing his breath, had reached the peak of effort and had even gone farther.

A group of men and women went by carrying baskets full of food and big bottles of wine. They were going to the gardens to celebrate the first of May. A girl sang and her voice was as clear as spring water. A little girl, her young breast already swelling, passed by me out of breath, and clambered on to a high rock. A pale and angry man with a black beard was chasing her.

"Come down, come down. . . ." he cried hoarsely.

But the girl, her cheeks aflame, raised her arms, folded them behind her head and, gently swaying her perspiring body, sang:

> *Tell me with a laugh, tell me with a cry,*
> *Tell me you do not love me,*
> > *What care I?*

"Come down, come down . . . !" the bearded man was shouting, his hoarse voice begging and threatening by turns. All at once he leaped up and caught her by the foot, gripping it fiercely. She burst into tears as if only waiting for this brutal gesture to relieve her feelings.

I hurried on. All these sudden manifestations of joy stirred my heart. The old siren came into my mind. I could see her—fat and perfumed and sated with kisses. She was lying beneath the earth. She must already have swollen and turned green. Her skin must have split, her body fluids must have oozed out and the maggots must be crawling over her now.

I shook my head with horror. Sometimes the earth becomes transparent and we see our ultimate ruler, the grub, working night and day in his underground workshops. But we quickly turn our eyes away, because men can endure everything except the sight of that small white maggot.

As I entered the village I met the postman preparing to blow his trumpet.

"A letter, boss!" he said, holding out a blue envelope.

I leaped for joy as I recognized the delicate handwriting. I hurried through the foliage, emerged by the olive grove, and impatiently opened the letter. It was brief and written in a haste. I read it straight through.

We have reached the frontiers of Georgia; we have escaped the Kurds and all's well. I at last know what happiness really is. Because it's only now that I have real experience of the old maxim: Happiness is doing your duty, and the harder the duty the greater the happiness.

In a few days these hounded, dying creatures will be at Batum, and I have just had a telegram which reads: "The first ships are in sight!"

These thousands of hard-working, intelligent Greeks, with their broad-hipped wives and fiery-eyed children, will soon be transported into Macedonia and Thrace. We are going to infuse a new and valiant blood into the old veins of Greece.

I have exhausted myself somewhat, I admit, but what does it matter? We have fought, my dear sir, and won. I am happy.

I hid the letter and hastened along. I too was happy. I took the steep track up the mountainside, rubbing a sweet-smelling sprig of thyme between my fingers. It was nearly noon and my dark shadow was concentrated about my feet. A kestrel was hovering, its wings beating so fast that it looked quite motionless. A partridge heard my steps, hurtled out of the brush and whirred into the air in its mechanical flight.

I was happy. Had I been able I would have sung out loud to relieve my feelings, but I could only make inarticulate cries. Whatever's happening to you? I asked myself mockingly. Were you as patriotic as that then, and never knew? Or do you love your friend so much? You ought to be ashamed! Control yourself and quiet down!

But I was transported with joy and continued along the track, shouting as I went. I heard a tinkling of goat bells. Black, brown and grey goats appeared on the rocks, in the full sun. The he-goat was in front, holding his neck rigid. The stench of him infected the air.

"Hallo, brother! Where are you off to? Who're you chasing?"

A goatherd had jumped up on to a rock and was whistling after me with his fingers in his mouth.

"I've got something urgent to do!" I answered, and continued climbing.

"Stop a minute. Come and have a drink of goat's milk to refresh yourself!" shouted the goatherd, leaping from rock to rock.

"I told you I've got something urgent to do!" I shouted back. I did not want to cut short my joy by stopping to talk.

"D'you mean you despise my milk?" said the goatherd in a hurt tone. "Go on, then, and good luck to you!"

He put his fingers in his mouth again, whistled, and goats, dogs and goatherd disappeared behind the rocks.

I soon reached the summit of the mountain. Immediately, as

though this had been my objective I became calm. I stretched out on a rock in the shade, and looked at the distant plain and sea. I breathed in deeply; the air was redolent with sage and thyme.

I stood up, gathered some sage, made a pillow and lay down again. I was tired. I closed my eyes.

For a moment my mind took flight to those far-off high plateaus covered with snow. I tried to imagine the little band of men, women and cattle making their way towards the north, and my friend walking ahead, like the ram at the head of the flock. But very soon my mind grew confused and I felt an invincible desire to sleep.

I wanted to resist. I did not wish to give way to sleep. I opened my eyes. A species of crow, an alpine chough, had settled on a rock directly in front of me, on the mountaintop. Its blue-black feathers shone in the sun and I made out very distinctly its large curved yellow beak. I was cross; this bird seemed to be a bad omen. I seized a stone and threw it at him. The chough calmly and slowly opened its wings.

I closed my eyes once more, unable to resist any longer, and sleep immediately overwhelmed me.

I could not have been asleep more than a few seconds when I uttered a cry and sat up with a start. The chough was passing at that very second above my head. I leaned against the rock, trembling all over. A violent dream had cut through my mind like a sword.

I saw myself in Athens, walking along Hermes Street, alone. The sun was burning hot, the street was deserted, the shops all shut, the solitude was complete. As I passed the church of Kapnikarea * I saw my friend, pale and breathless, running up to me from the direction of Constitution Square. He was following a very tall, thin man, who was walking with giant strides. My friend was in full diplomatic uniform. He noticed me and shouted from some distance, in a breathless tone:

"Hello, what are you doing nowadays? I haven't seen you for ages. Come and see me tonight; we'll have a chat."

"Where?" I shouted in my turn, very loud, as if my friend were a long way off and I had to use all the strength in my voice to reach him.

* Eleventh-century Byzantine. C. W.

"Concord Square,* this evening, six o'clock. The Fountain of Paradise Café!"

"Good!" I answered. "I'll be there!"

"You say you will," he said in a tone of reproach, "but you won't!"

"I will, for certain!" I cried. "Here's my hand on it!"

"I'm in a hurry."

"Why are you in a hurry? Give me your hand!"

He held out his hand and suddenly his arm came off from his shoulder and sailed through the air to seize my hand.

I was horrified by his icy grasp and woke with a start and a cry.

That was the moment when I discovered the chough hovering above my head. My lips seemed to be exuding poison.

I turned towards the east, riveting my eyes on the horizon as though wishing to penetrate the distance and see. . . . I was sure my friend was in danger. I shouted his name three times:

"Stavridaki! Stavridaki! Stavridaki!"

As if I wanted to give him courage. But my voice was lost a few yards in front of me and faded into the atmosphere.

I rushed headlong down the mountainside track, trying to deaden my sorrow by fatigue. My brain struggled in vain to piece together those mysterious messages which sometimes manage to pierce the body and reach the soul. In the depths of my being, a strange certainty, deeper than reason, entirely animal in quality, filled me with terror. The same certainty which some beasts—sheep and rats —feel before an earthquake. Awakening in me was the soul of the first men on earth, such as it was before it became totally detached from the universe, when it still felt the truth directly, without the distorting influence of reason.

"He is in danger! He is in danger!" I murmured. "He is going to die! Perhaps he doesn't realize it yet himself, but I know it, I'm sure of it. . . ."

I ran down the mountain path, stumbled over a pile of stones and fell to the ground, scattering the stones. I jumped up again with grazed and bleeding hands and legs.

"He is going to die! He is going to die!" I said, and felt a lump rise in my throat.

* Or Omónia Square. C. W.

Luckless man has raised what he thinks is an impassable barrier round his poor little existence. He takes refuge there and tries to bring a little order and security into his life. A little happiness. Everything must follow the beaten track, the sacrosanct routine, and comply with safe and simple rules. Inside this enclosure, fortified against the fierce attacks of the unknown, his petty certainties, crawling about like centipedes, go unchallenged. There is only one formidable enemy, mortally feared and hated: the Great Certainty. Now, this Great Certainty had penetrated the outer walls of my existence and was ready to pounce upon my soul.

When I reached our beach, I stopped to take breath for a moment. It was as though I had reached the second line of my defences and I pulled myself together. All these messages, I thought, are born of our own inner anxiety, and in our sleep assume the brilliant garb of a symbol. But we ourselves are the ones who create them. . . . I grew calmer. Reason was calling my heart to order, clipping the wings of that strange palpitating bat, and clipping and clipping until it could fly no more.

When I arrived at the hut, I was smiling at my own simplicity. I was ashamed that my mind had been so quickly overcome by panic. I dropped back into everyday reality. I was hungry and thirsty, I felt exhausted, and the cuts made by the stones on my limbs were smarting. My heart felt reassured: the terrible enemy who had penetrated the outer walls had been held in check by the second line of defence round my soul.

◇ 26 ◇

IT WAS ALL OVER. Zorba collected the cable, tools, trucks, iron scrap and timber, and made a heap of it on the beach, ready for the caique which was to load it.

"I'll make you a present of that, Zorba," I said. "It's all yours. Good luck!"

Zorba swallowed as if trying to hold back a sob.

"Are we separating?" he murmured. "Where are you going, boss?"

"I'm leaving for abroad, Zorba. The old goat within me has still got a lot of papers to chew over."

"Haven't you learned any better yet, boss?"

"Yes, Zorba, thanks to you. But I'm going to adopt your system; I'm going to do with my books what you did with the cherries. I'm going to eat so much paper, it'll make me sick. I shall spew it all up and then be rid of it forever."

"And what's going to become of me without your company, boss?"

"Don't fret, Zorba, we shall meet again, and, who knows, man's strength is tremendous! One day we'll put our great plan into effect: we'll build a monastery of our own, without a god, without a devil, but with free men; and you shall be the gatekeeper, Zorba, and hold the great keys to open and close the gate—like Saint Peter . . ."

Zorba, seated on the ground with his back against the side of the hut, continually filled and refilled his glass, drinking and saying nothing.

Night had fallen, we had finished our meal. We were sipping wine and having our last talk. Early the following morning we were to separate.

"Yes, yes . . ." said Zorba, pulling at his moustache and taking a drink. "Yes, yes . . ."

Above us, the night was starlit; within us, our hearts longed for relief but still held back.

Say goodbye to him forever, I thought to myself. Take a good look at him; never, never again will you set eyes on Zorba!

I could have thrown myself upon his old bosom and wept, but I was ashamed. I tried to laugh to hide my emotion, but I could not. I had a lump in my throat.

I looked at Zorba as he craned his neck like a bird of prey and drank in silence. I watched him and I reflected what a truly baffling mystery is this life of ours. Men meet and drift apart again like leaves blown by the wind; your eyes try in vain to preserve an image of the face, body or gestures of the person you have loved; in a few years you do not even remember whether his eyes were blue or black.

The human soul should be made of brass; it should be made of steel! I cried within me. Not just of air!

Zorba was drinking, holding his big head erect, motionless. He seemed to be listening to steps approaching in the night or retreating into the innermost depths of his being.

"What are you thinking about, Zorba?"

"What am I thinking about, boss? Nothing. Nothing, I tell you! I wasn't thinking of anything."

After a moment or two, filling up his glass again, he said:

"Good health, boss!"

We clinked glasses. We both knew that so bitter a feeling of sadness could not last much longer. We would have to burst into tears or get drunk, or begin to dance like lunatics.

"Play, Zorba!" I suggested.

"Haven't I already told you, boss? The *santuri* needs a happy heart. I'll play in a month's, perhaps two months' time—how can I tell? Then I'll sing about how two people separate forever."

"Forever!" I cried terrified. I had been saying that irremediable word to myself, but had not expected to hear it said out loud. I was frightened.

"Forever!" Zorba repeated, swallowing his saliva with some difficulty. "That's it—forever. What you've just said about meeting again, and building our monastery, all that is what you tell a sick man to put him on his feet. I don't accept it. I don't want it. Are we weak like women to need cheering up like that? Of course we aren't. Yet, it's forever!"

"Perhaps I'll stay here with you . . ." I said, appalled by Zorba's desperate affection for me. "Perhaps I shall come away with you. I'm free."

Zorba shook his head.

"No, you're not free," he said. "The string you're tied to is perhaps no longer than other people's. That's all. You're on a long piece of string, boss; you come and go, and think you're free, but you never cut the string in two. And when people don't cut that string . . ."

"I'll cut it some day!" I said defiantly, because Zorba's words had touched an open wound in me and hurt.

"It's difficult, boss, very difficult. You need a touch of folly to do that; folly, d'you see? You have to risk everything! But you've got such a strong head, it'll always get the better of you. A man's head is like a grocer; it keeps accounts: I've paid so much and earned so much and that means a profit of this much or a loss of that much! The head's a careful little shopkeeper; it never risks all it has, always keeps something in reserve. It never breaks the string. Ah no! It hangs on tight to it, the bastard! If the string slips out of its grasp, the head, poor devil, is lost, finished! But if a man doesn't break the string, tell me, what flavor is left in life? The flavor of camomile, weak camomile tea! Nothing like rum—that makes you see life inside out!"

He was silent, helped himself to some more wine, but started to speak again.

"You must forgive me, boss," he said. "I'm just a clodhopper. Words stick between my teeth like mud to my boots. I can't turn out beautiful sentences and compliments. I just can't. But you understand, I know."

He emptied his glass and looked at me.

"You understand!" he cried, as if suddenly filled with anger. "You understand, and that's why you'll never have any peace. If you didn't understand, you'd be happy! What d'you lack? You're young, you have money, health, you're a good fellow, you lack nothing. Nothing, by thunder! Except just one thing—folly! And when that's missing, boss, well . . ."

He shook his big head and was silent again.

I nearly wept. All that Zorba said was true. As a child I had been full of mad impulses, superhuman desires, I was not content with the world. Gradually, as time went by, I grew calmer. I set limits, separated the possible from the impossible, the human from the divine, I held my kite tightly, so that it should not escape.

A large shooting star streaked across the sky. Zorba started and opened wide his eyes as if he were seeing a shooting star for the first time in his life.

"Did you see that star?" he asked.

"Yes."

We were silent.

Suddenly Zorba craned his scraggy neck, puffed out his chest and gave a wild, despairing cry. And immediately the cry canalized itself into human speech, and from the depths of Zorba's being rose an old monotonous melody, full of sadness and solitude. The heart of the earth itself split in two and released the sweet, compelling poison of the East. I felt inside me all the fibers still linking me to courage and hope slowly rotting.

> *Iki kiklik bir tependé otiyor*
> *Otme dé, kiklik, bemin dertim yetiyor, aman! aman!*

Desert, fine sand, as far as eye can see. The shimmering air, pink, blue, yellow; your temples bursting. The soul gives a wild cry and exults because no cry comes in response. My eyes filled with tears.

> *A pair of red-legged partridges were piping on a hillock;*
> *Partridges, pipe no more! My own suffering is enough for me, aman! aman!*

Zorba was silent. With a sharp movement of his fingers he wiped the sweat off his brow. He leaned forward and stared at the ground.

"What is that Turkish song, Zorba?" I asked after a while.

"The camel driver's song. It's the song he sings in the desert. I hadn't sung it or remembered it for years. But just now . . ."

He raised his head, his voice was sharp, his throat constricted.

"Boss," he said, "it's time you went to bed. You'll have to get up at dawn tomorrow if you're going to catch the boat at Candia. Good night!"

"I'm not sleepy," I said. "I'm going to stay up with you. This is our last night together."

"That's just why we must end it quickly!" he cried, turning down his empty glass as a sign he did not wish to drink any more. "Here and now, just like that. As men cut short smoking, wine, and cards. Like a Greek hero, a *Palikari*.

"My father was a real *Palikari*. Don't look at me, I'm only a breath of air beside him. I don't come up to his ankles. He was one of those ancient Greeks they always talk about. When he shook your hand he nearly crushed your bones to pulp. I can talk now and then, but my father roared, neighed and sang. There very rarely came a human word out of his mouth.

"Well, he had all the vices, but he'd slash them, as you would with a sword. For instance, he smoked like a chimney. One morning he got up and went into the fields to plough. He arrived, leaned on the hedge, pushed his hand into his belt for his tobacco pouch to roll a cigarette before he began work, took out his pouch and found it was empty. He'd forgotten to fill it before leaving the house.

"He foamed with rage, let out a roar, and then bounded away towards the village. His passion for smoking completely unbalanced his reason, you see. But suddenly—I've always said I think a man's a mystery—he stopped, filled with shame, pulled out his pouch and tore it to shreds with his teeth, then stamped it in the ground and spat on it. 'Filth! Filth!' he bellowed. 'Dirty slut!'

"And from that hour, until the end of his days, he never put another cigarette between his lips.

"That's the way real men behave, boss. Good night!"

He stood up and strode across the beach. He did not look back

302

once. He went as far as the fringe of the sea and stretched himself out there on the pebbles.

I never saw him again. The muleteer arrived before cock-crow. I climbed into the saddle and left. I may be mistaken, but I suspect that Zorba was hidden somewhere about, watching me leave, though he did not run up to say the usual words of farewell, to make us sad and tearful, to shake hands and wave handkerchiefs and exchange vows.

Our separation was as clean as a sword cut.

In Candia I was given a telegram. I took it with trembling hands and looked at it for some time before I opened it. I knew what it said. I could see with a terrifying certainty the number of words, even the number of letters it contained.

I was seized with the desire to tear it to pieces without opening it. Why read it when I knew what was inside? But we no longer have faith in our souls, alas! Reason, the eternal grocer, laughs at the soul, as we ourselves laugh at witches and old women who cast spells. Or at eccentric old ladies. So I opened the telegram. It was from Tiflis. For a moment the letters danced before my eyes, I could not make out a word. But slowly they came to a standstill and I read:

YESTERDAY AFTERNOON STAVRIDAKI DIED FROM PNEUMONIA.

Five years went by, five long years of terror, during which time gathered speed, and geographical frontiers joined the dance, national boundaries expanded and contracted like so many concertinas. Zorba and I were carried away by the storm; though from time to time, in the first three years, I had a brief card from him.

One from Mount Athos—a card of the Virgin, Guardian of the Gates, with her big sad eyes and her strong and determined chin. Beneath the Virgin Zorba had written with his thick, heavy pen, which always scratched the paper: "No chance of doing business here, boss! The monks here even fleece their fleas! I'm leaving!" A few days later another card: "I can't go round all these monasteries holding the parrot in my hand like a travelling showman. I made a present of it to a comic sort of monk who had taught a blackbird to whistle *Kyrie Eleison* beautifully. The little devil sings like a real monk; it shocks you to hear him. He's going to teach our poor parrot to sing, too. Ah! the things that rascal's seen in his lifetime! And now he's become a holy father, our parrot has! All the best. Father Alexios, holy anchorite."

Six or seven months later I had a card from Rumania showing a very buxom woman wearing a low-necked dress.

> I'm still alive, I'm eating *mamaliga** and drinking vodka. I work in the oil mines and am as dirty and stinking as any sewer rat. But who cares? you can find here plenty of all your heart and belly can desire. A real paradise for old rascals like me. Do you understand, boss? A wonderful life . . . plenty of sweetmeats, and sweethearts into the bargain, God be praised! All the best.
>
> ALEXIS ZORBESCU, sewer rat.

Two years went by. I received another card, this time from Serbia.

> I'm still alive. It's hellishly cold, so I've been obliged to get married. Turn over and you'll see her face—a fine bit of female stuff. She's a trifle fat about the middle because she's cooking up a little Zorba for me. I am standing at her side wearing the suit you gave me, and the wedding ring you see on my hand is poor old Bouboulina's—nothing is impossible! God bless her remains! This one's name is Lyuba. The coat with fox-fur collar I'm wearing is part of my wife's dowry. She also brought me a mare and seven pigs—a funny lot they are! And two children from her first marriage, because I forgot to say she was a widow. I've found a copper mine in a mountain close by here. I've managed to get round another capitalist and am now taking it very easy, like a pasha. All the best.
>
> ALEXIS ZORBIĆ, ex-widower.

On the back of the card was a photograph of Zorba in splendid form, dressed as a newlywed, with a fur cap and a long new overcoat and carrying a swagger cane. On his arm was a beautiful Slav woman of no more than twenty-five, a wild mare with generous haunches, looking tempting and roguish, wearing high boots and graced with an ample bosom. Beneath the photograph was some

* A Rumanian maize gruel. C. W.

more of Zorba's pot-hooked writing: "Me, Zorba, and that unending business, women—this time her name's Lyuba."

All those years I was travelling abroad. I also had my unending business, but it had no ample bosom, no new coat, no pigs to give me.

One day in Berlin came a telegram: FOUND A WONDERFUL GREEN STONE. COME IMMEDIATELY, ZORBA.

It was the time of the great famine in Germany. The mark had fallen so low that you were obliged to carry millions of them about in a suitcase to buy even the smallest thing, like a postage stamp. Famine, cold, worn clothes, shoes full of holes everywhere—and the ruddy German cheeks had grown pale. If there was a slight breeze, men fell down in the street like leaves before the wind. Mothers gave their children pieces of rubber to chew to stop them crying. At night the police kept guard on the bridges across the river to prevent mothers from throwing themselves over, with their children in their arms, just to bring it all to an end somehow.

It was winter and it was snowing. In the room next to mine a German professor of oriental languages tried to warm himself by taking a long brush in his hand and, after the painful custom of the Far East, copying out some old Chinese poems or a saying from Confucius. The tip of the brush, the raised elbow and the heart of the writer had to form a triangle.

"After a few minutes," he used to tell me with satisfaction, "sweat begins to pour off me. That's how I get warm."

It was in the midst of bitter days such as those that I received Zorba's telegram. At first I was angry. Millions of men were sinking into degradation because they hadn't even a crust of bread to sustain their bodies and souls, and here came a telegram asking me to set out and travel thousands of miles to see a beautiful green stone! To hell with beauty! She has no heart and does not care a jot for human suffering!

But soon I was horrified: my anger had evaporated and I began to realize my heart was responding to this inhuman appeal of Zorba's. Some wild bird in me was beating its wings and asking to go.

Yet I did not go. Once more I did not dare. I did not obey the divine and savage clamor within me; I did no insensate, noble act.

I listened to the moderating, cold, human voice of logic. So I took my pen and wrote to Zorba to explain.

And he answered.

> You are a pen-pusher, boss, if you'll allow me to say so. You too could have seen a beautiful green stone at least once in your life, you poor soul, and you didn't see it. My God, sometimes when I had no work, I asked myself the question: Is there or isn't there any hell? But yesterday, when your letter came, I said: There surely must be a hell for a few pen-pushers like the boss!

Zorba has never written to me since. We were separated by even more terrible events. The world continued to stagger and reel like a drunken man. The ground opened and friendships and personal cares were engulfed.

I often talked to my friends of this great soul. We admired the proud and confident bearing, deeper than reason, of this untutored man. Spiritual heights, which took us years of painful effort to attain, were attained by Zorba in one bound. And we said: "Zorba is a great soul!" Or else he leapt beyond those heights, and then we said: "Zorba is mad!"

So time passed, sweetly poisoned by memories. Another shadow, that of my friend, also fell across my soul. It never left me—because I myself did not wish to leave it.

But of that shadow I never spoke to anyone. I talked to it in private, and, thanks to it, was becoming reconciled with death. I had my secret bridge to the other side. When my friend's soul crossed the bridge, I felt it was weary and pale; it was too weak to shake my hand.

Sometimes I thought with fright that perhaps my friend had not had time on earth to transform the slavery of the body into liberty, or to develop and strengthen his soul, so that it should not be seized by panic and destroyed at the supreme moment of death. Perhaps, I thought, he had no time to immortalize what there was to immortalize in him.

But now and then he was stronger—was it he? or was it just the more intense way I remembered him?—and when he came at these times he was young and exacting. I seemed even to hear his steps on the stairs.

One winter I had gone on a solitary pilgrimage into the Engadine mountains, where many years before my friend and I, with a woman we both loved, had passed some ecstatic hours together.

I was asleep in the same hotel where he had stayed. The moon was streaming through the open window and I felt the spirit of the mountains, of the snow-covered pines and the calm, blue night enter my mind.

I felt an indescribable felicity, as if sleep were a deep, peaceful, transparent sea and I was cradled, happy and motionless, in the depths; but my senses were so keenly attuned that had a boat passed on the surface of the water, thousands of fathoms above me, it would have made a gash on my body.

Suddenly a shadow fell across me. I knew who it was. His voice came, full of reproach:

"Are you asleep?"

I replied in the same tone:

"You kept me waiting for you; I haven't heard the sound of your voice for months. Where have you been wandering?"

"I have been by you all the time, but you had forgotten me. I do not always have the strength to call, and, as for you, you are trying to abandon me. The light of the moon is beautiful, and so are the trees covered with snow, and life on earth. But, for pity's sake, do not forget me!"

"I do not forget you; you know that very well. The first days when you left me, I ran over the wild mountains to tire my body out, and spent sleepless nights thinking of you. I even wrote poems to give vent to my feelings . . . but they were wretched poems which could not remove my pain. One of them began like this:

And whilst, with Charon, you trod the rugged path,
I admired the litheness of your bodies, your stature.
Like two wild ducks who wake at dawn and depart . . .

And in another poem, also unfinished, I cried:

Clench your teeth, O loved one, lest your soul fly away!"

He smiled bitterly, bent his face over me and I shuddered as I saw his paleness.

He looked at me for a long time with empty sockets where there had once been eyes. Now there were just two little pellets of earth.

"What are you thinking of?" I murmured. "Why don't you say something?"

Again his voice came like a distant sigh:

"Ah, what remains of a soul for which the world was too small! A few lines of someone else's poetry, scattered and mutilated lines —not even a complete quatrain! I come and go on earth, visit those who were dear to me, but their hearts are closed. Where can I enter? How can I bring myself to life? I turn in a circle like a dog going round and round a house where all the doors are locked and barred. Ah! if only I could live free, and not have to cling like a drowning man to your warm and living bodies!"

The tears sprang from his sockets; the pellets of earth turned into mud.

But soon his voice grew stronger:

"The greatest joy you ever gave me," he said, "was once at a festival in Zürich. Do you remember? You raised your glass to drink to my health. Do you recall that? There was someone else with us. . . ."

"I remember," I answered. "We called her our gracious lady. . . ."

We were silent. How many centuries seemed to have passed since then! Zürich! It was snowing outside; there were flowers on the table. There were three of us.

"What are you thinking about, master?" asked the shadow, with a touch of irony.

"A number of things, everything. . . ."

"I am thinking of your last words. You raised your glass and said in a trembling voice: 'My dear friend, when you were a baby, your old grandfather held you on one knee, and placed on the other the Cretan lyre and played some *Palikaria* airs. Tonight I drink to your health. May destiny see to it that you always sit in the lap of God!'"

"God has quickly granted your prayer, alas!"

"What does it matter?" I cried. "Love is stronger than death."

He smiled again bitterly, but said nothing. I could feel his body was dissolving in the darkness, becoming a mere sob, a sigh, a jest.

For days the taste of death remained on my lips. But my heart was relieved. Death had entered my life with a familiar and well-loved face, like a friend come to call for you and who waits patiently in a corner until you have finished your work.

But Zorba's shadow was always prowling jealously about me.

One night I was alone in my house by the sea on the island of Aegina. I was happy. My window was open on to the sea, the moon came streaming in, the sea was sighing with happiness, too. My body was voluptuously weary with too much swimming and I was sleeping profoundly.

Suddenly, just before dawn, in the midst of all that happiness, Zorba appeared in my dream. I cannot remember what he said or why he had come. But when I awoke my heart was ready to break. Without my knowing why, my eyes filled with tears. I was filled with an irresistible desire to reconstitute the life we had lived together on the coast of Crete, to drive my memory to work and gather together all the sayings, cries, gestures, tears, and dances which Zorba had scattered in my mind—to save them.

This desire was so violent that I was afraid. I saw in it a sign that, somewhere on earth, Zorba was dying. For I felt my soul to be so united with his that it seemed impossible for one of them to die without the other being shaken and crying out with pain.

For a moment I hesitated to group together all my memories of Zorba and put them into words. A childish terror took possession of me. I said to myself: If I do that, it will mean that Zorba is really in danger of dying. I must fight against the mysterious hand which seems to be urging mine to do it.

I resisted for two days, three days, a week. I threw myself into other writing, went out on excursions all day and read a great deal. Such were the stratagems I employed to elude the invisible presence. But my mind was entirely absorbed by a powerful feeling of disquiet on Zorba's behalf.

One day I was seated on the terrace of my house by the sea. It was noon. The sun was very hot and I was gazing at the bare and graceful flanks of Salamis before me. Suddenly, urged on by that divine hand, I took some paper, stretched myself out on the burning flagstones of the terrace and began to relate the sayings and doings of Zorba.

I wrote impetuously, hastening to bring the past back to life, trying to recall Zorba and resuscitate him exactly as he was. I felt that if he disappeared it would be entirely my fault, and I worked day and night to draw as full a picture as possible of my old friend.

I worked like the sorcerers of the savage tribes of Africa when they draw on the walls of their caves the Ancestors they have seen in their dreams, striving to make it as lifelike as possible so that the spirit of the Ancestor can recognize his body and enter into it.

In a few weeks my chronicle of Zorba was complete. On the last day I was again sitting on the terrace in the late afternoon, and gazing at the sea. On my lap was the completely finished manuscript. I was happy and relieved, as though a burden had been lifted from me. I was like a woman holding her new-born baby.

Behind the mountains of the Peloponnesus the red sun was setting as Soula, a little peasant girl who brought me my mail from the town, came up to the terrace. She held a letter out to me and ran away. . . . I understood. At least, it seemed to me that I understood, because when I opened the letter and read it, I did not leap up and utter a cry, I was not stricken with terror. I was sure. I knew that at this precise moment, while I was holding the manuscript on my lap and watching the setting sun, I would receive that letter.

Calmly, unhurriedly, I read the letter. It was from a village near to Skoplije in Serbia, and was written in indifferent German. I translated it:

I am the schoolmaster of this village and am writing to inform you of the sad news that Alexis Zorba, owner of a copper mine here, died last Sunday evening at six o'clock. On his deathbed, he called to me. "Come here, schoolmaster," he said. "I have a friend in Greece. When I am dead write to him and tell him that right until the very last minute I was in full possession of my senses and was thinking of him. And tell him that whatever I have done, I have no regrets. Tell him I hope he is well and that it's about time he showed a bit of sense.

"Listen, just another minute. If some priest or other comes to take my confession and give me the sacrament, tell him to clear out, quick, and leave me his curse instead! I've done heaps and heaps of things in my life, but I still did not do enough. Men like me ought to live a thousand years. Good night!"

These were his last words. He then sat up in his bed, threw back the sheets and tried to get up. We ran to prevent him—Lyuba, his wife, and I, along with several sturdy neighbors. But he brushed us all roughly aside, jumped out of bed and went to the window. There, he gripped the frame, looked out far into the mountains, opened wide his eyes and began to laugh, then to whinny like a horse. It was thus, standing, with his nails dug into the window frame, that death came to him.

His wife Lyuba asked me to write to you and send her respects. The deceased often talked about you, she says, and left instructions that a *santuri* of his should be given to you after his death to help you to remember him.

The widow begs you, therefore, if you ever pass through our village, to be good enough to spend the night in her house as her guest, and when you leave in the morning, to take the *santuri* with you.

ABOUT THE AUTHOR

NIKOS KAZANTZAKIS *has been acclaimed by Albert Schweitzer, Thomas Mann, and critics and scholars in Europe and America as one of the most eminent and versatile writers of our time. He was born in Crete in 1883 and studied at the University of Athens, where he received his Doctor of Law degree. Later he studied in Paris under the philosopher Henri Bergson, and he completed his studies in literature and art during four other years in Germany and Italy. Before World War II he spent a great deal of his time on the Island of Aegina, where he devoted himself to his philosophical and literary work. For a short while in 1945 he was Greek Minister of Education, and he was president of the Greek Society of Men of Letters. He spent most of the later years of his life in France. He died in Freiburg, Germany, in October 1957.*

He was the author of three novels which have been enthusiastically received in the United States and England: Zorba the Greek, The Greek Passion, *and* Freedom or Death. *He was also a dramatist, translator, poet and travel writer. His crowning achievement, which he worked on over a period of twelve years, was* The Odyssey: A Modern Sequel. *In Kimon Friar's magnificent verse translation, this modern epic was published in the United States in 1958 and was acclaimed by critics and reviewers in such superlatives as "a masterpiece," "a stirring work of art," "a monument of the age," and "one of the outstanding literary events of our time."*